Praise for *The Muse Of Freedom: A*

An Amazon #1 Bestseller in Renaissance Fiction
New Voices Award by Writers & Publishers Network
Finalist in the Global Book Awards

"AN ENGROSSING STORY about fiercely independent people... This ABSORBING
TALE of religious strife creates a vivid world that will draw readers in... "
~ **Kirkus Review**

"BRILLIANTLY TOLD. A story that will stick with you long after you've turned the
last page. FRESH AND COMPELLING. As relevant now as it was then."
~ **Janet Wertman, author of the *Seymour Saga trilogy***

"Larimore's LUSH, VIBRANT PROSE and SHARP EYE FOR HISTORICAL
DETAIL at once transported me back to Occitan haunts and castles. A must-read for
anyone who loves novels set in that alluring region of southern France."
~ **Glen Craney, author of *The Fire and the Light*, *The Spider and the Stone*,
and more**

"This story WILL CAPTURE YOU and not let go. History and DEFTLY-CRAFTED
STORYTELLING rolled into one."
~ **Rozsa Gaston, author of the Anne of Brittany Series**

"Jules Larimore has cast a spell on her readers with this WONDROUS FIRST
NOVEL. She is an alchemist, drawing on the poetic power of words, assembling a
colorful combination of characters to authentically explore the landscape of the human
heart; its yearnings, boundaries, expectations and limitations."
~ **Elijah Alexander, actor, Amazon five-star review**

"The author has woven an INTRIGUING STORY... This ranks right up there with
Gabaldon's OUTLANDER series & Auel's CLAN OF THE CAVEBEAR series, for
research, believability, historical accuracy, & fun! I can't wait for the next volume to
come out!!"
~ **Eve B. Mayes, Amazon VINE VOICES five-star review**

"YOU FEEL LIKE YOU'RE THERE. A very special historical novel... imbued within
it not only history but notions of religious freedom, images of landscape and town life,
and knowledge of late 17th century medical remedies... brought beautifully to life..."
~ **Amazon five-star review**

"BEAUTIFULLY WRITTEN... filled with love for the story, the characters, and the setting. As a historian, I know the context of the tale, but it was brought beautifully to life by Jules Larimore's detailed prose. A HIGHLY ENJOYABLE AND ABSORBING READ!"

~ **Barnes & Noble five-star review**

"A VERY PROMISING FIRST NOVEL where I escaped a hundred years before the French Revolution with delight, in tune with the perfumes, colors, and enchantments of Mother Nature!"

~ **Goodreads five-star review - France**

"I love the descriptions, conversations, and thoughts of this young man. It is AN INTRIGUING READ. I hope the author will write a sequel."

~ **Amazon five-star review**

"An EXTRAORDINARY, WELL-WRITTEN historical novel. The extremely well-done research of historical details, the mentioned remedies, as well as the pictorial scenes of the town life, the landscape, and the people, had an extraordinary impact on me. A MUST-READ."

~ **Goodreads five-star review - Germany**

"Engrossing read. DRAWS YOU INTO ITS WORLD, evoking the best and worst of the times in portrays. I CAN HARDLY PUT IT DOWN."

~ **Amazon five-star review**

"I really enjoyed the RICH HISTORICAL DETAIL and descriptions. The farther I got into the story the harder it was to put it down. It wonderfully captures a young man's search for his spiritual identity and the meaning of love."

~ **Amazon five-star review**

The LANGUAGE IS EVOCATIVE AND SENSUAL, which makes it a JOY TO READ."

~ **Goodreads five-star review**

THE MUSE OF
FREEDOM

A CÉVENOLES SAGAS NOVEL

JULES LARIMORE

Mystic Lore
Books
OJAI, CA

Mystic Lore Books
Ojai, California

First Published in the United States by Mystic Lore Books, 2022
For information on bulk discounts for book clubs, promotional, educational, or business use, contact us at;
https://www.facebook.com/mysticlorebooks or jules@juleslarimore.com

Notes on Plants, Cures, and Recipes

Details on plants, cures, and recipes in this novel are taken from various sources from the 1st-18th centuries and compiled to fit the story. (These can be found in the Bibliography). Some of the treatments and medical theory considered acceptable in the late 17th century, when this novel takes place, have now been disproved or even found to be toxic. Further, some helpful herbs may be confused with harmful and/or deadly substances. Thus, none of the information on plants, cures, or recipes in this novel should be considered health advice. The contents of this book is for entertainment purposes only and is not intended to diagnose, treat, cure, or prevent any condition or disease. The publisher and the author make no representations or warranties of any kind with respect to this book or its contents and disclaim all representations and warranties, including but not limited to warranties of healthcare for a particular purpose. In addition, the publisher and the author assume no responsibility for errors, inaccuracies, omissions, or any other inconsistencies herein. You understand that this book is not intended as a substitute for consultation with a licensed practitioner. The use of this book implies your acceptance of this disclaimer.

Editor, Laurie Chittenden. Book cover design, Gram Telen. Interior design, Jaycee DeLorenzo, Map Brushes, K.M. Alexander.

Identifiers: LCCN 2022913906 I ISBN - 979-8-9864488-0-0 (paperback) I ISBN 979-8-9864488-1-7 (hardback) I ISBN 979-8-9864488-2-4 (ebook)

Printed in the United States of America

to

Mary Bondurant Warren *1930 - 2021*
Historian and Author of The Bondurant Family Book Series

and

Militia (Lisha) Bondurant Larimore *1818 - 1891*
The last of my ancestors born with the "BonDurant" name, for carrying on the tradition of acceptance and compassion that I like to believe Jean Pierre Bondurant exemplified.

Note to Readers

This is a work of historical fiction inspired by the life of Jean Pierre Bondurant 1677-1734/5, yet much of the novel is a product of my imagination. Many of us—descendants and others—might have our own ideas of who Jean Pierre was and what he might have felt or done. This novel is my personal vision of the man after careful study of documented facts and in-depth research on the culture, politics, and historical events of the era. What I discovered was far different than my preconceived ideas. To learn more about which elements of the story are based on the few known facts, and for references to sources, see the Author's Notes and Historical Notes in the back of the book.

In this novel, you will see references to Protestants, Catholics, Roma, and others that were, and still are, considered to be derogatory. But, in many cases, you will also see the use of these disparaging words called out by certain characters as unjust and unacceptable. I chose to use these words to stay true to the times and as an opportunity to teach the importance of kindness and compassion.

Let the adventure begin!

Jules Larimore

"Since we pretend not to infallibility, let us not dogmatically determine that all but ourselves are in the wrong."
Jean Cavalier, Cévenol Huguenot and Camisard general

"Life is infinitely stranger than anything the mind could invent."
Sir Arthur Conan Doyle

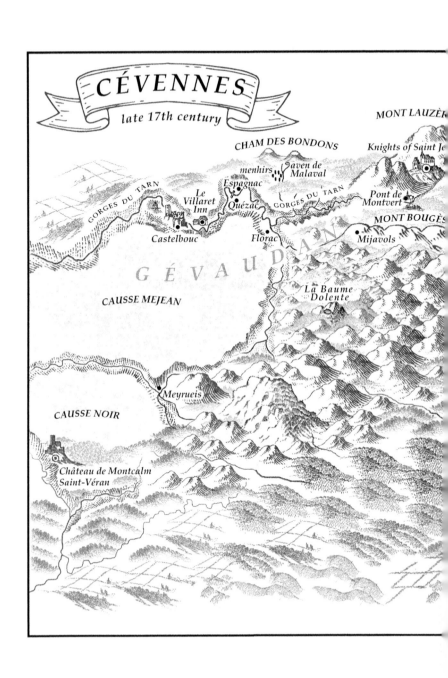

CÉVENNES

late 17th century

MONT LAUZÈRE

CHAM DES BONDONS

Knights of Saint Je

menhirs
aven de
Malaval

Espagnac

Le
Villaret
Inn

Quézac

Pont de
Montvert

GORGES DU TARN

GORGES DU TARN

MONT BOUGÈS

Castelbouc

Florac

Mijavols

G É V A U D A N

La Baume
Dolente

CAUSSE MEJEAN

Meyrueis

CAUSSE NOIR

Château de Montcalm
Saint-Véran

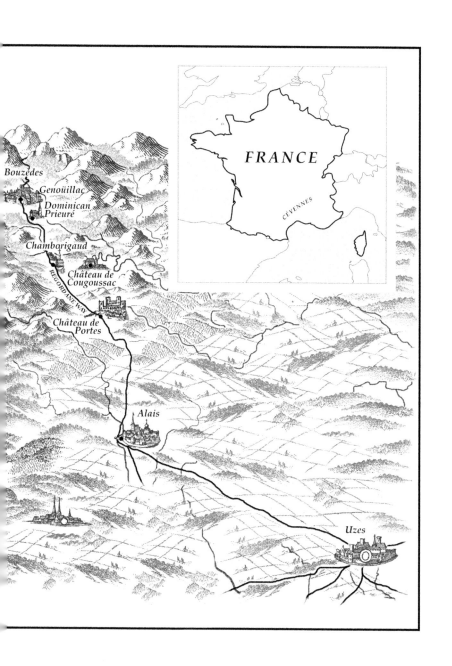

Bouzèdes

Genoüillac

Dominican
Prieuré

Chamborigaud

Château de
Cougoussac

REGORDANE WAY

Château de
Portes

Alais

Uzes

FRANCE

CÉVENNES

Contents

PART THREE

THE RECKONING

THE MUSE REFLECTS

The Gorges du Tarn, sheltering heart of the Cévennes mountains, was verdant that spring day after a morning rain, veiled in restless mists that kept old secrets hidden away. My homeland was a world apart from the lavish court gardens at Versailles, yet a majestic land where the deep greens of sweet-scented juniper and pine danced against the grays of moss-dappled stone cliffs. And baubles of amethyst orchids, ruby red poppies, and golden narcissus adorned and perfumed its woodlands and meadows. Few had chosen to build their homes in our remote, wild sanctuary protected by high cliff walls, but those who did came seeking peace and freedom. Much like the inquisitive young nobleman who had visited that day—the amiable Sieur BonDurant—an apothecary in training, traumatized by a childhood locked away in a Dominican prieuré.

On that fine May morning, in the year of our Lord 1696, it was easy to feel safe in the ethereal dreamscape created by glistening droplets of dawn's dew upon the oak and chestnut forests. Yet, with King Louis XIV's new Route Royale roads cutting deep into the peaceful heart, I sensed the dream would soon vanish with the morning mist and the *féerie* folk of the night.

Ushered in from the forest, a chilled breeze carrying aromas of earthy loam and something amiss blew through the window of my stone cottage, billowing the delicate lace curtains and turning pages in the old, illuminated tome I had opened on the table before me. I laid my hand over the fluttering pages, trying to keep the place where I had been reading. But the wind moved faster than I, and my fingers landed on a new page, pointing to a phrase I deciphered from the Latin manuscript.

You can lower yourselves to the level of the beast, but you can also be reborn as a divine creature by the free will of your spirit.

Such profound and powerful words. These divinely guided occurrences always carry a message, so I paid careful attention.

PART ONE
THE REVEALING

Dipsacus fullonum L.: *cardère sauvage*, teasel

The barbed, ovid head used to clean, align, raise, and reveal the nap of wool cloth thus softening its rough nature. The leaves bruised and applied to the temples allay the heat in fevers, qualify the rage in frenzies; the juice dropped in the eyes, clears the sight.

CHAPTER ONE
THE DAY OF JOYFUL MYSTERIES

Monday, 18 July 1695
Dominican Prieuré, Genoüillac, France
Hour of the Rosary

Jehan BonDurant dared not chart hope while still held behind the walls of this spiritual stronghold, yet the time to set out approached. The chapel doors of the Dominican Order of the *Frères Prêcheurs* stood open, and from his seat in the last pew, he stared out to the gardens, wilted and waning in response to the intense midsummer heat. Waves of humid air melted across the fields, cicadas thrummed and buzzed. Awaiting the moment he would walk into the sun and the shadows of his torment would cast behind him, he looked to the distant gates—the gates he hoped to walk through for the last time that day. Those gates had symbolically locked him in for eleven years, since the malleable young age of seven, and were now, finally, the gates that would open to freedom. But freedom from the prieré meant an unknown course lay ahead, and Jehan prayed that some guiding star would aptly lead his naif heart through the strange new world beyond the stone walls.

A faint breeze stirred past him to the frères and novices at prayer, cloaked and perspiring in their white woolen habits and caps. Jehan, too, wore the oppressive habit as one of several lay students forced to live at the *prieuré* because of their parents' refusal to give up the Reformed religion. The Bishop hoped students would join the Dominican Order by conversion and coercion. But Jehan was not convinced, not in the least. And he had let his unspoken rebellion to monastic life express itself in his growing locks. He was eager to leave for good and begin a joyful life. *Soon.* Soon Benat would arrive.

The nave reeked of muck-sweat despite the high-vaulted ceilings. At home, no one had associated bathing with the evils of nudity, as was the tradition here. Jehan tugged at his damp tunic where the white wool serge abraded his neck, longing for the serene embrace of cool water.

His eyes searched for anything to keep his mind clear, but the austerity of the prieuré's modest chapel had always unnerved him. The meager embellishments—a few small frescoes at the altars of the saints—offered no distraction, only frustration. The only lit candle was at the altar of the frères' patron saint, and only because of a significant bequest to cover perpetual maintenance of the altar's little lamp. Yet another pretense that, in Jehan's estimation, fell short of God's true glory. But, for today, none of it mattered. How could one pray, at all, on a day so important and too blessed hot for even a single candle?

He closed his eyes, merely appearing to be adrift in prayer, but his thoughts went elsewhere as he meditated on the rich inspirational triumphs of the great cathédrales depicted in the prieuré's old tomes. Their splendor floated through his mind, settling the flutter in his chest. He longed for the magnificence of those stained-glass, gilded marvels, illuminated by a thousand candles. Surely, his faith would be stronger in the presence of such miraculous triumphs.

Jehan's head slumped forward. As he drifted toward sleep, the nave melted behind his lashes. His awareness narrowed to the incessant sweat dripping off his brow and onto his hands. Even in this half-dream state, he sensed the peculiar emptiness when his wooden rosary slipped out of his hands, falling onto his lap.

Gradually, he came back to alertness, blinking, groggy. He lifted his scapular and wiped his hands on his tunic. When he picked up the rosary again, he stared at it, grasping at the realization that, today, his life would begin again and he could make it his own. His obligation to recite the Dominican prayers ended on this day, his eighteenth birthday, so all motivation to continue ceased and thoughts of home engulfed his mind.

He strained his neck around to view the gate again—*aw, no Benat yet*—then collapsed back into the pew with a faint moan. Benat, the *metayer* of the family's Château de Cougoussac, had agreed to make certain that the Dominicans would release Jehan without delay. *Ever faithful Benat*. He had been the one who always visited. Jehan's mother had come, just once, but that was years ago, in the beginning. He could never understand why his parents had abandoned him while they were still alive. Perhaps Benat, being a lifelong Catholic, was more comfortable spending time here. Whatever the reason, since Jehan's parents had passed, Benat was family.

Jehan tapped a thumb across his rosary beads and looked back to the nave where others, likewise, had succumbed to the urge to nap. Those still awake droned on in unison, "*Salve Regina, Mater misericordiae* . . . To thee do we send up our sighs, mourning, and weeping in this valley of tears . . ." He could never fathom why a prayer on Monday, the Day of Joyful Mysteries, should end in such a sad manner and vowed he would choose a different way of praying once at home. So many things he questioned, now that freedom was in sight.

The grating whine of the prieuré gates alerted Jehan. He checked the door again, but the glare of the midday sun washed out the two figures who had entered the *clos*. He could vaguely make out the rattleboned frame of the parish priest, Curé Gellion, from the Saint-Pierre Catholic church in town. *Why is he here? He cannot force me to stay. Not now.* And a second man, near the gate. A tall, middle-aged man in humble attire with the wide brim of his hat cocked to one side. *Benat!* Jehan's heart relaxed into a steady cadence.

Benat strode with confidence down the path ahead of the curé, who scuttled to keep up, his cumbersome black robes tangling between his legs. As they approached the chapel, the throbbing in

Jehan's chest surged again, and his temples pounded as if to burst. There was no way to know what trouble the curé would cause.

"Who are you?" Curé Gellion called out to Benat. "State your business here."

Benat stopped under the church portico outside the door, close enough that Jehan could see him wince before he answered. Benat turned and looked over his shoulder at Gellion. "Name's Benat. I'm here for Jehan BonDurant."

"Nnnnooo, no." Gellion stuttered and snarled, his face flushed. "*I'm* here to escort the young Seigneur BonDurant. I must show him how to serve the Lord in the real world. Prieur Chabert's teachings will only go so far."

The other students rustled and turned toward the disturbance outside. Curé Gellion was up to his old tricks, trying once again to take control where he had no authority. Jehan's shoulders tensed. He prayed Benat would not give in. *Not today.* Not on this joyful day of *émancipation.*

Benat gave a sedate response, showing a disregard for the curé's hysteria. "Monsieur Curé, what matters is that I know exactly who you are, and I've heard how you treat your flock. As for myself, I am a parishioner in Chamborigaud, where we are treated with respect. 'Twill be Jehan's choice where he is to take Mass. Your parish church is back up the road, and you know full well, this prieuré is Chabert's domain. Perhaps you have gotten yourself lost?"

Gellion squinted and shouted, "Do not question me. I have no need to give reason to you. The young seigneur must be taught to resist the temptations of the Reformed faith." He wagged his head as if in a fit of nerves and leered into the nave. Jehan glared back at him, determined not to show signs of intimidation.

"What else has Jehan learned during his years here, if not that?" Benat queried assertively. "He is no longer under the tutelage of anyone starting today. Not yours, nor Prieur Chabert's."

"The prayer is closing now," Gellion said as he took a step forward to enter.

But Benat swiftly leaned his hand on the chapel's door frame, blocking the curé. He stared at Gellion, his face just inches away.

Then, tapping his forefinger to his chest, Benat said, "*I* shall collect Jehan."

The youthful Prieur Chabert projected his closing with great poise in an energetic voice that echoed through the nave. "In the name of the Father, and of the Son, and of the Holy Spirit."

Jehan hastily crossed himself and rose to leave the chapel without delay, consoled to see Prieur Chabert step off the pulpit and follow him to the portico. Jehan was grateful for Chabert. Only a few years older than Jehan, he was an exceptionally young man to be appointed to the post of prieur. Chabert had spent his early years at the prieuré as a novice, so they had grown to adulthood together, and he had always watched after Jehan in the manner of a benevolent older brother.

As they stepped outside, Jehan pulled his hood around his face to ward off Curé Gellion's maliciousness.

"I am prepared to take my leave straight away," Jehan said to Benat.

Gellion clenched his fists, squinting like an angry fox. "Oh, no, you shall not," he said, his voice rising to a lurid squeak. "Not until we *give* you leave."

Prieur Chabert stepped in between, brandishing his unwavering confidence. He calmly laid a hand on the wily Gellion's shoulder and looked him directly in the eyes. "Jehan has his leave. He is no longer under the state's control, and he has made ready to do the Lord's work out in the world. Now, let him pass."

Gellion crumpled, giving in, then stomped down the path and out of the clos, dust enveloping his black robes.

Jehan kept his face hidden under the ample white hood. He folded his hands together and lowered his head in a silent blessing to the good Prieur Chabert. He would always hold profound respect for the prieur as a spiritual leader since, unlike the punishing abjurations Curé Gellion was known for, Chabert enticed Catholic conversions with a gentle, heartfelt enthusiasm. It was Chabert who had broken through the frozen ground of Jehan's traumatized spirit and had kept him safe from the more rancorous frères. And it would be a different world outside the prieuré gates without his protection and guidance.

After the air settled, the prieur accompanied Jehan and Benat toward the gate at a slow, steady pace. It aided in putting some distance between them and the obsessed curé, and allowed time for Chabert to dispense some advice. "Jehan, stay mindful of diversions. Whilst living here amongst us, you had to surrender worldly excitement and tame your passions. Yet now, I see the desire to explore is within you. Curé Gellion is overzealous at times, but he is right in that you have no experience resisting temptations. 'Twill be in your best interest to temper your desires and set a good example for the community."

"Thank you, Prieur," were the only words Jehan could muster. He fixed his eyes toward the ground as he and Benat passed through the gates and headed toward town. Exhausted by the tension, the advice seemed as if it were water pouring through a sieve.

Just beyond the clos walls, a current of fresh air moved up from the river, cooling Jehan's skin under the heavy woolen tunic and sending a revitalizing shiver through him. Sunlight reflected off the slow-moving water and danced through the trees along the river bank. A flock of ravens rustled and departed out of the trees, leaving behind a single bird in the reeds along the shore. Its iridescent black feathers sparkled as it snatched up a beetle and triumphantly cawed over its solo achievement. Like the rakish, jolly raven, Jehan was finally free to make his own way.

His lips parted, and he sighed. He pulled back his hood, brushing wet strands of hair from his face, and sensed a few tears blending with trickles of sweat. "Is this real, Benat, or a splendid vision?"

"'Tis real, Sieur. You are released. Now let's get you home."

BonDurant Townhouse Genoüillac, France
Early Afternoon

Jehan and Benat entered through the rear courtyard gates of the family's townhouse, the *grande maison de ville* at 42 la Grand Rue, one of two homes Jehan had inherited that day, along with three mills and some significant parcels of land. He scarcely remembered this place. Yet the country château, with its subtle majesty and life-giving lands, had stayed vivid in his mind, and it was there he wished to reside—far away from Curé Gellion, far from the prieuré walls.

While Benat patiently waited, Jehan lingered in the cool shade of a tall birch tree, coaxing memories, long subdued, to spring to life again.

He could envision it now . . . as a boy, his mother had insisted he enter this way and wash at the small fountain near the gate. She never wanted the salon's elegant black-and-white marble floors covered with soil from his gambols along the river. Cleanliness and purity were one in her mind. He would do anything to please her and, since she had passed, he wished to honor her as best he could.

He stared into the fountain where sunlight flickered upon the water, stirring up the past in small flashes—a tiny hand splashing in the water, the reflection of his young sister's face. *Françoise*! She had been less than three years old when he had last seen her.

"Benat. Have you news of Françoise? Is she still schooling at the Theyrargues Convent?"

"I have heard nothing, Sieur. She would be approaching her fourteenth year, would she not?'

Jehan tried to recall the day she was born. It was spring. The narcissus were in bloom. "I believe so. Last April."

"Then she is of the age to be released or, elsewise, take her vows."

Jehan could not imagine that she would choose to stay under the control of the abbess another day longer than required. Outrage welled in his throat for her, for himself, and for all children abandoned to religious confinement. He writhed and threw off the stifling scapular. Pulling at the tunic's neckline, he splashed fountain water across his face and let the cooling liquid run down his chest.

Soon. Soon he would shed the rough tunic for something more comfortable, more dignified—something to elevate his status. Though Prieur Chabert might disapprove of such finery, Jehan wanted desperately to shed *all* the Dominican rules that had held him down.

Benat removed his hat, rubbing his forehead as he stared toward the townhouse. "Perhaps your cousin knows more about your sister. He's managed all the family affairs since your father passed." Benat paused. An unsettled look in his eyes said there was something more. "Your mother . . . she had neither the strength nor the will to take on the burden of the *seigneurie*, and the houses, and the mills during the last year of her life."

"How is that?" asked Jehan. "I remember her as being strong and capable."

"'Twas the heartbreak. With you and Françoise gone to be educated by the church, then three babes in a row gone to the angels, watching your father take his last breath was too much for her to suffer. 'Twill be good for the estate to be back in your hands. Let us find your cousin so you can begin to set things right."

Jehan could only imagine how painful that must have been for her. He had no idea about the other children she had lost.

Benat motioned and they walked across the courtyard to the townhouse. He tried the rear door of the ground floor rooms used by Jehan's cousin, André BonDurant, for his apothecary shop. Locked— for the noontide closing. He then tried the door leading to the living quarters—also locked.

Jehan smirked and combed his fingers through his damp, tangled hair. "Well. 'Tis a wonderful welcome, is it not, Benat?"

"André is likely being cautious about roving thieves. There are many of 'em about after the famines." Benat cupped his hands to his mouth and called out toward the balcony, "André. André BonDurant. The seigneur of the house is home. Come, open the door."

André leaned out the balcony door. He still had his thick mane of dark curly hair and *Levantine*-like features—high cheekbones, dusky brown eyes, broad shoulders, and tall stature. Yet middle age seemed to be setting in far too soon.

Jehan leaned in to whisper to Benat. "He looks so much older than I had expected, yet I thought him to be barely past thirty years."

Benat tilted his head, studying André. "Hmm. A few lines around his eyes now, but that is to be expected after living most of his life amidst the death and destruction that besieged the region until recent times. The persecutions have aged many before their time, leaving even some of the young withered and listless."

André turned back into the townhouse and crowed. "They have arrived."

From behind him, came an elegant, dark-haired woman, great-bellied with child. She rested her hands on his shoulders, a smile beaming across her face. "Welcome home, Jehan. Do you remember me? I am the girl who used to distract Curé Gellion when he followed you around proselytizing."

"Lucrèce! Of course, I remember. So you have married André. I am ever so pleased. Yes, you saved me from Curé Gellion's clutches many a time."

"I see you will no longer require my assistance," she said. "You have truly grown into a man, fully capable of looking after yourself."

Jehan wished he could share her assurance. Had it not been for Benat and Prieur Chabert, he might still be fending Gellion off at this very moment. But her confidence bestowed a new lightness.

Lucrèce squinted a bit, with a studied expression. "Come closer, Jehan. Out of the shade and into the sunlight so I can get a better look at this man that you've become."

As he stepped forward, she leaned her elbows on the balcony railing and perched her chin on her palms. Her face beamed, her eyes radiant in the summer sunlight. In response to her pleasant attention, Jehan sensed an uncontrollable smile grow on his face.

"Such a striking resemblance between you and André, aside from your vibrant blue eyes and that infectious smile. Quite a handsome lot, all of you BonDurant *gentilshommes* with your rich, tawny skin tone. You will surely find a virtuous wife of quality before long."

Out of nowhere, two cherubic faces poked out from around Lucrèce's wide silk skirts and giggled. "Cousin Jehan! Cousin Jehan!" they chirped. "Come play cup-and-ball with us."

Jehan chuckled. These two could change his mind about his intentions to live at the château. Perhaps he would stay here at his townhouse, after all, at least a good share of the time. Innocence and joy would be healthy for his soul, having long since wearied of their deprivation.

"I shall be down shortly, Jehan," André called out, and then disappeared into the townhouse with Lucrèce and the little ones.

Jehan shifted in his chair, running his hand over the fine texture and rich colors of the tapestry upon the table. It was odd to be back in the salon of the well-appointed upstairs apartments. He had joined the other two men around a small card table, while Lucrèce and the children busied themselves in the family *solaire*.

"Tell me, André . . ." Jehan said, hoping to dispense immediately with any idle chat. "What do you know of Françoise? Will she be home soon?"

André poured them each a glass of wine with a disturbingly indifferent reaction. "We've had no word. We think she may have taken her vows."

Jehan's heart sank at the notion. He had expected the homecoming to be bittersweet, with most of the family passed and his sister locked away in the convent. But he had hoped Françoise would soon return. Once she was at home, he could learn who his real family was—who he was.

He glanced around the room to still his thoughts, admiring the wood paneling commissioned by his grandfather; the painting of his strict, yet kindhearted grandmother; the colorful embroidered linen curtains his mother had inherited. It set Jehan to reminiscing about the joyful times with his family—card games to pass the winter evenings, playing hide and seek with Françoise, chocolate drinks for the children, and for the adults, the *nouveau en vogue* exotic coffees from the Marseille port.

But André abruptly broke the spell with his practical thinking. "More income is needed to maintain the family properties. It would be good for you to learn the apothecary trade, Jehan."

"I was fascinated by the shop as a child and have often considered it. 'Tis certainly a noble endeavor to heal the sick. And some time away at medical school could help me forget my past misfortunes."

"Good then," said André. "You can be my apprentice. I could use a good worker."

Worker! Jehan could not bear the idea of more years of submission. He could feel the heat rise on his face at André's presumption.

After all, Jehan had already served the family well by his confinement to a stone slab in the prieuré, and all the while, André continued to live as usual, in comfort and style.

"I may want to learn your trade, and you may be my elder, but I am now the seigneur, not your indentured servant."

"Yes, yes, Jehan," André dismissed. "Now then, I shall have you take the room on the third floor . . . across from the laundress. That way you'll have a window toward the street."

Jehan wanted to curse André for his disrespectful proposal. He shook his head in disagreement while summoning the courage to speak up again. He grabbed the edge of the table, trying to steady the years of suppressed anger rising to the surface, then exhaled in a hushed tone. "The room across from the laundress? Have you run mad, André?"

Speaking his mind emboldened him and loosened an ill temper he never realized he had. He let his eyes blaze into André's, and insisted, "I shall take a bedchamber on the *family* floor."

He pushed his chair back, nearly knocking it over before Benat caught and righted it, then marched down the hall to inspect the chambers, with André and Benat following.

He paused at an open doorway, enraged blood coursing through his being, pounding in his ears. "Here . . . this one, facing the courtyard." A sense of empowerment began to settle in, and the throbbing faded. He took a deep breath of the potpourri-scented air and looked around the room. The old tester bed, with its gold and green embroidered Tree of Life canopy and curtains, invited him in. He stepped up on the side rail and let himself sink gently into the sheep's wool mattress. *Heavenly.* "I see you have moved my parents' bed and writing desk from the front chamber. *This* will do nicely."

"But this is my private chamber, Jehan," André objected, his voice taut.

Benat looked to the ceiling, keeping quiet.

"Well, naturally, this will necessitate that you lovingly share a bedchamber with your wife from now on . . ." Jehan allowed his tone to stay firm: like the young dog asserting his dominance over the pack leader, this required fearless assertion. ". . . as good peasant husbands do, and all husbands should."

"You cannot . . ." André responded until Jehan cut him off.

"Cannot?" Fully unleashing his defiance, Jehan stood tall, head to head with André. "You are living in *my* house by the grace of my late father and mother, and I shall *not* have you cast me down this way."

Benat broke his silence. "Sieur, there is a grand bedchamber waiting for you at the château. And your horse will be happy to see you, as well."

Jehan hesitated, weighing the matter for a moment, wanting to be practical and avoid a decision driven by heated emotion. His horse was his most valued asset. It meant freedom to travel and safety in a chase. Life would be different without the walls of the prieuré to protect him, so his horse was essential, though she needed the pastures of the countryside.

"André, we *must* have an agreement," Jehan said, trying his best to subdue his vexation. "I shall stay and be your apprentice, but I shall also spend time at the château whenever I see fit. You may instruct me whilst in the shop. However, I shall do my own determining about my life and the management of my properties, *including* this townhouse. As of today, you are my guest, not my master."

André's eyes widened, his gaze flitting around the room until he puffed and responded. "Alright then, Jehan, you may have the bedchamber."

The shock and disbelief written on André's face faded after a few brief moments, and he resumed his usual domineering swagger, hands on his hips, head cocked. "Now then . . . I have a council meeting to attend. Supper will be after Vespers, and you will need to be up by dawn to start in the distillery."

Jehan and Benat looked at each other, raising their eyebrows in the mutual realization that André would not readily be convinced he was no longer the one in charge.

The moment André set off for his meeting, Jehan sensed a new openness and fluttering in his chest, his mind brimming with images of herbs and potions. He was, in fact, eager to begin his apothecary training the next morning, in spite of how it might have sounded when he lashed out at André. It was something he had longed for as a child while watching André as a young apprentice with his great-grandfather.

"Sieur, now that you are settled, I should be on my way," said Benat.

"Of course. I shall walk you down. I want to take a look at the apothecary . . . to familiarize myself again."

On the way out, Jehan stopped by the solaire to fetch a spare shop key from Lucrèce. After a bit of convincing, she raised a brow and smiled as she handed it over. "I suppose André will appreciate your eagerness to learn. The only key I have is for the streetside door. He keeps the hallway door key on him at all times."

When Jehan reached the threshold of the front door with Benat, he paused to take a deep breath of the afternoon air. "Thank you for collecting me today," Jehan said. "I shall plan an outing to the château Sunday, after Mass." Though Gellion's church was the last place he wanted to be, it might otherwise cause a rout until the curé's obsession with Jehan faded a bit. Real freedom would need to come in measured doses—yet with every hindrance Jehan found it harder to restrain a seething urge to fight for it. "I suppose, for now, I had better attend the Church of Saint-Pierre or Curé Gellion will be beating my door down to drag me off with him."

"Surely enough, Sieur," agreed Benat. "And you will receive a hearty welcome at the château afterward. I believe you will enjoy learning the apothecary trade, but you will also need to master the skills required of a seigneur. It would give me pleasure to provide the necessary training."

Benat's care and concern settled Jehan a bit. Having been the family's loyal servant for years—since before Jehan was born, he was told—he trusted Benat's guidance. As métayer, he acted as steward of the seigneurie, possessing any skill a noblesse landholder might want to learn. During Jehan's childhood, Benat had been his patient teacher whenever his father was otherwise engaged—which, pitifully, was most of the time.

Jehan's mind cluttered with all he would need to attend to, now that the duty of running the seigneurie fell on his shoulders, but the things he had delighted in as a boy rose to the top. "I would, indeed, like to refresh my skills at riding, and hunting, and swordplay. I believe I have acquired all the mathematical skills and analysis needed for accounting and dealing with assets, thanks to Father Chabert's guidance."

"Oh, but there is also viticulture, milling, and chestnut harvesting," Benat added as he chuckled and headed off down the road.

Jehan waved, his heart lightened by the promise of new knowledge. "Sunday by midday, then."

Jehan stepped onto the ancient cobbled street of la Grand Rue—once the old Régordane road where travelers had passed since Roman times —and turned to study the front of the townhouse. *Now, this, I remember.* Two public entrances conveniently delineated private life from business life. The door to the right, from which he had come, led to the townhouse apartments. And the door to the left, where his new studies were about to begin, led to the apothecary shop.

He gazed up at the large three-story stone dwelling, cleverly embellished with several small, but elaborate sculptures. One peculiar carving illustrated a very sick-looking man with his tongue sticking out—every bit as intriguing now as when Jehan was young. A brief whimper of mirth formed in his throat, and his cheeks tightened into a smile. Smiles were such an odd sensation after his years of solemn existence. Still prominent above the arched doorway was the decorative lintel featuring a carved snake wrapping around three staffs.

The staff of Asclepius, the Greek God of healing . . . the symbol of the apothecaries and medics. Though something always seemed amiss —this carving had three staffs instead of the customary one—and he had yet to learn why.

He unlocked the apothecary shop's heavy wooden door and it groaned a little as he pushed. A cluster of small bells sounded with a dulcet tinkling that lingered in the stillness of the empty shop. Once they faded, it was utterly quiet, but his childhood recollections began to bring the place to life.

As his eyes wandered the room, he could hear the sounds of a busy day—the bustling about and chatting of patrons with prescriptions in hand. In his mind's eye, he could see them queuing along the oak cabinets that lined the walls, with rows of drawers that held a huge variety of potions and pills, ready-made for sale.

Above the cabinets, shelves climbed to the ceiling. Jehan's heart beat like a bee's wings as he eyed the jars of art and mystery that rested upon them—large, majolica ceramic jars labeled for the herb, oil, or other cures they contained. He had always been drawn to their radiant blue, gold, and green tin-glazing. Some displayed a coat of arms while others were adorned with mythological figures and swans set against a landscape. Once when he was young—when no one was looking—he had climbed the ladder and peered inside a jar to see its magical contents. He had been certain it contained some divine giver of life; some ingredient from God's forests or meadows.

Glass bottles of amber, verdigris, and crystalline clear caught the sunlight with a beauty that now sparked his devotion far more than the wafer held high at Mass. He ran his hands slowly over the various mortars and pestles that lay scattered atop the counters and tapped a finger on the brass scales, setting them teetering. He had no doubt the shop was well stocked and would have precisely the cures his own patrons might desire: all weighed out on this set of scales, in precisely the correct proportions.

Through an open doorway was the distillery, the room devoted to the distillation of oils, with a *bain-marie* furnace installed over a massive hearth. On most days, the hearth would be glowing with a crackling fire in readiness for the preparation of another batch. But today, with André away, the hearth was quiet and cold. On the one day, many years ago, that Jehan had been allowed to watch the process, a peculiar fusion of cardamom and thyme had scented the air. It must have recorded itself in his mind since the aroma suddenly awoke in his nostrils.

Forgetting all else, he lost himself in a strange euphoria, his eyes foraging the room as he beheld every detail and imagined himself creating the finest cures to heal the ailing townsfolk.

In his distraction, he stumbled and almost fell backward when he discovered the bizarre menagerie of dusty stuffed creatures hanging high among the ceiling rafters. To most observers, the crocodile, two turtles, and an assortment of petrified fish would seem more like an absurd flock of birds than beings of the land and sea. Jehan surmised it was his cousin's clever way to advertise access to the rarest and most effective ingredients from the furthest parts of the world, although he would find it difficult to give André the credit if he stood face to face with him.

Leaning against a cabinet, Jehan closed his eyes and pondered for a long while. Why had he fallen so easily into such spiteful envy of André? In less than an hour away from the prieuré, he had already lapsed into pride and greed, then wrath, and now envy. Could he not be free of these irreverent temptations? Was this his cousin's doing or perhaps his own? Jehan pressed his hands to his forehead and heaved a long, weighty breath. If only his Dominican upbringing would not lash out at him with such guilt at every minor offense of the cardinal sins.

"The shop is just as splendid as I remember," said Jehan, as he entered the solaire, finding Lucrèce quietly reading, a hand on her belly. He sat on the settee next to her and handed over the key. "And so is your alluring beauty."

Her cheeks blushed against her pale skin. "I thank you for the compliment. And you already know, from the foolish words I blurted earlier . . . I think you have become quite the striking gentilhomme." She looked down and brushed a finger over her supple lips, then drew a slow breath and looked up. "This prompts a discussion I had hoped to have in a few weeks, yet . . . I am feeling . . . we must have it sooner rather than later."

"Yes, Lucrèce?" Jehan asked, curiosity thrumming through him.

"Jehan . . ." She seemed to be having trouble looking in his eyes. "I think we should begin working on finding you a marriage match."

"What? I have just gotten myself free," he huffed. "I am not ready to be tied down to a wife." Yet he would gladly marry Lucrèce if André had not already thwarted that idea. He leaned in to taunt her, as he had done when he was a boy. "Of course, were I to find a wife like you, Lucrèce, it might be an entirely different matter."

She pushed gently on his chest—the warmth of her hand suddenly searing through his tunic and sending throbbing waves down his length. She quickly released it and stood.

That touch. Jehan clutched his head and ran his fingers through his hair. *I am slipping again.* He would never escape the prieuré if he fell into such lust every time he was near a woman. And a woman with child, at that. The knowledge of his sins already burdened him far too much to miss confession, and it had only been a few hours since his departure.

"Someday you will find your muse, Jehan. One your own age. One who will inspire and motivate you. Then you will finally feel freedom like you have never known. And I can help you on that account."

Jehan felt the need to move. He stood, then began a slow pacing. Lacking experience in controlling his lusts, he would need help—

somehow. Perhaps marriage to another, to this inspiring muse, would be the only way to quell his interest in Lucrèce. Was that the sort of freedom that she spoke of? "How is it that you can help? Do you not need a matchmaker?"

Lucrèce sat back on the settee. "Between André's family and mine, I have a large, finely woven *réseau* of prominent cousins and local *noblesse* from whom to seek matches. Since I never seek a remittance, many in the family have come to me for introductions."

He walked over to her and paused. "I can see how your charming words work well to persuade men and women alike." Yet he was prepared to stall as long as he could—if he could only manage to resist the enchantment she had held over him since a boy.

She nodded in commitment to the task. "Then I shall start correspondence with Sieur de Montcalm de Saint Véran concerning a match with his daughter Louise," she said cheerfully, then let out a sigh of relief. "She is of the right age, just twenty, and I am told she is quite becoming."

Jehan remained standing over Lucrèce, arms crossed, trying to build some resilience to her plans.

"I see from your look, you are not in full agreement," she responded. "I know it is an important decision, but do not worry, my friend. I shall arrange an introduction first, then you can decide. I've oft thought Louise would be a promising wife for you. She is your fourth cousin and her family holds many titles and great wealth. You are both descended from François de Montcalm. I must tell you, though, I am not certain where his family's loyalties lie. In the past, they were supporters of the Knights of Saint Jean who follow the Roman Catholic traditions, but they have also been strong defenders of the Protestant faith. I hear they are now *nouveau converti*, having voluntarily abjured to keep their fortunes."

"But might they still practice the Reformed faith in secret?" Jehan asked.

"We will only know more when you pay them a visit."

Jehan rejected the thought of embroiling himself with those who defied the law, but perhaps he should consider a family who could be compassionate to both sides of these religious divisions. He wasn't sure if there were many lifelong Catholics who would understand the entanglement of his family's history with the Reformed faith. He did not yet understand it himself. His arms dropped and he felt his resolve wane. "I would need to marry in the Catholic church or it would ruin me."

Lucrèce smiled, sweet and radiant, warming again the atmosphere that had gone cold and difficult. "I shall write to inquire on which medicinals they might be in need of. Surely, they will be wanting the Castlebouc honey from Menina Elise and her granddaughter. You can deliver them when Sieur de Montcalm writes back and is willing to extend an invitation. Patience may be required for his response . . . and for good weather. 'Tis an arduous ride to the Château de Saint Véran, and you will need to take every precaution."

"Very well, Lucrèce. We shall wait for their reply." Jehan prayed the wait *would* be long. He would have all the patience in the world.

CHAPTER TWO
ILLUSIONS OF THE TIMES

15 September 1695
Apothecary Shop, BonDurant Townhouse Genoüillac, France

Time spent in the apothecary's distillation room was among Jehan's favorite activities. But with September's warm temperatures, afternoons were not the most desirable time to work. He had risen before dawn and toiled over the blazing hearth fire to finish another distillation, trying to complete his day's work while the morning was young. Yet today he was motivated by more than just the heat. He wiped his damp brow on the sleeve of his work coat hoping that, after nearly two months of apprenticing, today would finally be the day André would trust him to go to Uzès market for supplies. No word had come from the Montcalms, and although the apothecary craft fascinated his mind to no end, Jehan still yearned for some new escapade.

The unmistakable scuffling of André's footsteps could scarcely be heard over the bain-marie furnace, but it was enough to catch Jehan's attention.

"The candles have nearly melted," André bellowed as he carried in two plates of bread, *charcuterie*, and melon. He donned a work apron so, surely, he did not intend to go to market himself. "You must have been up all night to get through this much work. 'Tis a good thing you are nearly finished. I will need you to go to Uzès since Lucrèce's babe will arrive any day. I cannot risk being gone just now."

There it was—exactly the chance Jehan had waited for, even though André had phrased it as a command for his own benefit rather than as a request or a mark of confidence. None of that mattered now, as long as Jehan had the freedom to set out on an adventure at last.

Nodding vigorously, he replied. "Yes, yes. Most assuredly, I would be delighted." He rushed to take his pack-saddle from the wall peg near the door. "I shall prepare immediately."

While Jehan loaded the pack-saddle and nibbled at his food, André pulled a map from the pocket of his apron and laid it on a table. He began discussing the particulars of the best route to Alais—the overnight stop to Uzès—when the bells on the shop door sounded. André was so absorbed in describing the mission that he did not look up to see the woman entering with a young girl in tow. The blush of dawn's light and an aroma of freshly baked bread followed them in. A conservative, pious woman, no doubt, in her dark drab attire, a white linen coif and simple lace collar her apparel's only ornamentation.

"Ahh . . . guided by the good Lord," she said. "This is the place, 42 la Grande Rue."

The little girl's face beamed with delight as she looked up at the door's bells and echoed them with a melodic giggle. "*Tanta*, Tanta. Look!"

The woman smiled, but shook her head and raised a finger to her lips in a gesture to silence the girl. "Quiet now, *ma poulette*." She stepped into the door of the distillation room. "Pardon, Monsieur BonDurant."

André raised his head with a startled glare on his face, appearing none too pleased to see the woman. He held a hand up to Jehan, signaling him to stay put. "I'll take care of this," he said, then strode into the front room and came to stand very close to her. Closer than seemed appropriate.

Jehan wondered who this woman could possibly be, but he held back in the distillery room, studying the interactions while he continued to pack. The wall lantern cast enough light on the woman's face that he could see a flush come to her cheeks. Was she here because she had an ague? Still, that did not explain why she and André stood so close.

"André . . ." The woman tilted her head, somewhat coquettishly, completely ignoring the little girl tugging at her skirt for attention. "You have changed little in the years gone by."

Jehan decided it best to stop packing and keep an eye on this puzzling situation. The flush in the woman's cheeks subsided, so it must not have been from fever. Embarrassment, perhaps? Or was she blushing?

"Marthe, what brings you to Genoüillac?" André asked in a sharp, but hushed tone.

She clutched her hands, appearing rather nervous. "I come seeking your services, André. Because I know I can count on you, my dear friend. Oh, how I deeply wish our meeting again, after so many years, could be under more favorable circumstances. Pardon for my coming so early, but I must use utmost care as I move about the villages."

Care? Why would this woman need to be careful? Jehan stepped a little closer to the open door.

"You most certainly do require care and *discretion*," said André. "It could prove dangerous should village folk recognize you as Pasteur Brousson's wife. You could have been sighted by some wretch hungry for a reward."

Pasteur? That explained her clothing. It had been ten years since Reformed pasteurs and their families had been allowed in the country. That would mean she was here illegally, yet Jehan had often heard talk that some still practiced in barns and in the forests. In his mind, everyone deserved the right to worship as they chose. But it was not usual for André to show so much concern over a Reformed Huguenot, so this woman must have been someone special.

"Is your husband preaching again around the Cévennes?" André continued, rubbing at the nape of his neck. "You know that will put us *all* at considerable risk. The King's *Intendant* will have me put to the wheel if he learns I've allowed a pasteur's wife into town."

By Holy Marie in heaven. Jehan inhaled to suppress uttering an

26

oath out loud. Did they truly believe he could not hear them? And they were leaving the poor child wandering the shop on her own.

"*Oc* . . . yes. I am aware there would be risk . . . if he were here with us. But do not worry, dear friend . . ." Drawing close to André's ear, she spoke with an intimate softness that Jehan strained to hear. "Claude is far away from town, deep in the mountains with his faithful. I had to take the chance to journey here, for my husband's sake. He lies ailing with a bout of consumption in a cold, damp cave. 'Tis the only place he is safe from the Intendant's dragoons."

"Hush, Marthe," said André. "I need not hear of his Reformed flock and their secret gatherings. If only you had abjured with me when we were young, our lives may be much different today."

The secret entanglement with these two went far deeper than Jehan cared to know. Deciding this unseemly interaction had gone far enough, he walked into the shop. "How can we help, Madame?"

André flinched and turned.

Marthe's eyes widened and she raised her voice again. "We are being taken care of, thank you. Monsieur BonDurant is, needless to say, the *best* apothecary in the Cévennes. We shall purchase his cures and depart without delay."

André was always malleable with a little flattery, and this Marthe woman seemed to be fully aware of that.

"Very well. I will help you," André groaned. "Jehan, check the streets. Ensure there is no one out there, then lock the door. This patron requires a private consultation."

While André did these consultations on occasion—for cases of syphilis or some other shameful ailment best handled in private—Jehan did not understand why he needed to check the streets. Was André afraid of missing another patron, even at this early hour? Or was it that he was about to dispense a cure without the proper prescription from a physician?

Jehan brusquely opened the door, setting the bells to jingling again. The long shadows of early morning retreated as the emerging daylight illuminated la Grande Rue. He surveyed every direction, observing what little he could see of the side streets and portals, looking out for meddlesome eyes from behind shuttered windows set ajar. But there was not a living soul in sight. He came back inside to the counter with the little girl skipping close at his heels.

André waved Jehan over. "Umm . . . Mar . . . Madame, you have not yet met the son of my poor deceased cousin, God rest his soul." He raised a hand with a flourish towards Jehan, rolling it palm up, indicating nobility. "This is Sieur Jean Pierre BonDurant. He prefers to go by Jehan to honor our grandfathers."

"Jehan . . . the name of many a troubadour," Marthe said. "I do admire a traditional *langue d'oc* name. Several years ago, when André and I were young, he spoke to me of your predicament. I am sorry you had to spend your youth at the prieuré. I believe anyone who has fallen victim to the state's oppressive powers deserves compassion. So . . . have the Dominicans now allowed you to come home for good?"

"Jehan has completed his schooling with our good Prieur Chabert," André answered before Jehan could speak. "So with this firm foundation, he is now apprenticing with me. Jehan, may I introduce Madame Marthe Dollier Brousso . . . um, excuse me . . . Beauclose."

Jehan stepped in and bowed his head. "Good day, Madame . . . pardon, was that Brousson or Beauclose?"

"Beauclose, indeed." She swallowed hard and did not look Jehan squarely in the eyes.

"But Tanta . . ." the little girl whispered, tugging on the woman's skirts. She gently squeezed the girl's hand and pulled her close.

Marthe took a quick curtsey. "What a pleasure to meet such a fine young gentilhomme in this town of country ease. And this is my niece, Elisette, whom I believe could spend the entire day here, captivated and enchanted by your shop."

Beads of perspiration formed on André's brow and his dark eyes held extreme concern as he spoke. "Jehan has been our Seigneur de Cougoussac since his émancipation."

"Fortunate indeed," Marthe said. "Sieur BonDurant, why are you not at court as the King commands of his noblesse? Why do you tarry here?"

"I often envision life at court. I hear the fashions are *truly* splendid," said Jehan, imagining the stunning, but costly, ensembles that the local tailor had informed him were required. "Yet it would strain our finances were I to become one of King Louis' courtiers . . . unless I can rebuild the former wealth of our seigneurie."

"Surely that will not take long," said Marthe. "Land is the best way to riches if you can manage them fairly . . . so as to keep good, loyal tenant farmers and staff."

"Jehan is well respected by his seigneurial métayer," said André. "He says Jehan has surpassed his father in the skill of oversight, although that would not be too hard given his father's inclinations when he was alive."

These inclinations—obsessions as André often called them—still mystified Jehan. His cousin would never explain what he meant, so it remained a secret. Perhaps it had to do with women or too much drink. Whatever it was, Jehan's father had drained a substantial portion of their assets. And this boasting about Jehan's skills was unnerving considering André had never offered any form of praise before.

Jehan would need to rein in André's expectations; unfulfilled they would only give him reason to criticize. "Yet my skills alone will by no means bring balance to the books. 'Tis most unfortunate that even the noblesse are being required to pay the new *capitation* taxes just as we have lost our exemption on the *taille* property tax."

André paid him no mind and moved to the counter where he began preparing a compound for Marthe. His fidgeting with the scales and shuffling of bottles attracted Elisette's wandering little fingers. He said nothing but pushed the little girl's hands away and gave her an annoyed, sidelong glance.

Jehan's stomach hardened with vexation at André. Perhaps conversation with others would be the only way to get his point across without sparking the fury he seemed to often feel towards André. He turned to Marthe. Fortunately, she provided quite the convenient audience while she waited for her medicinals.

"You see, Madame . . . while André speaks highly of my skills, we still have challenges ahead. Along with new taxes, our fixed rents fetch only a meager income, and as you must know, crops have been failing miserably with the ceaseless years of cold weather. With André and Lucrèce's growing family, our share of the crops barely suffices to feed our household, let alone return a profit."

André must have thought he was out of Jehan's sightline when he crossed his arms and began shaking his head, but Jehan could plainly see him out of the corner of his eye.

Marthe sniffed and raised her chin. "I am ever so sorry to hear, Sieur. Yet, God be praised for what we *do* have."

She was right. Jehan's shoulders dropped as he glanced towards the floor. He *should* consider what he was grateful for. "I do remind myself the worry over taxes and income is a fair price to pay . . ." A faint quiver came to his voice as bitter memories crept in and he trailed off in a murmur, ". . . so long as I am free from the grasp of the more ungodly frères." He cleared his throat and raised his mist-shrouded eyes, then took a deep breath. "At times, I am grateful my sister Françoise is safe with the nuns, though I miss her dearly."

A thought came to him that lifted his cheeks into a weak smile. "I may need to change how things are being done . . . devise new . . . solutions! I could . . . enforce the mill tax my father saw fit to drop. Elsewise, we might resort to surviving off chestnuts."

Marthe glanced into the distillation room. "Truly, Sieur?"

Jehan turned to follow the direction of her glare. *She must see the half-eaten plates of food.* Abashed by his own hypocrisy, a faint moan slipped inadvertently from his mouth.

"You would enforce yet another tax?" she asked. "The famines have been hard on all of France, including your poor tenants. I've met some of them and they blessed your father for offering them a reprieve. And concerning chestnuts, many people would be pleased to have them, yet even those were destroyed by ice storms in the high mountain villages."

André scoffed at Jehan, "Hah!" Then turned and smiled tenderly at Marthe. "You always could win a debate."

Again, she makes a good point. Had he learned nothing from his years of harsh living? And now he wanted to chain his tenants to a life of poverty to keep himself in high style? His thoughts restled in his head until some sort of instinctual defense won out. *Yet she knows nothing of the struggles that come with my title.*

30

"But, Madame, there is *so* much required of me as the seigneur," Jehan complained. "We could all be in debtors' prison were it not for André's apothecary trade and our tenants."

Marthe cocked a brow at Jehan, tapping her fingers on the counter in a most fitful manner. "You are luckier than many to have such a trade. And your status offers you the privilege of choosing to join André."

Clearly she did not understand the regulations placed on noblesse. It was not only the lower classes who were directed by their authoritarian king.

He shook his head hard. "No, no, my standing does little good in the matter. It limits me nearly as much as if I were a Protestant by forbidding me to legally practice my preferred profession as an apothecary. Or even in the direst of situations, to plow my own lands. That is why I am considering the tax."

She curtly turned away and fixed her eyes on André, watching him prepare the medicines while she spoke sardonically. "Well then, Sieur Jehan, if you cannot become a licensed apothecary, why are you studying the trade?"

It was as if the woman were discrediting his choices, joining forces with André in ridicule. Jehan tried not to let her tone fuel his feelings of worthlessness—the ones kindled by his abandonment and stolen childhood. They were always simmering just below the surface and, of late, it did not take much to spark those feelings into flames of anger.

"I have designs to attend University of Montpellier medical school, Madame. 'Tis also said to be forbidden to one in my position, yet I shall send a letter of appeal. Certainly, when I return to become prosperous and well respected throughout the region, the King will be pleased that I have more land to tax, and . . ."

André broke in just as Jehan took another breath to continue.

"Well now, Jehan, we must serve our patron and not hinder her departure any longer. What would *you* prescribe for her husband's consumption? Or have you not completed your reading on this ailment yet? The remedy would be . . . to discourage the phlegmatic humor."

Could André not let him answer even one question before firing another? Jehan's cheeks went afire. *Surely, they must be the crimson of fall heather.* The humiliation quickly roused his sleeping anger. He scowled at André as he persisted in his disparaging tone.

"You see, Jehan, that requires three parts elderflower and one part yarrow or goldenrod, as I have blended here, and hot, dry foods such as millet and onions. And . . . of course, the Castlebouc honey as well . . . best in all the Cévennes. Now, write up the advisory to go along with the formula so Madame can be on her way."

Jehan put his head into his hands and rubbed his temples for a few moments before looking up. "Since you alone, Master Apothecary, seem to possess *all* knowledge, *you* should assist your friend. Yet . . . you seem to have forgotten one thing . . . the blue lungwort in small quantities. Yes, cousin André. You *are* the clever one! But now I, too, must be on my way," he proclaimed, adding a generous dose of self-importance. He turned and stormed out of the room feeling the fury of a caged lion breaking free.

As Jehan stomped up the stairs to the family apartments, his fit of rage felt like a dose of arsenic poisoning his soul. André's pharmacopeias said frenzies such as these were often aided by allowing the full vessel to vent. It helped a bit to vent. But only a bit. Perhaps a method for other sorts of fits could bring full relief, such as the leaves of wild teazels, *Dipsacus sativus*, crushed and applied to the temples. Or those for purging melancholy and quieting the frantic person such as borage. Jehan needed more guidance on this affliction, but it would be better sought from someone other than André.

Jehan slowed his pace as he walked to his bedchamber, letting breath replace the bitterness that clenched at his chest. When he opened the old oak armoire, he stared, unable to decide which of his father's carefully hung garments would serve him best on his journey to Uzès. After the strained interactions in the shop, he found it difficult to concentrate. André spent so much of his time confining Jehan's life—his every move, every thought, every step he took. *What senseless hindrance.*

And it did not go unnoticed that André and this Beauclose woman had something to hide. Perhaps a past love affair? Jehan had enough to worry about and certainly did not need a scandal to tarnish the family's already questionable reputation. Over the two months since his release from the prieuré, he had developed misgivings about his duties as Seigneur de Cougoussac, including the new burden of accountability for his family's behavior. So much rested on his shoulders now. He had gone from living a simple, quiet monastic life—one that locked him behind cloister walls but provided for his basic needs —to reigning over the estate that would ensure the sustenance and safety for, not only himself, but also his family, a small staff, and the five tenant households that farmed his lands. At least while on his trip to Uzès, he could be a free man and leave the worry behind.

He leaned into the wardrobe toward a small lavender sachet hanging on the door. Though it was a hot, dry substance that was not considered fitting for his fiery condition of the choleric temperament, somehow it always soothed him as a child. He took in a long breath of its fragrance, sighed, and recited from his recent readings. "*Lavandula stoechas*. Helps the panting and passion of the heart and swimming of the brain. Restores strength lost, and by its heating faculty, comforts the brain to treat melancholy, and will cheer all the Spirits." Then he scoffed to the empty room, "How is that for you, Monsieur Master Apothecary?"

The morning was slipping away fast, so Jehan began to deliberate over the three ensembles inherited from his late father. While locked away in the prieuré and relegated to the simple Dominican tunic, his daydreams of fine clothes and fine living had helped lift his spirits. Yet, as seigneur, elaborate fashions were more than a mere diversion; they would grant him higher regard were he to join the other noblesse and bourgeoisie in flattering their King by imitation. Once at market, he would search for the finest quality ensembles of silk damask and elegant Alençon lace. But, for now, he would simply make do with what was here. Surely there was something better than a tunic or André's handed-down work clothes.

Jehan carefully selected and donned the most appropriate ensemble, one of twilled wool, dyed brown—the commoners' color. Its knee-length justaucorps had side pleats and no more than the necessary buttons, with a matching sleeveless waistcoat of the same length. He found it quite conservative for noblesse attire. Nevertheless, the somewhat elevated details would make the ensemble acceptable in higher social circles. He caressed the plushness of the wide, wine-red silk velvet cuffs covering from elbow to forearm, and studied the simple bobbin lace on the *chemise* sleeves flowing across the top of his hands.

After readying himself, Jehan went downstairs to the apothecary shop, where André was busy with another patron. Thankful to see it was not Madame Marthe Beauclose, he slipped quietly in and passed through the open door to the distillation room.

He gazed at his reflection in a large copper vessel to check the fit of his father's old ensemble. Although it was of high quality, it had been tailored for an older man. It was a bit tight across his well-developed shoulders and too loose in the waist, so Jehan took it in mind he would soon purchase one in a more exciting shade.

Perhaps a deep blue. Blue would be more befitting for a noble, or at least a chevalier, be it dyed by indigo or woad; it did not matter so long as it abided by Colbert's import policies.

He sensed soft-footed movement in the room, then caught sight of André's distorted face in the copper vessel, grotesque and bizarre, hovering in from behind. Jehan did not turn around, or even react, but instead continued to peer at his own reflection a bit longer. "I thought to wear this cravate in the new fashion." He placed the band of white linen fabric around his neck, twisted it, and tucked the end into a buttonhole. "I have seen wealthy import merchants traveling the Régordane road wear theirs in this manner. Seems quite practical."

Jehan turned to speak to André but found him oddly absent in a distant silence. "I am glad my father had the sense to order these knee breeches instead of the old-style loose slops many still wear around here. *Far* too much cloth to get caught up in stirrups and weapons." Jehan rubbed the tight-fitting wool fabric that covered his thighs, grown solid and sinewy in the past year. "These will be much better for my ride out to market."

He pulled up a stool and sat to put on the only pair of stockings he owned—pearl-gray woolen twill that he tied up with black garter ribbons. He had no boots that fit, but regardless, he added his father's lace-topped linen boothose along with his own well-worn, dark brown shoes sans the usual silver buckles.

André smirked slightly. "Well, that will do, but the boothose are just an unnecessary indulgence that may call you to the attention of bandits or *bohémiens*. What you will need is a *perruque*. I shall allow you to use mine until you can purchase one of your own."

Jehan clumsily removed the boothose and tossed them aside in frustration, then shot back a reply, "Why would I want to wear the 'unnecessary indulgence' of a perruque when I have a fine head of hair?" Jehan did not care for André's offer in the least. He had tried to tidy his long, dark locks to frame his face in waves, setting off his high, proud cheekbones and square jawline. But he knew, without a doubt, they were not the restrained locks of the perruques customarily worn by the noblesse.

"Jehan, from the conversations in the shop earlier, you clearly thrive on soliciting attention and lack any discretion concerning family matters. You cannot be so loose-lipped. 'Tis hard to tell who to trust in these times . . . Catholics, nouveaux convertis, the Reformed . . . each has an agenda."

Jehan ignored the lecture in order to preserve his patience. He took his father's sword belt and light rapier sword from a cabinet near the door and placed them around his hips. Then picked up André's carefully drawn map, folded it, and tucked it into his saddlebag. "Have you the list of herbs and spices to be purchased?"

André took a small parchment with notations from his desk and handed it over, then clasped his hands behind his back in his typical stance for dispensing fatherly warnings, "I do trust that your trip will be a success, and I'm thankful that you can go in my place. However, since this is your first time traveling the cities, there are things you should know for your own safety, aside from the usual thievery and road dangers." Jehan rolled his eyes at André but remained tight-lipped as he continued, "When you are in Uzès at market, don't let the charlatans swindle you out of good money. Believe me, they will try. And be mindful of the wenches. They will pilfer your pockets when you embrace or give you some woeful story to elicit your sympathies. Not a single *denier* for any of them, no matter how enchanting."

"Hmm." Jehan gave André a look from under his brows. "How is it you are so familiar with the ways of harlots?"

André folded his arms across his chest. "Never you mind that, Jehan. Just let me continue. You will need to watch for clipped coins everywhere. And upon arrival in both Alais and Uzès, go straight away to the earliest Mass. Make certain to go there before going to your lodging, do you understand? No one must think you're not of the King's religion."

"But of course, I *am* of the King's religion, as are you."

"But since you were first baptized in the Reformed faith, you must be careful," reminded André. "The Intendant Basville and his men are always suspicious of the *nouveaux convertis*, despite the many years you spent at the prieuré's school. And be sure to keep with the crowds in town so you don't attract attention."

"So many rules. I may as yet be back at the prieuré." Jehan stared out the window to escape the irksome instructions and envision what his trip would really be like. In his imaginings, he wandered the streets of the cities, seeking all things exotic and exciting—tasting, touching, tempting himself like never before. *My chance for a bit of freedom, and I plan to take advantage!*

André nudged Jehan's arm. "Here." He pulled up Jehan's hand and planted a small purse that emitted a muffled jangle of coins. "'Tis enough to take you through your trip, and for the herbs and other medicinal ingredients. And you shall need to keep your certificate of Catholic conversion close to your person at all times, lest you be detained." André rustled in the pocket of his overcoat and pulled something out, holding it between his fingers. "Oh, and this."

Jehan caught only a quick glimpse of the small silver object André held. Firelight from the hearth was captured in a glimmering, brilliant moment on a medallion of some sort. He could barely make out the details, since the carving was crude and simple. There was a flying bird, and maybe—a triangle—but there was no way to know for sure since André's thumb was covering it as he slipped it into the purse.

"Show it to Monsieur Jacques Arnaud, the innkeeper at Le Cristal

Blanc Inn in Alais. He was a friend of your father's and his inn is one of the few places to provide safe lodging for nouveaux convertis. I've marked the route on the map. 'Tis close to the cathédrale, so go directly there after mass."

Exhilaration over the upcoming adventures coursed through Jehan. And all the mystery around this medallion, and the so-called Madame Beauclose, heightened his realization that his world was about to change—it would no longer be quiet, or simple.

Jehan took the purse, tied it under his waistcoat, slipped on his black felt hat, and with a brisk motion, grabbed the saddlebag and headed out the door. "Farewell, cousin. I shall see you by the Sabbath."

CHAPTER THREE
REUNITED

15 September 1695
Château de Cougoussac, France
Late Morning

"Good day, Sieur," called out Métayer Benat to Jehan as he entered the grounds of Château de Cougoussac. The humble old two-wheeled chaise he rode in, pulled by a sturdy little *Mérens* cart pony, heaved and jolted as it rolled over stones jutting from the dirt road.

Benat was walking the floodplain field below the château where the tenant farmers, teamed with a dozen hired workers armed with scythe and sickle, were harvesting the millet crop along the river near the mill.

Benat stepped up to the road and removed his hat, wiping his moist brow as Jehan pulled alongside him.

"Whoa," Jehan called out to the pony.

Benat's graying locks gave away his decades of hard work, but his tall, hearty physique expressed an able, energetic, even youthful man despite his nearing fifty years.

"A pleasant surprise to see you, Jehan."

"As always, Benat. 'Tis good to see you as well." Jehan tethered the reins to the dash rail. "The hemp field is certainly looking fine. A worthy idea, indeed, to rotate it into the winter wheat field when not in use."

"Yes, quite a practical crop," Benat said. "The hurds that would otherwise be discarded can be used to freshen the animal's bedding."

"It might bring a superior price if we take it to the port markets for rope making," Jehan suggested, assaying his ability to contribute to the seigneurie management.

"Yes, Sieur. I agree. Could fetch an admirable price in Montpellier. But we should stay clear of Aigues-Mortes. Too many soldiers there guarding the Protestant women imprisoned in the portside tower. And too many husbands protesting for their release. Likely a chance of getting caught up in a tumult there."

Jehan leaned back in the seat of the chaise, honored that his suggestion met with Benat's approval. "We have a plan, then. Montpellier it shall be." If only André could offer a tiny dose of the respect that Benat showed.

"Yes, Sieur. And our farmers will keep their share for weaving and papermaking, will they not?"

"Certainly," said Jehan. "I had thought to reinstate the mill tax, but have given it consideration and decided not to do so. I had a bit of a lesson this morning, and it reminded me of what Prieur Chabert has taught from scripture; 'The hard-working farmer that laboureth must be the first partaker of the fruits.' Our farmers are of great import, and we must show them their worth." He looked off to the field and waved to the group with earnest enthusiasm, catching the eye of a few, while the others kept to their work. "I am so pleased you are beginning to replenish the wheat and millet stores. Quite an accomplishment after the last few years of foul weather and failed harvests."

"Faith was required, Sieur, to bring us these rewards. Along with countless days of hard work. Yet we always honor time off on holy days for those who wish to take it."

"I am grateful, Benat . . . to all of you. Please share that with the others. I see you have much to do until after the harvests, but when time allows, I look forward to more lessons and training."

During his stay in the Dominican prieuré, Jehan had yearned for the times when, as a small boy under Benat's instruction, he learned the skills of riding, hunting, and fishing. In the last few months, since his release from the prieuré, he had relived those memories every Sunday afternoon on his brief visits to the château. Of late, they had focused on elevating his skills at marksmanship and swordplay to prepare him for business out on the road. Benat had made it clear his young seigneur needed to be equipped to defend himself in case he was commissioned to the King's troops—customarily an obligation of firstborn sons of noblesse. Within a short time, Jehan had learned that merely wielding a weapon would not guarantee his salvation. He needed the same *savoir faire* Benat exemplified for respect, tolerance, and negotiation—talents that would go a long way in this land of diversity and division.

"I must be in Alais before supper, so I have come for my horse," Jehan explained. "She offers a much more comfortable ride than André's old cart and pony." He jostled the pony's mane and let out a laugh.

Jehan's senses were heightened in anticipation of his first adventure with his horse. The air was sweeter, the sky bluer. It had been for his sixteenth birthday that his father had purchased Luisant, a stunning Andalusian palfrey. She had been trained and waiting for him upon his release from the prieuré school. The splendid horse was his father's last expression of love before he passed and had come to represent the family he had hardly known. She responded well to Jehan's affection and had become a reliable, protective companion that gave him the confidence to venture out alone.

"I'll have her saddled and brought up right away," Benat assured. "In the meanwhile, perhaps you would like to see the new cook for fresh bread and cheese for your travels. Although she is Reformed Calvinist, she is from a fine, trustworthy family. I've known 'em for years and she's like a daughter to me. I believe we can keep her here out of harm's way as long as we are discreet."

"Yes, we must use discretion," said Jehan. "'Tis best she resides here in the country where she will not be closely watched. I am coming to understand that the Reformed are still under scrutiny from the Intendant Basville. Light was clearly shed on that fact for me just this morning."

Jehan gazed up at the château positioned on an immense hill, built over one hundred years earlier with defense in mind—when the Wars of Religion raged and the region was a Protestant stronghold. From what Jehan could gather, the countryside must have been relatively peaceful during the last few years while the King's dragoons were busy fighting in King Louis' war against the Allied Nations. Fears had calmed a little, and Benat was now in the practice of leaving the château gates open during the day. Still, a rider was slowed by the circuitous front pathway, which caused both horse and wagon to maneuver with agility.

He tugged at the pony's reins, leading it through the lower gate-house and up the steep winding path, content that life was falling into proper order at last. *All excepting André's controlling nature.* But Jehan refused to let that have power over him any longer. Instead, he chose to savor recollections from his youth here on the château's lands as he made his way up the hill—recollections of the freedom and aliveness he felt when he had explored the surrounding fields and forests and, glided down the river's cooling waterfalls. Here he sensed the true magic and beauty of life—the trilling of larks, the chattering and laughing of the fox, the spectacle of blue columbine en masse, and the fragrance of lily-of-the-valley after a spring rain.

When he was young, the view from the château's third floor windows made him feel as if he were a bird soaring over the Luech River, the fields, the mill, the vineyards on the lower slopes, the grazing pastures at the upper end of the valley, and the tenant farmers' diminutive hamlet.

Over the years, Jehan's ancestors had installed a series of terraces and high walls around the château. One wall wrapped the entire hill to protect a forest of chestnut, walnut, and mulberry trees, along with a *magnanerie* for breeding silkworms. As he rode past the trees, memories darted through his mind. This time it was the treasured moments with his grand-father. Silver hair glinting in the sunlight, telling tales of the féeries who lived in the woods. The much loved Pierre BonDurant, kind-hearted *avocat* of law, had always been available to serve the community yet managed to make more time for Jehan than his own father had. Grandfather Pierre had named the chestnut trees his 'bread trees' for the consistent food they provided, and the mulberry his 'gold trees' because they fed the silkworms, which brought excellent income. And he was always sharing lessons he had learned from his own father—Jehan's great-grandfather, a respected physician—about which wild plants to harvest for medicine.

The pony's hooves clattered up the cobbled incline until they came to the gate of the walled courtyard where the tiny chapel doubled as a guardhouse. As they passed through the gate and into the courtyard, several hens—of silver and russet—clucked and scattered. Jehan drew a deep breath of the fresh, dry air, and let out a hearty sigh at the sight of his treasured country home. He cherished his Sunday afternoons here. It was within the walls of this three-storied stone building, not the walls of the prieuré, nor those of the townhouse, that he had been most nurtured and protected as a child.

At the far side of the courtyard, the kitchen garden was yet plentiful with late summer vegetables. The last of the tomatoes and beans were ready to be crocked and put up. His stomach rumbled a little when he spotted the cabbage and sweet onion starts that would be ready just before the frosts and make a nice pot of *garbure* soup. He could almost taste the savory broth that was a favorite from his early childhood.

He secured the cart and pony at the small stable next to the dovecote and headed across the courtyard to the kitchen door. As he walked, he wiped his soiled shoes across the dewy grass and contemplated a fine new pair of black leather boots. With his head down and eyes focused on the ragged appearance of his cracked brown leather shoes, he put one foot in front of the other until, suddenly, his foot hovered over a mound of fur. He stopped—realizing it was Benat's hunting dog sprawled atop the stoop—and quickly pulled his foot back, then stumbled. At the last second, he leapt over the dog and into the kitchen in something resembling a clumsy three quarter beat minuet.

"Oh, *mon Diu!*" The new cook startled and grabbed a broom, holding it high as if Jehan were some desperate rogue ready to attack.

"Who are you?" she demanded, prepared to thrash him if he advanced.

Jehan steadied himself, then paused. He closed his eyes and he took a deep whiff of the enticing aromas that filled the room. The malty scent of hot bread blended with that of the fresh-cut herbs strewn about the kitchen floor.

He chuckled and gave the cook a winsome smile. One he had learned worked well for disarming others. "Now that smells like home!"

It seemed to relax the cook a bit, and she lowered the broom. Jehan studied her for a moment with an evaluating eye. She was a slightly stout woman near the age of André, with dark curly hair and a fair, rosy complexion—apparently capable of demanding work, as all was in order here.

"I am your Seigneur."

When her eyes widened and she gasped, he tried to contain himself but an odd half laugh, half hoot escaped. He was not upset with her, but apparently she feared the worst.

"Oh, *perdon, mon Sénher.*" Her face flushed, and she gave a deep curtsy.

"My, how I am surprised at the great number of people still speaking the langue d'oc," said Jehan. "I spent years locked away with very little news, but thought, surely, I would find more had changed. Old habits never seem to waver with resolved Cévenol folk."

Despite the fact he found nothing reprehensible about speaking the old language, he wondered if he should be more stern on the matter, considering the consequences. "'Tis not that I am opposed to anyone speaking the langue d'oc. I would like to learn, myself, one day. But we truly must use care to speak only the King's French outside of the château. Particularly the children. No need to give the frères an excuse to devise more punishments. Sadly, I have witnessed it myself . . . a slight slip of the tongue and one could be beaten, or worse. Now . . . I presume you are the cook. Please tell me, what is your name?"

"My name is Biatris Gasquet, *Sénher*. *Oc*, yes. Cook for Château de Cougoussac. How can I be of *servici?*"

"A little bread and cheese would please me. I am about to set out on a journey and I have quite a thirst this morning, so I will also need my *costrel* filled with wine."

"Do you not prefer fresh *aigua* . . . umm, water, Sénher? Our spring water *es purmèr* . . . not dirty, and better than a *mal de cap,* a bad ache in the head, in afternoon sun. We have only wine from early harvest." She tilted her head and gave a little smile. "'Tis still in *fermentacion,* and wineskin could *explosiu.*"

Jehan enjoyed the forthrightness of this new addition to their household. "Thank you, Biatris. Water will do quite fine. Indeed, I wish not for an explosion of wine on my clothes. Your skills and knowledge will be appreciated around here."

He looked down at the large oak table where a butter crock was beckoning in a swirl of creamy deliciousness. For a moment, Jehan restrained himself from temptation, but that conditioned response passed as he reminded himself that now, as Seigneur de Cougoussac, he was free to do as he pleased. After his morning with André, he considered a small gesture of defiance appropriate—it was time to establish his domain. He reached down and scooped a generous finger full of the sweet butter and filled his mouth, eliciting another wide-eyed look from Biatris, just as Luisant's whinny outside the door called to him.

Jehan licked his lips and hastened out to see Benat and his beloved horse standing in the courtyard, her coat of pale, dappled chestnut glistening from a recent brushing. He loved Luisant's revered dun Andalusian coloring with her contrasting dark mane, tail, and lower legs.

"Luisant!" He held his arms out for their usual embrace, wrapped them around her neck, and rubbed between her expressive eyes. "Together again, my brilliant one."

She caught the scent of butter and tipped her head up to lick his fingers.

He burst into joyous laughter, alive and elated by the course his life was taking. "I have decided. I must reside here full time from now on." How could he not, when life was far more pleasant here in the country? "Let André and his family have the house in town. I no longer care. *This* is where I shall thrive."

"We are always glad to have you," Benat said with a warm, gentle laugh of his own.

Biatris stepped out in a hurry, her sabots clattering on the stone steps. A beaming smile animated the rosy apples of her cheeks. "Oc, Sénher! Very glad. You are talkful, and it will help me to learn your *lenga*." She loaded the saddlebag with the costrel, a round of pélardon cheese, and a small loaf of *pain de Beaucaire*.

Jehan nodded at Biatris in approval, and at last, he was ready to venture off down the Régordane Way.

Chapter Four
Outrage on the Pilgrims' Path

15 September 1695
Régordane Way, France
Midday

The narrow sheep *drailles* through the forest were sometimes used by Saint-Gilles pilgrims to bypass toll houses along the Régordane Way. Jehan took advantage of these paths on his journey to market, relishing the solitude and hypnotic kaleidoscope of sunlight between the leaves, only now and then interrupted by the sudden movement of a startled deer or fox.

He rode in contemplation, reflecting on how a pilgrim's journey compared to his. Perhaps, as they traveled, they walked in meditation, focused on gratitude felt for God's splendid creation and bounty. *Surely they pray.*

A heavy sense of guilt suddenly assailed him when he realized his delay in offering his own prayer, so he reined in Luisant to a stop.

Lifting his head to the heavenly realms, he folded his hands at his heart, then whispered, "Lord, be my guide, and may Saint Christopher protect me on the journey I am about to take. Keep me free from harm to body and soul, and keep me always mindful of Your presence and love. Amen." He crossed himself, perceiving a lightness in his body never there before—certainly never while in a church or chapel. Was it something about the forest? He quickly disregarded it, picked up the reins, and signaled Luisant to move on.

After some time, the path emptied back onto the main road, just before Château de Portes, the most massive, foreboding château fort in the Cévennes region. When it came to the toll stop at Portes, there was no option around it thanks to its late deceased ruler, Marie-Felice de Budos, Marquise de Portes, who had routed all direct paths to Alais through her land. She was a notorious woman who had mercilessly tried to convert Reformed Cévenols by using powder, bullets, and cannons. Even Prieur Chabert had found her tactics extreme and told of the times she had incited riots by unjustly confiscating livestock and imprisoning the innocent.

Thanks be to God, Prince de Conti has inherited these lands.

Jehan drew in several slow, steady breaths before he reached the armored sentries at the Portes tollgate. He had heard the inspection here was seldom a pleasurable experience for anyone, so it was not time to let his emotions take hold. He decided a display of his best noblesse decorum, presented with calm and confidence, might ease the encounter.

"Greetings valiant Knights of the Way." Jehan touched his hat in salute, and the guards returned the gesture, tapping the visors of their helmets. "You are looking most stalwart . . . and well-prepared, like Chevaliers Pariers of old. We are most grateful for your courageous protection of travelers along this route."

As Jehan had planned, the rare compliment seemed to beguile the guards, their looks and nods to each other, indicating their appreciation.

"Sieur, we thank you. We are honored and wish you safe travels," the collector said, bowing as low as his breastplate would allow, again and again, while entirely forgetting to take the toll.

One might take advantage of the collector's distraction, yet Jehan handed it over, hoping he could count on these men in the future. "Here, my fearless friends. The required share for the Prince, along with a few extra sous for your own pockets." Their eyes widened in surprise and delight, their amiable grins giving him some assurance he was now in their favor.

"Tell the Prince that I, Seigneur de Cougoussac, give him my regards and wish him good health and great fortune."

"I would, Sieur, however, we see little of him," replied the collector. "He has a gallivanting nature and leaves the region to manage itself . . . a great relief after so many ghastly years under the Marquise."

"'Tis fortunate we have more peaceful times," Jehan said. "Let us pray it will stay that way. I bid you a good day, my friends."

A contented smile spread across the collector's face. "Godspeed, Sieur," he said, and the other guards bowed their heads in respect.

Jehan tipped his hat and rode on, relieved to have made it past Portes and feeling blessed to have the coin for safe passage. He quickened the pace, settling Luisant into an ambling gait as they began the long, easy descent into the L'Auzonnet valley.

This portion of the road quickly became his favorite, expansive and free, with sweeping views of the verdant Lower Cévennes mountains. Topped with jagged serras ridges, the mountains were dressed in lush emeralds, viridians, and chartreuse, accented by rustling amber grasses signaling the approaching fall. With a deep breath, Jehan caught the scent of newly cut wheat and dry earth from harvested fields that dotted the landscape. Truly a glorious sight after last year's famines.

The next tollgate was at the bridge over the L'Auzonnet River. A note on André's map said the keepers at this humble house had a reputation for kindliness and enjoyed engaging with the many travelers. As Jehan arrived, a balding elderly man, skin mottled from years in the sun, ambled out with bones creaking and crunching.

"Welcome to our relay stop. We have much to offer a weary pilgrim. 'Twill be six sous for the road tax, but there is fresh water at the well. For nine sous, we have feed at the trough for your horse, and we can arrange a bed should you need rest."

While Luisant took in a bellyful, Jehan sauntered over to the well to refill his costrel. Once his horse lifted her head and appeared satis-

fied, he walked back and led her to a shady spot near the river to rest
and eat his midday meal.

"Have you all you require?" called out the old man from uphill.
"Should you be hungry, I provide a potage free of charge for all
pilgrims."

"I have all that is essential, for today. Yet I thank you kindly," said
Jehan. "I appreciate your generosity, Monsieur."

For today, the bit of freedom he was enjoying satisfied him
immensely—despite the family secrets that had come to lodge in the
hollow place in his heart. If he could only learn more of his father's
inclinations, then he might come to know himself.

He knelt at the river's edge to wash, then pulled his meal from his
saddlebag, and took a seat on a nearby boulder. As he bit into the delicate, milky goat's cheese Biatris had packed, he felt a sense of indulgence while its subtle fruitiness dissolved on his tongue.

"Oh, quite elegant indeed. We are living the high life now," Jehan
announced to no one but his horse, quite satisfied with her company
alone.

Relaxed into the sereneness of his surroundings, his daydreams led
his mind wandering and weaving through tales and legends of the
Régordane Way, and the great divergence of people who had come
along the route. He dreamed up images of roving troubadours of old,
and of the Knights Templar and Knights Hospitallers who had traveled to southern ports for passage to the Holy Land. He imagined all
the ancients and what he had learned of in his lessons on history;
Mycenaeans building their beehive tombs, Gabali widening narrow
footpaths into roads for transporting iron, and Romans working to
move and fit every stone that now made up the roadway.

Although the road had been rather quiet so far that morning, he
wondered with curious excitement who he might encounter on his journey. There could be all manner of traders and merchants transporting
salt, spices, wine, oil, cheese, grains, silk, weapons—*even jewels*.
There might be journeys taken by entertainers—bohémiens, magicians,
and jugglers—and certainly, there would be shepherds juggling their
straying sheep. Monks and frères might head south to honor Saint

Gilles or Marie de Magdala, or north to honor the black virgin of Le Puy. Saracens and Jews, Catholics and Protestants, paupers and nobles, laborers and vagrants all shared this communal roadway. Jehan preferred to hold a utopian image of cooperation between this mixed bag of voyagers, yet he knew it wasn't always the reality.

"Hmm." *Cooperation* . . . What about the cooperation—or was it conspiring—that had gone on with André and Madame Beauclose earlier that morning? And what about the mysterious silver object from André? *Is it a méreau? Or a medallion?* There was no waiting for the privacy of the inn to find out. Jehan's curiosity had to be satisfied that very moment, so he reached under his waistcoat for the coin purse.

His pulse quickened as he pulled out the shining little artifact. Its brilliance delighted him. He turned his head one way—then another—studying all sides, as if it were a tiny patient undergoing an examination. He quickly ascertained it was a medallion crafted to hang on a cord or chain. Its oval body was domed a bit and cast with primitive patterns which pierced through the piece. He could decipher an equal-sided cross. It seemed familiar, but he couldn't name it. Below the cross was a dove flying downward. He knew from his teachings at the prieuré, a dove in that position represented the Holy Spirit. Adding irony to the mystery of the medallion, there was a silversmith's stamp on the backside—*Maystre 1688 Nimes.* Jehan let out a merry little hoot, thinking it some sort of jest.

Enough time wasted. He returned the medallion to his purse, then paused when he remembered he hadn't offered grace before his meal. He still felt utterly chained to the Dominican rituals. But now there was no time for an after meal prayer either. There simply could be no more lingering. He needed to be on his way so, at the least, he would arrive in Alais in time for Vespers.

Jehan led Luisant back up to the road and jumped into the saddle, eager to venture on. As he prepared to leave, a horrendous thundering reverberated off the surrounding stone-lined ridges. Once he realized the sound was coming from behind him, he spun around to see a transport coach filled with riders racing down the road—heading directly toward him. In an instant, it occurred to Jehan the driver intended to run the toll stop. He panicked and froze.

"Out of the way!" the driver bellowed.

Luisant reared and squealed, then bolted back towards safety in the clearing near the river. Jehan tried to bring her under control when a low-lying branch knocked his hat from his head and left his hair strewn across his face. Every muscle in his body tensed. Luisant reeled and stomped until the coach passed and she had shaken off the fear.

Jehan brushed his hair out of his eyes, then reached out to stroke her neck and assure her. "'Tis safe now, Luisant. No cooperation from *that* rebellious fool, eh, my brilliant one?" He leaned forward, resting his head against her strong, warm neck—to calm himself as much as to settle his horse. "Thank you for your quick instincts, my *fille*."

He dismounted her, then secured the bridle in one hand and reached for his hat with the other. "Seems instincts are something I should use more of myself instead of dreaming the day away."

Alais, France
Early Evening

Jehan slowed Luisant and stopped atop a rise, his destination within view. The city of Alais lay at a distance, where hills folded one over the other. Once a Protestant stronghold, her temples had been destroyed, and control was now in the hands of the King's Intendant Basville. The battles between religions had taken a tremendous toll on her, both sides leaving scars that hindered the flow of life.

He observed the Gardon River as it wound around the city. The water glinting fiery colors of late afternoon sun, like iridescent scales of a healing Aesculapian serpent knowing she was a city still in need of recovery.

From his vantage point, he could make out the King's new fort, glowing pink in the languid late summer sunset. It was just five years young and was a bold, bright statement fixed against blackened buildings that had been set ablaze to root Protestants out of their sanctuary.

Relieved to be nearing his destination, Jehan searched ahead to spot the Pont du Marché bridge into town. Just before the bridge, there once stood a Dominican Presicadou, notorious for heavy-handed inquisition of Knights Templar—men who had valiantly protected Christian pilgrims en route to the Holy Land, yet were labeled heretics by the Roman Catholic church. Jehan recalled from his lessons at the prieuré that the Presicadou had been destroyed in the flood of 1600, giving way to the fertile fields that now flanked the river. And local legends said it was God's punishment for inflicting torture on fellow Christians. Jehan weighed the paradox of that divine twist of fate while he continued down the road and into the valley.

As he neared the bridge, a rustling and the sound of labored breathing off to his left caught his attention. He turned to see a woman running through the northern field, desperately parting dried stalks of late summer corn out of her way. When she rushed out in front of him, he pulled at the reins, trying to miss her, and brought his horse to a swift halt. The woman stumbled and fell, sliding onto her hands and knees, dusty road gathering between her fingers. Gasping and choking on inhaled dirt, she turned her head toward Jehan with pleading eyes. She bore a hideous burn, in the shape of a cross, on her smudged and sweaty face. His gut tightened, and he pulled back in the saddle. Without hesitation, he began to dismount when a middle-aged man came up from behind and vigorously pushed him back towards the saddle.

"Sieur, stay put, please," the man implored with the look of a concerned father.

"What? Leave me be!" Jehan resisted and struggled while Luisant snorted and stomped at the man.

"'Tis a clearing of the heretics. You must make yourself scarce or dragoons will be after you besides." The man held a firm grip, but there was compassion and concern in his eyes.

"And what of this poor woman? This is lunacy, she is injured," deplored Jehan.

"Save yourself, Sieur!" The woman waved him away while she

scrambled to her feet. She ran off up the hill calling back, "My fate is sealed with this mark on my face."

"She must go into hiding quickly," said the man, "or she will have no chance of survival. And you cannot be seen assisting her, or it will be the end of you."

"Dragoons would have no cause to harm me. I am of the King's religion," Jehan said.

"Oh, but they have mistaken our good Catholic friends for Reformed many times. Follow me, straight away, if you want to remain unscathed."

The man ran away from the field toward a thicket of trees where several other travelers huddled, and he signaled Jehan to join them. Jehan was reluctant. He had seen no dragoons, but heeded the warning and joined the group in the cover of the trees.

Squinting in the dim light, through the lower branches, he eventually caught sight of at least a dozen mounted soldiers crashing through the field in the far distance. They rode high on their immense steeds, their brilliant flame-red uniforms and trailing fatigue caps waving like battlefield banners were a warning to all.

Jehan had listened to tales among the prieuré students of marauding mercenary dragoons and their atrocities, and overheard talk of feral soldiers that plagued the Cévennes. But he had no memory of seeing severe tactics like this before. The frères had always diminished the persecution stories, telling students they were hearsay, merely exaggerated rumors. Jehan trusted the frères version since the soldiers commissioned to Genoüillac were always so complacent—as long as they had plenty of food and drink.

Shrieks shot through the air, sending startled gasps up from the group of travelers and Jehan's breathing into a shallow, rapid rhythm. Luisant was not holding. She jounced her head, her tail swished, and her ears were back. Dragoons were driving their horses toward what seemed like countless peasants running through the field, knocking some to the ground and injuring them.

"Is there nothing we can do to stop them?" Jehan asked the group next to him.

An elderly man blew out a breath, rattling his lips. "'Twould be futile! Best not enrage them any further. Just stay clear."

Jehan knew the King intended to rid the land of heretics and was determined to oversee conversions to the Roman Catholic faith. Yet this was ludicrous. He thought the Grand Alliance wars had sent the fiercest dragoon units off to foreign lands, so he never expected to bear witness to anything like this.

The dry stalks of corn trembled and crackled as dozens of peasant farmers emerged from the field and onto the road, some crying, some cursing. They fled in all directions, but the dragoons on their horses encircled the peasants and only a few managed to escape.

Time seemed to bolt into an accelerated pace, gathering momentum when a curé came running across the bridge from town, waving an immense iron crucifix and panting hard.

"Abjure now . . ." he cried out between breaths, "to save your souls and prevent this torture!"

With crucifixes tied to the end of their carbines, soldiers poked at the peasants' faces while screaming raucous commands.

"Kiss this and show honor to the King's religion, otherwise the Intendant will have you all sent to the galleys or locked in the tower," barked the captain.

Luisant started weave-walking side to side, agitated by the shouting and screams. Jehan stroked her neck but dared not speak aloud to calm her.

"Kiss it like it was yor maman!" screeched one soldier.

"No, like your lover," yelled another as they all roared in laughter.

Repelled by the dragoons, the peasants backed into a tight circle. A large cloud of dust spun into the air as the commotion escalated. Riotous insults being slung by the soldiers made the peasants' choking and coughing almost imperceptible.

One dragoon swung his carbine back and gave a scathing blow to a woman's face using the flat side of the attached crucifix, knocking her to the ground. A man standing nearby tried to come to her relief. The dragoon turned, then rammed the crucifix-turned-bayonet into the man's stomach, leaving a wound Jehan thought, in all likelihood, would be mortal. The dragoons heaved the two victims upon the back of a horse, with no care given to their injuries.

A flush of seething heat moved across Jehan's face as his shock transformed into anger. It was all he could do stifle a scream of outrage. With an instinctive impulse to aid the injured using his new healing skills, he jumped down off Luisant and rummaged through his saddlebag.

The man who had called him to safety among the trees placed a hand on Jehan's arm. With a pained look in his eyes, he whispered, "What is your intention, Sieur? There is nothing to be done without risking your life."

"I could help these people," Jehan answered frantically. "I carry a little oak bark powder, good for cuts and infections. Willow is the most effective treatment I have with me for pain."

But the man shook his head in disapproval, his eyes swelling with tears. "I lost my son this way . . . while going to the aid of our Reformed neighbors."

Jehan realized the man was right, and it would be prudent to bide his time there on the fringes. These dangerous soldiers were not inclined to want, or need, their victims aided—even by a medic obediently sworn to the Church of Rome.

"Thank you, Monsieur. I am grateful for the warning," Jehan said.

As if this cyclone of chaos around them had created a change in the weather, the clouds overhead swirled like molten silver and gathered over the valley, turning twilight to deepening darkness. Rain burst from the sky as the grim procession moved across the bridge and into town.

Jehan mounted Luisant and proceeded behind them, leaving plenty of distance, as did the other travelers waiting to enter the city. Like cowering hounds trained with a harsh hand, good folk had become accustomed to these incidents and remained stifled, even paralyzed, afraid to be drawn into the violence.

The dragoons prodded their prisoners on, pushing them down the old rampart stairs and into the market square with the curé close at their heels. Upon the commotion, several citizens rushed to the streets with lanterns. The light gave a pallid glow to the peasants' faces.

"Torches! Bring me torches," yelled the captain to the man closest to him.

Jehan shivered at the unnerving scene. Remaining wary, he stayed on the rampart as they made preparations for a public display of conversion by torture. He pulled down the brim of his hat to ward off the rain and conceal the shock on his face—a move of certain benefit at this highly uncertain moment.

A small crowd formed, some cheering on the persecutors, some looking on in horror with hands folded in prayer, or clenching their fists as if trying to control their growing rage.

Jehan pulled the map from his pocket with André's directions to the Cathédrale Saint-Jean-Baptiste and realized they led straight through the market square. He clasped the small scrap of parchment, rain dissolving the ink. Raindrops—like the sorrowful tears of the persecuted peasants. If only the rain could wash away the blackness, the evil, of these dreadful dragoons.

The curé stood nodding and praying over the captives. Jehan could only trust their fates would be assisted by Divine Providence and was about to ride away when, abruptly, the curé screamed, "Abjure, you *barbets*! Abjure." His eyes lit with a maddened glare, and he swung a large confessional crucifix into the group of captive peasants. They threw their arms up to protect their faces, some stumbling and falling to the ground.

"You are infected by heresy. You vile Huguenots," the curé derided, waving the crucifix at them. "Ours is the one true religion, and I am tasked with saving your souls by the avenging power of the Holy Spirit!" Cries, jeers, and curses went up throughout the square, intensifying his mania. He flew into an uncontrollable frenzy, growling and kicking at the heads and backs of the peasants who had fallen.

Luisant flinched, the skin on her shoulders rippling, and Jehan gripped the saddle, scarcely able to take a breath.

"Renounce Satan and cast out the spiritual forces of wickedness that rebel against God," the curé wailed out, in an attempt at exorcism, his lips pulled back and contorted as he held the crucifix high and stomped on their hands.

Jehan's heartbeat thrashed in his ears, and an overpowering urge to deter the violence sent a powerful rush of rage through his body. He grasped his sword hilt and sat tall in his saddle.

A few swarthy bystanders jumped in to pull the crazed curé off the peasants. "Cease now," one man shouted as others took hold.

Jehan sat back, releasing his sword and crossing himself.

"Unhand me," yelled the curé.

"You're to be a man of mercy and honor," said the man. "These are righteous men and women even if they don't show up and drop coin in your confessional or pay for indulgences."

"As Judicial Vicar, I am the one to decide their fate," the curé howled. "Depart or I shall have you arrested as well."

"You are to provide them with a trial, are you not?" asked the man.

The men continued to restrain the curé and admonish his behavior while he made demands for arrests, but the dragoons ignored him and focused on securing iron cuffs and chains on the rest of the captives.

Jehan knew he must remove himself from this cruel scene to resist a rescue attempt that would only lead to disaster. A twinge of panic ran through him, causing his arms and legs to weaken. He looked around for his way out. There it was—a ramp to the right, heading to a side street. He clicked his tongue and nudged the reins, signaling Luisant to move along.

Guilt muddied his conscience like the mire left by the rain as they hastened down the ramp toward what looked like safety. But it was a tangled path through a labyrinth of narrow back roads, and each new turn in the drenching darkness caused more uncertainty. Was he on the proper course, or was he getting himself lost? He came upon a busy intersection with a sign reading Rue Peyrollerie.

High on a ladder above this main road, a lamplighter was at work igniting street lanterns that swayed on cables in the gusty wind. Jehan looked to the left and caught sight of the illuminated cathédrale tower above clay-tiled rooftops. Eager for sanctuary after the enormity of the day's unexpected events, he took the turn.

Luisant still appeared agitated, her tail whipped and nostrils flared as she dodged debris floating in puddles along the congested, noisy street. Foul odors from the nightman's latrine haul and the reek of rotting fish mixed with a faint scent of charred wood. The fetid smells overwhelmed Jehan and soured his already nervous stomach.

The streets were cleaner the further they moved from the riverfront, and the rain abated, but the odor of seared wood grew more pungent as they progressed along the road. A few blocks from the cathédrale, he discovered the source—a large burnt-out shell of a building. The continuing light rain seemed to be the culprit in renewing the sickening odor. Jehan brought Luisant to a stop and noticed a wooden sign, remarkably unscathed, near the street's edge that read "Temple du culte Protestant".

He could find no justification or logic for destroying a building of such grand magnitude and cost—nor in the outrageous behavior he had just seen. He could not, in any way, buy into the extreme fervor of these maddened Romish leaders trying to justify their actions in the name of God or for the common good.

Glancing up to the lintel, he studied the words carved there.

My sheep hear my voice, and I know them.
They follow me and I give them eternal life.

At once, his memory was triggered—it was the time when Curé Gellion showed up at the prieuré to share news about the burning of Reformed temples around the region. Gellion had been particularly entertained, clapping his hands in delight as he told a ghastly story of Catholic villagers who dug up skulls from a Reformed cemetery to play *pétanque*. Jehan scrambled through his mind for the details. It must have been ten years earlier. He recalled it being near the time of his lonely, agonizing eighth birthday—the first one not celebrated at home with his family.

Because he held only a few recollections of those early days, he questioned how many other disturbing experiences he might have suppressed. The rain tapered off as he regarded the old temple, considering why his family had abandoned him and not come to see him on that birthday. The frères had convinced him no one cared enough to visit, but when those cloistered clowns spoke, their eyes held the same wicked glare he had just seen in the eyes of the pummeling curé. Was it possible his young mind had found it safer to blame his parents than to rebel against those rod-carrying frères? A dizzying sense of confusion came over Jehan. But when the first bell for Vespers tolled, he broke away from his thoughts and rode swiftly on, fearing there could be danger in arriving late to Mass.

It was a short distance to the outwardly unimpressive cathédrale, encircled by shops and townhouses. The heaviness of disappointment came over Jehan upon seeing the austere Romanesque facade, as rustic and plain as the old village churches. He had so very much looked forward to something grander on his first visit to a true cathédrale.

Two finely attired, but rain-soaked men stood near the steps of the cathédrale handing money to a boy holding a lantern, whose mop of wet blonde hair flowed from under his woolen cap. The boy promised to keep watch over their horses as they entered the portico.

"You shall have three more sous," said Jehan to the boy. "As long as my horse is here and unharmed when I return."

"Thank you, Sieur. I shall see to it." The boy took a deep bow and tipped his cap, his hair falling about his tidy face.

The last bell before Vespers rang out in a pompous echoing off the lime-plastered walls of surrounding buildings, causing a painful vibration deep in Jehan's ears.

"Here is one sou now to secure our agreement." Jehan dropped a coin in the boy's hat, then tied Luisant to a tether ring on the stone wall. In that moment, it was as if he tethered *himself* to the avowed stability of the Roman Catholic Church, truth or not, for good, or for bad.

He stopped at the portico to leave his sword in the weapons house along with those of the parishioners, then removed his hat and shook off the rain. When he walked into the vestibule, his mouth dropped open as he looked upward, thoroughly spellbound, and a chill ran down his arms. Much to his surprise, the interior of Cathédrale Saint-Jean-Baptiste resembled a glorious, mythical palace—just what he had hoped for. He took a few more steps and his heart leapt. Had he entered the kingdom of heaven? He genuflected and almost fell over as he looked up again. There, high above, was an artifice of deep blue midnight sky teeming with golden stars and a band of angels. Perhaps these stars might guide his soul in its searching and calm his fears.

Jehan queued with others at the font, dipped his fingers in holy water, and crossed himself. He entered the pews from the Epistle side aisle, taking a rear seat for the most magnificent views.

Exotic incense filled the air, its smoke suspended in candlelight, and before long, Jehan was lost in his imaginings. Was this elaborate space, reaching high toward the eternal realms, the place where he would, at long last, feel a true connection to God? He waited for the prayers to begin while the curé chattered on about something. Utterly absorbed in the magic of these surroundings, Jehan was unaware of the nature of the curé's message until his voice elevated, reverberating off walls, and into bones, shattering the tranquil harbor Jehan had entered.

". . . and rid this land of the heretical pests that plague us!"

Pests? Plague? What had these people done to deserve the treatment he had witnessed? The phrase on the Protestant temple lintel flashed into Jehan's mind, and he deliberated on its meaning. *My sheep hear my voice . . . they follow me. Of course!* Just what the bishops, and the King, were afraid of, and what incited them to violence—that people would follow a direct path to God. He clenched his jaw as the revelation rolled through his thoughts. They wanted control over the people by keeping the path to God a narrow journey through their own tightly governed gates. *I pray, someday, I shall find my own path . . . hear God for myself.*

Without warning, the heavy wood and iron main doors burst open. An eruption of local curés and Cistercian frères preceded the branded, wounded, and shackled peasants that had been rounded up in the market square. Their restraints clinked and rattled, and their mournful eyes called out for mercy as they clutched to each other with all hope fleeting.

Cries of alarm resounded throughout the nave, as dragoons, still mounted on their horses, pushed the procession from behind. The echoing clash of hooves against the stone floor, and the prisoners' wails, turned heaven to hell. Stench from wet horses and unbathed soldiers had the congregation scrambling to cover their faces with cloaks, and hands, and hats.

A harsh clanking from below the pulpit drew Jehan's attention to the silver Eucharist platter that the lay minister had let slip from his hands. Wafers of bread had scattered across the floor, and the horses were trampling over them.

The body of Christ! Had these soldiers just let their horses trample the Real Presence of Christ? Or, as he suspected, was there no real presence after all.

"'Tis better late than ne'er 'tall," shouted the captain. "Intendant will be pleased!"

At that, another flare of anger burned through Jehan. So much anger in one day—far deeper than any he'd ever held toward André— and he now understood why this vile policy of persecution needed to change. *But how can any one man possibly make a difference?*

Jehan could no longer be a witnessing party to more cruelty, but it would be dangerous to be seen leaving. So he needed to take measures. He waited for a bit until the mob moved into the transept crossing—where the display of savage bedlam would screen his exit.

When the moment was right, he crept out the side aisle holding his hat to his face, silent as midnight, adept as a cat, and out through the unguarded door to retrieve his sword. It was potent and natural, almost instinctive—these movements of stealth and ruse in the face of subjugation. *It must be in my blood.* Yet how could he use it to help these victims of this inhumanity?

Chapter Five
Gentilshommes' Lounge

15 September 1695
Le Cristal Blanc Inn, Alais, France
Evening

The brightly lit inn was abuzz with talk of the marketplace incident and the sacrilegious invasion at Mass. Jehan removed his rain-soaked hat, gave it a shake, then squeezed through the crowd of patrons—past merchants, traveling traders, and townsfolk. The loquacious talk and gaggling melded into a loud murmur of voices and the clink, clink of glasses, mugs, and bottles.

A Saracen trader called out, "Samples of the latest herbal tea for calming . . . all the way from India . . . samples here."

But most seemed to prefer the house wine, a rough dark red let down with water. Jehan looked around the tables for the plat du jour. The supper orders seemed to be lagging—there was not a single plate or bowl in sight. He suspected the upheaval had excited stomachs, and the patrons were not much interested in eating, but he hoped the kitchen had at least a comforting potage and some bread.

The smell of fear permeated the room. The people crowded in clusters, aggravating the young serving woman as she navigated through the commotion, rolling in a fresh barrel of wine.

"Mademoiselle tapstress," shouted one of the patrons, raising an empty glass in her direction. "We need more wine served here."

"Come now, messieurs, mesdames, you're draining these bottles quick as an eyelid's beat," she said as she brushed an errant curl of golden hair from her face. "Help me lift this barrel onto the counter and I will refill your empties."

Suddenly, shy as a squirrel, Jehan could not bring himself to move. His attention was drawn to the woman's delicate fingers as they tucked the strand of hair under her linen and lace *fontange* coif assembly. He stood mesmerized by her allure, and missed the chance to assist her alongside the other men who jumped right in. As he began to explore her with his eyes, several customers blocked his view, so she was only visible waist up. Jehan studied her delicate heart-shaped face, framed with those luscious honeyed curls. He reasoned she was the loveliest serving girl he had ever seen in his woefully limited experience. His eyes roamed the upper knolls and vales of her petite but well-defined form, not quite hidden under a sheer silk neck scarf.

Realizing he was daft at not moving to her aid, and compelled to right his blunder, Jehan combed a hand through his hair and decided to pursue her immediate attention.

He inched through the crowd toward her, heart throbbing as he came nearer. He knew he appeared a bit unfashionable, perhaps even a bit disheveled in his handed down noblesse attire. But, when the young woman turned and held his gaze with a beguiling smile, he was mantled in momentary confidence, feeling vigorous and handsome, all shyness now set aside. Trifling with her would make for a fine distraction from the day's dreadful events. So, he pushed past the others who stood between them and approached her as she continued to stare into his eyes.

"Pardon, Mademoiselle," Jehan interrupted, offering a smile full of innuendos he hoped she would read. "Jean Pierre BonDurant, Seigneur de Cougoussac to see your innkeeper, Monsieur Jacques Arnaud, if you please."

"I don't please at all with these nervous cats in the house." She raised an eyebrow and rolled her eyes at the crowd, then smiled. "But

I will find him for you, Sieur. Good reason indeed to leave these fools to their chattering."

Jehan kept a watch on the young woman as she faded into the shadows of a darkened hallway. When she opened the door to a back room, a stream of light filled the unlit space. There was a brief glimpse beyond the door, revealing nothing more than a view of a sideboard, although several muffled voices perked his ears.

He waited, remembering André's words about the medallion. *'Show it to Monsieur Jacques Arnaud, the innkeeper at Le Cristal Blanc Inn in Alais.'* With great care and caution, he maneuvered the odd little medallion out of his money purse and slipped it into his pocket without notice. Sleight of hand was a skill well learned at the prieuré when trying to acquire apples from the frères' stash.

Jehan rolled the medallion over and over in his pocket in curious impatience, but without too much delay, the serving girl reappeared with the innkeeper a few steps behind. Deep thought etched the already deep lines of the man's middle-aged face as he quietly shut the door behind him. Jehan's eyes followed the young woman when she passed by. He turned back to see the innkeeper had paused while approaching—appearing to be studying Jehan in a quick analysis. He reciprocated the silent interrogation, wondering what benefit this man could possibly be to him on a simple trip for supplies, or at any point, for that matter.

How had his father come to know this man? Did it have something to do with those inclinations that André had talked about? Jehan surmised the need for discretion in the interaction, so he pulled the medallion out in a closed fist, holding it to his side as he stepped toward the innkeeper.

"I am Jacques Arnaud, innkeeper. How may I be of help?"

"Monsieur." Jehan gave a slight nod. "Sieur BonDurant de Cougoussac. I understand you are an acquaintance of my late father," he said as he concealed the medallion in a handshake.

"Not too loudly, Sieur. I have already been informed of who you are." Monsieur Arnaud said in a hushed tone. He squinted his eyes and looked around the room. "Prudence is required in public. Wait till I take you to the gentilshommes' lounge where you can speak of such things." He did not look at the medallion but instead rubbed his thumb over the carvings, then handed it back to Jehan. "Your father was regarded by some as a man who could bring tribulations to family and friends alike."

Monsieur Arnaud's words sent a shot of resentment through Jehan, stirring the unhealed wounds of abandonment. It left him to consider what pain his father might have caused for the others caught up in his unrevealed misdeeds.

"Come along with me to the lounge, where you can relax a bit," Monsieur Arnaud instructed. "'Tis only open to your fellow noblesse. And you should find no prying eyes or curious ears there."

Jehan hesitated for a moment to obey this stranger, but the secrecy behind the closed door piqued his curiosity. He took a deep breath, and opening to the uncertainty, accompanied Arnaud down the hallway.

Monsieur Arnaud peered over his shoulder as he walked. "You may enjoy spending the evening here in civilized discourse, and it will give you a reprieve from the anxious crowd in the front room. Your father would have you . . . listen . . . and learn."

They entered the lounge without introductions, and the innkeeper seated Jehan at a large communal table, covered in a most luxurious embroidered linen cloth, before bowing his head and slipping out. The other men in the room were involved in conversation and ignored the new arrival, which suited Jehan fine for the time being.

The serving girl hastened in with supper and a bottle of wine. Her attentiveness and the much needed meal delighted him, so he gave her a smile and blinked his eyes in slow, cat-like contentment.

The room was inviting and pleasantly dry, its wood paneling reminding him of the Genoüillac house salon. The men sitting around the dining table appeared to be friendly enough, and the familiar incense of the crackling pine logs burning in the hearth mingled with the aroma of the succulent stew placed before him.

While the evening passed, Jehan studied the men's features illuminated by the fire's merry pulsating. He filled his belly with the hearty stew and requested a pear brandy to finish off his meal. He would spare nothing for a comfortable evening to help forget the tragic scenes of the day. And just as he had hoped, the young serving woman assisted in the task of distraction. Surely there could be no sin in a few flirtations with this young woman who bore no ring or other signs of betrothal. She may not be the muse he sought, but she was quite pleasant indeed.

She continued to flit in and out, her golden locks glimmering in the candlelight, time and again asking if he had all that he needed. The next time she came by, she rested her hand on the back of his chair and peeked around at him. "Anything more that you desire?"

"Thank you, Mademoiselle. Your generous care to my needs is *much* appreciated. Nothing more at this moment . . . yet . . . perhaps later."

He would be pleased, indeed, to let her take care of other needs, but he thought it sensible to stay focused on observing the evening's business. He smiled and gave a longing look from under his eyelids each time she came by, hoping to maintain her interest.

The quiet conversation among the group of five seemingly well-educated men—wigged, powdered, and primped—filled his mind with new ideas but left him with conflicted feelings as the scholarly debates over Papist versus Reformed ideologies ensued with definite leanings against the state religion.

The youngest man, dressed in a bright, popinjay green velvet justaucorps, caught Jehan's full attention when his tone turned duplicitous, ". . . and you all agree, do you not, that ever since the King let Chancellor Louvois influence him on these outrageous persecutions, that nothing has prospered in our country. Even with Louvois' passing, his policies live on. The King has certainly cursed himself by not reversing those tactics."

A few of the men raised their brows and tipped their heads in Jehan's direction, seeming to signal uncertainty over whether they could trust him.

But that did not stop the young fellow in green. Barely skipping a beat, he went on. "You've had plague, famine, a crisis in the economy, and more taxes to make up for all the administrative incompetence."

Jehan tried to heed Jacques Arnaud's words of advice to listen and learn, but he struggled to control his reactions to the brazen talk against the King and his advisors. Every muscle in Jehan's face twitched while the man continued.

"They have drained men from farm and factory to enlist in camps and battlefields for the follies of this never-ending war with *all* of Europe. And they have forced incredible numbers of Reformed citizens to leave with their much needed skills and money. I hear some have taken up on the ships of enemy fleets. They say that there are nine thousand or more Huguenot soldiers now in the service of The Dutch Republic and England."

"Yes . . . Monsieur Fallere," agreed a somber older man. His considerable size caused his breathing to be labored between words. "The emigration of hundreds of thousands . . . has put many of the trades at a near standstill . . . but you flame the fires of our emotions on the subject, Fallere . . . and we have a guest."

"Not to worry," said Fallere. "I'm sure Monsieur Arnaud has been presented with the requirement for entrance from this young gentilhomme, has he not?" He looked directly at Jehan for the answer.

Jehan nodded, taking a deep drink of his wine—as if he'd had nothing to drink all day—and hoped this Monsieur Fallere was referring to the medallion.

The older man wheezed in another deep breath before resuming his thoughts. "The wars and import tariffs . . . *have* greatly affected our ability to export our own goods . . . or import much of anything . . . and most of Europe has united with retaliatory import dues."

Jehan sat quietly, examining the cut and exotic fabric of the older man's clothes, trying to glean a little of who he was. Could he also be a traitor to the King? It came to Jehan—the man's garments, and his concern over the trade wars, suggested he was a wealthy draper merchant whose survival depended on imports and exports.

After some awkward moments of silence, the one they had called Sieur Sollier—a middle-aged man whose calloused hands exposed him as a hard-working country noble—spoke up. "Well then, if we are to be frank . . . and this young man is to be trusted . . . 'tis my opinion that should the King continue to allow these savage dragoons to act as monstrous followers of the Beast, then he is a bigoted tyrant." Sollier took a long drink, emptying his goblet. "He should put a stop to these persecutions."

While Jehan agreed King Louis had allowed his dragoons to get out of hand, he honored his King and found Sollier's remarks utterly disloyal. *Wasn't the King anointed by God? The Sun King. How could he be the cause?*

Jehan could remain silent no longer. "Surely, it is the royal advisors who have influenced him. As Monsieur Fallere says . . . Louvois . . . or perhaps Madame de Maintenon and the Assembly of Clergy."

Sollier gave Jehan a steely glare, lifted a pitcher of wine, and filled his goblet. Taking another deep drink, then continued, "'Twas the King's *choice* to support the Romish bishops. He knows they are hoarding riches and kidnapping the innocent children of the Reformed who refuse to abjure, forcing them to grow up with the Dominicans. And, in case you did not realize, it is all by the King's direct order. The clergy who encourage persecutions are, indeed, the most vile hypocrites. But the King *chooses* to send soldiers to assist them, saying it is needed to pluck the children from the arms of heresy and procure them a happier education in the bosom of the true religion. He could put a stop to it if he wanted."

"I know all too well about the children being taken from their parents," Jehan remarked sullenly. "'Tis where I spent most of my youth. But I never realized it was by the King's direct order." Had that been his own fate yet he had no recollection? But the frères had always told him he was a *rejeton*, his parent's rejected offshoot—his schooling with the Dominicans was the deal his parents had made so they could be rid of him and practice their Reformed faith in peace. But had he been misinformed? He heaved a seething breath and his cheeks tightened while trying to prevent a display of emotions.

Sollier's tone became more empathetic. "And were you happier in the bosom of the Dominicans?"

Jehan looked at his plate and shook his head slightly.

Sollier turned his questioning toward another of the gentilshommes. "Have you an opinion, Sieur Monteaux?"

"Indeed I do," answered Monteaux. "Thankfully, when my son was forced to attend school with the Dominicans, the prieur did not outrightly kidnap him. He continues to live with us but reports frequent occurrences of caresses when alone with the frères. I become infuriated when I think of it!" Monteaux's gold rings sparkled from the nearby firelight as he waved his hands, animating his vexation, and the elaborate plume on his hat bobbed whenever his head moved from side to side. A heavy layer of powder made his face appear almost ghostly, were it not for the rouge painted on his cheeks. "I have paid a small fortune to the Roman Church in fees and fines, all under the guise of education for my son. As you are all aware, I converted some years ago and attend Mass regularly. And now I wonder what the point is." He closed his eyes and shook his head. "This madness is taking the life from me," he whimpered.

"Surely most of you know," Sollier continued, "I fervently believe it is our right, as free men, to make all our own choices. The Edict of Nantes was put in place by the King's grandfather for that very reason, to have equality for all regardless of how one worships."

"But now the King's Revocation of that edict has taken away your freedoms," said Fallere, "with the noblesse told they should no longer worship in their château chapels unless they are Catholic. Are you not all upset by that?"

"Of course!" said Sollier. "We are not fond of being told how to live. It has set a grievous precedent." Sollier's brow creased in an insinuating sideways glance, "And what about *you* and *your* freedoms, Fallere? You always speak in terms of how the rest of us should think rather than your own thoughts."

Fallere did not answer, strangely enough after all that talking. But as soon as Sollier turned to speak to the other men, Fallere cocked his head and gave a sneering, closed-mouth smile.

"We should be free to choose our own style of worship," Sollier said. "Including those of us who choose to live outside the yoke of Popery. The Romish church has strayed from the ancient teachings of the Good Book, which prompts many of us to choose another path. But we must take heed. There is a rise again in *mécontents* and assemblers up in the mountains . . . in the 'Desert' as they are calling it. 'Tis a vicious cycle . . . the King's dragoons terrorize, then the rebels retaliate, stirring up more reasons for the Intendant to send in the dragoons, leaving many of us caught in the middle. I have information that the Calvinist Pasteur Brousson managed to make his way back into the country from the Dutch Republic and has been busy leading assemblies up there again. So, we must weigh our actions with careful consideration now."

"Brousson," Jehan interrupted. "I believe I have heard that name."

"Most everyone has," snapped Sollier. "Have you been hiding in a cockloft somewhere? Brousson has been inflaming the people, telling them that Babylon is near end times, and God is on their side."

Jehan wondered if Sollier was annoyed by the interruption, or if it was merely misdirected tension.

Sollier leaned across the table toward Jehan, shaking his head. "Do you not know that he has a price on his head? Up to 5000 livres now, and with rewards such as that, it is no wonder there are false brothers and spies everywhere. When testimony is rewarded with gold, *anyone* is likely to be labeled a heretic." Sollier slammed his wineglass down with a thud, splashing drops on the table and across his hands.

Like blood from an execution.

He dabbed at the splattered wine with his linen napkin, and roared a curse. Bounding up from his chair, he knocked it to the floor, then marched to the door and pulled it open. "Mademoiselle, we have a spill. Station yourself in here now, please."

The serving woman was swift to right Sollier's chair and clean up the wine. After he took his seat again, she went to sit in the small *bergère* armchair near the fireplace. Settling into the deep burgundy silk brocade cushion, her eyes focused in Jehan's direction with a scintillating smile on her face. Lifted eyebrows and smirks appeared on all the men as they glanced between the woman and Jehan.

Odd . . . that they allow the tapstress to stay in the room. The gentilshommes room. And that was not all that seemed strange at this gathering—this first foray into political life. Jehan studied the young man in the brilliant green velvet ensemble, this Monsieur Fallere, who had grown rather quiet. *Peculiar choice of clothes for the steamy September weather.*

Sollier put his hands together for a few moments, fingers steepled and pressed against his lips, then took a deep breath and continued in a calmer tone. "Brousson's *Mystical Manna* pamphlet is being passed around throughout the land, drawing Intendant Basville's malefic attention. All the prophesying and fanaticism of Brousson's Calvinist followers could adversely affect our own cause to worship in peace." He surveyed the eyes of each man in the room before he continued. "Hence, we may need to distance ourselves, my friends. And yet, at the same time, we cannot ignore the depraved malicious deeds of the Catholic clergy."

Jehan was becoming suspicious that André's purpose in having him attend this meeting was to influence his opinions. *Why would that be?* Was André practicing the Reformed faith right under his nose? All this talk of fanaticism had Jehan fearing for his sister's safety at the convent. And with drink causing his head to swirl like the flames in the hearth, it loosened his lips.

"'Tis true, there are malicious clergy, as I myself witnessed at the market square today. Yet what of the good nuns and novices at the hospital convents that have provided a place for the poor and infirmed. Can we wrong them for those virtuous deeds?"

"Virtuous deeds. Absurd," Monteaux cried out, setting off snorts and grimaced faces among the men.

"The hospitals are yet another way for the Romish church to have control over the province," said Sollier.

Monteaux leaned an elbow on the table and put his forehead into his hand while the men muttered over each other.

"Let me introduce myself," said a tall, thin man at the far end of the table, his face gaunt and pale, but with a wholesome glow about it. "I am Raymond Brun. What did you say your name is?"

Jehan hesitated, looking around into the eyes of the group, not sure who he could trust. "Jean Pierre BonDurant," he answered as if it were a question. Being from the mountains himself, he was not prepared to use his langue d'oc name for fear that some in the room might take *him* for a mécontent.

"Hmm, BonDurant," said Brun. "Would you be relation to Jean Pierre BonDurant who spent a month in the King's Uzès prison tower in '79? He was a stubborn man, refusing to convert, leaving a wife and young child at home whilst he was wasting away in prison. But he did a fine job for the cause."

"I . . . am not sure if that was my father. I have heard no stories of imprisonment."

"Seigneur de Cougoussac . . . wife was Madame de Barjon. She used her own money to hire an avocat and paid the fines to have him released."

Yet another secret! Jehan looked to the ceiling, wishing he could escape the shame, and breathed a long sigh of discontent before speaking to Brun. "Madame de Barjon was my mother, so I am sorry to say that . . . in fact . . . that man must have been my father. And he also did a *fine job* of leaving me at the Genoüillac Dominican prieuré for eleven years." His father's betrayal to his familial duties carved deeper yet into Jehan's wounds, and now his loyalty to him was all but gone. "My father passed a few years ago and finally abjured after the King's edict against false religions. Although I have been told he held out for several days after my mother and grandparents converted. I do recall he could be rather obstinate." *Absent and obstinate, that is all I recall.*

"Then you must want retribution for your confinement in the prieuré," coaxed Monteaux. "You must know what those frères can get up to. 'Tis ungodly what some do to the children."

Yes, I know all too well.

"Let me fill your glass, Sieur BonDurant, with some good Bourgogne wine," said Brun. His chin lifted, he raised his glass in a toast. "As the King's physic Fagon would say, '*To your health.*' At least one of his advisors has some worthy strategies."

Jehan raised his goblet then threw back his wine. The room seemed to be moving when he noticed the young woman rustling about in her chair near the fireplace. While the other men stayed focused on conversation, Jehan's attention moved to her. As she shifted the layers of her skirts from one side to the next, a bit of her silk stockings made an appearance, revealing delicate embroidery over her ankle. She moved about restlessly, causing the end of a blue silk garter ribbon to drop to the floor. In his mind's eye, Jehan languorously followed the ribbon up her pearly stockings, until he sensed her watching him. He looked up. Her brows came together and she gave a little pout. Was she expressing disappointment? Perhaps she wanted to be alone with him. He tipped his head towards the men, then frowned to let her know the men would occupy him well into the night, and she would have to wait for another evening.

The wet stones of the narrow back alley glowed from the flames of their noxious torches. The peasants surrounded him holding staffs, pitchforks, and muck-rakes, the chains on their ankles and arms creating a grievous clanking. Jehan took a few steps back away from the mob when someone grabbed his shoulder from the rear. He jerked, and the scene faded.

The scent of snuffed candles and smoldering coals filled his nostrils. Gasping, he woke in a frantic start. He lifted his pounding head off the table, then twisted and swung his sword arm back to fight off whoever was behind him.

The light of a solitary candle blinded him for an instant, a field of white swallowing his vision. He pulled his free hand up to cover his eyes, but an image of the flame still burned. After a few blinks, he could see his hand empty of any sword, and the gentilshommes' lounge empty of either peasants or the men with whom he had just shared the evening. An oscillating image of a woman's smiling face came into view.

"Did you enjoy your evening, Sieur?" The young serving woman had come to rouse him. "Now then, no more trying to take blows at me. We must get you off to bed."

As Jehan pushed off from the table and attempted to stand, he doubled over from the sloshing, squeamish feeling in his stomach. "Ginger. Can you bring a ginger tea for my stomach?"

"No, Sieur. There are no such medicines on the premises. Now, off to bed." She slipped her free arm under his shoulder and around his back. Her small, warm body, scented of rose water, pressed against him as she helped him to his feet. He gazed down at her in a wanton stupor, remembering the evening's flirtations.

"Yes, Mademoiselle tapstress, let us go off to bed."

"No! Not us, *you*, Sieur Jean Pierre BonDurant."

The two weaved and tottered as she struggled to support his robust frame, nearly a head taller than hers.

"I would never share your bed," she said, "unless as your wife. And besides, your wand holds no magic with all the wine you've drunk."

"Awh, but I am sure you fancy me. Will you not place your kindness on me and be my paramour? I shall be your Jehan. That is the name I shall hear you say when you are desirous of me." He was heading into deep waters but fuddled by drink, he had no concerns in the least about the consequences.

"Oh, *Jehan*. You're not thinking clearly, *Jehan*. I would like to call you by that name, but you don't even know mine . . . or the slightest bit about me. I will certainly *not* be your paramour, but should you persist, your love will give me authority over you and you will become my vassal for life." As she teased him, her arm squeezed a bit tighter around him.

"I would like to know more about you. Tell me your name then, Mademoiselle taptress . . . my sweet dove. We can fiddle about whilst you tell me your entire story," he said, pulling at her chemise ties that had come untucked.

She slapped his hand and pushed him back down to the chair where he landed with a limbered jolt.

"I am Colette Brun de Entraigues, not the 'tapstress'! But titles are no matter . . . unless . . . you are to take me for Demoiselle de Cougoussac."

Her arms crossed her chest under her breasts in a feigned show of anger, and Jehan could only notice that it made them spill from atop her stomacher like ripe peaches ready for picking.

"I am serving here this evening because Monsieur Arnaud was overwhelmed with the clamoring crowd and he is a dear friend of my father's. You met him this evening . . . my father . . . Seigneur Raymond Brun de Entraigues. I must decline to lie with you this night." She gave a little giggle. "Although your ardor has ignited a flame, that is to be saved for my wedding night."

"Awh, but Mademoiselle. . ." Jehan reached for her again, and again she pushed his hand away.

"Your bed-chamber is up two flights and down the hall to the third door. Surely you can find your way. And . . . Jehan," she looked at him with wistful brown eyes. "Should you come looking for me, your time will be wasted."

She left, closing the door behind her, and the room enveloped him in a cold, silent darkness. Some appetites were not to be satisfied without much patience and frustration, and he had been deluded to think otherwise. He folded his arms on the table and laid his throbbing head down on the soft velvet cuffs of his justaucorps—where the fragrance of lavender, and the unforgettable familiar scent of his father, lingered—and drifted off to sleep.

CHAPTER SIX
INTENDANT BASVILLE'S ORDERS

16 September 1695
Protestant Townhouse, Alias, France
Mid Morning

The door to the townhouse gave a feeble moan as Intendant Basville opened it only wide enough to leer out across the road. The lurry of noise and activity in front of Le Cristal Blanc Inn was distracting him from his task for the day, but he suspected there was a scheme afoot. From his vantage point, the bright morning light allowed him to clearly view the group of men gathering outside, preparing for their departures.

He strained to make out their conversations over the din from the adjacent plaza—already filled with people, carriages, carts, and beasts —and over the screams and laughter coming from within the townhouse behind him. He felt a heat rising in his body and loosened his cravate as he stepped out onto the portico, leaving the door open. It always agitated him to no end that his failing hearing made it hard to collect information from a distance.

His new informant, Monsieur Fallere, was among the group at the inn, so he would take care of gathering the particulars. *Stands out like a lizard, though, in that bright green velvet.* Basville's jaw tightened at the young spy's indiscreet appearance. *Vexes me to no end*! Fallere would need to be reprimanded for being so careless.

The Intendant recognized a few of the seigneurs—Monteaux, the flamboyant one; Brun, most certainly one to keep an eye on; and then there was the draper merchant. Yet the others—one middle-aged and one younger man—he could not identify.

The older of the two unknown men pulled the brim of his hat down low, hiding his face, then patted Monteaux's shoulder and stepped into the northern bound relay coach. With the crack of the driver's whip and the clatter of hooves on cobbles, the coach was down the street and out of sight within moments.

Basville watched the draper merchant step forward and the innkeeper signal a hackney carriage. As it pulled in, it momentarily blocked his view of the men. Its driver steadied the horses when the carriage tilted, then lurched under the draper merchant's massive weight as he climbed aboard.

When the sun rose in the sky and began to light the townhouse side of the street, Basville stepped back into the foyer, hoping not to be seen, but left the door slightly ajar. The sound of his royal dragoons inside—carrying out their task of persuasion on the Protestant family who lived there—was drawing a few onlookers in the street. He could hear the soldiers in the next room cackle and hoot as they talked about plucking hair from their victims' heads, and of their plans to sell the family's furniture and books for booty.

One of the women pleaded with the soldiers, panting between her words, "Can we please stop . . . dancing now . . . Monsieur?"

"You dumb-fogged?" one soldier growled. "Course not you loon. You'll be dancing, and worse, for days unless you abjure. So, come on now, abjure. If you do, you'll have a two-year exemption from any more billeting, or . . . " the soldier erupted in wild laughter that echoed through the townhouse, "would you rather we burn your feet in the fire, or make you stand naked in the street where you can revel in the mockery of every passerby?"

Pleased to know his soldiers were managing to make progress, Intendant Basville focused his thoughts back on the dealings outside.

He peered out the half-open door and saw Fallere, green as a gooseberry, emerge from around the hackney carriage.

Fallere headed toward the townhouse and stopped shy of the portico.

"Fallere. Come closer. You know I do not hear well."

"Intendant." Fallere tipped his hat slightly and stepped up on the portico. "Sieur, you do realize you've already been seen, do you not?"

"Simply keep your eyes cast down the street as we talk . . . and your voice down, but loud enough that I can hear over this rout. I need more information about the two men I do not recognize. The one setting off in the long-distance coach, heading north, and . . . who is that awkwardly dressed younger man?"

Fallere grew an arrogant smile. "Ha!" he said, tilting his head back. "The younger man, yes, those clothes are quite mockable."

"At least his color choice allows him to blend into a crowd," Basville said, folding his arms across his middle-aged paunch. "You should take note, since your green velvet ensemble is too expensive for a truffle farmer's son. You're encouraging suspicions. People will wonder where your money is coming from."

"Well, remember, I do have noble family on my uncle's father-in-law's side. And if I am to fit in with the noblesse . . . " Fallere swept his hand up and down again with a flourish, "I must play the part."

"Stop now. You look as showish as Monteaux. Keep your eyes out to the street, as I requested."

Fallere did as instructed and ceased his jocular display long enough to give up the information. "The man heading north is Sollier, from the Ardeche region, new to the group, and quite radical. I could not tell if he is actually Protestant."

"Be clear, Fallere. What do you mean you couldn't tell?"

"Well, Sieur, he took both sides. He scoffed over restrictions, yet also advocated for suppressing the Calvinist preachers and their cult in the mountains who are making trouble for others. He could simply be one of the noblesse who wants to hold up in their châteaux, living as they see fit, and not be bothered as long as they continue their financial support of the diocese and pay their taxes. You know, they are not accustomed to being told what to do."

"And, what more did you learn?" Basville clutched the door frame, grumbling through clenched teeth, "Be quick with it, and then move along."

"Yes, Sieur. They confirmed Brousson is back inciting a new wave of Huguenots, and, mark my word, they will be back at it, creeping around at night to combat the supposed errors of Catholicism."

"Brousson! That man is a throne in the flesh." Basville drew his sleeve across his forehead, wiping at beads of sweat that had begun to rise. "We thought we had put down those seditious Cévenol fanatics a few years past. But now there are rumblings, and he will certainly stir them up again. Miserable wool carders and peasants!"

The crash of shattering glass startled the two men. Basville promptly leaned his head out the door and wrenched it in the direction of the noise. A front window of the townhouse had just broken; glass still fragmenting and falling to the street. A dragoon struggling with a woman to take her nursing baby from her arms flashed in front of the window, then disappeared into the recesses of the townhouse.

The woman could be heard crying out to her Lord and Saviour, then whimpered, "I will convert, Monsieur, just give my child. I must have my child."

"Success!" Basville felt a lightness in his chest but tried to remain sullen.

"How is this success, Sieur?" asked Fallere.

Basville heaved and grunted. It was like teaching a schoolboy with Fallere. "We know these *dragonnades* are a deterrent to resistance and rebellion. You heard how it worked on that woman. However, we have a house full of resistors here, so I am billeting these dragoons until every last one of these Huguenots convert."

More bystanders started to form outside the broken window, but Basville paid them no heed. His eyes still keen on the goings-on in front of the inn, he watched Brun hand a leaflet to the younger man, who quickly stuffed it into his pocket.

"Hmm. The other man, the one with such poor taste in clothing . . . who just took that leaflet . . . what do you know about him, Fallere?"

"He's Jean Pierre BonDurant. Must've recently inherited his title, Seigneur de Cougoussac. Don't yet know much about him. He seemed to come to the defense of the King and the Catholic church even though his father was imprisoned in the King's tower when he was young." Fallere's calculating eyes took a sidelong glance at the men. "Just now, he told me he'll head back to Genoüillac, near Mont Lauzère, after he goes to Uzès' market. He could be a good source for us, since he'll likely hear news of the illegal assemblies in the mountains."

"Stay with him then. If he is nouveau converti, he must demonstrate good faith and be loyal to the King's cause. See if you can persuade him to join you and provide us with more information." Basville felt a flutter of anticipation in his stomach at the possibility of rooting out the lawbreakers, once and for all. "The mountains are mostly impassable and hard for our soldiers to maneuver, so they must know the precise location of these assemblies. We must hunt down *all* the heretics who break our laws. Every last one." He could feel a crooked smile grow on his face for the first time in what seemed like years.

"I will need to determine where his loyalties lie," said Fallere, "so I know whether to pose as a Huguenot or a Catholic loyalist. Still, do not worry. I will handle it and report back with accurate information on the assemblies," he vowed, then stepped off the portico, going to stand in the street near the bystanders.

"See that you do. And get rid of that green justaucorps! I do not need your foolishness to cause me more problems."

Basville wondered what more he would be forced to bear before his job of converting the Languedoc region was finally finished.

CHAPTER SEVEN
NEW INSIGHTS

16 September 1695
Outside Le Cristal Blanc Inn, Alias, France
Mid Morning

The intense mid-morning light that blazed outside the inn caused Jehan to shield his eyes. His head throbbed as he said his good-byes to the remaining gentilshommes from the inn, Monteaux and Brun. The commotion at a townhouse across the street was not help-ing. *Dear Lord.* He had never been so drunk on so little wine before. *Must have been the brandy.*

He started to pull the leaflet Brun had handed him from his pocket, but when he noticed Fallere on the stoop of the townhouse, he promptly stuffed it back down, eager to see what this new acquain-tance knew about the goings-on there.

"Monsieur Fallere," he called out. "There seems to be much merri-ment and frolic over there. 'Tis quite early in the morning for that." But Fallere did not seem to hear him.

The thought of festivities and drinking made Jehan's head pound even harder, but he didn't want to miss out on a chance for some lively entertainment.

As he walked nearer to where Fallere stood on the stoop, he could see a man's face peering out the slightly opened front door of the townhouse—a humorless, thin-lipped, hardened face of a man in black clerical-looking attire.

Before Jehan reached the townhouse, a thrashing sound startled him and he reeled in its direction. A cloaked woman rushed up the street toward him, her layered skirts flailing against her legs. She paused in front of him, cutting him off before he could reach Fallere. Her face hidden by the hood of her cloak, she said in a low voice, "I would not go near. They may have you join in their devil's revelry . . . on one side or the other. You will have to make a choice."

"Pardon, what do you mean by that?" Jehan squeezed his temples, the excited throbbing in his veins triggering his headache again.

"Simply, if you value your life, stay clear of entanglement." In a quick moment, she slipped down an alley and was out of sight.

Just then, Fallere began walking over in Jehan's direction.

"Fallere. What is all this celebrating so early in the morning? I think last night's drink is playing tricks on my mind . . . I thought I saw a soldier taking a babe from its mother."

Meeting Jehan halfway, Fallere snatched him by the elbow and steered him back across to the inn. "'Tis not what you think. Those are innocent people being tortured by the dragoons billeted to their house. And yes, they have taken a babe from its mother. To force her to abjure. You will need to distinguish the difference between frolicking and torture if you are to survive in the city."

"So it is a dragonnade?" Jehan felt the heat of embarrassment race up his neck, across his face, and to his ears. "I can only blame my ignorance on the drink, or my want of knowledge, or both. Being raised in the prieuré, we had little to amuse us there, and now I am far too eager for diversions for my own good."

By the time they had walked back to the inn, the stable boy had brought up Luisant and she was ready to go. Jehan mounted, then gripped the saddle to steady himself. The ache in his head had dulled but the exertion made it whirl through his head. A fly buzzed around his face, apparently drawn to the rank scent of last night's liquor oozing through his skin. He swatted a few times but missed.

Fallere turned to the stable boy and showed him a coin. "Bring up my horse, swift as you can." Then with wide, unblinking, reptilian amber eyes he looked up at Jehan. "Sieur, I will ride with you to Uzès. We can begin plans to meet with Brousson and learn what we can about putting an end to this madness. You will need to take me to the mountains to find him."

Jehan wasn't clear if his meaning was to put an end to the persecutions—or put an end to the uprisings. "I do not know Brousson or begin to know where he may be." He swatted at the fly again as he recalled the uneasy feeling he had with Fallere the night before. And those eyes— there was something unnerving about them. "And just how *would* you put an end to this? I wonder what little good we, as individuals, can really do."

"The mountain people have resisted before. They will likely convene again and retaliate," Fallere said. "So is it a plan? Shall we ride out to find one of these assemblies?" He gave Jehan a hard stare while the irksome fly circled between them. Without looking, Fallere snatched it out of the air. He opened his hand and studied the dead little pest with those strange amber eyes of his, then flicked it to the ground.

"Those assemblies are *illegal*, Fallere." Jehan felt a knot in his belly and was sure it had little to do with the drink. His gut was telling him to reject Fallere's scheme. "I am sorry, Monsieur Fallere, but I must be on my way. I have much to do. Perhaps another day."

There was something not right about Fallere's behavior, and it was too early in these days of newfound freedom to be consorting with one encouraging unlawfulness. Jehan lifted the reins and nudged Luisant with his legs, turning her toward the Route d'Uzès.

CHAPTER EIGHT
TO MARKET

16 September 1695
Place Aux Herbes , Uzès, France
Midday

Jehan crossed himself with holy water as he left the late morning Mass and hastened down the stairs, saddlebag over his shoulder, toward Uzès' Place Aux Herbes market square. Upon arrival into the city, he had secured Luisant at a livery stable so he could attend Cathédrale Saint-Théodrit to offer prayers for victims everywhere of wrongful persecutions, past and present. But still, an unsettling heaviness lingered in his heart.

Eyes cast down as he walked and hands still trembling, the gravity of his journey's events brought a heavy cloud of disquiet, stealing the joy he had expected on this first visit to the vibrant Uzès international market.

When he entered the market square, even the pandemonium of fascinating sights and sounds, and the trails of exotic odors, could not immediately clear his head of the jangling—that incessant, dreadful jangling of the manacled and shaven chain gang he had seen shortly after leaving Alais.

He had come upon them as they were being marched across the

kingdom to the galleys in Marseille, and he was sure to stay several paces behind until they turned off onto the Route d'Nimes. Jehan had heard of this parading of law-breakers through city streets, but was shocked to see—chained alongside savage culprits and snarling criminals—were men in magistrates' clothing, men who were clearly gentilshommes, and even a few women and octogenarians. He could only assume the more virtuous appearing people were convicted of violating the laws of religion. The sight of them might have filled the King's baser supporters with delight, but it struck utter terror in Jehan, and likely in their coreligionists or anyone with a compassionate heart.

He paused to take in the array of color throughout the market stalls before him, hoping it would lighten his heart. There were the reds of wild raspberries and of pomegranates cut to display their tiny ruby-like seeds; the energetic yellows of lemons, dried mustard, and chanterelles; the dark majestic purples of plums for filling custard galettes and of dried lavender for scenting; the myriad greens of olives, artichokes, lovage, and rosemary. And there, on the far side of the square, a marvelous display of herbs and spices in rich, earthy hues of every sort imaginable beckoned him.

Long, slow breathing let him drink it all in, and a murmured prayer of thanks for the wondrous diversion seemed to ease his trepidation a bit as he walked toward the stalls.

Before he realized it, he was caught in the midst of the frenzied—but amusing—commotion at the heart of the market. He nimbly side-stepped several scrawny dogs dancing around the stalls, barking at squawking caged chickens, then turned and swerved from the stench when a fishmonger dangled foul-smelling fish and a basket of sardines in his face.

"Eww!" Jehan had to push the man back away when he tried to come closer.

"Fresh fish," the man screeched in his ear. "Bargain on a catch o'day."

"Smells as if it were from last week. Charlatan! You won't swindle me."

From behind Jehan, an impatient baby started to cry. He turned to see its nursemaid bartering over orange-scented confections. He smiled at the little one, then looked up to see a liveried lacquey carrying a cushioned stool, following his well-dressed mistress who sat every few minutes fanning herself.

The babel of many languages, the magnificent clothing, the beautiful variations of skin tones, and the clever, melodious cries of the vendors begin to brighten Jehan's mood. This was a place of exploration and discovery for him; a place of normalcy and routine for others as the world around them was once again moving toward upheaval.

He dodged and darted until he finally made his way to the stall displaying herbs and spices. There he found a spectacular array from the Levantine and the East, which he presumed came by way of the Montpellier port. Some were processed into powders, but André preferred the fresh whole varieties. Jehan remembered from his readings that the fresher they were, the better they retained their potency until time to distill tinctures, create infusions, or pulverize them into salves.

From a large tin bowl on the spice merchant's table, he picked up amber crystals of myrrh and frankincense gum, holding them to the light to examine their clarity and color. As he came upon each of the items on André's list, he dipped into the jute sacs containing their exceptional treasures and indulged in the aromas of their contents—warm, spicy cinnamon bark, pungent ginger roots, sweet seed pods of cooling anise, and complex green cardamom, the scent of which reminded him of the forest.

Jehan noticed a shallow basket of small amethyst-colored flowers and lightly touched one delicate petal. "It seems early for crocus," he said to the woman running the stall.

"Not too early for these," she replied, her voice thick with a peculiar accent. She removed the lid from a ceramic jar and tilted it toward him, revealing a bounty of saffron stigma threads. "An early blooming from the Spanish Pyrenees. See what lovely threads they produce. The deep red are the freshest."

After he examined each item on his list for quality, he asked the spice merchant to weigh and package his numerous selections, including some of the saffron threads from her jar.

Once she had packaged the first few items, she stepped a little closer to hand them over. But then, wrinkling her nose, she gradually backed away and pulled the *lappets* of her white linen hood across her face. "May I suggest a bottle of lemon oil to go along with your choices?"

"'Tis not on my list for today, but I thank you," he replied.

"A trick you'll thank me for, Sieur. Sip a little and rub it on your skin, and no one will know you were . . . hmm . . . *bezopen* last evening."

"Bezopen?" Jehan tapped his chin. "I have never heard this word, bezopen."

"'Tis Dutch . . . how do you say, *overmatig drinken*? . . . uhm, swilled, yes swilled in drink. 'Tis tried and true by our merchant ships for this, and for *scheurbuik* . . . pardon, for scurvy."

"Ahh, yes, the lemon oil would be a wise purchase." He took the bottle with a label that read 'Dutch East India Company' and dabbed a little of the refreshing oil on his tongue.

As the woman prepared the spices, he pondered the King's trade policies on such imported items. France could grow lemon trees in these southern regions, but not enough to support a thriving industry. The restrictions and tariffs would probably never stop the imports. The demand was simply too great and the Intendant too obsessed with his persecutions to enforce the regulations. Jehan was beginning to think the King had his priorities all wrong. Instead of investing in wars and the persecution of innocents, he could be spending to bolster the struggling economy.

If the woman was right, and he was rather odorous, he knew this would be the time to quell it before he arrived at the high fashion shops. He walked around the side of the stall to get out of the main flow of the crowd, then loosened his cravate to apply the crisp, pungent liquid to his chest.

While there, he noticed a table of assorted apothecary caskets and bags. He was attracted to a smaller one; well suited for travel with a handle and leather straps for tying to his saddle. The past few days had taught him many lessons, and one very important lesson was to be better prepared for treating injuries and ailments. This small bag would allow him to be equipped with a variety of remedies, so he added it to his purchases and loaded them all into his saddlebag.

Jehan continued perusing all the wonders that the market offered, but he did not bother to stop at a stall selling precious stone powders, potable gold, and antimony. *Better left for the alchemists.* Despite the inclusion of these earth substances in many medical writings, he found it hard to believe they truly held curative powers. He had formed the opinion that there was simply no essence of life to be found in them, not as there was with cures from plant matter.

He was far more interested in the merchant he saw across the way. A white turban wrapped the man's head, and he wore long colorful robes typical of a Turkish merchant from the Levant Company. Jehan stepped around a group of men blocking the way and found the merchant was holding out a basket full of poppy tears; slightly oval, bricks of amber resin the size of his palm.

"Glimpse into the future, my friend." The man's mustache lifted to one side in a playful half-smile.

"The future?" Jehan had heard that, as well as providing healing and pain relief, opium could conjure visions. "Do we really want to know the impending events about to unfold?"

"Dervishes use often . . . claim bestows one with sight of future happiness. One livre each. Good price to take you to better place."

Jehan swallowed hard, shocked by the price the man wanted, and uncertain whether it was a fair rate. It was on the list, but he had far more important purposes for opium than visions. He could create cures for coughs, eye inflammation, frenzies, and extreme pain such as earaches. The prospect of practicing with these remedies animated his heart and helped him to put the terrors of the last few days out of his mind. But he was *not* about to overpay the man. He knew he had to start low.

"I shall take the lot, but at eight sous each . . . that is two livre, four sous for all six of them."

The merchant scoffed and countered. "Three livres for the lot."

Jehan hesitated. It was, in fact, quite the miraculous cure, and he knew it was hard to come by. He hoped he was not making an error, but he ceded the negotiations.

He nodded and reached into the purse inside his waistcoat for the payment. Just as he handed it to the man, he saw a flash of bright green across the square. *Fallere?* The flash was definitely a man in a green velvet ensemble, like Fallere's, who then slipped behind the arcade column near the bookseller's stall. But Jehan couldn't be sure of his identity just yet.

He finished his transaction with the opium merchant, then walked over to investigate the books—*and* the man in green. The bookseller's stall would give Jehan suitable cover to keep an eye out in case Fallere, or whoever the man was, showed up again.

Picking up a gazette from a stack on the bookseller's table, he said, "I see you have the latest *Nouveau Mecure Galant* by de Vise." He held it near his face and flipped through a few pages, intermittently scanning the crowd while reading de Visé's latest articles on fashion.

There it was again—the flash of green—out of the corner of his eye. He glared over his shoulder toward it to confirm. Indeed, it *was* Fallere, the only man diswitted enough to wear green velvet in the heat of September. *Scoundrel! Quit following me.* As soon as Jehan caught Fallere's eye, he turned and disappeared into the crowd. *Like a slippery green lizard.*

Something was certainly incongruous with the man—on many levels. Why would Fallere be stalking him? The night before at the inn, and just that morning during the dragonnade upon the townhouse in Alias, he talked as if he were a Protestant, so why would he need help finding his way to an assembly? A memory sparked about the dragonnade. A realization really—now that his head was clear—of what he had seen. *Fallere was actually talking to the clerical-looking man . . . before I walked up . . . was that the Intendant?* So, Fallere wasn't just a bystander. And perhaps not a Protestant after all. Perhaps a spy. Did Fallere hope to implicate him as a secret Huguenot for some reward? *Best to stay clear of him.*

Jehan turned back to the bookseller, knowing he should finish his business and move on before he had to interact with Fallere. "I see de

Visé has commented on which styles are *à la mode* for winter. Style is so ephemeral and I am needing some guidance. I shall have one copy of this issue of the *Mecure*."

"And what about an edition of Moliere or Rabelais?" The bookseller pulled up two small books expertly bound in embossed leather, tinted in exquisite colors and gold gilt. "One cannot help but admire these beautiful fanfare bindings."

Jehan was taken by the bindings but wasn't much interested in comedy or satire, so he sorted through several stacks until he found, very near the bottom, wrapped loosely in a scrap of linen muslin, a book titled *Systema Cosmicum*. He pulled the book out and felt a smile grow on his face.

"I may prefer this Galileo."

The bookseller appeared thunderstruck, then grabbed at the book. "No, I am sorry, that book is not for you."

Jehan pulled it back away from him and smiled, delighted at the discovery of such a rare find. "Ahh, yet astronomy fascinates me. I understand this book is banned. Monsieur . . . I shall not report this should you relinquish it for fifteen sous along with . . ." Jehan scanned the table for the féerie tale book he had seen a few moments earlier, ". . . this edition of *Le Conte des Feés* for my niece and nephew."

"I would have it go for over five livres," the man said as he rubbed his wrinkled brow. "However . . . as long as we have an agreement . . . and there will be no report."

"I vow there will be no report," Jehan said in agreement.

The bookseller let out a huge breath, and sounding rather annoyed, he said, "So be it then. Wonderful choices, Sieur." He hastily wrapped Jehan's new acquisitions in a scrap of muslin while the two discussed where to find the textile and clothing vendors.

A bell marking midday began a deep, resonant tolling, interrupting their discussion. It came from the direction of a cylindrical tower, several stories high and beautifully embroidered, with many small fenestrelle windows from top to bottom. Jehan could see it was the Cathédrale Saint-Théodrit tower. Another bell joined in from a different tower, then another, and within moments there was a sweet-sounding cacophony of peeling throughout the city.

As Jehan looked up at the towers, they reminded him of last evening's story about his father's imprisonment. He raised his voice to be heard over the tolling. "There are so many towers. Monsieur, please tell me which one is the King's Tower."

"'Tis in that direction. You can just see it over the tops of those buildings. What is your interest? Do you know someone locked away there? A heretic or thief?"

"No . . . rather . . . I have heard stories."

"Dreadful place. I know of a way to get letters in and out . . . if the need arises."

"Thank you, yet I hope not to have a need. Seems best to stay clear of anyone deemed a heretic or thief."

"All the same," the bookseller said. "Keep it in mind. I can help with many matters along these lines. My card is in the books." He tipped his hat. "Monsieur Jean Giraud at your service."

Jehan wondered for a moment what other matters he was referring to. Something other than the illegal delivery of secret letters?

He was tucking his new gems, and the edition of the *Mercure,* into his saddlebag when a parade of begging frères staggered out of a nearby tavern. Jolting and bouncing against one another, they moved into the crowd holding out sacred pictures, rosaries, statues of the Maries, and other religious devotionals and trifles, and asking for donations.

Jehan came face to face with one teetering frère who would have needed a barrel of the lemon oil to temper the reek of wine. He pushed the frère out of the way, disapproving of his asking for money only to drink it away, and moved on down the street. *Such injustice.* Had they been citizens, and not holy men, they would have been fined for their drunkenness.

With a few short paces along the cobbled street and a few brief moments of reflection, he realized his own arrogance—after last evening, who was *he* to be casting stones? The lemon oil had cleansed him of the noxious odor, but certainly not of his sin.

According to the bookseller's instructions, all the items on Jehan's list—the clothing, and shoes, and accessories—were available in shops down a side street. So it took some additional walking, but he didn't mind. It gave time to weigh the importance of each item in light of all he had witnessed on his journey. He recognized that his strong desire to be a man *à la mode* had waned over the day, as both the new discoveries—and the unnerving, heinous acts—now preoccupied his mind.

When he reached the row of *haute couture* shops, a pair of dandies, fashionably dressed, looking like plumed and laced ladies carrying swords, strolled out of the tailor's shop. Jehan smiled and tipped his hat, enjoying how androgyne fashion had become. It allowed a taste of freedom for those who enjoyed crossing boundaries. Yet that freedom could be lost at the whim of the King since, on any given day, he might dictate yet another manner of dressing.

Jehan peered in the shop window to see a small sign reading *modes d'hiver* in front of the latest winter fashions. He found them stunning; men's ensembles in the finest damasks and velvet plush, chemises with the distinctive Le Puy lace, *balandran*-style cloaks with silk linings. But he found he had no taste whatsoever for the outrageous prices. While studying the extravagant details, he could not help but wonder if others would think him foppish and overly pompous— the way he thought of Monteaux, or worse, like Fallere.

He watched as a woman of lower means inside the shop counted out 300 livres for a dress of printed linen with raised ornamentation mounted on silk.

"For your mistress?" the tailor asked.

"Oh no, Monsieur, it shall be mine." The woman held the dress to her body and studied herself in a tall mirror. "I hope to elevate my status. Perchance, take up a job in the household of a duke or marquis, or at least in a fine shop such as yours. And I believe this gown will help."

Jehan shook his head and sighed, knowing her purchase would likely leave her with nothing for her basic needs for quite some time. It was then he realized just how obsessed the King and Colbert had made the entire country with their policies commanding new styles for the noblesse every spring and winter, and promoting the widely held belief that one was of little significance if they did not keep up with the latest courtly fashions. All this elaborate clothing no longer seemed of much importance to Jehan. Not if it left people impoverished and beholden to the King's fancy.

It was settled in his mind—a high-style ensemble was simply not as pragmatic as the medicinals, tools, and weapons he would need if there were more conflicts on the horizon. He decided the textile stalls held all he needed for commissioning a practical ensemble by the Genoüillac tailor, and at a much better price.

He returned to the market square where he made his choices—fine wool serge twill, one lot in dark blue and the other a rich gray, watered ribbons, bits of lace, and a cleaning brush. *That should do*. He was feeling a bit loaded down with all his purchases and reckoned he should take leave and return home before sunset.

On his way to the livery, an assortment of pocket tinderboxes enticed him into the cutler's stall—complete with flint, fire striker, and hemp matchcord. He had never seen these in Genoüillac. "Now that's an essential device," he said to the vendor. He chose one, and tired of haggling, immediately paid the man full price as marked without any negotiation.

For a few moments, he also considered a dagger from the array of weapons on display. He ran his fingers along the table, sliding them over grips of mother-of-pearl, and white jade, and embossed silver. The quality was admirable, but he decided against a purchase when a pair of modest silver buckles caught his eye, rectangular in shape with round studs on each corner.

"I would like to purchase this pair, Monsieur, however. . . they are *nothing* exceptional, so I will only pay half the price marked."

The cutler nodded in easy agreement, likely because he had taken advantage on the price for the tinderbox.

Finally, Jehan had his first pair of silver buckles. The city streets were full of fanciful buckles—on the elite and their servants, and on the tradespeople who, when not at work, dressed to imitate the higher classes. It was odd that one should feel so emasculated over lacking a pair of buckles, yet this was one small indulgence in fashion that seemed quite necessary to fit in.

By Jehan's measure, it had been a successful afternoon at market. He had acquired everything on his list and restrained himself from too many unnecessary purchases.

He departed the square, and just as he turned a corner en route to the livery, he saw Fallere, yet again, in the block ahead, leaning out from an alley and looking down the street in the opposite direction. When Fallere turned his head in Jehan's direction and appeared to catch sight of him, Jehan ducked into a deep entryway alcove.

"This audacious man is a plague on me," Jehan said under his breath. He backed firmly against the door, clenching his jaw.

He waited as Fallere came closer, the clicking of his shoes on the cobbled street growing louder and louder. Jehan stood rigid, motionless, holding as still as the stones in the surrounding walls.

There had to be a reason Fallere was stealing about, spying on him. Who was Fallere working for? Why was he trying to coerce him into attending an assembly?

A haunting memory flashed in Jehan's mind—of a time when one of the unscrupulous frères came looking for him. Could Fallere have the same intentions? Was he in danger from this man?

Jehan thought hard, trying to recall their interactions that morning. Fallere had no sword as far as he could remember, but perhaps he concealed a dagger or pistol.

Poised to intercept Fallere, he was aching to move. He was prepared to use his swordsmanship skills, learned after weeks of intensive training with Benat. *But only if he is a genuine threat.* Yet he did feel threatened, and rage at this incessant pursuer was creeping in. His hand moved to the hilt of his sword.

When the infamous man in green passed by unwittingly, Jehan lost all self-restraint and moved impetuously, swiftly, out behind him. He skillfully drew his sword in silence from the leather-wrapped wood scabbard and aimed at Fallere's back without him being aware. But Jehan's foot kicked a large pebble that clattered out into the street.

Fallere recoiled at the sound and started to turn, but Jehan poked the blade into his loathsome green justaucorps, causing him to squirm. *Slimy green lizard.*

He looked over his shoulder at Jehan with those cold, unblinking eyes. "BonDurant, I was searching for you," he said, then licked his lips as if preparing to eat his prey.

"Resist the temptation to move, Fallere. And tell me why you are lurking about. You shall approach me like a proper gentilhomme, or leave me be."

"I do not fancy death, BonDurant. Will you *please* remove the blade?"

Jehan was locked in the grip of such infuriation that he could not move.

"Come now," Fallere said. "Is *this* the act of a proper gentilhomme?"

Jehan knew he was right. It was not proper, and he could be arrested for drawing his sword when there was no real threat. But Fallere's voice was eerily calm. It made Jehan afraid to back down. The man was stealing his freedom, just like the frères.

"I had only hoped that we were more alike than you let on the other night," Fallere said. "That you would guide me to an assembly of good, brave Huguenots." Fallere turned his head away from Jehan before he spoke again. "You want to see an end to the persecutions, do you not?"

Absolutely, Jehan wanted the persecutions to stop. But he certainly didn't want to go against the King's law by attending the illegal assemblies. Jehan found it difficult to read the truth when he could no longer watch Fallere's eyes. How did he propose to end the persecutions? By aiding the Huguenot worshipers? Or was it by assisting the King's officials in ridding the land of them entirely? Perhaps Fallere did, indeed, want to help the innocent worshipers, so Jehan softened the push of the blade.

"I have told you, I have no designs to join an assembly," Jehan said vehemently. "I see no way you and I alone could possibly put an end to the persecutions. Yet I might open my mind if you will propose how, exactly, it could be possible."

"But, BonDurant, I know no one else in the mountains who . . . "

Jehan pushed the sword a bit firmer onto Fallere's back and felt his face heat as he resisted the urge to unleash his simmering anger. "I do *not* trust you, Monsieur Fallere. You are not acting as a man of honor, and you do not explain yourself about ending the persecutions. Be gone with you. And if I ever find you following me again, I may use this blade to tear your fine clothes into *very* fine shreds."

Jehan poked at Fallere's back, trying to force him along. He flinched but stood his ground. So Jehan grabbed his arm, spun him around, and brought the sword to Fallere's chest.

"I mean what I say," said Jehan. "If you would like a meeting with me, you should send a letter requesting one. Doubtful, though, that I would honor any such request after this. Be gone, now!"

Jehan stepped back and crossed his arms across his chest, sword still high in his right hand, while he watched Fallere slink down the street, glancing back over his shoulder again and again like a boy sent to his room.

Perhaps he had been too hard on Fallere—let his annoyance and past fears ruffle him needlessly. Jehan slid the sword back into the scabbard as he questioned his own behavior. Had all that Benat taught about savoir faire and negotiation been for nothing? Jehan's rival emotions tried to wage war in his head until he realized the cause of his folly was not Fallere, but was bred by the violence of the past few days.

CHAPTER NINE
TRUTH OF THE MATTER

17 September 1695
Château de Cougoussac, France
Evening

Jehan stepped outside the front door of the Château de Cougoussac as the sun set. Benat joined him, placing a calming hand on his shoulder as the two looked out across the fields

"'Tis my favorite part of the day," said Benat, "when the birds begin their eventide dance."

Swallows wheeled toward the violet mountains, dotted with evening's first hearth lights, until they were inky flecks against a fiery apricot sky. It was a much needed antidote to the troubling scenes from the trip that Jehan had begun to share with Benat.

"Yes, a time of enchantment and serenity . . . at last," Jehan said as he took in a long breath of the country air, sweet and calming as a mother's embrace. "The sky is such a canvas of prolific color, setting off those tiny heaven-bound souls as they glide free. I envy those little creatures." A breeze brushed over his face. Tufts of wood smoke across the valley spoke of the coming chill of the night. He turned to Benat. "Will you take some air on the terrace with me before our meal?"

"Certainly, Sieur." Benat pulled the door shut, then folded his hands behind his back as they began their stroll across the graveled fore-court.

Jehan shuffled the gravel under his feet as he walked, the crunching and crackling not helping to still his unsettled thoughts. There was more he needed to say beyond the brief retelling of his trip to Alais and Uzès, and many more questions he longed to ask. Exhausted from the experience, Jehan rubbed his forehead and looked off over the fields again.

"I am truly sorry, Sieur, for what you witnessed on your journey," said Benat. "I had hoped that none of us would ever see such cruelty again after the terrors of the Revocation times."

"As did I." Jehan was grateful for Benat's gentle invitation to unburden himself further. "And I realize now I need to be wary of responding, in turn, in a cruel manner. I acted against my better nature in dealing with Fallere." Jehan let out a long breath. "I am utterly disillusioned after my encounters . . . and now, I find little importance in the trivial things I valued just a few days ago." He turned to look at Benat, hoping he had wisdom to offer. "I do not understand this world of divisiveness and intolerance, or the motivations that drive such severity. Is it that one man's hatred breeds hate in others?"

Benat hesitated, as if he were weighing the words he was about to speak. "We can never truly understand this world. We can only take heed of the dangers and the secrets, and do our best to survive."

"These secrets . . . there are so many," said Jehan. "I am still certain that Monsieur Fallere carries secrets. I believe he has insidious plans of some sort, either to lure me into the fold of the assemblers, or perhaps to turn in Pasteur Brousson for the reward. Yet . . . of greater concern to me . . . what about the secret of my father's arrest? Why did . . ."

A golden eagle's call interrupted in a soft whistling wip as it circled high above the field.

"Look, a golden." Jehan said. "Seems to be observing its possibilities from a distance. 'Tis not going after the rabbits grazing in the field. It must be waiting for the fox to come out of hiding."

They studied it for a few moments until Benat, in his astonishingly intuitive way, translated its message. "The eagle has a lesson to teach us. Perhaps it is best to fix attention only on secrets that bring good things about . . . and wait for them to come out when the moment is right. Some secrets revealed will bring relief and redemption. Others are better cast off, never to be discovered . . . should you wish to live a contented life."

Yet these secrets burned like a curse in Jehan's soul, and he yearned to know more. "I understand how that can be, though I *must* learn the reason for my father's imprisonment. Please . . . tell me what you know."

Benat hesitated, his face graven and staid.

Jehan looked hard into his eyes, searching for honesty. "And I have more questions . . . why was I held in the prieuré? Why did my parents stop visiting?"

Benat took a deep breath. "The hard truth, Sieur . . . is your father was a resistor and was arrested for trying to stop the destruction of the local Protestant temples ordered by the King."

Jehan's throat tightened at this news. Compassion for the persecuted was one thing. He understood that. He, himself, had felt compelled to help the dragoon's victims in Alais but it had also become clear it may have meant his own death. What good could he be to the victims then? It seemed utterly foolhardy for his father to have involved himself the way he did, taking such a risk when he had a family at home depending on him.

"What more about my father, Benat?"

"He was a man who angered easily and had no trust of lifelong Catholics, like myself. Thus he shared little with me. Yet your grandfather confided in me for many years. He knew me well and trusted that I would always be loyal to your family."

Benat stopped and turned to look directly at Jehan. "This much I do know, Jehan. . . your parents did not abandon you. Without a doubt. I thought André would have explained this to you by now."

"He has not. But he would not unless I asked. And I have not asked because I cannot trust him to be truthful. His motives always seem to be in his own best interest." Jehan's brows and shoulders grew taut. "What happened, then? Was I forced to live at the prieuré by my parents choice . . . so they could continue to worship in the Reformed faith?

"Sieur, you were one of the children stolen by dragoons," answered Benat.

Jehan's chest clenched in disbelief, and he grew restless in his stance. He had been like the innocent baby in Alais, ripped from his parent's arms.

"Your family did what they could to keep you at home. They paid a pension, or rather a bribe, to a former prieur who threatened to take you when you were only five years of age. Although the edicts stated that seven years of age was the requirement, some clergy would make these sort of threats to acquire more money for their coffers."

"But the prieuré is so austere," said Jehan. "There are no outward signs of wealth as in the grand cathédrales."

"The austerity is but a feeble disguise for the controversial flow of funds. That bribe your family paid worked for a while. But a few years later, out of spite, Curé Gellion reported all Reformed families who did not show up for Mass at *his* church."

"Gellion. Iron-hearted babbler," Jehan groaned. He paced away from Benat, then back again, grinding the gravel beneath his feet. His heart was about to rip open as anger radiated from his chest. "Were the families punished?"

"Yes. But only because Gellion wrote to the Intendant and petitioned for dragoons to be billeted around Genoüillac. The soldiers forced their way into your townhouse, and after six weeks of tormenting your family, they took you away to the prieuré.

"So the stories I heard at the inn are true." Jehan pressed a hand to his twitching cheek as forgotten memories tried to take hold, dancing like ghosts in an outer darkness.

"And my sister? What of her?"

"They managed to keep her at home, but only until her seventh birthday when, by law, they were required to let the Abbess take her to the convent. They saw the trauma it inflicted on you when they fought to keep you home, so thought it best not to resist for your sister's sake.

"I am confounded as to why I have no remembrance of it. But

after I witnessed the same horrors yesterday in Alais, I am beginning to understand." Jehan clenched his teeth. "Those vile miscreants. Did I tell you? They, too, took a nursing infant from its mother, forcing her to abjure." He made the sign of the cross, looking skyward. "I pray to the Blessed Virgin they gave her poor child back . . . so it does not have to live in terror."

Benat closed his eyes for a moment and sighed, shaking his head, then cleared his throat. "After you were taken, your family came here to live; to escape the eyes of the King's soldiers and any Genoüillac neighbors hungry for a reward. Your father was so infuriated he would rage through the château, threatening to kill all the curés and frères in order to get you back. Your mother feared you would both end up dead. So, for that reason, she asked him to stay away from the prieuré and tried to visit in his stead."

"I don't remember her visiting more than a few times." Jehan fell silent and stared toward the mountains as they disappeared into the fading light, recalling the endless days of waiting. That he remembered well. The waiting that had turned to hunger—a hunger for lack of food, lack of family, lack of love—powerful hunger that had paralyzed his will.

Benat patted Jehan's shoulder and eased him back around. Candlelight from the windows cast a warm, benevolent glow across Benat's face, and Jehan could read deep compassion there as he weaved the story together.

"After a few months, they would no longer give your mother permission to see you. She continued to try for years, and would stand outside the prieuré's gates weeping and hoping to catch a glimpse of you."

"Not given permission? I . . . I had no idea." Jehan blinked back the tears that began to cloud his eyes. They were the first tears to the surface for nearly a decade; since the time he had finally given up on his family.

"Do you remember Pierre Miguet, the former prieur before Chabert?"

"Not well. Only that he did not want to be bothered, and would send me off with the frères."

"When you first arrived, Prieur Miguet promised you trips to see the great cathedralés and their magnificent objects if you would study to be a devout Catholic and give up your family. After that, he never allowed your mother to visit again. Your parents and grandparents all finally converted over a year later in a failed attempt to get you back, but I have been the only one since given permission to visit."

Jehan shook his head, his thoughts scrambling to understand. "'Twas my doing, then?" He took in several shaky breaths and his throat tightened. He was suddenly shackled by his own misdeed, the burden of it somehow heavier than the weight from abandonment. "I sent . . . I sent my own mother away?"

"You are not to blame," Benat said.

Jehan could see his own anguish reflected in Benat's misty eyes as he spoke.

"They seduced you with their illuminated manuscripts, and sparkling votives, and promises. The frères beat you with whip and rod, making you do penance for the heresy of your parents until you were convinced that they were evil." Benat held a hand to his heart. "When I came to check on you, I saw the marks on your young body. You only wanted to do what you were told was right before God's eyes. Now you know, Jehan . . . your family *did* truly love you. All this secrecy is an ancestral curse that you are not bound to. You can choose your own path."

Jehan's taut shoulders loosened. A wave of emotions rolled through him like a frozen river thawing, yet strewn with broken ice that he must straddle. He inhaled deeply, thinking about his choices in that moment. He could, at the least, cling to the good Benat had pointed out in the long withheld story.

The scent of pistou caught on the breeze and perked Jehan's nose, distracting him as he wiped a sleeve across his damp eyes.

"*Sopar* is ready, *mes bons òmes*," Biatris called out. She appeared silhouetted in the doorway, the flickering light from inside casting an angelic aura around her motherly figure—a comforting sight, to be certain. "Has Benat told you the blessed news about Lucrèce's babe? 'Tis a boy. Little André. God's blessed joy arrived just yesterday."

"Another child in the world that could be taken from his parents,"

Jehan mumbled as a chill ran through him. "It feels like sad news at this moment." But then, he inhaled deeply, allowing himself to imagine the shining face of the new tenderling, soft, and rosy, and cooing, and his entire body relaxed into acceptance.

Benat's eyes lightened. "Perhaps you can help the children to stay intent in the Catholic faith so they will meet no malice. You can be their shepherd, always leading them to safety."

Jehan gave a half-hearted shrug. "Yes, that is the least I can do . . . keep them from harm. I cannot continually relive my past without constant despair, so what is important now is the future of the family. I must choose to steer my thoughts thus. First and foremost, I shall set to the task of securing my sister's release. I worry the assemblers may try to burn the convents again in retaliation, as they have done in the past."

He walked toward the house knowing, in truth, his guilt and grief would likely emerge time and again, entwining him, holding him down, making real freedom illusive. But he was ready to end the anguish of the revelations for the time being.

"Biatris, won't you join us for supper? We are all family now, after all. I want to show you and Benat my gratitude for your service."

She curtsied, slightly lifting her white apron, now stained by broth and basil, her *chatelaine* tinkling a delicate melody of keys, tiny scissors, a needle case, and a thimble. "Oc, delighted, Sénher. I will see you upstairs in the family solaire . . . perdon, in *our* family solaire," she said, beaming.

Jehan, too, looked forward to spending time in the solaire. He had not seen the room since a boy, being too busy with training out of doors while on his short visits over the last few months. He remembered the solaire as a merry place where his extended family would gather. And now, he would finally have family again.

There was already a connectedness—a growing bond of trust—in their little trio despite differing beliefs and backgrounds. His heart warmed knowing he no longer had to spend his evenings alone with only the shadows on the prieuré walls for companions—the shadows that had haunted his lowly life for far too many years. Mutual respect and tolerance were key to living harmoniously, and Jehan was determined to play his part. Perhaps it would help make up for so many years lost in the mire created by the Revocation and ease the tenuous times ahead.

Brilliant candlelight, made dazzling by an abundance of crystals and the blazing hearth fire brought hope to every corner of the *solaire* as light pushed darkness to the far reaches of the ceiling. The old Persian rugs in rich reds and golds gave a sense of warmth and welcomed Jehan home. He would gladly spend his evenings here from now on.

He laid his linen napkin across his lap and bowed his head to join the others in silent prayer. They each had their own way of praying—Benat in the local Catholic tradition, Jehan in the Dominican tradition, and Biatris in the way of the Calvinists—thus individual prayer suited them well.

Biatris had set out an evening meal of soup, pain crestou, olives, and honeyed figs served on his grandmother's fine Rouen porcelain. When Jehan finished his prayer and looked up, he noticed something different about Biatris. She had dressed in her Sunday finery, modest though the outfit was, and it came to him that this was truly a special event for her.

She smiled—a smile that was all heart, sincere and warm and joyful. No longer playing the role of serving woman, she passed him a wickered bottle of wine.

Jehan's mind busied itself, preparing for the evening's opportunity for honest discussion. Disheartened with his Dominican upbringing, he was becoming curious about other notions, and it was a perfect time to ask for differing views from his two tolerant companions.

"Benat, do you feel the 'Real Presence' of Christ in the Eucharist?" Jehan asked. "I was told all these years to trust it is there . . . the true body and blood of Christ. But I have never felt it, and do not know by what measure to determine its presence."

It felt good to open up; to have those with whom he could share his thoughts, although he could see a look of discomfort on Benat's face and his posture became rigid.

"Sieur, this must only be between the three of us," said Benat. "I have felt his presence and I believe it is a matter of faith whether you actually experience it in the Eucharist. Otherwise, all would recognize it and not question. But I would caution not to ask these heretical questions in the presence of other Catholics. I am among the few impartialists in our region, but I ordinarily keep my thoughts to myself."

"While in Alais, I witnessed the Eucharist bread being crushed underfoot by dragoons, so it set me to wonder. To question. Truth is, I have not trusted Curé Gellion for some time. And after all I have witnessed, I may trust no clergy ever again . . . perhaps with the exception of Prieur Chabert."

"You are not the only one to question," said Benat. "The concept of the 'Real Presence' in the Eucharist comes, not from scripture, but from a doctrine instituted as a response to the Cathars. Thus, its validity has been debated over the years."

Jehan looked toward Biatris. "Do the Protestants practice the Eucharist?"

"Oc. Yet a different way for we Calvinists. But no matter. We should all have a right to choose our beliefs. You as well, *mon sénher*."

"Outside of our Catholic church," said Benat. "Some think the Eucharist is simply a place to focus one's mind in remembrance of Christ while meditating on communion with him. Others see it as spiritual nourishment."

"Can we not use other devices for this meditation? The clouds in the sky," Jehan waved his hands in the air as he spoke. "The sound of a waterfall. Things that we do not ingest? Is his presence only found in a wafer of bread and a cup of wine doled out by a curé?"

Biatris and Benat looked askance at each other with eyebrows raised. Perhaps they were a bit astonished, but then a smile crept onto both their faces.

"Well, Sieur, I have felt the presence at other times as well," said Benat, "and you will, as well . . . if you have faith. You will know the presence when the time comes . . . when you no longer question."

They continued their lively, open-minded discussion on spirituality throughout the meal. One that was deeply personal and free from the political animosities that hung in the air at the gentilshommes lounge. When they had emptied their bowls, Biatris stood, pushed in her chair, and began clearing the table. "I'll leave you now to your talking. I've much to do. *Bona nuèch, mons bons òmes.*"

"Good evening, Biatris. And I thank you for the delicious meal. The honeyed figs were an unexpected delight." Jehan did not have the heart, or the vivacity, to scold her again for using the langue d'oc. He was tired, and she had as much right to her free choices as anyone.

She left the solaire with one hand juggling a tray of dishes propped on her hip and a candlestick in the other. The comforting clap of her sabots against stone steps faded as she descended the stairs.

After her departure, Benat skillfully guided the conversation away from religion and on to everyday matters.

While the men took an after supper brandy, Jehan delighted in showing his new purchases. He was glad he had been sensible with his choices, omitting the courtier style frippery. But a part of him still longed to acquire bright new possessions. He had dreamed of it for years, using the dream to hold out hope while waiting for his release from the prieuré. It was a hard dream to let go of, but it was time. There were other priorities now.

He presented the respectable quality textiles that he had chosen, draping them atop a chair near the fireplace. "On one of my trips soon to Genoüillac, I shall visit the tailor to commission a few ensembles and meet with the shoemaker for some riding boots."

"I can help you with the new boots," offered Benat eagerly. "I'll show you techniques to design and make your own, start to finish. I have all the tools to do the job. And we can spend time on winemaking."

"I shall gladly accept your instruction." Jehan replied, delighted by Benat's enthusiasm for passing on his skills. "And I purchased this Galileo book for my endless curiosity. One, I believe, that has been banned. I nearly bought a dagger, but worried it was frivolous. Yet after this trip to market, I feel my sword alone is no longer sufficient protection. It might be a practical purchase in the future."

"Sieur . . . I have been waiting for the right moment to share your grandfather's collections, and I believe it is time. His library is in the far reaches of the third floor and has been locked for years, since your father had no interest. You will find your grandfather's volumes and treatises on law and many of your great-grandfather's pharmacopeias on the healing arts and medicine. They could be of good use in your endeavors."

Jehan gave a single decisive nod to signal his enthusiasm. "Splendid," he cheered. He had yearned for the freedom found in such uncensored writings. His Dominican schooling had provided only a narrow view of the world, but now these books would finally endow him with the knowledge to make truly informed decisions.

His heart raced, and a blitheful energy buzzed through him. He deemed it was no strange illness in need of a cure, but simply his insatiable eagerness for truth.

Jehan carried a basket of tallow candles while Benat held his lantern high. He rattled the key in the library door's rusty lock, struggling to get it to budge. At last, the lock declared surrender with a grating whine and a slow turn of the key. It took several kicks and shoves from them both to open the stubborn door that was party to the resistance. It seemed as if the library still wanted to conceal long forgotten mysteries or secrets, yet they were determined the time had come for it to divulge its wealth of knowledge.

Upon entering, a musty smell seeped into Jehan's nostrils and a cloud of dust took flight, swirling in the light from their lanterns. As he cautiously waved his lantern around the room, their surroundings gradually became visible.

"Here," said Benat, "we can light the chandelier."

He pulled over the library steps and climbed up. Jehan held up the basket while Benat took three of the candles, placed them in the chandelier, and used a rushlight sparked off his lantern to ignite them.

Jehan set the basket on the floor and turned to study the room. It was a narrow, crowded space with ceilings higher than the room was wide—more than twice head-high. At the opposite end of the room, a wooden-mantled fireplace and a soaring mahogany longcase clock with moonphase dial filled the narrow wall. On the right wall were two tall windows, and on the left, floor-to-ceiling oak shelving with neatly stacked books of all shapes and sizes. Jehan ran his hand across the spines of one collection, wiping away the years of dust and studying the gilded titles.

He stepped to the space between the windows where a rosewood Mazarin bureau, with its delicate ebony marquetry, was positioned. It had many drawers and compartments to explore, and, oddly, one leg had been cracked and was now tied up with bracing.

"I remember this bureau from when I was a boy, although it was in the *solaire* at that time." Jehan took a seat on the chair in front of it, and blew the dust from its leather writing pad. It had a shallow knee-hole that he recalled allowed the writer to sit sideways, with sword still strapped to one side. "'Tis a shame to be in this condition. It was my grandfather's most beloved piece."

"Yes, unfortunately your father took out his anger on it one evening, and had me move it here to hide his shame. I can send Biatris up tomorrow to tidy up, if you like."

"No need for her to work on the Lord's Day," said Jehan. "Have her wait till I return and I shall assist her. Tomorrow I need to take the supplies to André and pay a visit to Lucrèce and her babe."

"Indeed, Sieur." Benat said. "The harvest *fête* begins tomorrow after Mass at the Place du Colombier. Since we will need to hire more workers for the chestnut harvest, perhaps, while you are in Genoüillac, you can contract four sturdy men or women."

"Certainly. I will take care of it."

Jehan lifted the rear of his justaucorps and sat down in the odd little walnut and leather desk chair, with its horseshoe shaped back. He picked up a small journal and flipped through its pages, seeing it was his grandfather's estate ledger and personal commentaries. Other volumes sat neatly atop the bureau. He scanned them and reached for a small stack, pulling a *Book of Psalms* from the bottom. As he looked down to read, a strand of hair fell over his eye and down his cheek.

"I still cannot bring myself to return to the prieuré for worship," he said, peering up from under the dark lock. "And Curé Gellion's parish church is out of the question." He opened the cracked leather binding and pressed back the pages, one at a time. "I would like to take Mass here in the private chapel before I leave. Is that possible?"

"Without question, Sieur. Even though the chapel was built as a refuge for your Reformed grandfathers, they never regarded the sect or creed of those who wished to worship here. We have Catholic worship as well. The *vicaire* from Chamborigaud is assigned to give us a mid-morning Mass."

"Then it is open to all in the valley?" Jehan asked, continuing to focus his eyes on the book, running his fingertips across its fragile, yellowed pages.

"Many faiths have shared in its solitude over the years, including a Saracen family from Tagnac. It is a true chapel of ease."

As Jehan looked up, he pushed his hair away from his face, wishing he could push back his trepidation. "I would like it if the chapel can remain open to all." But, in a dark corner of his mind, he could still hear the cries of the persecuted and see the hardened face of Intendant Basville. "What if we are exposed to the Intendant? We will certainly have trouble then."

"I highly doubt he will bother with the private chapels of the noblesse," Benat said. "He has much larger concerns."

Benat's eyes were not entirely convincing as they fixed on the warm lantern light, then grew vacant. Jehan was not sure if he was reading veiled uncertainty or mere exhaustion from the long evening.

"Sieur, I believe we could both use some sleep. So, then, I will see you for worship in the morning." Benat picked up the basket of candles, bowed his head, and turned to leave.

"Thank you for everything this evening. Your support and loyalty mean much to me." As Jehan shifted in his chair, he heard a crinkling in his justaucorps. He slid his hand in his pocket and felt a crumpled ball of parchment. "Oh yes," he mumbled. *The leaflet from Sieur Brun at the inn.*

"Pardon, Sieur," said Benat. "What was that you said? I could not hear."

The reading of the leaflet's contents could wait. Benat appeared rather weary, so Jehan would let him get off to bed.

"Only . . . will you please leave me a few more candles? I shall likely be here exploring these texts till late into the night."

Benat laid two candles on the table and bid him adieu.

Jehan waited until his footsteps had faded down the hall. He removed the leaflet from his pocket and spread it across the bureau's top, rubbing and massaging until it lay flat enough to read. He scanned the parchment. Published by a collective of Languedoc noblesse, it offered contrasting views of two Calvinist theologians who were refugees in the Dutch Republic.

The LAST HOPE of the NOBLESSE
A DECISION for SURVIVAL OF THE CLASS

Anonymously published
by a
Languedoc Collective of Noblesse

Do we **Choose the Radical Path of PASTEUR JURIEU** *who writes;*
The Reformed should ***Violently*** *oppose Universal Toleration.*
Such a Doctrine is a Conspiracy against Truth. Our Creed is the only True Faith.
Pierre Bayle now embodies complicity with the French court,
denying we should use open ***Resistance*** *to the King and State.*
He is a traitor to the Reformed who commits Religious Heresy.
OR
Do we **Choose the Peaceful Path of PIERRE BAYLE** who writes;
A Correct Life is more important than a Correct Belief.
Even the best Creed will not Save the Soul from Damnation
if its Deeds have been Evil and if there is not
a ***Universal Toleration*** *for all,*
be they Huguenots, Jews, Mahometans, Pagans, or Catholic.
The Cause of our Calamities are Louis XIV's ill Counselors
who advise that our Reformed Parents' Children are to be raised as good Catholics;
This makes the Children of the Oppressed a generation of Rebels at heart.

The result will be mutual slaughter,
something GOD cannot have intended.

OUR LAST HOPE *is in the hands of* **WILLIAM de ORANGE,**
Stadtholder of the Dutch Republic, King of England and Ireland,
Champion of the Reformed Faith,
as he conducts negotiations to end the War of the Grand Alliance with
Louis XIV.

Jehan carefully rolled the leaflet, ruminating on what this meant to him. He could see how children of the oppressed could easily become rebels; rebelliousness was trying to take root in his own heart, despite knowing it could be perilous and bring the same fate his father's resistance had. But his heart spoke louder of his true nature—he agreed wholly with this Pierre Bayle's concept of Universal Toleration and a peaceful path, and prayed that William de Orange could help remedy the sorry state of affairs in France. Fallere must have known about the vengeful and bigoted doctrine of this Pasteur Jurieu when he said the Reformed were likely to convene again and retaliate. This all made it sound as if rebellion was truly close at hand.

Possession of this leaflet was dangerous in itself. It needed to be hidden. He could feel his pulse quicken in time with the tall clock that hovered over him, with its chubby little moon face watching his every move.

He felt around the kneehole of the bureau, recalling his grandfather showing off a hidden compartment. On the underside, the cold metal of a latch halted his searching fingers. He pulled, and with a little pressure, there was a soft click and a small door in the back sprung open. But when he tried to slide the leaflet inside, there was resistance. So, he reached in and felt around until he grasped an object that fit quite neatly into his hand. From its hiding place, it emerged—a dagger—of unusual and exquisite design.

CHAPTER TEN
SECRETS LEFT UNTOLD

24 January 1696
BonDurant Townhouse, Genoüillac, France
Afternoon

As Jehan opened the rear door to the apothecary shop, an icy wind wrested it from his hand and flung it wide, causing a vortex of snow tendrils to whirl into the room. While juggling a stack of his great-grandfather's medical books, the wind competed with him as he tried to shut the door and leave the weather behind. But within moments, he easily won the skirmish using the strength he had built working the fall harvest alongside his tenant farmers and laborers. Once inside, even the chill of the distillery room provided relief from the biting cold.

He set the books on a nearby worktable and brushed melting snowflakes from his face. Having prepared ahead for a day of experimentation, he was ready to get started. He rubbed his hands together to warm them, then sorted through the books to find the first recipe; one he had never seen in André's pharmacopeias. It was a most practical recipe for the use of the poppy tears that had been sitting in a jar since his trip to Uzès market the past fall. He thumbed through until he reached the black ribbon marker.

~ English Drops for epilepsy ~
Take tears of poppies, 6 ounces, cut small and put in matrass,
pour in Spirit of Wine to the height of four fingers, stop the
vessel, and digest for three days in moderate heat . . .

He took down the rounded glass matrass flask from an upper shelf, holding it by its long narrow neck and removed the stopper. Then followed the steps up to 'digest for three days', leaving it on the mantle above the distillery room fireplace. Once it was in place, he reviewed the rest of the recipe.

Distill in an alembic of this and Spirit of Human skull; mix
equal parts.

"No! That I shall never do," he said outloud. André and he were in agreement on at least one thing—they would never use human body parts, even those from mummies. He would just have to make do with distillations from powder of animal bone, or horn, or pearls.

Hearing the children's laughter upstairs, Jehan decided he'd had enough experimenting for the day. He looked forward to time with André's family, since recent heavy rains and ice had prevented his last few weekly visits. After making his way to the hallway, he leapt up the stairs two at a time, and headed to the *solaire*.

Warmth radiated in a wave when he stopped in the doorway. A fire blazed in the massive hearth, heating the ancient stone floors and bringing some relief to his tingling fingers and toes.

Lucrèce sat focused at her spinning wheel, the spokes and bobbins a blur as her foot rapidly plied the treadle, her fingers nimbly drawing out wool fibers just a bit at a time.

André was lucky to have this lovely, capable, intelligent woman. He had the best of all worlds—he had Lucrèce, and the apothecary trade, and his council position that brought him high regard. How was it that André was so worthy? What had his cousin done to be so blessed? This jealousy Jehan felt had not fully settled, but with each visit to the townhouse, his prayers for relief were gradually being answered. The questions had become less of a torment and more of an unanswered puzzlement. He only hoped that André appreciated Lucrèce enough that he was not spending time with that Marthe Beauclose woman.

Jehan did not want to startle Lucrèce, so he called out before entering the room, "Good afternoon, Lucrèce. André is very fortunate to have such an industrious wife."

Her dark brown eyes regarded him for only a moment until she returned them to her spinning. "'Tis good to see you after so long. First time in the new year, is it not? Please slip off your boots and cloak in the hall."

He did as she asked and set his hat on a table near the door.

Jeanette, the laundress, stood near the fire and rocked Lucrèce's baby, little André, in her arms as he chewed and slavered voraciously on her forefinger.

"My, how the babe has grown," Jehan said. "Has he teeth already?"

Jeanette nodded. "And sharp they are, Sieur."

"Lucrèce, where are Dominique and Pierre? I was hoping to read to them again from *Le Conte des Fées*. I always enjoy how amused your children are by the stories."

Lucrèce's vivacious smile spread across her face. "The nursemaid has taken them to their room for an afternoon rest. I think you fancy those féerie tales as much as the children do."

"Well, the tales do come from folk legends, which many say are true. What about the water spirit, Mélusine? I understand even Luther believed in her."

Lucrèce burst into a melody of laughter, with Jeanette joining in. She looked tenderly at Jehan and explained, "Yes, and many Reformists believe her to symbolize the seductress. They say she is a diabolical Catholic superstition. In truth, féerie tales are simply stories to keep the children, and we ladies, entertained while we spin and weave, nothing more. Yet they do often have a worthy moral lesson."

She stopped plying the wheel, and the whirling bobbin gradually came to a halt. After removing it, she laid it in a basket brimming with other bobbins, thick with fine wool yarn. "Jeanette, please wind these off and take the skeins to the dyer in the morning. Ask him to distribute them to anyone in need this winter."

"Gladly, Madame. Your kind and generous heart is always appreciated in town."

Lucrèce stood and straightened the plush layers of her blue silk velvet gown. It was unadorned yet refined. She was lovelier than ever, with long spiraled tresses of sable hair cascading out of her coif and over each side of a white woolen shawl. One would never guess she was a mother of three.

She took the baby into her arms while Jeanette hurried off with the basket of bobbins, then moved to the settee by the fire, and arranged herself, and her skirts, so as to comfortably support the little one. Her ivory skin glowed in the bits of sunlight that streamed out from around sporadic winter clouds and through the windows. Patting the empty spot next to her, she looked around at Jehan and said, "Come sit and warm yourself. Tell me, what brings you into town in this weather?"

He took the seat beside her and brushed the baby's soft cheek, noticing how dark and rugged his hand was in comparison. "I am eager to work on some new formulas I have come across in great-grandfather's books, and collect any mail that has arrived. And . . . I have drawn up a letter of application for medical school. I shall need André to sign as my reference. Where is he?"

"He is playing cards at Monsieur Narbonne's," Lucrèce said, humming softly to the baby between her words. "You should join him there. Monsieur is hosting a Roma group for the winter and they entertain nightly in exchange. Everyone in town tells me there is great merriment."

"And this has not attracted the attention of Intendant Basville? Are they not worried he would enforce the King's edict against giving bohémiens refuge?"

"No one seems to be worried." Lucrèce turned her head and addressed Jehan's eyes with a look of somber determination. "And they prefer to be called Roma, not bohémiens." She turned back toward the baby, appearing to relax again as she rocked him and hummed a bit more before continuing. "You well know the soldiers stationed here in town mind their own business as long as wine and silver flow their way. They believe their only duty is to protect the city from attack, so they won't summon Basville. Rumors are blowing like chaff in the wind about the Intendant sending dragonnades up here to the mountains again. Yet, it seems unlikely he would attempt it while the roads are so difficult to travel."

Lucrèce paused and ran her finger gently down the baby's nose several times, making the little fellow's eyelids heavy.

Jehan had grown tired of discussing dancing, and cards, and Basville, so he changed the topic to the one that weighed on him most. "What other news have you? Has there been any word about Françoise's release? I have written weekly since fall and warned her of the threat of rebellions against the convent, but have received no reply."

"I did receive news, and I know you will be disappointed, but she has decided to take her vows."

"What? No!"

"Shhh." She held a finger to her lips and whispered. "Quiet now, the babe has fallen asleep. Your sister was not comfortable responding directly to you since she scarcely remembers you. She says to tell you she is happy, that God is her family now, and the convent is well protected by armed sentries. She is also very sorry that your experience did not hold the same joy as hers. Jehan . . . sometimes it is best not to let yesterday take up too much of today."

He dropped his shoulders and exhaled, trying to release the discouragement and accept his sister's decision. Who was he, anyway, to think he should persuade her against her will?

"I suppose . . . you are right, Lucrèce. I am relieved to know it is her own choice, and that she is safe. It does lighten my heart somewhat to know she is content."

"Concerning other letters, I still have had no word from Sieur Montcalm about meeting his daughter to consider a marriage proposal," Lucrèce said in a soft voice. "'Tis a far distance to his château and the couriers do not travel often in the winter. But I did just receive a letter from your uncle, Pasteur Barjon. Do you remember him? Your mother's brother?"

Jehan summoned what recollection he had of his uncle. There was fondness, certainly, for although he had dressed in black robes like Curé Gellion, Pasteur Barjon was a compassionate contradiction to the Catholic curé. "Yes. A gentle man as I recall."

"Here it is." She took the letter from a side table, cracked open the seal, and pulled back the many entangled folds of the parchment, one at a time, then studied it for a few minutes. "He was forced to flee to Switzerland upon the King's banishment of all Reformed pasteurs, so he never uses our names in the letters, nor his, to keep from any implication. But I know his handwriting, and he asks how our new Seigneur is faring now that you are back home."

"That is a wise thing, to use no names. How are he and his family getting on?"

"They all seem well," Lucrèce answered. "He wishes you to know you are welcome to join their Calvinist camp. He says they can use young, sturdy men when they find a place to settle and build permanent homes, especially one trained as an apothecary."

At first, his uncle's offer annoyed him. Certainly, it would benefit their group to have another able-bodied man, but it held little benefit for Jehan.

"I am not sure why he thinks I would risk imprisonment to leave the country and join them. I have no reason. Surely he knows I am a Catholic, though admittedly not as devout as Curé Gellion would have me be. And I have my properties here which require my full-time attention."

Yet perhaps his uncle had gotten word of Basville's increasing persecutions and had a sincere concern for Jehan's safety. That was of comfort. "Though it is good to know he asks after me. 'Tis a fact that I have come to feel disillusioned with the spiritual education I received at the prieuré . . ." Jehan paused when he saw Lucrèce give him an odd look—one of surprise but great interest. "At the same time, I am not wanting to embrace the Reformed faith. 'Tis far too dangerous. Although I am rather curious to learn more about it."

Jehan got up from the settee and went to the windows. None of the day's tidings made him very cheerful. He rubbed his forehead, then raked his fingers through his hair, eyes fixed on the wintry scene outside. "Snow is getting heavy. Seems I will not be going back to the château this evening. I should settle my belongings into my bedchamber."

Jehan had joined Lucrèce back in the solaire and spent the better part of an hour encouraging her to get out in the world again, but his persistence was going nowhere.

"Lucrèce, truly, you should join us at Monsieur Narbonne's to watch the dancing. Your nursemaid can tend to the children. What harm could there be?" He simply could not understand her reluctance when she had the opportunity. He knew it was her choice, and he shouldn't keep pressing her, but this was just like the game she played when they were young. She would make him nearly beg, then finally give in with a twinkle in her eye.

But this was no longer a game. Concern was plainly engraved on her face when she glanced at the clock, her brows raised and cheeks hollowed.

"Are you worried for your safety?" Jehan reached through the side slot on his justaucorps. "I shall protect you. I have this splendid dagger now," he said, pulling it from the scabbard on his belt.

She leaned back, her eyes as wide as an owl's. "I know that dagger. It belonged to your grandfather. Where did you find it? We thought he had it well hidden."

"'Twas in his desk."

"Best not show it around town. It will only stir up some trouble. I do not know the reason why, but when your grandfather returned home with it after a trip to Castelbouc, he said he would hide it because there are things in your family's history that are best left untold."

All these secrets! "Benat said something very much like that." Jehan wondered what she knew about the medallion that he now wore about his neck. He loosened his cravate and reached down his chemise.

"What are you doing, Jehan?" she asked in a fretful tone.

"Can you explain this?" He held up the silver medallion with its cross and dove. "André gave this to me. It allowed me entry into the gentilshommes lounge at Le Cristal Blanc Inn in Alais last fall. Does this have anything to do with the dagger?"

"No. Nothing. But do not go showing it around town either. Almost five!" She stood, quick as a startled cat, causing the baby to stir. While cradling him in one arm, she began twirling a lock of hair with her unencumbered hand. Clearly, she was nervous about something. "'Tis getting late. Enough talk of this and of Monsieur Narbonne's soiree. I do not need that form of entertainment. But you go on now."

Jehan stood and followed her as she moved toward the door. Hoping to bear sway on her decision, he met her eyes squarely. "You are such good friends with Narbonne's wife, Suzanne. I would think you would enjoy seeing her. And . . ." He tilted his head down and put on a boyish look from under his eyelids, ". . . I cannot leave just yet. I shall need to have supper first."

"I wasn't expecting you for supper. You must go *before* then," she insisted, writhing her face into a frown. "'Tis for the best. Likely, the Narbonne's are serving something other than drink alone since André spends day and night there. Some sweets or cheeses, in the least. I shall need you to stay late and accompany him home so he does not end up in the gutter."

Jehan reluctantly reached for his hat on the table near the door. He was searching for something more to say when she picked up his boots, pushed them against his chest, then took his hat from his hand and patted it on his head.

The jostling woke the baby, and he started to whimper. "Go now and have an enjoyable time," Lucrèce said in an anguished tone. "I shall not expect you till *very* late."

Jehan had never seen Lucrèce like this before. He knew her well, and this was not like her at all. She had always been so welcoming, so caring, but something had her rather anxious. Or—perhaps she had simply tired of his company.

CHAPTER ELEVEN
ROMANI SPIRIT

24 January 1696
Narbonne Townhouse, Genoüillac, France
Evening

Winter's first blanket of snow was a fresh start for Genoüillac's streets. Welcomed by the townspeople, it cleansed away the filth and dung, and filled the cobbles, making the short walk to Monsieur Narbonne's quite pleasant for Jehan. It was strangely quiet as he passed through the south gate of the city ramparts to the outlying townhomes, despite several small groups of people about. Muffled voices, and icicles, and the downy white blanket across the roads, made the town seem otherworldly, almost magical.

Everyone who was out seemed to be heading to Monsieur Narbonne's *soirée*. There was an air of excitement and a sense of comradery among the chatting neighbors who were usually at odds, arguing over whose religion was most righteous, or who should be imprisoned for disobeying the King's laws. No one seemed to care that it was illegal for Narbonne to harbor the Roma, or that they were complicit by attending the dancing. As long as they had this entertainment to pass the evening and forget the divisions between them, they seemed happy.

There were twelve others in total ahead of Jehan, queuing in front of the house, all dressed in their finery for this exceptional occasion—fur-lined capes and muffs and plumes abounding—and all exchanging pleasant greetings.

He glanced down at his new blue serge ensemble, and—for a moment—wished he had added some embellishments. But the moment passed in a heartbeat. *No. 'Tis just fine.* He thrust back his shoulders and walked on to join the others at the doorstep.

Monsieur Laurens, the hatmaker, rapped the iron door knocker. They waited in silent anticipation. From outside the house, all was quiet, and Jehan wondered if the soirée had been called off.

"Have the soldiers been out patrolling yet tonight?" Jehan asked. "Could they have put a stop to the jovialities?"

"Oh, they have been patrolling alright," said Monsieur Laurens. "Straight to the inn. We heard them singing some merry tunes when we walked by, so they are well on their way to being liquored, as per usual. I believe Narbonne has paid them a courtesy fee, as one might say, to overlook these things. And likely does so on a regular basis since they are too close for comfort with their quarters just down the mill street."

The group of townspeople all stood again in silence, waiting, with eyes flitting about and brows raised in curiosity. Jehan could hear no revelry, just a faint murmur of voices. Nothing—until the door cracked open and lively, uplifting melodies flooded into the street, sending an energizing vibration to his very core.

"What a rare pleasure this will be," Jehan said to the others as he removed his hat and shook off the snow. Some of the group smiled and nodded in agreement, in perfect time with the music. Some stood wide-eyed with sparkling grins, and a few laughed and hooted.

Once the door had opened wide, the *valet de pied* appeared from behind it, donning a fine emerald velvet justaucorps detailed with gold shoulder bands and trim. Each of the guests requested to visit Monsieur Narbonne and Madame Suzanne, then provided their name, which the valet called out as they entered. It was only a formality since the valet knew each and every person from their frequent visits to Narbonne's boutique, which was located inside. Surely there were no worries about these people being road bandits.

The housekeeper scuttled out from the ground floor salon. "Madames, messieurs, welcome," she said, and curtsied.

Jehan noted that even she had dressed well for the occasion, although a bit garish, in multi-colored layers of striped taffeta over damask and touches of lace.

"Please leave your cloaks and weapons in the boutique," she said. "And join the others in the salon for music and dancing. Or you may visit upstairs where you will find card playing in Monsieur Narbonne's room or fortune-telling in Madame Suzanne's red room across the hall."

Then the housekeeper leaned toward the group, cupping her hand, and whispered, "If nature calls, there are convenience chairs on each floor in the dressing rooms."

Her comment elicited some faint giggles among the group as they squeezed into the crowded entry. They all did as instructed; some headed to the salon and others made their way up the spiral staircase to the room of their choosing.

The townhome was exquisitely furnished, but Jehan found it rather small for the home of one renowned as a man of significant influence and power. Narbonne primarily used it for his trading business, housing the boutique to resell exotic goods purchased from merchants traveling the Regordane Way, from port cities to Paris. Yet, how did that bring in enough money to hold such influence? It puzzled Jehan for a moment until he remembered André's ramblings about the many homes Narbonne possessed, including a few châteaux in the country and a couple of townhouses in the larger cities. The display of luxury goods required to furnish each one surely taunted his guests into purchases. *These soirées must be a strategy for success.*

Jehan found his way to the salon and stood in the doorway, bouncing up on his toes as he strained to view the Roma dancers and musicians over the heads of the other guests. Not able to see to the front where they performed, the green and gold velvet brocade draperies covering the tall windows invited his eyes upward to the sparkle of an elaborate crystal chandelier. The warm candlelight frolicked over the exquisite gowns and ensembles; it made the beautiful all the more graceful, the ungainly more tolerable, and smoothed the garish in soft, creamy shadows.

A preponderance of redolent perfumes mingled in the air, drawing Jehan's attention. They vied with the underlying muskiness of the room as it heated up, jammed with titillated bodies.

"Pardon. Pardon, please." Jehan tried to move past those standing in the rear. But the music was too much competition for his normal tone of voice, and no one responded. He placed a hand on the man's shoulder in front of him, trying to ease him out of the way. The man turned, and Jehan saw it was his neighbor, Alexandre Nicholas, the locksmith.

"There are a few spots by the windows," he said, speaking loudly enough to be heard over the merriment. "And you can greet our hostess who sits nearby there."

"Ohh . . . good evening, Alex."

"Haven't seen you for quite a time, Jehan." Alex gave him a friendly clap on the back. "Good you are getting out for some diversions. Just over there," he said, pointing the way through.

Jehan moved toward the windows where, close by in the corner, Madame Suzanne sat poised on a fashionable canopied bed receiving her guests, as was the style in the elegant Parisian salons. She had dressed in a splendid cochineal-red damask gown trimmed with layers of gold braid fringe. She must have had her lady's maid devise a scaffold of wire to support her mountain of lustrous auburn hair, various ornate laces, and watered ribbons into the courtly fontange atop her head.

"Good evening, Madame." He bowed slightly and moved closer so he could speak without shouting. "Thank you for opening your home tonight. 'Tis wonderful that you have offered shelter to the Roma, and I believe I speak for the entire town when I say I am grateful for the amusement."

"'Tis our pleasure, Sieur BonDurant." Madame Suzanne greeted him with a charming, cordial smile.

"I wanted to ask, how is it possible we could not detect the music from the street?"

She wiggled her eyebrows. "Well, Sieur, you are quite astute. Look behind the draperies and you will see my trick."

He put his hand to the heavy draperies; his fingers relishing the weight of the sumptuous, velvet pile in the deepest emerald, vacillating with an interwoven gold ground in a majestic pattern. *Another measure of Narbonne's success.* He pulled them back to find, edged between the windows and the exterior shutters, were pillows—top to bottom.

"Ah," he said. "Quite clever."

"Yes. 'Tis a stratagem I learned from the Reformed pasteurs for eluding the authorities." She fluttered her painted fan about her face as it had become dewy despite a layer of powder. "There is an excellent spot, just there, for taking in the entertainment. Go on now. We don't see you out much and it is time you had some enjoyment."

Jehan nodded, then moved to the spot between the windows, close to the musicians. He settled in, leaning against the wall where he had a full view of the dancers.

Delighted with the music, his pulse quickened with its rhythm as he studied the movements of the women. Their hips swayed as they spun, their arms wove about their heads with wide waves of their hands. Suddenly, they were shaking their brilliantly colored, layered skirts and their shoulders, while tossing their heads and intricately tapping their feet. The men moved around them with fast, furious footwork, clapping, snapping, patting knees and thighs in a dizzying, spontaneous display that expressed freedom with great passion and joy.

Jehan felt a weightlessness, as if his soul rejoiced at the sight, and it loosened his inhibitions. He thumped his feet to the rhythm of the tambourine and moved his head to the melody being chanted by the violin and cobza lute.

Truly inspiring. Any painter would be glad of heart by the play of candlelight on the stunning colors and patterns of the dancers's clothes and headscarves, and the glinting gold ear and finger rings.

The tune ended with a dramatic climax, an instant of silence, and an eruption of applause and delighted exclamations. Jehan clapped until his hands stung.

The musicians took a break at a table set out with wine and trays of cheese, sausages, chestnut pudding, and almond biscuits. His stomach was encouraging him to join the musicians for some food, so he began to head over. Just as he did, one of the dancers, a young woman about the age of his sister, glided with grace across the parquet floor in his direction—large soulful eyes staring at him, captivating and gentle.

"Sieur. You have not been up to have your fortune read." She came so close he could smell the fresh, clean scent of her skin. "My name is Syeira. Will you join me in Madame's room upstairs?"

She was petite next to his tall frame, so he bent his head down to look at her eyes while they spoke. "Well . . . I . . . my name is Jehan. I was about to have something to eat."

"There is a tray upstairs as well. Come, you will not lack, and I can see you want to know your future."

It was true. With the new dilemmas that presented themselves earlier that afternoon, he wanted to know, even if the future held strife.

"I would like that . . . to have my fortune read. But I did not bring coin to pay you. May I bring payment tomorrow morning?"

She looked deeply into his eyes with a serious expression and said nothing. He was not sure if she was angry or if she was reading his trustworthiness.

After a long, awkward moment, she finally spoke. "I see you are an honorable man. Tomorrow will do." She took his hand and pulled him through the crowd and up the stairs. He let this tiny young woman —yet a girl, really—guide him along and up the stairs without resisting. And not even a sip of wine had touched his lips. If Syeira could trust him, a total stranger, he would accede and relinquish himself into her hands.

A waft of noxious smoke trailed out into the hall from the card room as they passed by. Jehan could see some of the men in the room puffed away on long-stemmed clay pipes. And, to no surprise, André—sitting with a view of the door—was one of them. Yet another bad habit

Jehan would never emulate; not unless he was starving. *Waste of money and fresh air.* André nodded and winked with a smirk, obviously thinking Jehan had intentions for the girl. *Just like André.* That was the way his mind worked. But Jehan had learned his lesson about respecting the ladies.

Syeira and Jehan settled across the hall in the red room at a small table. Her eyes glittered behind the single guttering candle that sent shadows dancing around the room, setting the mood for mystery and the hair raising on his arms. Her earrings dangled just above her shoulders, grazing the bare skin near her neck where a long rope of red coral beads hung.

"Why are you not wearing a *dikhlo*, Syeira? I understand that young Roma women of your age are usually married."

"Sieur, we are here to learn about you, not me."

"I am only curious as the subject of marriage has come up for me in recent months."

"You give yourself away. Say no more until I read your palm." She clasped both his hands and pulled them close under the candle. "I noticed you favor your right hand. Yes?"

"That is true." No one had ever paid such close attention to his behavior.

"Your left life line shows the past. You see, it's shorter than the right . . . broken . . .not so clear. Your life has been unstable, and you've had little confidence. But the present is most important."

"And what about the future? Do you see whom I am to marry?"

"You must realize . . . the present is what will create your future."

"Hmm. The present." Jehan had begun to realize how important it was to take heed of consequences while in the present moment—before he took action. Could this be what she meant? But it was something he lacked experience in. The experience that would have come if he hadn't been under such rigid control as a child.

Syeira continued for a while, explaining the right life line, the Mount of Mars, the Mount of Venus, and how they defined him as a traveler who liked to return home, a man with moral courage, tenacity, physical vitality, and with a great capacity for love, warmth, and sympathy for others.

"And do you see love?" he asked.

"The heart line is here." She placed her tiny finger toward the top of his palm. "It is straight and of good length. You need harmony, affection, and you love nature." She ran her finger gently across to the outer side of his hand. "But there is this break . . . the lines on Mount of Mercury show two loves, one much deeper and longer than the other."

She continued delving into the meaning behind every last line in Jehan's palms until two women appeared at the door, ready for their turn at a reading. He thanked her and promised to return with his payment in the morning, then decided he had enough for one evening. After all, men in his profession knew physical vitality also required rest and fresh air.

He descended the stairs and recovered his hat and sword from the boutique, pleased to make it to the door with no one noticing. When he opened the door, Curé Gellion—crouched as if he had his ear to the door—rolled onto the floor at Jehan's feet, sprawled half inside, half outside with his legs still in the snow.

Jehan hopped back away from the floundering curé. "What is the meaning of this?" he demanded.

Gellion sneered and quivered all over. He rose to his feet on the stoop and smacked the pure white snow off the hem of his black cloak. "Prieur Chabert, come quick," Gellion shouted. "I told you so! You hear that music, the clamor, the bedlam. They *are* harboring those bohémiens. And they need to be stopped."

Prieur Chabert was walking away from the scene, about to turn around the corner of the building, in the direction of the prieuré. But he paused and called back. "And, I told you, Gellion. I spoke to the soldiers already. They do not want to get involved."

Curé Gellion cocked his head, eyes askance with disdain. "Your efforts are useless, as always, Chabert. I have summoned Leyris, the King's regional councilor." Then he howled, spitting scorn with every word, "I am *going in*! On *his* authority! To rid the house of these *vermin*!"

There was no time to waste. Jehan closed the door, bolted it, and rushed to warn Madame Suzanne.

"Pardon, I must get through. Leyris has been summoned." Jehan had no difficulty parting the crowd as soon as they heard that name. Some of the Catholics immediately headed to the boutique—to retrieve their cloaks and duck out, he was sure. "Leyris is on his way," he shouted while the music and dancing continued.

Madame Suzanne slid off the silk damask covers of the canopy bed, then ran to the stairs, telling the people not to worry, that she would find Monsieur Narbonne.

Jehan moved back to the hallway to keep an eye on the fleeing guests who had unbolted the door and left it standing ajar. Gellion had stayed in the street, glowering, but Leyris had arrived in full official regalia. Jehan moved against the wall, not daring to show any resistance, as the councilor marched in and toward the salon.

Leyris stopped in the salon doorway, motionless, staring for several minutes at the Roma women still dancing in the far corner. A blank look came across his face and his body went slack. He looked as if he was entranced; under some magical spell of his own creation.

Narbonne flew down the stairs and grabbed Leyris' left arm. "You have no official order to enter my house," Narbonne shouted.

"I shall go where I choose," Leyris said in a snide tone, struggling to turn and watch the dancers.

Narbonne slapped Leyris across his cheek. He looked stunned; his eyes wide, he tilted backward as if he would fall. He had little time to react before Narbonne took him by the collar and shoved him out onto the street.

Every vein in Narbonne's face and neck bulged as he stepped outside. "You have trespassed where you *should not* have dared. I swear by almighty God, the Roma people will *not* be leaving my home! I will be providing them shelter for the winter despite any ludicrous edict against it." He wagged a finger toward Gellion and Leyris. "And none of you have a say in the matter."

Jehan hoped the law would, indeed, be on Narbonne's side. He was said to have friends in high places, and trespass was a serious offense, after all, perhaps more so than harboring Roma.

He quickly followed Narbonne into the street, standing close to the simmering turmoil.

Several of the Catholics ran to Curé Gellion; some chirping that they had been acting as spies, some asking if they would need to atone for their sins. But Gellion was backing away, his face gone ashen, only able to make shrill little utterances about getting the soldiers until he fled around the corner, slipping and sliding on the ice.

Leyris seemed to have lost all of his senses from the blow. Nearly catatonic, he froze in place outside the house and babbled, "'Tis a rendezvous of all the villains of the village. The women dance, but they do something else. They have the most beautiful eyes in the world. Take care, good people, they will capture the heart."

Jehan was in agreement about their eyes. They had drawn him in as well, but he could not say they captured his heart, for he was still a free man, and they were certainly not villains.

Leyris spread his arms and looked to the sky as if he were calling on the heavens. "They move the tender passions," he muttered. His cheek had just begun to swell, but his entire face flushed. "Their dances warm the soul . . . and the body."

At that, Narbonne's eyes blazed, his face so red Jehan feared for his health. He grabbed Leyris' hat and threw it to the ground, then pulled off his wig, tossing it aside. "I will be back with my sword," said Narbonne. "And that fine shaft of metal will help you meet your maker, Leyris, if you do not leave town by the time I am back."

The guests continued to flow into the street, turning into a hungry, mocking crowd, while Jehan held his place in front of the house.

Prieur Chabert came to Leyris' aid, picking up his hat and wig, then placing them in his hands. "I think you best leave now," he advised.

Jehan scanned the crowd for André wondering what his involvement in this might be. As a council member for the city, he could be arrested if he showed support for Narbonne against Leyris. What would happen to André's family if something happened to him? Would they suffer as his mother had after his own father had been jailed?

A bit of jostling was happening in the crowd, and Jehan could see it was between those of opposing faiths. He overheard talk of plans to ransack the church and prieuré the next day, so he walked over to the group.

"I do not believe that is a good idea," he interrupted, addressing the most outspoken man whom he knew to be a stalwart Protestant. "'Tis not the Christian way. Remember, my friends, we must turn the other cheek."

The man let out a hearty laugh and looked at Jehan with a sardonic grin. "Seems Leyris forgot to turn his other cheek."

Out of the corner of his eye, Jehan saw André and a few of his friends leaving from the boutique door just around the corner of the building. They managed to slip off up the street without much notice paid to them, likely moving their card game to another location.

Relieved about André, and feeling his pleas to the mob were pointless until they sobered up, Jehan walked away in the direction of the townhouse, his feet sinking into deepening snowdrifts. Suddenly the rabble turned on him with their scoffing and jeering, calling him the Prieur's Papist coward. He gritted his teeth and continued to walk until he felt a hard impact and an explosion of cold snow on his back. A round of cheers went up. He reeled around to see the scoundrels firing rounds of snowballs—too drunk to get lucky again and hit their target—and two soldiers escorting Leyris out of town, away from the brewing defiance of the populace.

Chapter Twelve
Clandestine

24 January 1696
BonDurant Townhouse, Genoüillac, France
Late Evening

As Jehan entered the rear gate of his townhouse, soft lantern light from the ground floor stable illuminated the snow-covered courtyard. Wood smoke scented the still, crisp air, making him eager for the warmth of his bed. He hesitated when he noticed an unfamiliar carriage, with a light accumulation of snow, tied along the side wall. A scramble of recently tread tracks led to the rear entry. Who would possibly be visiting Lucrèce while André was still at Monsieur Narbonne's? The windows were shuttered as usual, so he could tell nothing more from outside.

As Jehan walked, his stomach rumbled, distracting him from the mystery of the guests. Hunger pangs alerted him to the fact he had not eaten a single morsel while at the soiree.

Upon entering the stable, he found Luisant had two new companions sharing the large horse stall with her. He stroked her brilliant coat, a pleasant balm after the wildness of the evening. "So, my fille, I see you have visitors. I wonder who their masters are."

Jehan brushed the long black main out of Luisant's eyes. She looked at him, tilting her head, then nuzzled her nose against the horse next to her, as if she understood. He took an armful of hurds from a barrel and spread them around the stall, hoping to keep the horses a bit warmer on this blustery night. "*Bona nuèch*, my brilliant one," he said to Luisant, practicing the langue d'oc Biatris had been teaching him.

When he entered the townhouse through the connecting door, he found the hallway sconces blazing, a sure sign that guests had been welcomed. He started his usual leaping up the stairs two at a time. But several strange voices upstairs stopped him midway.

He waited, keeping as still as possible. The voices were muffled and much too hard to discern. He strained to hear until—silence. Then a beautiful harmony started, drifting down the stairs, at first barely a whisper, then filling the air with an aura of majestic reverence.

"The earth is the Lord's, and all it contains;
And they that dwell therein.
For he has founded it upon the seas,
And surrounded it with many beautiful rivers.
But his mountain is a holy place.
Who shall ascend to the mount of the Lord?
Who will be there?"

He recognized it from Psalms. But they were not singing in Latin, as required. By law, singing Psalms in French was forbidden. And these words were a bit different somehow than the scripture he had learned at the prieuré. If they were heard from the street, they might be arrested. *I might be arrested!*

Yet the words spoke so beautifully of creation and divinity. How could this be wrong? Like wings, the singing lifted him and drew him up the stairs.

"The one that hath clean hands, and a pure heart;
Who hath not exalted vanity, nor sworn in deceit.
One such as this shall receive God's blessing,
And God his Saviour, will provide mercy and righteousness."

He crept up to the landing, then stood outside the salon, leaning an ear within an inch of the closed door, taking in the inspiring words.

When the singing finished, only one voice spoke—of God, and of the old believers. "We must be ready to build up God's church and renounce the errors and deceit of Catholicism."

A clandestine assembly . . . in my own house?

Jehan opened the doors and rushed into the midst of the assemblers—Lucrèce, Jeanette, an older man who looked like a poor farmer, three other women whose husbands he had seen at Narbonne's, and there, next to the fireplace, was the rump of a man dressed in pasteur's attire as he squeezed into a secret compartment built into the paneled walls.

"Wha . . . what is happening here? Lucrèce?" Jehan was so taken aback he could scarcely get out the words. "Are you a secret Huguenot? And . . . and who is this man embedding himself in the walls of my house? Explain this to me." He tried to sound commanding, but it was something he was not capable of with her.

He stomped toward the compartment—the candles around the room flickering from the sudden movement—but before he could reach it, the pasteur's rear view disappeared into the recesses behind the paneled walls.

Lucrèce moved to block the opening with her ample skirts, while the others moved to the far corner, cowering a bit.

Jehan had not meant to frighten them. Yet how could they think *this* was the place they should gather? How could Lucrèce be involved and endanger the entire family?

He took a few more steps toward Lucrèce, causing her to stand tall and firmly hold her place.

Resisting the tightness that gripped around his eyes, Jehan probed for information. "Is this why you were so anxious to send me away earlier?"

"Ladies, you should go now," Lucrèce said before answering.

She was stalling, and it was only making matters worse. It rendered him as a tyrant, and the thought of that caused his empty stomach to go acrid.

The women moved carefully around Jehan and out the doorway, but the older man still stood quietly in the corner, clutching his hat.

"You as well, Moyse." said Lucrèce. "I will need you to meet the pasteur in the rear courtyard and get him safely home."

A bewildered expression came across the older man's face, until she explained further in a hushed tone. "The pasteur will move through the passages in the walls."

"Passages?" Jehan said. *What is this secret they have kept from me?*

"Yes. They are the ones your grandfather built when the troubles began with the dragonnades. They lead to the stable, and the pasteur knows to wait there and ready the horses."

The man she called Moyse scooted around them with pleading eyes, bowed, and backed out the door.

Relieved to see the others go, Jehan took a deep breath and wearily shook his head. It was all so much to fathom at this late hour. "It seems I set the fear of God into that man."

"Most likely," said Lucrèce. "Moyse BonDurant is a gentle man. One of your poor cousins who lost his wife recently. He is solid in his Reformed faith and committed to assisting the few remaining pasteurs who refuse to leave the country."

Jehan stepped back from Lucrèce and glanced around the room, wondering if there were more concealed passages. "My grandfather built that escape route? I can scarcely believe he would risk holding Reformed prayer meetings."

"But he did. Perhaps you do not realize . . . the symbol carved above the front door is not simply a staff of Asclepius. If you look closely, you'll see embedded in it is the Greek letter *tau*. As in Ezekial's vision, it is meant to bring God's protection from the wrath of our persecutors. Other Reformed know its meaning, and they know they are welcome here."

Jehan's stomach soured in a mix of disbelief and escalating anger. A throbbing in his temples warned him to steady his response. "Do you mean to say we are shouting it to the world that herein are Huguenot assemblies?"

"The soldiers, and the curé, and other Catholics all think it is just the sign of the apothecary, nothing more."

"Does André know about these assemblies?"

"He does. The medallion he gave you . . . that is our secretive symbol of the Reformed faith. All of our husbands are aware that we meet for prayer. But they are also aware that the local authorities pay little attention to what women are up to, as long as the men show up for Mass."

"I had my suspicions about André. But you, Lucrèce?"

"Yes. You see, it is we women who are the keepers of our families' true faith while the men navigate the political realms, complying with whatever the King and state require. They must maintain the outward impression of good nouveaux convertis. By spending time elsewhere, they stay innocent to what would be judged as heresy."

"And is this why the wife of a pasteur came to see André for cures last fall?" Jehan had wanted to protect Lucrèce from any betrayal André may have committed, but there could be no more secrets. "I was afraid to mention it to you for fear he had a romantic entanglement with her."

"Marthe was here?" Lucrèce asked.

"Yes, she went by the name Marthe Beauclose, but I would swear André slipped and used the name Brousson. Is she the wife of Pasteur Claude Brousson?"

"Yes. She and André knew each other when they were young, so she trusts him." Lucrèce folded her hands across her heart, and her lips trembled. "We fell on hard times while you were away, and this has been the only place for us to meet for worship."

"I am terribly sorry for that," Jehan said. After everything Lucrèce had done to protect him from Curé Gellion when he was a child, he never liked to see her unhappy, but this could bring the wrath of the dragoons on them all. "You *should* be allowed to worship as you choose," he told her.

The corners of Lucrèce's mouth lifted ever so slightly.

It was clear she was trying her best to smile at his acknowledgment—which made his next words harder to say. "Yet now that this house belongs to me, you put us all at risk. If they condemn me, they will take *everything* and you will no longer have a place to live."

Lucrèce was always a proud soul but now appeared like a scolded child, dropping her folded hands, and then her head. "I do not mean to cause you trouble."

"I must tell you, there was an attempt to stop the soiree at Monsieur Narbonne's tonight. Curé Gellion called in Leyris, but Narbonne sent them all running. No one was arrested, but the officials are on high alert now, so please use *great* discretion and care in everything you do."

"If you claim no knowledge of our prayer meeting, I believe all will be well," Lucrèce said, not looking quite convinced herself as she pressed her lips together.

"I cannot claim something that is not true. As in the Psalm you were singing, I cannot reckon with deceit, so the less I know, the better. 'Tis all the more reason for me to live at the château. I have had too much deceit in my life already. Lucrèce . . ." He paused to make sure she understood him clearly. "I hope to have no more deceit from you . . . especially you. Please, always speak the truth with me."

Tears welled in her eyes, and Jehan sensed her remorse.

It was difficult to see his dear friend so sad. He moved closer and took her hands into his, wishing he could take the sadness from her, and upon himself.

"The hymn you sang . . . it was so inspiring. The last part seemed to hold a message for me. Perhaps one day I would consider joining you for your worship. But, if I do, I could not bring myself to deny that I was part of it. I cannot lie. Instead, I would have to place myself at God's mercy."

CHAPTER THIRTEEN
THREADS OF RED

25 January 1696
Narbonne Townhouse, Genoüillac, France

Jehan and Lucrèce had talked late into the night about the balancing act of the life she and André led. It stirred a deep compassion within Jehan for their situation, and he was beginning to understand why André regularly bounced from an overconfident, domineering boor to a man who drowned his fears with liquor and gambling. Both were devices for coping in a world where he had very little control. When André had finally stumbled home, Lucrèce had buoyed him off to bed, abetting his incapacity.

By early morning, the winter storm's dark clouds passed, along with any remnants of resentment Jehan held over Lucrèce's prayer meeting. He realized he should pull down the sails on his criticisms of André, who had, after all, taken on the heavy burden of family, business, and a city council position all at the same time.

Setting out for Monsieur Narbonne's to repay Syeira, Jehan walked Luisant down a back lane—boots and hooves clattering crisply over the cobbles where snow had melted and rendered them clean. Patches of rich earth shone through low spots in the drifts, trying to reclaim their right to breathe, softening the sharp scent of the snow with the musk of new life.

As Jehan put another foot forward, his breeches snagged on a dried, brown teasel—a remnant of summer past growing along the roadside—holding him prisoner in its grip. He clenched his teeth, viciously tugging and jerking at the thing, trying to release its spiky talons, until his jaw began to ache. At that, he realized a rough approach to the problem simply would not do. Like much of what he was learning about life, a patient, thoughtful, gentilhomme's manner had a much better effect. He slowed and took care to ease the barbs from the wool fabric, one at a time. His annoyance softened and, once he was free, he was at ease again, clearly seeing the message behind the prickly thing.

Luisant gave him a gentle nudge and he resumed his walk, the brisk air and clear blue sky overhead aiding his thoughts, now more lucid than ever about exploring the Reformed faith. Lucrèce had piqued his interest by stories of the new prophets up in the 'Desert' and their visions. And now his imaginings concocted designs to attend their assemblies—high in the mountains—while on the trip she was planning for him come spring. He weighed it out in his mind. Should he seek out this Pasteur Brousson to hear the amazing sermons that brought so many to follow him? Or should he keep his pledge—the one he made to that annoying Monsieur Fallere from the Gentil-shommes' lounge—that he would never attend one of the Reformed assemblies?

He arrived at Narbonne's, hoping to meet briefly with Syeira then depart for the château. He rapped the knocker and waited. Shortly, someone opened the door barely a crack; without the same grand welcome as the evening before.

Through the crack, he could see the valet with Monsieur Narbonne leaning around his shoulder. Narbonne dismissed the valet, then opened the door only a bit wider.

"BonDurant . . ." He sounded distressed. "Did you hear?"

"Here what? I saw the scene with Leyris."

"A group vandalized the church *and* the prieuré last night after you left. I am hoping I am not blamed for their actions. They became a riotous mob that could not be stopped. I went to rouse the few soldiers who weren't in a drunken stupor, but it was too late."

"Good Lord in heaven!" Jehan crossed himself. "I think I know exactly which drunken rascals did this. I heard them talk, but did not think they would go through with it. They mocked and taunted me, trying to start a fight. I knew it best to stay clear."

"Yes, best to not get in the middle of this quagmire. Pardon my lack of cordiality and manners this morning." Monsieur Narbonne rubbed his forehead and opened the door a bit more. "I've been overly vigilant after last evening's calamities. I suppose the soiree was a mistake . . . that it wasn't worth the disruption it caused."

Jehan talked at some length to reassure Monsieur Narbonne that the townspeople truly appreciated his generosity and hospitality, and that his stance on offering shelter to the Roma was commendable. After some time, Jehan explained he was there for Syeira; how he still owed her money for his fortune reading, and how he needed to be off soon.

"She's helping cook with preparations," said Narbonne. "But I will send her out straight away."

He closed the door and left Jehan outside, holding on to a restless Luisant; her tail switching and head nodding.

"Easy, my fille. We will be on the road soon."

Within a few minutes, Syeira appeared at the door, a dusting of flour across her cheek and down the apron covering her brightly hued clothing.

"Good morning, Sieur BonDurant. I pray you slept better than those of us here."

"Well, I also had a few unexpected events come up last evening, but today is a new day. And I have your payment."

He reached into the purse tied under his overcoat and held out several coins.

Syeira's dark eyes widened as she stepped out onto the stoop. She cupped her hands, and he dropped them in, clinking and jingling on their descent.

"I thank you, Sieur."

A smile flashed on her face—the first smile Jehan had seen from the tiny young woman. She had worn such a solemn look the night before, even while dancing. But then a moment later, it was gone.

Her eyes darted around as if she were thinking. "This is much more than anyone has ever paid for a reading. 'Twill go far to purchase food and supplies when we travel this spring."

"You are very deserving of this money. Although you did not give me every answer I sought, I learned a great lesson from you. As you said, the present is what will create my future. I realize now, I must *choose* to create a better future and not let my past, or poor choices in the present, decide it for me."

"Yes, your future is in your hands," Syeira said, a tiny smile playing again on her lips as she jangled the coins. Suddenly, she frowned, crossing her arms over her chest. "Last evening you asked why I was not wearing a *dikhlo*. And now you give me so much money. I hope you do not have notions."

"Notions?"

"Notions that you can buy . . . umm . . . certain favors." Her face became expressionless again.

Favors? "Oh, you mean . . ." He stopped himself from saying it out loud.

If she were truly angry over these notions and favors, she concealed it well. He had not yet learned to make head nor tail of how the feminine mind worked, and there he was again, blundering his way into giving the wrong idea about his motives. Perhaps, one day, he would make sense of it.

"Pardon, Syeira. No, I do not have notions. Not at all."

Jehan watched a flush grow across her cheeks. Clearly, he had embarrassed her. She tilted her head down and looked at him through long, dark lashes like a scolded puppy.

"I did not mean to mislead you." He tried to assure her, but he did not want to offend either. "You are very beautiful, but I was only curious since the subject of marriage has weighed on my mind. You see, my family is trying to match me with a distant cousin, Louise de Montcalm, and marriage is something for which I am certainly not ready. I need to find my way in this perplexing world before I can do that."

She took a deep breath and sighed. "'Tis much like our family. As you are noblesse and your family wants you to marry into your kind, my people are *lăutari* musicians and we marry only other lăutari. So I must wait to meet a good one. I was afraid you had interest, Sieur, and that would only make trouble. Yet, surely we can be friends."

"Indeed, we can. And please call me Jehan." He took a satchel from the saddlebag on Luisant and held it out to her. "Perhaps this will make your life easier. I have gathered some sausages and smoked fish from our pantry. These should keep until time for you to be on the road again. And if your people would like work, I will have tilling and sowing come early spring. At Cougoussac, near Chamborigaud."

"Thank you, Si . . . Jehan, for sharing the wealth you are blessed with. A truly noble man is one who uses his money to show such compassion."

Jehan drew a deep breath, relieved that she now understood his intentions. He had stumbled in the first months away from the prieuré. Without its rigid structure, he had readily fallen into sin. But it was becoming easier to walk a straighter course as he grew accustomed to the outside world. He had learned it was possible be near a beautiful woman without falling into lust, and now he could take joy in the benevolence he offered to his neighbors, avoiding the sin of greed altogether.

"If there is ever any way we Roma can help you . . . if ever you are in the high mountains, look for our marks. Red threads. We tie them to trees or wrap them onto small bundles of twigs along the road. It is how we find our way back to our camps or the caves."

"Perhaps I will. I have decided to seek out one of Pasteur Claude Brousson's assemblies. In the spring when the weather breaks. So I may indeed see you up there one day."

PART TWO
The Remembering

Lillium convallium: *muguet*, Lily of the Valley

The flowers of the Valley Lily distilled with wine and drunk in the quantity of a spoonful comforts the heart. The water aforesaid doth strengthen the memory that is weakened and diminished.

CHAPTER 14
LIFE BEGINS AGAIN

8 May 1696
Château de Cougoussac, France

Jehan trotted down the back steps, saddlebag in hand, and into the château's kitchen for his weekly meeting with Benat. The breaking dawn cast a whimsical pink hue around the walls, adding to the promise of the spring day. Decisions were made, reluctance pushed aside, and today, life would re-emerge in time with the burgeoning spring flowers.

"You're quite early, Senhér Jehan," Biatris said as she set out a plate of aniseed biscuits. Her jovial face was always a welcome sight. "I'll prepare a pot of tea. Benat should be along soon."

The rear door creaked open and the rising sun flooded the room. Benat entered with a bounce to his step and an affable ease to his face.

"Already here, Biatris, and ready to start the day."

Benat's mood seemed to echo Jehan's; happy for spring and for life to begin again with purpose, hard work, and a little well-earned pleasure. Jehan enjoyed the communal convivality, but was ready for new adventures on his own.

He waited for Benat to settle in before sharing his news. "Lucrèce has sent a note with a reply from the University. They have denied my entrance to medical school."

Benat's mouth twisted with a look of bewilderment.

Jehan hastened to explain. "Apparently, with our family's long history of ties to the Reformed faith, and my father's act of resistance, they are unsure if the King would approve."

"Can you not petition Prieur Chabert or Curé Gellion to write a letter to the King?" Benat asked.

"I have already approached Prieur Chabert, and he has agreed, but it will take months, perhaps years, before an approval can be in my hands. Then many more months will transpire as the University considers my application again. I have decided, life must move on. I know enough to practice as an apothecary, so for now, that is where I shall concentrate my efforts."

Biatris set a cup of tea out for each of them, but Jehan was not sure he needed to be any more alert than he already was. Nevertheless, he sipped, taking pleasure in her hard work and devotion.

"The Montcalms have also replied," he said, embracing the warm teacup between his palms. "And they will gladly accept a package of remedies. So, I shall set out today to pick up the Castelbouc honey before heading to Château de Montcalm at Saint Véran. The mistral winds are quiet so far this spring, so it will be a good time to travel."

Benat tapped his chin. "Sieur, I thought you had no interest in a match with Louise de Montcalm. Is it not the real reason Lucrèce and André are sending you?"

"I have indeed been reluctant. We actually received their letter over the winter, so I was able to use the weather as a reason to postpone. But now I have resigned myself to stay open." Jehan buttressed his decision with a long breath. "The dowery would be significant and help rebuild the estate. So perhaps a match to Mademoiselle de Montcalm would be wise. Though, I am not entirely ready to exclude other possibilities. I shall simply pay attention to God's messages for me and seek guidance. Now then, Benat, would you be able to help me set a course?"

"Well, I've never been to Castelbouc. I suppose you'd take the road to Pont de Montvert, then the river road. Biatris knows better than I."

"There is a route, more direct," said Biatris. "And safer. Drailles along the mountain crest. There are signposts . . . *Rota de Cresta* . . . perdon, Sénher, Route de Crêtes. Someday, I'll tell you legends of the magic heroines of the mountains. Women with special powers, part fée, many believe. 'Tis something in the waters that makes them so."

Jehan chuckled. "I would rather take my chances with the féerie folk than with the King's dragoons."

He listened intently as she continued, making a mental note of her detailed directions. As intrigued as he was by the mention of féeries and magic, her instructions on how to reach his destination had to take precedence.

"Sieur, are you quite sure you will not take your sword?" Benat's forehead gathered and his eyes held all the pain of a worried father. "There can be dangers out on the road."

"I have other protection." Jehan was confident that his grandfather's dagger would be enough. His sword was such an annoyance, and there would be no one in the mountains he needed to impress.

"Jehan, please. Though you're taking a route where the soldiers are no threat, you never know about wolves . . . or even rebels. Word is, there are Reformed rebels planning to come after the properties of Catholics, like they did the night of Monsieur Narbonne's soiree."

Jehan took a simple black ribbon from his pocket and pulled his hair into a queue before he responded.

"They are more likely to come after me if I appear an arrogant Catholic noble ready to wield a sword." He reached into his saddle-bag. "This is it, Benat. This is what I shall take."

Jehan held out the dagger with its well-worn leather scabbard, banded at both ends by bronze. The bronze hilt had a bulbous center inlaid with strips of bone. "I found this marvelous dagger in grandfather's desk."

Benat lifted it gently from Jehan's hand and pulled it from the sheath, revealing a delicately engraved steel blade. "Ahh. I wondered where this had gotten to. I had meant to tell you of it when I first showed you the library. I was certain it was there somewhere."

"Do you know where it comes from? It looks nothing like the daggers I saw at market."

"'Tis said to have belonged to the great-grandfather who brought the BonDurant bloodline to the Cévennes. The story told says he came from Aragon."

"How would you know he was from Aragon?"

"'Tis only a story. Nonetheless, you can see the carvings. Your grandfather studied these for many years to determine the dagger's origin. This ornamentation is of Mudejar origin . . . Moorish . . . but, at the same time, you see praise for Jaime I, King of Aragon, and also the Hebrew inscription, "*Yeshuat Hashem Keheref Ayin*", which means "God's salvation comes in the blink of an eye".

Fascinating. Though it was yet another secret that his family had held. *Is that why it was hidden?* Perhaps his grandfather worried a Jewish connection would bring shame or punishment. It seemed an honorable heritage, yet he knew many a king and pope had attempted to destroy the Hebrew culture. Being a known Protestant of Jewish descent would likely double the risk of death or the galleys if caught by the Intendant's men.

Benat continued to assist Jehan in preparing for his journey. He offered a belt for the dagger, and reminded him that a nobleman's finery would make him an easy target for robbery or aggression, just as much as a sword.

With that in mind, Jehan readied himself in a work chemise and selected the simple gray ensemble. He located his rosary and the special medallion that had gotten him entrance to the Gentilhommes' lounge. Holding them side by side for a moment, he knew, someday, he may need to choose between them. He placed the medallion around his neck, tucking it into his chemise. Then put the rosary in his coin purse and gathered the journal from his grandfather's library, along with a writing kit he had also found there—with quill, pine soot ink stick, and inkstone. Jehan hoped his dagger would suffice to sharpen the quill, since he planned on taking note of any special healing techniques the *sage-femme* in Castelbouc was willing to share. After loading everything into his saddlebag along with a package Biatris had prepared, he said his goodbyes.

Route des Crêtes Cévennes Mountains, Gévaudan, France

The journey along the Route de Crêtes had invigorated Jehan thus far. To be alone in this ridgetop wilderness was a pleasing change to his routine. He rode upon Luisant with a warm breeze on his face, intoxicated by the nature that surrounded him. Alert to the divine blue sky and every hue of green imaginable, he let go of all worry.

He studied the swaths of juniper and pine amongst the beeches on the highest slopes and, in the valleys below, the gnarled holm oaks where truffles grew. Newly sown fields of barley and wheat spread across undulating mountain tops. The draille he rode on followed the ridge for leagues, disappearing only in the far off distance. Chestnut groves often lined the hillsides, terraced by low walls, with only a few small stone buildings here and there.

This land. Too poor to host cities, but too rich to abandon.

Off in some valley, he could hear the gentle melody of sheep bells from the spring *transhumance*—the sweet symphony of the Cévennes.

"Whoa, my fille." He brought Luisant to a stop, then jumped down onto thick meadow grasses dotted with early purple orchids. He threw off his hat and gray justaucorps, then sat in the soft grass—a delightful relief for his buttocks after time in the hard saddle—and scanned the lower foothills.

L'Espinas relay was visible in the distance. He looked further until he finally caught sight of the flock, flowing like a school of white fish up a draille from their winter homes in the distant foothills. Looking to the sky, he flung his arms wide and inhaled a long, steady breath, relishing the fresh, vernal air. *This land, with its splendid remoteness. Ever so welcoming to a soul in search of freedom.*

Jehan had encountered but few people along the route until the time when sunset painted ridgelines deep purple, and pale blue mist settled in the valleys below. As he began to turn off at the signposts for lodging at Mijavol, he stopped for a moment to watch the light of several lanterns dancing in the distance.

He continued on, descending a path down the mountainside a short distance until he came upon the tiny village. After locating the rustic hostel, he tied up Luisant and knocked at the small, battened wood door. When it opened, an older man with an amiable round face, in tidy hempen clothing and wooden sabots, greeted him. Jehan ducked as he entered to avoid the huge timber lintel.

"*Soi urós que pòditz vénguer. Vos pregui, siitz com a casa.*" The man chattered in the langue d'oc so quickly that Jehan could not keep up. "*Aquí que l'assemblada de Brousson? Del temps qu'èra per pradas, consagrava fòrça temps a pregar e a recitar. Anuèch.*"

Jehan shook his head and shrugged his shoulders, hoping the man would read his confusion. More lessons from Biatris would have helped immensely, but at least he understood the bit about an assembly with Brousson. That was of great interest, but Jehan had no idea how to ask the man where and when. Perhaps the beekeeper in Castelbouc would know more. He prayed she would speak at least a little of the King's French. It was interesting that people here seemed as free with sharing information as he was often accused of. 'Loose-lipped', as André would say.

The man pointed to himself, saying, "Chaplet. *Que soi* Chaplet."

Jehan nodded. "Jehan BonDurant." Then pointed to himself and tipped his hat.

The pantomime was helpful in getting Luisant secured in the stable. Afterward, Chaplet showed Jehan to a box-bed in the main room.

"*Bona nuèch. Mercés*, Chaplet," said Jehan in an exchange of goodnights with the man before he climbed a ladder to the loft. At least Jehan had learned enough to express his gratitude to this kind man.

After such a freeing day on the road, Jehan could not bear to close himself into the confines of the bed. He kept the bed's door ajar and listened to the night sounds drifting through shuttered, but glassless windows. Mingled in the cool night air were the calls of a nightingale and a distant owl.

He got up to open a shutter and peered out at a treasure trove of stars twinkling across the heavenly night sky. Which one of those millions of stars would be his guiding star, pointing him in the right direction on his spiritual journey? Which one would lead him to his muse? Surely there was a path that would bring him the kind of freedom he longed for, but the questions remained for now. He laid back in the bed, and just as the rustling of the chaff mattress stilled, a beautiful, otherworldly sound began, floating through the window on the breeze. It seemed a sort of celestial harmony, faint at first, then growing louder, and then softer again. The angelic sound moved through him with a pleasing vibrancy—a gentle, soothing charm that was coaxing him to sleep.

9 May 1696: Mijavol, Route des Crêtes Cévennes Mountains, Gévaudan, France

Jehan bolted up to a rooster's crow, thumping his head on the top of the box-bed. "Silly bird."

Perched in the open window, it lifted its head to sound its alert a second time. Just as he ran over to shoo it from the room, memories of a nightmarish sleep came to him. Dreams—filled with loud groans and sobbing, wailing and shouts. In the darkness of night, the torturous dragoon attacks upon the people in Alais had been reenacted in his mind. The evening had begun so peacefully, he could not imagine what prompted these night terrors.

Then he remembered the specter of his grandfather Pierre. *Why had he been in that horrible place?* Jehan sat on a stool near the window and clutched his head, trying to call the images to mind. As his grandfather had appeared, the gruesome visions of the dragoons vanquished. With his hands outstretched, he offered his magnificent dagger, but he had a warning. He spoke, yet not a word passed from his lips. 'This will bring God's salvation for yourself and for those under your protection. Though if your soul seeks to find its way to the heavens, where it will be free, you must always do the least harm. Merely raising the dagger will often suffice. Yet before you do, let love guide your choices and consider what lies outside of yourself. Try to understand others' motivations and offer them reason and compassion. You should never use it for revenge or theft, or in anger or jealousy. Only for good deeds.' Then his grandfather had faded into the night sky, joining the other souls who had found their way to freedom.

The instructions and the knowledge that the dagger could only serve a noble purpose lightened Jehan. But the horrifying memories of the dragoons still lingered. All he could do for now was to push the thoughts aside and make haste in getting back on the road to Castelbouc. There was so much country yet to travel, and he would need to find lodgings before nightfall. That would readily occupy his mind.

Gorges du Tarn Cévennes Mountains, Gévaudan, France

As Jehan began his descent from the mountain peaks into the Gorges du Tarn, he looked out across the landscape, lingering on its details. The river below took a sinuous route, hemmed in by soaring, craggy, sun-dappled walls of karst and limestone. Pockets of mist nestled in a multitude of deep ravines, with wisps taunted away by eddying currents of air. Enlivened by the sight, a tingling sensation slid down his neck and across his arms.

Fog that clung to a cliff across the gorge thinned, revealing a stream that cascaded through a great crevice. Alluring, yet fierce, as it tumbled and splashed on its way to the river, it held a powerful energy that he found keenly perceptible, its lilting resonance drawing him further into these wondrous, but wild, natural environs.

No need for finery here, and glad of it. His simple, travel-ready attire was suiting him well, as long as he could be wrapped in this resplendent, unfettered nature.

Before setting off again, he surveyed the way down to the Tarn River. At the bottom, he could make out the Pont de Quezac and just across the river, the Route Royale—the newly expanded road built for the King's troops. Jehan's destination for the evening was the Le Villaret Inn, which was positioned directly along this main route, as most inns were. But for years, the road had not been wide enough to accommodate troops. Now the inn sat squarely along the path of their occasional patrols.

By late afternoon, Jehan had arrived at the Pont de Quezac. It was the last possible crossing point over the Tarn before reaching the inn. This began the portion of the journey that would no longer guarantee reliable refuge. It seemed peaceful enough—there were no signs of foot soldiers or mounted dragoons—but he knew the sanctity of this haven would be threatened whenever soldiers were out.

Luisant drank her fill alongside the bridge while he indulged in the shade of an old plane tree. His eyelids grew heavy as he stared at sunlight scattering across translucent blue-green waters that glided peacefully over millions of large pebbles.

It must dishearten the people. In the distant past, they had been like the fish frolicking in the crystal clear river water; unaccustomed to being easily seen, practicing any faith of their choosing. But now they could end up captive, laid upon the King's table, if they did not outwardly follow the Catholic faith or practice the utmost discretion. Like the fish, hiding among the rocks was often the safest choice.

Jehan was grateful for Biatris' advice to take the Route des Crêtes, and for the joys of the peaceful journey thus far. He could not imagine the frenzy of nerves it would induce had he taken the Route Royale the entire way.

After a brief rest, he crossed the bridge and headed west along this road. It was much like the main roads around Alais; neatly placed stones on a track wide enough for large carts and coaches.

It was less than half a league before Jehan came to the Le Villaret Inn, where he would acquire his night's lodging and stabling for

Luisant. It was just across the river from Castelbouc and, from outside the three-story stone building, it sounded like quite a lively place. Most probably, it was the only spot for miles where shepherds and farmers—who spent most of their days isolated in quiet solitude— could gather with friends.

Upon entering a small makeshift foyer created by wooden screens, he could hear several conversations, but could not make out their meaning. It seemed certain he would pick up more of the langue d'oc by the time he returned home, and, though a bit difficult, it would eventually be of great merit.

He stepped into the common room—the air redolent with sweet onion and savory garlic—to find several folk enjoying their evening meal. They all wore simple work attire, most of the men in open-collared white chemises. If he wanted to blend in, it seemed prudent to remove his cravate—the most prominent vestige of his class—so he quickly did so and stuffed it into his saddlebag. When the people glanced in his direction and grew quiet, he returned their inquisitorial looks with a smile.

"*Bonser*." Jehan said, greeting the innkeeper as he came by with a tray full of empty clay mugs and pewter tankards.

A short, well-muscled man, his arms looked equipped to carry a mule across the room.

"Have you lodging. Uhm . . . *lotjament*? And can you provide stables, *éstables*?"

"*Oc*. And I speak the King's French, if easier. 'Tis important for business, you know." The innkeeper winked and gave a quick nod.

"Ahh, grand," Jehan said, relieved. Perhaps conversation would be easier than he had feared, but an attempt at speaking the langue d'oc might help him fit in.

"How many nights?"

"Two, *doas nuèchs*, please."

"Where are you traveling? You have business here?" The innkeeper pursed his lips and regarded Jehan from head to toe. "You look trustworthy, but we never know these days."

"I am to purchase honey in Castelbouc for our apothecary in Genoüillac."

"Aha, you want to see Menina Elise, our *sage-femme* healer." The innkeeper waved a hand, signaling to his patrons, and they went back to their chatting.

"Yes. That would be the woman," Jehan said. "Do you know a boatman who I can hire to take me across the river?"

"Simos is our *batelier*. He stands by, ready to ferry at the landing. Go there very early and you should not need to wait long." The innkeeper set the tray aside on a back counter, then picked up a quill and opened a record book. "We'll get you registered, then settle your horse. Which name would you like to use? With our road now part of the Route Royale, the King's tax collector requires us to keep a record. An X will do."

It seemed the innkeeper could be trusted to use discretion, if one needed. For now, Jehan saw no problem with establishing a presence around the Gorges du Tarn. He knew he needed a legitimate business reason to be in the area, in case he were stopped while traversing to an assembly.

He gave a crisp nod, then took a deep breath, dipped the quill in the inkpot, and signed using his own name.

The establishment felt comfortable so far. It was simple but welcoming—except for the two younger men in the rear, giving him sideways, cynical glances.

CHAPTER 15
SAGE-FEMME

10 May 1696
Le Villaret Inn to Castelbouc, Gorges du Tarn Gévaudan,
France

Jehan began his day at dawn, setting out early, just as the innkeeper had suggested. He left through the rear door to check on his horse and was greeted in the stable's courtyard by morning mists and a bank of bright fog. Once he saw Luisant was well supplied with water and feed, he set out to meet the boatman.

As he walked the path to the river's edge, gossamer threads of sunlight broke through the mists, illuminating the shoreline. Quite different from the riverside location where he had rested the day before, here the bank was wide and of fine sand that sparkled as rays of sunlight passed over. Mercurial emerald water lapped gently in the light breeze. *Such an ethereal otherworld.* It lulled and embraced him with its allure.

Although the mists still hung low across the river, they parted at spots higher up, revealing the steep cliffside and a few rooftops belonging to dwellings that clung precariously on the heights. The fog swirled up the cliff above them and opened to expose a gargantuan structure perched like a golden eagle watching the river scene. It was the ruins of an ancient château, and it seemed to survive as a reminder of the hamlet's need to fortify.

With no sign of the boatman, Jehan looked around for a bell. On a nearby tree he noticed a large mouflon ram's horn tied up with plaited reeds and a wooden sign nailed to the tree reading, '*batèu tres deniers*'. He walked over and lifted the hefty, curling object, fitted with a mouthpiece, and blew. A rude sputtering was all it emitted at first. He tried again, eliciting a lofty bellow that echoed across the walls of the gorge.

"*Ohé. Es aquí*," came a distant voice through the fog.

Minutes seemed to stretch on with no sign of anyone, nor any sound. Perhaps the call had not been from the boatman.

An instant later, the front of a flat-bottom boat glided like magic out of the mists, skimming silently as the water birds drifting by.

Jehan's awe set his skin to tingling.

When the rest of the boat came into view, he could see the boatman—a thin man in a large-brimmed hat—standing as he dipped a long pole into the river's depths.

"Are you Simos?" asked Jehan.

"Oc, Simos."

The boat slid onto the sand and came to a stop.

"Use care getting in. And sit *vos prègui*."

Jehan situated himself with agility and settled in. Simos pushed the boat off, and they glided with only the gentle lapping of water to fill the silence between them. But Jehan was craving to learn more about this enchanted place.

"Simos, what makes the sand here so magical? It sparkles like gold. Is it gold?"

"'Tis mica in the sand, no gold," Simos said, with a croaky laugh that rivaled the bullfrogs bellowing among the reeds.

Jehan gazed down and a strand of hair fell across his face. *I must seem quite naïve.* He drew a long breath and flung it away as Simos continued.

"Only treasures in these mountains are iron, sometimes a little silver, but most precious are *las baumas*, the caves, for protection. Are you in search of treasures or protection?"

"Neither . . . just a little honey from Menina Elise. Though after witnessing the violent dragoons in Alais last fall, I suppose we should *all* consider protection."

"This is the best place, then . . . even with the new roads. And above, on the *causses*. Better than near the cities. The Cévennes have always offered haven. There've been Celtae druids and their menhirs, saints and their miracles, Knights of Saint Jean and their hospital, and thousands of Cathars during the inquisition. With all the caves, you can find safety, but you must always be cautious."

Jehan's eyes glazed over as the boatman talked. He had wanted to know more, but his mind was a little overwhelmed and bemused by all these bits and pieces of new knowledge.

Simos skillfully brought his boat to the opposite shore; to a small wooden platform anchored at a stairway carved into the cliffside.

"When you are ready, there is another horn . . . just above, near the stair landing," he said.

"*Mercés*, Simos. Here you are then." Jehan handed him the three denier fare, stepped out, and looked up at the wet, moss-covered steps, climbing high into the mist. The ascent would need to be taken with great care. His mind raced with the possibilities of what he might find when he finally reached his destination.

He turned to ask Simos if he knew about Pasteur Brousson's assembly, but he was gone—disappeared into the veil as quietly as he came.

Where could one possibly grow a garden in this troglodyte hamlet? Jehan could not imagine it.

He walked past dwellings that clung to craggy terraces just below Causse Méjean; carved into the steep limestone cliffs of the gorge, tight and jumbled, up a narrow, circuitous path. Trees and shrubs had taken hold in every available nook, leaving no space that Jehan could see for growing the herbs Menina Elise was known for.

He came to the last house just before the cobbled path faded into a narrow wooded valley. A small sign hung outside, '*Sage-Femme de*

Castelbouc'. High on the door was a large, flat, pale yellow flower with a rosette of thistle-like leaves. *A cardabelle?* He had heard stories of these miraculous flowers—with their special property of closing up shortly before bad weather—but he had never seen one before.

The moment he lifted the bee-shaped iron door knocker, he heard a growl. He spun around behind him, but there was nothing there. The growl came again. And this time it was clear—it came from inside the house.

"Remus, you hush now." A woman's muffled voice came from behind the door, accompanied by the sound of scraping metal as an eyehole opened. A large hazel eye surrounded by withered skin peered out at him. "Are you BonDurant?"

"Indeed, I am. Have come from Genoüillac for my cousin, Master Apothecary, André BonDurant."

"Back now, Remus." The door creaked open a few inches, and an elderly woman peeked out, coif neatly containing her ash-white hair. "Jehan BonDurant?"

"Yes, Madame. Would you be Menina Elise?"

"Oc, yes, yes. Welcome, young Sieur BonDurant. I've been expecting you. André's wife described you well in her letter. You *do* look very much like André, yet a bit taller." She reached a hand out the door. In it was a scrap of coarse linen, dyed a golden yellow. "Here . . . take this. You must hold this scarf to signal my dog, Remus, that you mean no harm."

Once Jehan had the scarf in his grip, she opened the door, and a large gray wolf-dog looked out from around her skirts, still softly growling.

"Offer him the back of your hand with the scarf."

The dog wasn't the only one whose hackles were up. Jehan felt the hair lift on the back of his neck as he held out the scarf. Remus sniffed, rubbing his cold nose on Jehan's hand.

"He's picking up our scents. Yours and mine and Amelia's from the scarf," said Menina Elise.

Amelia? He was just about to ask who Amelia was when Remus began vigorously licking his hand with a large, coarse tongue.

"There now. You and Remus are friends," she said. "Come in and we can go to the garden to gather your order."

They passed through the common room of the tidy, modest house, where a multitude of herbs and flowers hung. Tied in bundles with hemp twine, they dangled from wooden pegs set into the stone walls, and on ropes strung between rafters.

Menina looked over her shoulder as they walked through the room. "I used to look forward to André's visits when he was young. He was athirst to learn about our more unusual plants, but he seemed to lose interest in recent years."

"If I may, I would like to learn. My studies have been limited to the more common varieties that André can easily access at the markets."

When they turned a corner to a back room, a splash of green foliage appeared through a window in the rear door, so intense it seemed to brim over into the house. *The legendary garden?* Menina scuttled along, her plump figure in knee-length skirts and sagging stockings disappearing out the door. Remus nudged Jehan's hand, herding him along, so he followed her out to find a most exquisite medicinal garden.

Aah. Perhaps the only spot in the village for such a garden. He counted eleven raised beds, with a variety of flowers and herbs, formed using *plessis* fences of interwoven branches. Set on a gentle slope, the garden was enclosed on all sides by cliff walls and houses. *How splendid.* Protected from poachers and mischievous plant predators, it was Menina Elise's own little Eden.

"I have the list André sent with his wife's letter," Menina said. "I'll harvest while you tell me all the news of late." She smiled as she picked up a basket, going first to a bed abounding with a tall plant that had nettle-like leaves and whorls of bright yellow flowers. "'Tis seldom we cross the river for dinner at the inn to get what little news comes to these outlands. Though, we have heard rumors . . . that there was another Reformed pasteur put to the wheel."

The wheel. It brought a lump to Jehan's throat.

"I am afraid that is true. 'Twas two months past," he said as he pulled his journal from his saddlebag. "Apparently, there are many

Reformed pasteurs still active despite the restrictions. I am told Pasteur Brousson is one who shares a good message, and I am hoping I can attend one of his assemblies while here. Do you hear word of them?"

Menina's eye widened. "Oh no! I wouldn't even think to *discuss*, let alone *attend*, those assemblies."

She brusquely turned and scurried to the next garden bed. Jehan followed along. She seemed quite rattled; her smile had faded.

"No, no," she said, emphasizing the dismissal with a shake of her head. "I was baptized Catholic, and I will *stay* that way. I wouldn't want my practice prohibited. The people here need me. Who would deliver their babes?" She wiped her forehead with the back of her hand and grimaced. "There are many who would brand all *sage-femme* healers as witches."

"I thought the era of witch hunts passed many years ago," said Jehan.

Her eyes went distant as she spoke. "They were worse when I was young, but the Abbé du Chaila would gladly use it as reason to torture or burn an old lady like me."

"The Abbé du Chaila?"

"The Inspector of Missions for the Gévaudan parishes, stationed in Pont de Montvert." She turned and continued cutting, no longer looking at Jehan. "He is the Intendant Basville's sadistic liege . . . a very evil man from a noblesse family with a reputation of stealing, and assault, and defying the law, and . . ." She puckered her lips and slashed a stem with extra effort before she continued. ". . . he has an aversion to women, I am told."

She abruptly turned to Jehan, standing rigid, her jovial face turned ashen. "Sieur, you must take care with whom you discuss the assemblies. I know about your family . . . that they abjured but still practice the old faith. Yet they have always been so careful . . . except your father. He was the rebel among them."

Jehan nodded, knowing the truth in that. He had not meant to disconcert her. It was wrong of him to assume all folk here would be of the Reformed faith. He thought for a moment about what might amend his wrong. "I shall take care. I give you my word. And now, may I offer you a bit of good news?"

Menina's brows raised, then she went back to collecting while conversing. "Oc, I could use good news."

"I have seen pamphlets announcing that William de Orange and the Allied Nations hope to meet soon with King Louis and his ambassadors in Rijswijk . . . to discuss peace. There are plans for the negotiations to include a reinstatement of the Edict of Nantes, so there is renewed hope for an end to the persecutions."

"That would truly be a blessing." Menina sighed, crossing herself with a handful of bittercress. "It has been dreadful, at times, to live in a land so divided. I have seen the worst of times and thought they were over, but there are rumblings about that worry me."

Jehan did not want to heighten her worry by telling her of the dragonnades he had witnessed. Since the reward for Brousson had been doubled the fall past, some fool would likely be hungry for it, sooner or later, and the dragoons would be sent to find him. It all made Brousson and the assemblies even more intriguing. *The connection with the Divine achieved there must be boundless.* Why else would it threaten the King and the Roman Catholic church to the point of taking such measures?

Jehan knelt on the ground and removed his writing supplies from his saddlebag. He poured a few drops of water from his *costrel* onto the inkstone and ground in a bit of the ink stick. Dabbing his quill, he began to take careful notes in the journal as Menina Elise harvested and explained the healing properties of the three plants she had gathered.

"First, we have yellow archangel, *Lamium galeobdolon.* For spasms of muscles, to clean and stop bleeding of wounds, relief of swelling, treatment of coughs and tumor." She crushed a leaf and waved it in the air. "Whew! Smells like a weasel though. Next, bittercress, *Cardamine impatiens.* The young shoots and leaves are good for rheumatism and gout, a purgative for cleansing, a nervine for restoring vigor. And, also, nourishment if lost in the forest. Finally, I give you rhubarb, *Rheum rhabarbarum.* The special Siberian variety for the effects of indulgent consumption of meat."

After Menina Elise packed the cuttings into muslin bundles, she explained, "You will need to go to Amelia for the honey and the wild flowers. She is in the forest."

"Amelia? You mentioned her before. Who is Amelia?"

"My granddaughter. She is tending the bees now, preparing another lot of honey. And you, Sieur, will be of great assistance if you take another basket of jars for her to fill. Follow the stone path on up, then take the footpath to the right, into the forest. And be sure to keep the yellow scarf in your hand."

"Why is that? Do you plan to have your dog lead me on?" Jehan wasn't so sure Remus had taken to him enough to be alone together.

"No, but he has a brother, Romulus, who watches over Amelia."

"I see." Jehan squeezed the yellow scarf securely in his hand. *These dogs must not sense my trepidation.* "'Tis good to know they are here for your protection."

"Now hurry along. We will settle the payment when you come back. If you would, please bring back all the baskets she has filled with honey. There should be three in total. They are much too heavy for me these days, and that will allow Amelia to continue her work."

"Thank you, Madame. I gladly will."

"And remember, Sieur BonDurant, use caution with whom you discuss the assemblies. 'Tis not that I don't believe each has the right to worship as they choose. I do. However, if you must know about them, it will be safer to ask Amelia. She has many friends . . . on all sides."

CHAPTER 16
HOLY WOMAN

10 May 1696
Castelbouc Gorges du Tarn, évaudan, France

Jehan followed the stone path through the forest where dwarf holm oaks thickened, craggy as the surrounding boulders, dressed in plush layers of lichen. They brought a shifting darkness and cooling dampness to the primordial, unblemished, virgin forest. As he ventured onto the smaller dirt path to the right, chestnut trees gradually took the place of oaks, and sunlight filtered through the treetops.

He thought he heard rustling down the hill, toward the river, but was distracted by a soft melody that drifted through the trees.

"*E los romius que passaràn. Prendràn d'aiga senhada.*" There was a pause. Then a slow, gentle, "*aaaaaaa, eeeeeee, iiiiiii, òòòòòòò, ooooooo*" The intonation resonated through him like a chant from the prieuré. "*Prendràn d'ai . . .*"

"Woraeech." A horrid sound interrupted the resplendent song. The screech had come from out of the woods on the downhill side of the path. Jehan turned to see an enormous wild boar heading toward him. He dropped the basket of empty jars—glass clinking and clattering— took a few steps back, stumbled, and slammed his back hard against a tree. Instinct seemed to take hold, and he swiftly pulled his dagger from its scabbard. His chest tightened and, for a moment, his legs felt as if they would crumble under him. From his position, he would have to go for the throat, so he readied for an underhand thrust.

Suddenly, a savage half-bark, half-howl came from up the path. Jehan stayed poised with dagger in hand, daring only a quick glance from the corner of his eyes to see a burly boned white wolf-dog charging toward the boar. The dog slid to a stop a short distance from the wild creature.

Romulus?

The boar halted, but then edged toward Jehan.

He frantically waved the yellow scarf, not sure if it would work. "Romulus . . . "

The dog seemed to recognize the signal and moved between Jehan and the beast; snarling, baring long white fangs, eyes blazing with fury. The boar growled and grunted back, then tried to charge Romulus, who pounced and snapped in return.

Jehan moved behind the tree, standing ready with his dagger, while the two persisted in charging at each other.

The boar was amazingly fast and agile for such a lubberly creature. It backed up for another charge when its rear legs slipped on wet leaves and undergrowth, losing its footing, causing it to hurtle down the steep hillside. Romulus stilled and watched, breathing hard, but his nose wrinkled and his fangs still flared. The boar slammed into a tree near a cliff's edge, flipped, and regained its footing, then bolted deep into the forest.

Jehan's chest ached from the pounding. He and the wolf-dog looked at each other for a long stupefied moment, until the dog stepped toward Jehan and sat. It tilted its head and its eyes softened.

"Romulus?" Jehan returned the dagger to its scabbard and, clutching the yellow scarf, held out his hand.

The dog nudged and licked his hand, in the same way Menina Elise's dog, Remus, had. Jehan took a long breath, his taut shoulders melting with relief. Romulus wagged his tail and gave a single soft bark, then began tugging lightly on the scarf.

"Do you want me to follow you? Can you take me to Mademoiselle Amelia?"

Romulus released the scarf, wagged his tail, then took off down the path. Jehan hastily replaced the jars into the basket, then grabbed it, and did his best to keep up. After a bit, he had to stop to catch his breath. Resting a hand on his knee, he looked at the ground for a moment. When he looked up, he saw streams of sunlight playing through the trees and Romulus sitting amidst a village of the oddest, petite little houses, made of knotty, bumpy logs standing upright with pieces of schist for roofs. They were scattered upon terraces that held a steep hill in its place alongside the path; nestled among unfurling maidenhair fern and poet's narcissus that filled the air with a sweet perfume.

"Romulus, have you brought me to a féerie village?" Jehan laughed softly at himself, but a part of him wanted to believe it could be so.

A figure stepped into one of the dancing beams of light. It appeared to be a woman. *Or could she be fée?* Romulus went to sit by her side. *Amelia?*

She certainly did not dress like other women; her clothing was as if she stepped out of a time long past. Her white sleeveless surcote over a faded blue linen gown reminded him of the scapular he had worn at the prieuré. A silk veil, the azure color of a summer sky adorned with stars, covered her hair. And a second, whisper-thin white veil laid over her entire face and head. Barely visible under the sheer veil were penetrating eyes that lit up as he approached. She stood solemn as a statue, except for those brilliant hazel eyes. In one hand, she held a long knife, curved at its tip, and in the other, a smoldering clay pipe.

"I see Romulus took care of scaring off that mischievous boar again," said the woman.

"Mademoiselle Amelia?" Jehan brushed his hair away from his eyes.

She smiled and lifted the translucent white veil. "I know you. Do I not?"

"No . . . well . . . I do not believe we have met." *Her voice, though.* It seemed so familiar. Jehan studied her face for a moment. He did not recognize her, yet there was a sense of knowing this woman. "Perhaps we have, but pardon, Mademoiselle, I cannot seem to recall."

"You must be Jehan BonDurant, come for honey. I see Menina sent you up with more jars. I will harvest your honey so you can be on your way." She laid her knife in the basket he held, then took it from him and turned away.

Jehan was perplexed and had to ask, "Before we go to the hives, will you tell me about these little houses? Is it féeries that live here?"

Amelia turned back around with a soft giggle. "Well . . . this is where I dance with the féeries." She held her arms out—basket in one hand and pipe in the other—and spun around three times, saying, "In this very spot!" She stopped her spinning, caught her breath, and gazed at him, raising her delicate eyebrows. "I must confess, Sieur BonDurant. I mislead. These little houses *are* the beehives."

"Aaah," said Jehan.

Then at the same moment, they both broke out laughing in uncontrollable delight. Hers was a laugh like the sweet, silvery tinkling of small magic bells; a laugh like he imagined a féerie would have. The more she continued, the more he could not stop. It seemed as if a breeze stirred from the leaves, wrapping them in a divine, joyous felicity.

Amelia stepped up onto a terrace as her melodic laugh faded. She set to task, explaining the details of collecting the honey as she worked.

"The first necessity is a sheer head covering that protects your face but allows you to see. That is why I wear the second veil."

Yet that didn't explain the blue veil, and he didn't feel the time was right to ask, so he nodded to express his interest and listened quietly.

"The beehives we call '*bruscs*'. And can you guess about the clay pipe?"

"To calm your nerves?"

A playful smile came to her face. "And just as it calms a person, it calms the swarms. Watch as I blow smoke into this crevice at the bottom of the log."

She placed her hand round the bowl of the pipe and blew into the hole created by her fingers until trails of smoke left through the mouthpiece and into the log. When she removed the schist stone that made up the roof of the little bees' home, the golden treasure was revealed—a network of combs dripping with rich honey.

"See how sleepy the bees are?" She removed the schist slab from another log, then picked up the first log and placed it on top.

Jehan could see Amelia's svelte, but muscular arms through the tight-fitting sleeves of her linen gown. It was quite the heavy log for a woman to lift, yet she did it with no outward sign of effort.

Once it was in place, she said, "I tap the log below, causing the queen to leave for the lower one, and then the other bees follow." She ceased the tapping, her eyes intent on the activity in the hive. "Now . . .we wait."

They watched until most of the bees had moved along to their new home. Then, using her knife, she cut the top half of the combs and began filling the first jar. Once full, she handed it to Jehan.

"In the basket, under the jars, there are squares of waxed linen and twine," Amelia said as she removed the sheer white veil and set it aside.

After securing the full jar with a covering, he placed it into the basket, and held out his hand, ready for the next. Soon, a rhythm developed as they silently connected in the ceremony of the harvest.

Finally, the basket was packed, and she handed it to Jehan. "Would you please take these other batches to Menina as you leave?" she asked, pointing to two baskets on the ground nearby, loaded with filled jars.

Jehan picked up the other baskets, but his feet would not move. He was in no hurry to go. He had all day before another night's rest at the inn, and being with her, watching her work—was pure joy.

"Sieur, is honey the only thing you came for?" She tilted her head with a look of curiosity. "Are there any other cures you seek?"

"'Tis all." He continued to gaze at her and noticed a sort of light all around her, not from the rays of sunlight, but emanating from her.

"Are you not ready to be off, then?" She folded her arms calmly across her chest and returned his gaze with a ruminating look that probed deep, as if she wanted to read his thoughts. "Tis nearing the time I customarily spend in prayer."

She had made herself clear with her words—that he should leave —yet something in the way she looked at him said differently.

"I am happy to respect your devotion to prayer, and will be on my way if you prefer, but I do delay for good reasons. I am obligated to take your honey to Sieur de Montcalm in Saint Véran, yet I do not set out till sunrise tomorrow. So, you see, I am in no hurry to go, and I am happy to assist you and learn more, if I may."

"You want to learn more of the bees? Or perhaps of wild plants?"

"Yes, I do. Both," said Jehan.

Already he felt such ease with Amelia. It was hard to resist an urge to share his pent-up worries over the match to Louise de Mont-calm. He could hear André's voice in his head telling him to be more discreet, yet her eyes called to unburden his fears.

"My trip to Saint Véran . . . 'Tis for more than honey."

"Is that so?" Amelia asked, providing an opening for him to share more.

"My family has suggested a match to Sieur de Montcalm's daugh-ter, but I have much to discover before I choose to marry. . . about healing and cures for my apothecary training, and divinity, and so much more. So, yes, I am eager to learn all I can."

He repositioned the baskets in his hands and mumbled, "I have promised to stay open to their ideas, but I want to be free to make my own choices."

"I understand, Jehan. I wear the veil of chastity because I value my own freedom. A soul united with God answers to no one." She slowly blinked her tranquil eyes then smiled. "I am accustomed to spending my time alone, in solitude and contemplation, however, I suppose it will do no harm for you to help me work."

Jehan set the baskets down, ready to assist. "Are you . . ." he swal-lowed, "a holy woman?"

"I am." Her gaze met his, then languidly drifted to the forest floor, the stars on her blue veil moving with elegant grace as she lowered her head.

Those stars. A portent from God? Jehan's skin tingled. His heart

JULES LARIMORE

beat like the fluttering wings of a dove, eager to fly home. Was his
path to be guided by this woman? "To what order do you belong? In
all my years as a student with the Dominicans, and since, I have never
seen a habit like yours."

"I do not pledge myself to any order," Amelia said. "I live alone in
a cottage a bit down river. Some would call me a gnostic because I
seek direct experience . . . an inner knowing. My practices are most
like a Beguine, or a Free Spirit."

"A Free Spirit? But that is heresy, is it not?" Jehan had heard
stories from the frères—the horrific burning of the mystic Marguerite
Porete and the trial of Meister Eckart, both some three hundred years
past.

"I choose my own beliefs rather than accept those forced upon me.
So, yes . . . those like myself could be called *airetikos* . . . heretics.
Church elites use the label because they fear they will lose power and
wealth should too many choose their own beliefs. Yet they read the
very same scripture as I that clearly says, 'And there are diversities of
ministries, but the same Lord'.

"I have no knowledge of this passage," said Jehan. "Could it have
been intentional that the Dominicans left this out of their teachings?"

"Ahh, exactly. It seems many of the clerics often choose only
passages that satisfy their own agendas. The more ministries there are,
the fewer tithes they receive. And they are often the same clerics who
are afraid to follow the tenets of the Christ, since to be 'poor in spirit'
would mean to give up their possessions and to renounce self-will and
all preconceived views and prejudices." Amelia sighed, turning her
eyes toward the treetops.

Her boldness both surprised and fascinated him all at the same
time. He put a finger to his chin and gazed at her. "May I ask . . . what
are these beliefs of *your* own choosing, Mademoiselle Amelia?"

A broad, receptive smile spread across her face. "You see, I
believe that a single, true theology exists which was anciently given
by God to humankind, and which threads through all religions. 'Tis
those common threads that will unite us. We need only stay open to
Wisdom. And to the enchantment of our world." She paused, her
expression gentle.. "And . . . what of you, Jehan BonDurant? What do

you believe?" Her eyes held patient respect, offering space for his words.

Jehan's thoughts spun through the recesses of his mind. There was no brief answer. "I am struggling to find what I believe." He looked down and kicked at a few pebbles among the ferns as his thoughts began to formulate. "I know I value peace, and freedom to choose, and equity, and compassion, but the only doctrines I have learned are those of the Dominicans. I was taken from my parents at such a young age, I had no opportunity to learn any others."

"Your parents . . . were they of the Reformed faith?

"Yes. But the Dominicans baptized me into the Roman Catholic faith, so I am a nouveau converti by force. I want to learn all I can of the old teachings . . . and the new. Please . . . tell me more about your beliefs." He moved to sit on a nearby boulder, intently focusing on her next words.

"I am one of many who vow to no one other than myself. I follow the two children of the Sophia Wisdom . . . the Anointed One, the Christ . . . and Saint Marie de Magdala, the Apostle to the Apostles." She held her palms out and looked off into the trees as if she were studying God's creation. "I vow to live humbly, and with love, within the realms of nature." Turning her face to the sky, she placed her hands over her heart. "To heal the sick and lame. And to be a peace-maker. To stay meek and pure . . . looking within to transform my mind and heart into a holiness that can only be bestowed by Spirit." She paused and looked back to Jehan. "The Holy Spirit is within us, engraved not on stone, but upon our hearts. It has always been such, and the Christ helps us to remember it."

Jehan nodded, beginning to understand. "So, the Holy Spirit will teach us. Not the curés, not the King. And yet they continue their persecutions, saying theirs is the one true religion. I have witnessed horrific deeds by the King's men, the likes of which you cannot imagine."

Amelia's brows raised, dismay filling her eyes as Jehan continued.

"It has most certainly caused my worldview to change. I once thought courtly dress would be the balm for my childhood tragedies, but now I fear material possessions could be the apple of Sodom." He raked his fingers through his hair, his habitual reaction to frustration that he knew he must get control over. Yet the injustices gripped at his heart. "I pray the peace treaties will force the King to stop."

"Peace treaties? That is hopeful news." She tilted her head and her face shifted as a cautious smile lifted one corner of her mouth. "Shall we walk in the forest? It will calm your soul. I will show you how I find the Cévennes saxifrage, the little stone breaker, we call it. Best cure for stones of the kidney. 'Tis quite rare and can only be found nearby."

"Splendid!" Jehan was ready for the mood to lift again. "I am ever so grateful that you are willing to share your knowledge."

Walking side-by-side they went deep into conversation about the healing properties of nature's rarities found near Castelbouc. They spent the rest of the morning foraging for wild plants, roots, and rhizomes. A delicious calm stole over Jehan's mind, now sated with new knowledge on healing and divinity. He had the pure soul of the student—released from worry over practical pursuits to indulge in reflection on solemn and eternal mysteries. His heart soared as if a bird freed from its cage as they talked of philosophy and religion, nature and the stars, of the evidence of a God in the laws of creation which give harmony to the universe.

Late into the morning, they sat atop boulders in the sun near a small stream where orange speckled butterflies and iridescent blue dragonflies hovered over the water, and occasionally darted around them. Jehan sat quietly, gazing into Amelia's eyes. It was as if they could see into each other's souls. As if they truly knew each other deeply without actually knowing each other at all—at least in this lifetime.

What is within your heart? he thought he heard her ask.

He cleared his throat. "What was that you said?"

"I did not speak, but I was wondering."

He felt his face flush. "You are wondering what is in my heart?"

She smiled with a brilliance dancing in her eyes. "You know my thoughts well." She bit her plump lower lip, bringing out a blush like scarlet wine.

"Amelia, there is something so different about you . . . and a sort of light around you. I am not sure what it . . ."

A distant bell started to toll, intruding in his moment of revelation, and he could not help but frown.

"'Tis the noontide bells from the Benedictine monastery at Sainte-Enimie," Amelia said. "I see you are unhappy over it, and I think you may be, even more so, when I tell you I use the bells to signal my time to pray and meditate."

"I would enjoy more time for learning, yet I am happy for you . . . that you have your time for devotion. It does make me think, though, of sounds I heard one evening during my travels here. They were beautiful, celestial sounds . . . unearthly melodies that echoed through the mountains. I drifted to sleep listening to them, but then awoke the next morning with an eerie remembrance of the nightmare that followed. 'Twas one of loud groans and sobbing mingled with prayer and psalm-singing. It brought back frightful memories of the dragonnades I witnessed in Alais."

"Oh, Jehan, I am sorry you had to witness those atrocities." A slight, wistful smile came to her face.

She used my given name. She must feel safe with me. A closeness, a bond of sorts was already forming. He could feel it.

"Though I do believe what you heard . . . the melodies, then the sobbing . . . was a Reformed assembly. There are many near Mont Bougès in the caves, which gives them the sound of angels aloft."

"I have been hoping to attend one of Pasteur Brousson's assemblies. Do you know of them? Menina Elise tells me you have friends who might help, though she seemed rattled by the notion."

"When you return from Saint Véran and your visit with the Montcalms, I shall introduce you to those who can guide us and keep us safe." She reached out and touched his hand. "We can go together."

He looked at the mutable spangling of color radiating in her eyes —tiny splashes of green, blue, and brown—his heart full, knowing he was on a remarkable path of discovery.

Jehan set the yellow scarf and the baskets with honey and saxifrage onto Menina's kitchen table. As soon as his hand was free, Remus nudged at it. Menina began inspecting the jars of honey, holding them toward the light without saying a word.

Jehan tousled and rubbed between the dog's ears while he spoke. "I shall set out for Saint Véran tomorrow at dawn to deliver a portion of the honey and herbs to the Montcalm family. Then I shall return. Amelia is willing to make arrangements for us to join her friends at an assembly."

Menina frowned and pinched her whiskery chin. "Hmm, is that so?"

"I can pay you in full now. But would you be willing to store the portion I am to take to our apothecary until I return from Saint Véran? It would lighten my load a great deal."

"Oc. 'Twill be good to have you back . . . to help and such. I hope you will plan to stay for a while." Menina counted the jars silently, then turned back to Jehan. "Yet I do not, in the least, like the idea of you two putting yourselves at risk. Your family would not be happy with me if you were harmed while visiting."

"I am certain Romulus will watch after us," Jehan said. "We became well acquainted today, and he is a fierce protector. If necessary, I have this for protection." He slide his dagger from the scabbard on his belt and watched Menina's eyes widen.

"That dagger. It . . ." She stopped abruptly and walked to the door. Then, opening it, she said, "Do you see the cardabelle flower on my door? 'Tis closed right up."

"And what about the dagger?"

"We can talk of that later, when you return. You have other dangers in store to worry about since this flower foretells that there will be rain for your journey. 'Twill make it hard to avoid the abysses up on Causse Méjean. Some say it is the devil's land. Take care on your journey, young BonDurant."

Jehan put his dagger away and headed out the door. His throat tightened with apprehension, but there was no way to avoid the journey now.

CHAPTER 17
THE ABYSS

11 May 1696
Castelbouc to Saint Véran, Gévaudan, France

Sunrise filtered through the forest in shades of salmon and pink,
occasionally obscured by tufts of fog. Jehan led Luisant up the
lacets of the narrow circuitous stone path leading to Causse Méjean,
saving her energy for the expanse of the plateau. After Menina Elise's
warning about foul weather, he was not sure what the day held in
store. But when the colors of dawn gave way to windows of blue sky
through the trees, he sighed with relief.

"The weather should be clear, my fille," he said to Luisant, patting
her neck, though his uncertainty was not only about the weather.

Once they reached the highest point along the corniche, the forest
acquiesced to the plateau and the stone path became a dirt draille.
Jehan could see dark clouds stretching across the horizon of barren,
flat grassland. He halted, looking out over the ominous landscape. It
was a wasteland compared to the nourishing forests and waterfalls of
the Gorges du Tarn below. He choked back his reluctance and
mounted Luisant, grateful at least for the easy ride across the plain.

He had traveled for some time, but it seemed to go on and on—

nothing but an expanse of gray, boiling clouds bearing down close to the endless, rolling land of grass, scrub brush, stone, and an occasional bevy of roe deer. The route was well marked with signposts, fortunate indeed, since there had not been a single living soul along the way to ask for directions.

The journey seemed to be taking forever—although he knew it had been only a few hours—and the landscape was far from pleasant company. His gaze darted around as he grew anxious, wanting to get to Saint Véran quickly and have the trip behind him.

Finally, a new sort of terrain broke the dreadful monotony; clusters of chaotic rocks and a few curious round depressions, like empty ponds. He veered off the draille, then dismounted to take in the view from a small rise, hoping to find a shorter route. He held Luisant's bridle and began to walk, but she resisted.

"Come now, Luisant. We deserve a brief respite."

He poured some water from his costrel into his cupped hand and offered it to her, but she only took a quick lick. When he stroked her neck a bit, it seemed to calm her, yet still, he had to tug to get her to follow him.

Just before he crested the rise, the land in the distance came into sight, drawing his full attention. He took one more step and stopped. Scanning the stark landscape, intent on his task, he gave little attention to the loose rocks underfoot. Pebbles scattered down the front of the rise—clicking, clacking. Only when the sound began echoing and growing fainter, as if going down a well, did he delay no further in looking down. He gasped—a sharp, choking inhale. *An abyss!* He jerked back from the edge, dropping Luisant's bridle.

After a deep breath, Jehan cautiously lowered on one knee and peered over the edge. *Menina was right.* It was as if he peered into the depths of hell. The cavern seemed to go to the center of the earth. On a ledge lower down, he could see a few bones scattered. It quickly became clear why both people and wildlife stayed far away from this place. Something, or someone, who came here had not made it out alive.

Jehan stared into the abyss and wondered whether there was a deeper meaning behind this terrible landscape. *Yet another portent?*

Or a knight's trial? He needed to be worthy of true love, yes, but could he find happiness deep in the pit of the far off land of Saint Véran, with Louise de Montcalm, never to have his freedom again, his soul dying a slow death?

When he noticed a deepening gloom about him, he looked up to see the sky an eerie violet hue with scowling clouds. A flash and a clap, as if from a giant's hands, came from behind—he startled and turned while Luisant whinnied and stomped the ground. Only moments later, thunder rumbled and shook the earth. Large drops of rain fell from the sky, little by little—a drop on his arm, then his back, then face, then more, and faster—until he was being pummeled by huge pellets of rain. The ground beneath them could give way at any moment in this heavy rain. He jumped to his feet and pulled Luisant away from the edge, and back to the draille as quickly as he could.

They made it safely to the main draille, and he paused, trying to catch his breath. He rubbed his forehead and debated about turning back or continuing, as strands of wet hair fell about his face. He whipped his head around, annoyed by his hair. Or was it the absurdity of traipsing across this alien land to deliver honey and consider marriage to a woman he had never met? *How did I get myself into this?*

He weighed his choices as logically as he could; he had to be getting close to Meyrueis, the halfway point along the journey to Saint Véran, surely closer than back to Castelbouc. So he continued on, walking Luisant beside him. It grew so murky and dark that, at times, he could barely follow the draille. Cold rain and muck were all that seemed to exist. The world grew smaller and more closed in every step of the way.

Stay open. He tried to remind himself.

By the time he reached Meyrueis, at the confluence of three rivers, the rain had subsided, but he still could not mollify his doubts. "Shall we stop, and perhaps turn back after a rest?" he asked Luisant, wishing she could make the decision. Yet the shame he would feel if he did not follow through weighed on him. His family, or at least André, would never let go of his failure.

A clock tolled for one long moment as he came to a main intersection of roads. Set atop a round stone tower as old as the Templars and troubadours, the clock read half-past nine. He had made good time despite the storm. He came to the intersection with the Camin Ferrat, where a jumble of signposts pointed in all directions—to the market square, to the *Juderia*, to the hat boutiques, to a multitude of hostels and inns. The largest sign read, 'Way of Saint Guilhem du Désert to Gellone. Tomb of Saint Guilhem and relics of the Holy Cross'. That explained all the businesses—they were for the Catholic pilgrims passing through.

Jehan noticed a nuncheon vendor with his cart nearby and approached him. "Monsieur, can you tell me which is the road to Saint Véran?"

"Why would you want to go to that awful place? No one goes there."

"I have a delivery for Château de Montcalm."

The man's eyes narrowed. "All I know is to continue in the direction of Lanuéjols and beyond, until you get to the Dourbie River, then head downstream. But I must warn you, people say the Montcalms have a reputation for changing coats quite frequently. These days, one can never tell if they are to be trusted."

Jehan nodded in thanks for the warning. It truly was getting harder every day to tell who was Catholic and who was secretly practicing the Reformed faith.

A Jesuit prieur pushed between Jehan and the nuncheon vendor, followed by a string of students marching behind solemnly. Dismal black scapulars flapping in the breeze, rosaries bouncing from belts, and faces painted with sadness were enough to drive Jehan on—even though there were nearly three hours of travel ahead. His costrel was still half full, and he had a bit of soggy bread, so he stopped only long enough to water Luisant at a trough and clean the mud from his shoes.

The weather had held, and Jehan had traveled the remainder of the way without incident. No more mud and muck and cold, but the apprehension over the pending meeting weighed heavily.

Following the Dourbie River, he rounded a bend, and the Château de Montcalm became visible ahead. Perched like a dragon's nest on an outcropping of high cliffs, it overlooked the river and the small village of Saint Véran. Teetering boulder towers surrounded it like colossal gargoyles guarding their fortress. And amidst them were thousands of chattering and hissing griffon vultures.

As he came closer, it seemed they were all laughing at him, knowing he was a fool for making the journey to such a foreboding place. He sneered and hissed back at them. "Take that, you gruesome creatures!" Many of them took flight, yet some remained, giving him a strong sense that he was not welcome.

Château de Montcalm's valet led Jehan from the stables to the kitchen, where he left the jars of honey and the requested tinctures. They passed through the armory, and the valet ushered him to the great hall.

When they entered, Jehan's eyes were drawn to the massive timbered arches supporting unplastered stone walls. Ancient tapestries covered two opposing walls. And on the end walls, prodigious ancestral portraits brooded over a young man and woman sitting at a table of great length, their backs to the door. Both were bedecked in a way that would have once impressed Jehan: colorful silk damask attire, elegant lace trimmings, and jewels set in rings and brooches. The young man wore a towering powdered wig and black silk beauty patches over white face paint. The young lady was a rather lovely creature—under all that rosy rouge and bright vermillion lip coloring —with golden curls in a high fontange. These two certainly did not have the appearance of pious Protestants.

"Pardon, Monsieur Louis-Daniel," said the valet. "Sieur Jean Pierre BonDurant, Seigneur de Cougoussac, here to see the Sieur de Montcalm."

Jehan stepped toward the table, but neither of them turned around, too intent on their intimate game of cards.

The valet cleared his throat, apparently hoping to get their attention.

The young man glanced over his shoulder, then raised his left hand and snapped three times while holding a fan of cards in his right. "Here, boy. Tell us why you seek our father."

Biting back a haughty reply, Jehan reached into the pocket of his justaucorps and pulled out the letter of reply from Sieur de Montcalm. He stepped up to the table, putting himself in the peripheral view of the pompous young Monsieur Louis-Daniel, and held the letter squarely in front of his face.

Louis-Daniel grabbed it from Jehan, ripping its edges while hastily opening it. He pursed his lips, then tossed it to the floor. "Seems this boy is here to consider your hand in marriage, Louise," he said to the young woman by his side.

"And your father has accepted my visit," said Jehan.

"Oh," she said, sucking in her cheeks and widening her eyes.

So these are the social graces of such high-borns? That face she made was quite childish, and her brother was certainly an ill-mannered lout.

Jehan wanted to offer his version of gentility, so he stepped around next to Louise's chair and bowed slightly. "I am pleased to make your acquaintance, Mademoiselle Louise."

"So you are Sieur BonDurant of Cougo . . . what?" Louise looked him up and down and frowned, apparently disappointed by his drab ensemble and muddy, unpolished boots. "Where *is* this place where you are the seigneur?"

"Far off, in a land very different from this."

"Louise never leaves Château de Montcalm," said Louis-Daniel. "So do not have any ideas about trying to take her away."

Louise threaded her arm around Louis-Daniel's and smiled. "No, I shall never leave my little brother. He will be *our* seigneur someday soon. As soon as father passes. And I shall stay here by his side."

Two women bustled into the room carrying great platters of food, filling the air with heavy, savory aromas. Louise snapped her fingers at the women and tipped her head toward Jehan, causing them to scurry to set the table for three with silver and delicate china.

Louise turned to look at Jehan again, this time her gaze resting on his face. She reached out and took Jehan's hand with a smile that looked a bit mischievous. "Perhaps, in your offer for betrothal, you would live here with us. Oh, yes, that would be pleasing. All three of us."

Heat rose on Jehan's neck and he pulled at his cravate. He was not prepared to speak of betrothal, or living in this godforsaken place, without properly courting first. He had just barely walked into the room.

"Actually, Mademoiselle," Jehan said as he eased his hand out of hers, "my purpose today was to get acquainted before asking for a betrothal. And to bring medicinals that your father ordered."

Louis-Daniel grunted and cocked his head. "Good! Then you can be on your way."

Louise looked at her brother with a disturbingly coquettish expression. "Ohhhh, brother. Let him at least stay for our meal."

"I thank you, but I cannot stay." Jehan was quickly feeling her brother's poor manners were fortuitous. The situation had been uncomfortable from the start, and Jehan would gladly be on his way.

Louise grabbed his hand again. "Sit. Here by me."

He resisted, but she pulled harder until he plunked into the chair. He stared at the elaborate arabesque stone relief on the enormous fireplace, taking pause. She had displayed such eagerness. Could it be that he was her first suitor?

The meal should be a simple one if the Montcalms were following Catholic tradition. It was Wednesday, the day for fasting in remembrance of Christ's betrayal, so they would abstain from meat. Yet, when the lids were taken from the platters and tureens, and a roasted rabbit stared him in the face, it was clear that fasting was not what they had in mind. An opportune moment was presenting itself to learn their true religious leanings.

"I understand your family has been supporters of the Reformed faith for many generations."

"That was then. This is now. My father is the only one left who has not abjured," said Louis-Daniel. "Fool!"

His answer took Jehan by surprise. The quantity and type of food was incongruous.

Louise filled a plate to overflowing and laid it in front of him. "Eat now, Sieur BonDurant. We have roast *lapin* with cardamom, ginger, and pepper; river trout with blood sauce; a tarte of onions and goat cheese; and boiled cabbage with saffron."

"I thank you, but I prefer not to eat such a meal today." His stomach had been accustomed to simple meals for so many years; nothing more than soup or pottage and bread, and there was no use of heavy spices in Biatris' kitchen. It certainly was not the meal to have before heading out on the road again. "I am also a practicing Catholic, so it is a day of fasting for me."

Louis-Daniel curled his lip to one side, and looked askance at Jehan. "Oh, stash it. We do not want to talk about religion. Religion does not need to dictate how we live or eat." He awkwardly crossed himself, waving his hand in more of a circle than a cross. He elbowed Louise, and she followed suit with a giggle.

So Catholic in name only, glutton in practice.

Louise finished a bite and dabbed her mouth with an embroidered linen napkin. Flourishing her hand toward the floor, she asked, "Are you not a fan of our new Turkish style carpets? They are just the sort King Louis has at Versailles."

"Well . . . I . . ." *She acts as if she, herself, is a royal.*

Jehan watched the two of them devour their food, as he muttered ever so quietly, "Choked with cares and riches, and voluptuous living." How could he have ever been so desirous of the sort of riches the Montcalms had?

When Louis-Daniel pushed his empty plate away, Louise nudged at his shoulder. "Come, brother. Let us amuse Sieur BonDurant."

They walked to the far end of the hall where a grand, gilded harpsichord stood. Louis-Daniel took the bench before it, while Louise picked up a lute leaning against a chair and sat.

"Lully's *Dies Irae*," Louis-Daniel said to his sister.

He tapped the nameboard three times, and they began. They both played well, but it was a sorrowful composition, and they played in such a maudlin, exaggerated manner that Jehan could not bear to listen for long.

The two were so engrossed in their own performance, enraptured in sullen gazes, that Jehan took the chance to comply with Louis-Daniel's command to be on his way and slipped out the door, heading for the stables.

"You did not stay long," said the stable boy. " I haven't finished brushing out your horse."

Jehan smiled at the boy, who looked no more than twelve. So diligent and hard-working, so mature—not like his master. "I thank you for tending to her, but I shall need to be on my way."

"Of course, straightaways, Sieur." The lad immediately began saddling up Luisant.

Jehan leaned against the stable wall and perched the sole of his boot against it for support. He crossed his arms and waited, tapping the boot's toe against the wall.

After several minutes, the boy must have sensed Jehan's impatience and asked, "Where you heading out for, Sieur?"

"Castelbouc. Do you know the quickest route? It seemed I was given directions here that had me circle round a bit."

"Oh, yes, Sieur. I would go by way of the Ravin des Rajals," said the boy as he finished up. "Follow the signposts to Lanuéjols, then on to Meyrueis. Then . . ."

"Thank you kindly. I will know my way from there, but your knowledge has been quite helpful."

Jehan nodded and mounted Luisant.

The stable boy handed over the reins and warned, "Take care to walk your horse up the ravine. She might easily break a leg."

Jehan headed up the ravine through the dark wood that gave the Causse Noir its name—a place so dense a man could walk along the treetops without ever touching the ground. A stream ran over boulder upon boulder, creating a melodic waterfall that carried off the morning's rain. The path was laid with small stonework, so footing seemed stable, but it was so narrow that walking Luisant behind him was the only option.

He had not gone far when the trees began to rustle wildly. A ferocious wind blew up the ravine from the river below, carrying a chill and damp that could only mean trouble. His muscles tensed and he looked up, trying to see through the trees. There was not even a flicker of sunlight or blue, but a raw scent of thunder hung in the air. He waited and listened. A flash pierced the miniscule openings among the leaves, and scarcely a second later, thunder shook the earth under him. *These storms.* Luisant tried to side-step away from the sound, but he held her tight. He could hear the rain burst in torrents on the treetops, yet there would be a few more minutes before it would inundate below the canopy.

He tugged on the reins. "Come, Luisant. We should make it to the top of the causse before this worsens."

She may not have understood his words, but at least she would read the tone of his voice. If he could sound assured, she would stay calm.

As they continued the ascent up the stone path, even the sturdy canopy of trees could not stop the deluge. Water cascaded from his hat, and his clothes became drenched and heavy. The gentle stream turned swollen, gradually becoming a raging torrent.

The stone path became slippery, and the way narrowed even more, as mud slid down the ravine. Jehan's mind raced with strategies to overcome the hazards, but all he could do was to slow the pace.

A crashing noise echoed down the ravine from higher up. *Thunder?* No, something like thunder, but it was different. A sickly feeling overwhelmed his stomach. He had heard the noise before. During a Cévenole episode. A wall of raging water, overflowing the streambed and lapping across the path, surged down toward him carrying several large rocks. He moved in front of Luisant, spreading legs and arms in an attempt to shield her.

One of the large hurtling rocks hit a boulder and ricocheted out of the water directly at them. He yanked Luisant out of the way and tried to step back, but the rock hit his calf with fierce pain. He flinched and lost a foothold. His body flung violently backward and his head jerked against a boulder with an eruption of pain . . .

CHAPTER 18
HEALING HEARTH

11 May 1696
Castelbouc Gorges du Tarn, Gévaudan, France

Jehan shivered, shaking loose the deep chill in his bones, as the golden flames in Menina Elise's broad hearth began to warm him. Amelia lowered to her knees onto the tile floor beside him, then cleaned the wrenching cut on his lower calf. To the other side, Romulus and Remus laid curled together, peering up with eyes half-lidded, looking nearly as tired as he felt.

Amelia began to construct a compress by applying a poultice between squared layers of linen. Even with the fog that hung over Jehan's thoughts, he speculated about this odd technique of applying a poultice to the linen instead of directly on the skin. She eased the patch of layered cloth over the raw wound, and he flinched, setting off a raucous bout of coughing.

She held the cloth in place and looked up at him with concern in her eyes, her heart-shaped face luminous in the firelight. His cough eased as he studied her features. Her blue veil with delicate gold stars was missing from her head, but a white linen turban of sorts confined her hair. All except for a single curled strand—light chestnut with sun-kissed ends—that had slipped down the nape of her neck.

Once the cough subsided, she asked, "How did this happen?"

Jehan's throat burned, his memory muddled and clouded. "'Twas as I made my way back here . . . in the dark wood . . . of the Causse Noir." He coughed a bit again. "Menina and her cardabelle flower predicted right. It . . . it rained. A freezing rain. And, at times . . . in torrents. It caused the ravines to flood." The room appeared to sway before his eyes, so he closed them and tried to recall the rest.

"And how did you injure your leg?" Amelia asked.

"I remember a careening rock. It hit my leg and took my feet out from under me. I believe I . . . I must have hit my head. But I can't seem to remember anything. Only flashes of knowing that I must return here. Nothing other than that . . . not until I found myself staring at the *cardabelle* on your door."

"How could you possibly have made it back?" Menina asked, holding a granite mortar bowl while Amelia scooped more of the mixture with a small marble spoon.

"I . . . I do not know. Perhaps Luisant found the way. She was nudging and licking my face when I became aware that I had made it here."

Amelia looked off into the room and nodded as if she were trying to read the lines of an ancient tome in her mind's eye. "Old lore says horses . . . and all animals, for that matter . . . can follow the earth's magnetic energies and find their way. Humans, too, if we pay attention. The works of Guillaume de Nautonier and the Englishman, Gilbert, may provide evidence."

Menina cocked her head toward Jehan. "We have much to learn from my granddaughter. In her mere twenty years, she knows more than anyone in the Gévaudan. She studies the tomes and manuscripts our family has collected for many years, but as a child who grew up half-wild, she also learned the secrets the forest teaches."

Jehan caught a mischievous glimmer in Amelia's eye as a faint smile played on her lips.

He began to feel clearer, stronger, and leaned over the bowl Menina was holding and looked in. "What is in your treatment? Some secret from the forest?"

"Our favored poultice for these sorts of injuries," said Menina.

"Warm water and honey in flour of flax with *achillée*, the soldiers' grass, for infection and closing. And *ceraiste*, the mouse-ear chickweed . . . be sure it is the one with hairy leaves. That is for pain and swelling. You'll want to record this recipe in your journal, along with the use of the marble spoon. Wounds heal faster this way. Some special property of the marble, I suppose."

"I thank you, Menina Elise. These are certainly different recipes than I have learned from André thus far. He uses various balsam or comfrey tuberose recipes."

"If you are injured like this again while out on the road," Menina said, "you can ask at any inn or house for garlic and vinegar to make a poultice. And there is always wine. These will be more painful, but they'll work."

"Crushed leaves of the plantain are a good cure if you are far from anywhere," Amelia said. She looked up at Menina Elise, lowering her voice to a near whisper, "I know it's been years, but you have kept some of Papa's old clothes, have you not? Jehan will need something dry to wear."

"Oc." Menina scuttled to the cabinets on the far wall.

"Jehan, please hold this compress in place," said Amelia.

He placed his hand over it as she let go. Then she began preparing more strips of clean linen, much longer than the first. She rolled a tiny piece of parchment, with some sort of words and letters too minuscule to read, and held it in place over the compress while wrapping the strips of linen around his leg. When she finished, she whispered, "*Ha brachah dabarah*," as she held her hand gently over his leg.

Was this some sort of magic? His mind grappled with the thought. Could she be a féerie, after all?

"What is that you have placed in the dressing?" he asked. "And are those langue d'oc words?"

"The words are Hebrew, meaning I speak the blessing," Amelia answered. "Sometimes they are written as *Abrax Abraca*. I use these things all together . . . the poultice, the spoken words, and the pure parchment with a written blessing in Hebrew and *charaktêres*. They serve as an abstersion, a purificative. I focus all my thoughts on your healing and bringing God's blessings, and send those thoughts from my hand onto the wound."

"*Charaktêres*? Thoughts through your hands?" These things seemed incredulous to Jehan, but a spark ignited his mind, his imagination triggered.

"Every word we utter, every thought we have, is an act of creation," Amelia said. "These are a few of the ancient healing mysteries I can share with you . . . if you are willing to learn." Amelia kept her hand in place on the dressing and gazed up at him, her countenance serene, but her eyes smiled.

"Most certainly, I am willing." *Willing and delighted.* The last traces of his confusion and fatigue seem to be vanishing at the very idea of learning these mysteries.

"The c*haraktêres* are characters from old healing practices, meant to call on God and the angels. Our souls carry this ancient knowledge . . . we need simply to open our minds to the remembering. All of these techniques I use are written in an old recipe book that has been handed down through Menina's family. A note in the margin says '*Corpus Hermeticum Aegyptia Gnostikoi*' but it is crossed out with '*Liber Medicinalis*' written next to it. I suppose the church might consider the second source less heretical, so it was safer to cite that one. We have both in our library."

"I know nothing of these sources," said Jehan.

"There is something else important to understand . . . you also play a part . . . you must keep your faith strong and know that you will heal." Amelia then rose from the floor and took the other chair near the hearth. "Someday I shall show you the recipe book. But, for now, tell us more of your trip."

He was reluctant to shift his thoughts back onto his journey, but he could tell she was truly interested. "I had not expected it . . . the poor weather or the sparse terrain of the Causses. 'Tis not a place I would advise venturing to."

"Oh, we all know better," said Menina as she finished sorting through the cabinets and closed the doors. "One can die of thirst there even in a rainstorm since all the water goes straight into those monstrous holes and the caves below. We have all we need here, so there has never been a need." She headed to a doorway just off the common room and paused. "You can use this bedchamber to put on these dry clothes. And I'll make up the bed for you. You need to recover before heading out again."

"I thank you Menina, yet I should not . . ."

"Jehan, what was the Château de Montcalm like?" Amelia asked.

Her question kept him from raising doubts about the appropriateness of staying the night, but he responded, glad for Amelia's attentive ear. "'Tis is a foreboding place, like a dragon's nest perched on a steep slope. The place was covered with so many griffon vultures, the likes of which I have never seen."

Menina poked her head out from the small bedchamber. "Must've been something dead attracting them."

"Or someone dead," he said. "The place had a sensation of being inhabited by spectres."

Amelia bit her lower lip, the way she had done in the forest when he had heard her thoughts. "We are glad you have returned safely," she said.

"By God's good graces, Luisant and I made it away from that wretched place and back here. I am certain she is as grateful for the dry spot alongside your goat as I am for this place by your hearth."

Menina appeared again from the bedchamber, humming as she walked. "There now. The room is ready for you. Bring your clothes out to me after you've changed, and I'll hang them to dry." She seemed rather pleased to have someone to tend to.

Jehan moved carefully on his painful leg as he walked to the room. He accommodated all her instructions while thoughts swirled in his head. Should he not be making his way to the inn before evening? Where would Menina sleep? And Amelia?

He came out and handed Menina his wet clothes. "It does not seem proper for me to stay the evening, so I shall head out to the inn soon."

"Nonsense!" Menina scoffed and tossed her head with a sardonic smile. "Amelia always sleeps at her cottage, and I have another bed in the dormer room. I let anyone in need of healing stay, and no one dares to cross me on that point."

"Very well, then," said Jehan as he nodded, conceding to her plan.

They all took their places around the fire again; he and Amelia in their chairs on either side of the hearth, Menina cozied up in the high-back oak settle across from it while she separated flower cuttings into two baskets.

"Jehan." Amelia leaned in toward him. "Were you well received by the Montcalms?"

"Despite my uncivilized appearance when I arrived, they welcomed me for their mid-day meal. But after the meal and nearly an hour of little conversation, it was time to leave."

"Was it not enjoyable?" asked Menina. "I had always heard the Montcalms were well cultured."

"Certainly, they are well cultured, regardless of living on an isolated rock in the middle of such formidable land. Louise accompanied her brother on the lute while he played Lully's *Dies Irae* on harpsichord. I am not sure why they chose that piece. It was a truly sad composition."

Menina muttered a bit, then cleared her throat. "Odd as can be . . . that was the piece commissioned for Queen Marie-Thérèse's funeral, from the sixth penitential psalm. I suppose it's their way of saying their enemies made them dwell in a place of darkness and they're asking for mercy to save them from those hellish pits."

Her sarcasm made Jehan snicker.

"Seems you are feeling better, Jehan," Menina said.

"Yes, indeed."

"Jehan . . . have you decided? Will Louise de Montcalm become your betrothed?" Amelia asked, her face nearly expressionless, guarded even.

"Louise was very welcoming . . ." Jehan tried to answer as politely as he could. It seemed a life locked away in that remote fortress, with Louise's simple wit and her rapacious, controlling brother of questionable principles, did not resemble freedom in any sense of the word. "But neither Louise nor anyone in their family shares my interests. I do not think a betrothal to her is wise, so I will be returning home bearing the news my family does not wish to hear."

He thought back on Lucrèce's succinct words, 'Someday you will find your muse. One who will inspire and motivate you. Then you will finally feel freedom like you have never known.' But the tiresome discomfort he felt while visiting the Montcalm's was as concise as those words—there was no flame of the muse ignited in him by Louise, whatsoever. Without question, it was not Louise. *However, life in the forest, in prayer and meditation, studying nature's remedies and seeking enlightenment* . . . He swallowed hard and felt a heat flush his face . . . *with the sweet songs of an angel by my side* . . . *that would be freedom.*

"Amelia . . ." Jehan fixed on her eyes, the flames from the fire dancing within their mosaic of color. He knew already—even though they had spent only a few hours together. His gaze was as unwavering as his heart. *Yet, no, no. It could never be.* He combed a hand through his wet hair and stared at the fire.

When he turned and looked at Amelia again, she sighed—a delicate sigh of understanding. "I see. I see exactly . . ." She paused for a long while, and it seemed her eyes delved into his thoughts. A smile came to her face—one with an assuring quality that seemed to confirm she knew exactly how he felt, even without speaking.

She brushed her fingers lightly across his forearm as she stood. "When you can find no solution to a problem it is perhaps not a problem but a truth to be accepted, a blessing in disguise. Now then, you must be hungry," she said. "I have a soup on the fire that will finish soon. Would you like tea, for now?"

He coughed again, and before he could answer, she took the kettle from the trammel hook in the fireplace and filled it with more water. He did not say a word, his throat burning after so much talking. She moved about the room, collecting leaves from one in the plethora of dried bundles hanging from the rafters. After tossing the ingredients in the kettle, she hung it back in its place on the trammel hook.

"*Pinguicula vulgaris*, the violet grassette," she said as she sat back in the chair. "The cough should be gone by morning."

Amelia took the lid off the soup cauldron and stirred its contents.

"That smells delectable," Jehan said in a raspy tone. She turned toward him with a humble smile and slight bow of her head, touching a hand to her heart. He read her appreciation, and it warmed his heart.

"*Bajanac* soup," said Menina. "Amelia's is exceptional. She uses wild spring greens and sweet onions with the chestnuts."

Jehan smiled and crossed himself while he thought back to the times he disparaged the idea of living off chestnuts. After the egregious display of rich foods at the Montcalm's, he was grateful for the simplicity of her soup. "Thanks be to God that I am blessed with such a wonderful meal . . . and the assistance . . . and lovely company of two *very* fine healers."

CHAPTER 19
DESERT MEETING

13 May 1696

Castelbouc Gorges du Tarn, Gévaudan, France

Warm afternoon sunlight poured through the bedchamber window. Jehan squinted and pulled back the bed coverings, then rose, placing his feet gently on the rush matting, testing for lingering pain from the wound. All seemed well as he walked to the window that overlooked Menina's garden. He opened it, and took a long breath of the sweet mid-day air, perfumed by the abundance of aromatic plants just outside; rosemary, sage, violet were the scents he could pick out. His clothes lay neatly across a chair, so he dressed and walked to the common room in search of Menina.

"I heard you stirring," she said as she walked in from the garden, carrying a basket brimming with fresh cuttings, and slipped off her muddy sabots. "You are looking better after your long rest yesterday."

"And I feel much better. No cough or fever, and the pain in my leg has greatly diminished. I feel nothing unless . . ." He pushed a finger on the spot and gritted his teeth at the discomfort. ". . . unless I poke at it, and then it is only a bit tender."

Menina clucked her tongue while brushing his hand away from his leg. "Well, don't poke at it. Remember Amelia's words. Keep those in your mind, and have faith."

Using the technique Amelia had taught, he laid his hand gently over the wound and concentrated on its healing while Menina ordered her plant cuttings across a counter.

"Last night, you told me Amelia sleeps in her cottage," said Jehan. "Does she live there with her parents?"

"No. Her parents have not been on this earth for many years. My son lost his wife in childbirth and then . . . when Amelia was but a few years old . . . he was sentenced to the galleys. It was after attending worship outside a Reformed Temple that had been destroyed." Menina's voice quivered, and she inhaled deeply. "Within a short time, we received word that he was killed in an attempt to escape. Amelia has been with me ever since."

"I can understand now why you want nothing to do with the assemblies."

"Exactly. There is no reason to risk my life over it. Amelia was too young to feel the hatred I felt by her father's unjust death. But because of his suffering, she is dedicated to keeping peace with people from all sides." Droplets formed on her forehead and she wiped it with the back of her hand. "About the cottage . . . it is nothing more than a library with a bed. My family built it many years ago in the forest. To protect their collection of manuscripts and tomes from thieves . . . or from destruction at a given ruler's whim."

Menina worked quietly for a time, then turned back to Jehan. "Amelia wanted me to tell you . . . go to the inn at dinner and ask for Jean Cavalier. She will meet the two of you there."

"So, she will take me to an assembly?"

"Oc. That is her intention, although I tried to reason with her. She will have Romulus, but be sure to have that dagger with you in case there is danger."

"When I was here last, it seemed you had something to tell me about my dagger, but you never finished."

Menina nodded, her expression quite sober. "I suppose you don't know . . . I was the one who gave it to your grandfather . . . many years ago. It had been in my family for generations. Since the thirteenth century, I was told. The man who owned the old recipe book left it behind."

"I did learn from Lucrèce that my grandfather came home with it after a trip here. And my metayer, Benat, told me something of this man. That he was one of my great-grandfathers, and he may have come from Aragon."

"I'll tell you more of him, but you must know, this story has been handed down and I don't know how much is true. It's best not to share these stories, or they may cause strife for us all." Menina walked to the table and sat. "Here, settle in. You have awhile before you need to be at the inn."

Jehan joined her at the table, the anticipation of learning more exciting his heart. He wrapped his hands around the smooth edges of the chestnut-wood bench and leaned in as she began.

"During the tragic Albigensian Crusades, when the Cathars were persecuted for their simple worship of God, they had to flee the areas around Toulouse and Carcassonne. Many came here to our Cévennes, where they thought they could be at peace in this remote wilderness. Yet here we are . . ." Menina took a deep breath and shook her head. "Over four hundred years past and, once again, the King's beasts are on the prowl for innocents."

Jehan tapped his foot against the oak floor, finding himself growing impatient with Menina's roundabout story. He tried holding back, but his curiosity won and he could not help interrupting. "Was my ancestor one of the Cathars?"

"No, not this man from Aragon. Though your grandfather said you have other ancestors who were Cathar, as do Amelia and I." She paused and her wrinkled lips contorted into a frown. "Remember now, Jehan, you cannot be talking to others about this. And never put it in writing. 'Tis far too dangerous."

"I understand. The Dominicans believe Cathars were the worst of heretics."

"Now then, this man from Aragon was a physician for the Tren-cavel family, the noble rulers of Carcassonne, who supported and protected Cathars. The story told says this physician was a Sephardic Jew who came to France in the service of his King Jaime I of Aragon on a mission to escort the widow of Roger de Trencavel, Vicomte de Béziers. The widow and her children had to go into hiding after Trencavel died in the Eighth Crusade, and my family sheltered them for a time. But one day, mercenary soldiers tracked them down, and they left in such a hurry that the physician left the dagger . . . and his recipe book."

Jehan pulled the dagger from its sheath and laid it out on the table. "What made you think this man was my ancestor? And why did you decide to give it to my grandfather?"

"'Twas the owner's name. Yohanan Ben Durant."

Jehan felt the hairs on his arms raise. "That sounds so much like my name."

"Oc. Your grandfather believed it could have been the father of his oldest known ancestor. It would explain the long line of physicians and medics in the family."

Could she also know about the medallion André had given him? Jehan hooked his forefinger around the cord on his neck and pulled it out from his chemise. "Do you know about this as well? André's wife tells me it is a secret symbol of the Reformed."

He held the medallion out but she pushed his hand away.

"Keep that hidden, Jehan. But not on your person. 'Tis not for displaying in the company of any Catholic. Even myself. And certainly never show it in public. If the Intendant's dragoons find it on you, they will immediately place you under arrest."

He reached into his justaucorps and under his overcoat to stuff the medallion into his purse. "So it has no attachment to this Yohanan Ben Durant?"

"No, but I saw it on your father once when he was staying at Le Villaret Inn . . . just before he joined a group of angry young men and women in trying to block the burning of a Reformed temple. I suppose you know how that turned out."

"I only learned last fall that it cost him a month in the King's dungeon and substantial fines."

Menina rose from the table. "So, now then, please, Jehan, promise me you will protect Amelia. "

Jehan was not eager to use the dagger. His fascination with

weapons and swordplay had left him after the incident at the market in Uzès with Fallere. And his grandfather's message in the dream rang true to his heart. He ran his fingers over the blade, perceiving the engravings, trying to absorb their meaning, to hear their words.

"*Yeshuat Hashem Keheref Ayin*," he said. "God's salvation comes in the blink of an eye."

At that moment, he could not envisage drawing the dagger, or a sword, ever again—unless it was the only option to save a life. *Or protect Amelia from harm.* He tried to think of who might want to harm her, and to no surprise, an image of Fallere's face triggered in his mind, hovering around behind walls and market stalls. The man did seem rather untrustworthy, but perhaps he meant no real harm. But what of the Intendant? Might he come after her as a heretic? *He very well might.*

Jehan looked up at Menina then gave a quick bow of his head. "Upon my honor, I shall do everything in my power to protect her."

Le Villaret Inn Gorges du Tarn Gévaudan, France

Jehan made his way through the inn's crowded common room to join the young man with large, lively blue eyes, hoping this meeting would not set him up for more pressure to choose a side as had the one at Le Cristal Blanc Inn.

Jehan cleared his throat. "The innkeeper tells me you are Jean Cavalier."

He looked much younger than expected. More a boy, really, than a man—three, perhaps four years Jehan's junior. The young man did not look up until he finished pouring wine from a tankard into the last bits of soup in his bowl.

"I am," he said, narrowing his eyes. "And you're Amelia's new friend?" He tossed his long, sandy curls behind his shoulders, picked up the bowl, and gulped, then wiped the dribbles with a linen napkin.

Jehan found himself staring, not over this odd habit of drinking one's soup, or over the notion of adding wine. There was something else. Something familiar. *Aha, yes.* He was one of the young men who had watched him on his first night at the inn—just as intently.

He broke his focus on the young man when, in the far corner, a group of men with musical instruments pulled small three-legged stools around in a circle and began to tune. Merry dissonance drifted in the air for a few minutes as the instruments came to life—a bodega, an auböi, a flute, a hurdy gurdy, a violin—then fell into a slow, pulsing melody. The evening was certainly starting off far more light-hearted than the night in the gentilshomme's lounge.

"Call me Cavalier." The young man said, swaying his head to the music. He raised his voice a little as the music grew louder. "Amelia taught me the power of my words, so I go by my surname now . . . to empower me."

"That is quite the handy surname to have," Jehan projected over the music. He smiled and nodded. One as young and as handsome as Jean Cavalier could use all the help he could get if faced with bullocking scoundrels or menacing dragoons. Yet, there was something about his proud features; the long, narrow, elegant nose, and the way he held his chin high, that gave him the confident look of a young Grecian warrior.

As the ballad picked up momentum, someone in the room sang out. Others jumped from their chairs and joined in, and Cavalier began clapping.

Jehan leaned in, hoping he could be heard over the spritely tune and joviality. "When is Amelia coming?"

"She'll meet us outside at sunset," Cavalier shouted. "She prefers not to spend much time here with the usual lot. They're a bit too bois- terous for her." Cavalier moved his head closer to Jehan, keeping his voice very low, almost too low to hear. "We need to look for the notes. They will be in the table linens."

Cavalier turned and shouted, "Clean linens, please! *Serviètas, vos prègui,*" waving his hand toward the innkeeper.

The man was busy lighting tallow candles and grease lamps as the light from the windows was fading, but he stopped and came promptly with two linen napkins folded neatly into squares.

"What do you mean, the notes?" asked Jehan.

Cavalier frowned, looking from under his brows and shook his head, making it clear Jehan should not have mentioned the notes out loud.

He watched as Cavalier put one napkin on his lap, making a movement as if he were unfolding it, then briefly looked down and slid something in his pocket. "A clean napkin for you," he said, handing the other to Jehan.

Jehan looked around, checking to see if they were being watched. When he confirmed that everyone was too taken with the music to notice, he went through the same motions to uncover the note and read, 'The sad one calls for the fair at the time of light'.

"Don't leave it behind." Cavalier jumped up, grabbing Jehan's arm. "Come, we must go."

"Certainly . . ." Jehan stuffed the note in his pocket and threw down a few coins for Cavalier's meal. He waved at the innkeeper as he followed Cavalier out the door. A sense of aliveness coursed through Jehan's body—the same aliveness that had been missing from his life for years, but had become familiar again of late.

As Jehan and Cavalier stood outside the inn, they watched the last bit of sunlight slip behind the corniches of the gorge. In the distance, the light of a single lantern was making its way up from the river.

"'Tis not only your life you risk when others hear our plans," Cavalier said. "But hers as well. You know there is an eye and ear in every place."

A heat rose on Jehan's neck and across his face, the embarrassment cutting straight through his excitement. Had he not learned from his lesson with Fallere that discretion was paramount in these times?

"I should have known better than to speak out loud just then. I thought . . . well . . . I am learning quickly that not everyone here is of the Reformed faith, as I had presumed."

"Mostly they are, and those who aren't have tolerated us . . . until recently. Of larger concern are the Intendant's soldiers and spies that can now easily make there way here on the King's new road."

Jehan strained to see who approached with the lantern. Gradually, Amelia's placid face became visible, like the floating face of an angelic apparition, the light framed it in a golden aura under a hood that hid her hair. He began to make out the dark clothing she wore—nothing like her blue gown. *Intriguing.* She could have been a man in the loose breeches and cloak.

Romulus was easy to spot, his white fur luminescent in the dusk. He kept close to Amelia until they were a few paces away, then darted toward the men, tail wagging, and nudged at their legs.

"Have you word?" Amelia asked when she stepped up beside them near the portico.

"We do. They will hold it at La Baume Dolente at the twenty-second hour," said Cavalier. "That will take over two hours on horseback. Jehan . . . I'll go to the stables and bring your horse round with my cart and pony. They trust me here. I'll let them know I offered . . . since you were leaving at the same time. You and Romulus keep watch over Amelia."

Jehan waited until Cavalier headed through the gate of the stable's courtyard, then turned to Amelia. "How would he know the message meant La Baume Dolente? He is so young. He seems inclined to take charge, but does he know what he is doing?"

A smile lightened the reserve on Amelia's face. "He knows. He has been to every assembly of Pasteur Brousson's since he was a young boy. His dedication to the cause came after he attended an assembly where the dragoons committed abhorrent acts. He has learned when stealth is required and knows these lands better than most."

"Yet, all the message said was, 'The sad one calls for the fair at the time of light.' How would he know what that meant?"

"'Tis a code he has worked out with the pasteurs and others. He is a smart young man with many years of education. 'The sad one' is surely enough, La Baume Dolente, the sad cave. That could be ascertained without difficulty, so it may not have been the best choice. The 'fair' is the assembly. 'At the time of light' refers to the lamp, which is another name for the Word of God. And there are twenty-two letters in the Hebrew alphabet that are said to compose the Word of God."

"Ahh, I see. I would say the code still works well. The Intendant might guess the sad one is La Baume Dolente, yet it is likely he will search for the assembly at dawn . . . at the time of light."

Le Villaret to La Baume Dolente Cévennes Mountains, Gévaudan, France

Even by traveling via the new, well-constructed Route Royale along the Tarn, it seemed as if it had taken over an hour to reach the outskirts of Florac—half-way to their destination. Once the waxing moon rose and clearly lit the wide road, Jehan sidled his horse up to the old farm cart, where Amelia sat next to Cavalier as he drove.

Romulus jumped up from the back, perching his front paws on the side rail, his tail wagging, so Jehan reached over and gave him a quick pat on the head. "My new best friend."

A muffled giggle came from behind Amelia's hood. She turned to look at Jehan, and in the dim light, he saw she was recomposing her face.

"Amelia, how do you feel about the Calvinist Reformed faith?" Jehan asked. "Do you think it offers something for you that other practices do not?"

She reached back and rubbed Romulus behind his ears. "I know it is meant to offer communion with God, without the intercession of a Popish clergy. Yet Calvin named specific clergy as the only inter-preters of God's secret will, which seems just as restricting. But I try to stay open and not judge the spiritual practices of others. This is my first assembly, as well, and I will need to learn more before I can ascertain my feelings. 'Tis the reason I came with you."

"Menina told me of your father . . . that he worshiped the Reformed faith," said Jehan.

"And I suppose she told you of his demise because of it. It has taken me many years to be ready for this day."

"I admire your courage, Amelia," said Jehan. "I am sure it cannot be easy."

Cavalier leaned forward, eyes focused toward Jehan."I believe you both will find comfort in Brousson's words, the way I have. Certainly you will join our movement once you've witnessed the ecstatic joy to be had," he waved a hand exultantly toward the sky, "and proclaim to follow the Children of God."

Amelia looked sidelong at Cavalier. "You tell me this every time you come to Le Villaret on your evangelizing visits. Yet, you know I am not a follower. I am merely a humble knight in service to God, wielding my medicines to help those in need."

Cavalier chuckled. "A knight, eh?"

It amazed Jehan how easily she spoke her mind. He found her devotion to liberty of thought and deed most agreeable. This was the sort of freedom he sought. It held promise, but under the King's growing absolutism, it also meant incredible danger.

"Just wait until you hear Brousson speak, Amelia," said Cavalier, his tone still bright with enthusiasm. "Then tell us how you feel."

She inhaled deeply and let out an annoyed huff. "I have always questioned such adherence to being guided by another person instead of directly by the Holy Spirit. It matters not whether it be a pasteur, or a curé, or an abbess, or a prieur. I cannot commit to join your Children of God. There is only one thing I can commit to."

Cavalier cocked his head, leaning an ear closer. "Tell us, Amelia, what is that?"

"That I will spend my life studying all faiths. I have never attached myself to any one creed since doing so can lead to disbelief and prejudice of all the others. And, I may miss the good that lies within the other faiths . . . but perhaps you might bring Jehan into your fold."

The flash of white in the moonlight told Jehan that Cavalier was smiling. Perhaps he was hopeful of a new recruit—and perhaps he would soon have one. *We shall see.* Jehan had always wanted to hear Pasteur Brousson, yet now he looked forward to spending time as Amelia's devout student. He was finding it was her convictions and guidance that held his interest most—in a profound, vehement, even fierce sort of way.

Past Florac, the road they took narrowed, and Jehan reined Luisant to the rear. They traveled upland with the little cart creaking over ruts and stones, maneuvering lacets as they switched back and forth, until the road leveled out on a land of rolling fields and clusters of trees.

They turned onto a barely distinguishable farm road through a field of rustling barley. When the road ended at the edge of a forest, Cavalier said, "We dismount here." He jumped off the bench and brought the reins around while Amelia stepped down. Romulus leapt off the cart and followed as Cavalier took the bridle and led his pony between the trees.

As Jehan dismounted, he noticed the gentle movement of something around the thin trunk of an immature tree. *A ribbon*? Whatever it was, it appeared almost black in the waxing moonlight. He looked closer. *Is that red*? *Red threads*? Just as Syeira, the fortune teller, had mentioned. '. . . *look for our marks. Red threads. We tie them to trees . . .*'

"Cavalier, look here," Jehan called out as softly as he could and still be heard. "There is a twist of red thread on this sapling. Was this left behind by Roma?"

Cavalier turned and squinted. "I'm certain that it is. I see their marks often. They know all the best caves and have shared their locations with us."

Jehan's heart began to race, knowing he had to be more diligent. If the Roma could be around, what about spies? The rear was now his responsibility, so he looked back down the road, making sure no one had seen them.

Their little procession moved on into the quiet of the forest. Moss-draped pines softly filtered the moonlight and their scent mingled with the comforting incense of wood smoke from distant hearths. The pine straw over the forest floor muted sounds, giving a sense that all was well. His years of learning Aristotle's logic at the prieuré had him reasoning it was a false assurance. Yet, just for tonight, he wanted to relax into the enchantment, so he brushed the thought aside.

Amelia slowed her pace and fell back next to Jehan. Now and

then, her eyes would light up when the moon pierced the forest canopy and sprinkled across her face like tiny stars.

"The forests were God's first temples," she said as she looked up. "My heart cannot resist their sacred influences . . . the ancient trunks reaching high, their mossy boughs mingling with the heavens. And the cool . . . and the silence."

Recognition of her kindred soul warmed Jehan's heart with a sense of ease, a sense of floating. "I feel that way, as well. There is a sacredness in the forest. And there is something about the sound of the breeze . . . like an invisible breath that sways the treetops as if they bow in reverence."

Amelia touched his arm and peered up into his eyes. "The Spirit is here . . . with boundless majesty. These are God's ancient sanctuaries where humble worshipers hold communion with their maker."

"Yes, and without thick stone walls to confine us." Jehan thought of the great contrast, the chasm, between this place and the decrepit prieuré chapel of his youth.

"Nature is the place where we can continually worship in tranquility with the presence of the Holy Spirit." Amelia lowered her voice to a near whisper, "I am curious about these assemblies in the wilderness. I would like to see if the presence of so many people, under the influence of a pasteur, will amplify the presence or discourage it."

They caught up with Cavalier at a small stone stable where he had brought in the pony and its little cart. "The way ahead is a draille down along the face of the mountain, so you'll want to settle your horse here."

Jehan moved Luisant inside and, while tying her to a hitching ring, his eyes were drawn to a cache of pitchforks, pikes, and a few pistols and blunderbusses. "Cavalier, these weapons. Why are they here?"

"Brousson has made efforts to keep our movement peaceful. He says he has given up carrying a sword and is resolved entirely to cast himself on Providence. So he has instructed us to come unarmed."

A sinking sensation suddenly came over Jehan. Now, what was he to do? Should he remove the dagger concealed under his waistcoat? He did not want to imagine the regret and sorrow he would feel if he left it behind and something happened to Amelia. Nor did he want to face the wrath of Menina—or his own guilt. He took the saddlebag off Luisant and slung it over his shoulder, leaving his dagger concealed. He had seen for himself what the dragoons could do, and decided not to take any chances.

"Amelia," Cavalier said as she stepped inside the stable. "Could we have Romulus stay to watch Jehan's horse and my pony? Wolves have been rather active in this area of late."

"Certainly." She knelt down and whispered something to Romulus. The dog moved to sit just inside the door, his profile rigid in the moonlight.

They left the animals behind and, with the full benefit of the moonlight, made their way down the cliff toward the cave. Singing gradually filled the air ahead of them. Sweet harmonies like one of the psalms Lucrèce and her friends sang at their prayer meetings. When other melodious voices started up from behind, Jehan turned brusquely and tried to stifle a gasp.

"'Tis just the other followers," said Cavalier. "The singing helps them find the way."

Two bulky men stood positioned as sentinels outside the cave. "*Qual son aqueles dos?*" one asked.

Cavalier walked on past, but one of the men—eyes as sharp as the dagger at Jehan's waist—stepped across the path, blocking Jehan and Amelia.

"*Las claus d'aur e d'argent obren totes las portes*," the man said.

It seemed instinctive when Jehan put a protective arm around Amelia's shoulder and eased her behind him, letting his own solid physique send a warning. He could not understand everything the man had said, but made out enough to know he would take a bribe. Jehan lifted a hand slightly—toward the purse under his waistcoat—wondering if he should show his silver medallion, or give up a coin. He stopped; realizing he could not let them get even a glimpse of the dagger.

"I'll tell them you are with me," said Cavalier. "That you've come to join our cause."

Amelia reached out and tugged at Cavalier's sleeve, her eyes filled with agitation. He turned toward her with a side nod and spoke to the men in the langue d'oc.

"What did they say just then?" Jehan asked her.

"He told them we are healers . . . here for their safety. And that we want to experience the rapture."

After a bit more conversation between Cavalier and the men, she leaned her head toward Jehan. "The man says they can use us. That there are always a few who receive injuries on the journey here. But we need to stay at the back. The spots near the pasteur are only for their true brethren."

The entrance to the cave was a wide, yawning opening, with a trickle of water flowing out and descending gently into a small stream. They stepped over it, using caution to keep their foothold on the damp, moss-covered stone.

Inside, nearly twenty people had gathered in front of a large boulder, tucked to the left side of the large chamber, with a few more shuffling into what little space remained. Upon the boulder, rested a pewter platter with the sacramental bread, a chalice, and a squat glass bottle with wine. A man climbed atop the boulder and stood—just behind the platter. Lit by feeble torchlight, he wore the coarse, dirt-stained garb of a peasant. When he raised his arms in a welcoming gesture, it became clear it was Pasteur Brousson.

"And so the Lord spoke, 'My dove, that hide yourself in the clefts of the rock and the mountain caves. My dove, show me your face and let me hear your voice, for your voice is sweet and your face is comely. Rise up, my love . . . my fair one . . . and come away with me.' Join us, my doves."

Pasteur Brousson's ardent, inviting words pulled at Jehan, lured him, drew him further into the cave, with Amelia and Cavalier close behind. Jehan lifted his right hand, readying to make the sign of the cross—but he halted, his jaw tightening. The response was annoyingly ingrained in him. He glanced around to see if anyone had noticed, but it seemed no one had.

The three continued to work their way deeper into the cave, moving around behind the others, backing up against the cold stone wall where they could observe the entire group. From their hempen clothing, wooden sabots, and frail physiques, the lot of them appeared mostly to be poor, simple folk. Farmers, shepherds, carders. They spoke amongst themselves in the langue d'oc, although Brousson spoke to them in the King's French. The service commenced with more psalm singing, then by reading the Bible, which everyone seemed to possess in some form or the other, but mostly in tiny, pocket-sized editions that could be easily hidden.

A mysterious quiet fell over the people.

"What is happening?" Jehan whispered to Cavalier.

Nearby heads turned his way, with raised brows, frowns, glares.

Cavalier leaned close to his ear. "The sermon is about to begin. And now you've gone and set yourself up as an outsider. So, be careful."

Pasteur Brousson shut his Bible then looked out at his flock. "I pray for God's mercy, grace, forgiveness, and cleansing. Keep our minds open to the Truth, and our hearts Spirit-filled, for we know you desire us all to show love for our neighbors."

The pasteur's benevolent words struck a harmonious chord in Jehan. He folded his hands together, receptive, attuned.

Pasteur Brousson raised his arms, palms toward his flock. "Well, my brothers, is it your desire that I announce to you the Word of God, and that I administer to you the Sacrament of His Covenant?

"Oc! Amen! Oc!" The faithful expressed resounding ardor that echoed through the cave and quivered through Jehan. It was a new sensation, leaving him eager, even a bit excited, to see where this new experience would lead.

"I see you persecuted daily," Brousson began. "Yet know this . . . he who is faithful unto the end shall be saved, such as our martyrs who have been lost on the wheel, and in the dungeons, or on the galleys, and, in heaven, he shall receive a glorious crown of life."

Amelia put her hand near her mouth and spoke under her breath, "What about she who is faithful?"

Cavalier put a finger to his mouth to shush her, but Jehan could not help smiling indulgently at her. She connected with his eyes, her upturned lips returning his smile.

"We pray for our King, who is badly advised," continued Brousson, "to see the truth of the gospel. We ask for God's mercy and divine protection for the faithful in caves and in foreign nations. Bless the Grand Alliance, and the good King William de Orange of the Dutch Republic and England, who are enlightened by the truth of the Reformed faith and fight our own King's soldiers against the tyranny we live under. Keep us out of Babylon, dear Lord."

Pasteur Brousson scanned the crowd as if he were looking for reactions to his reference to the war—the war that drudged on and had all the European nations defending themselves against the absolutism and aggression of Louis XIV and his armies. With this sort of talk, the pasteur would easily gain many a sympathetic ear, since the French leaders waged war against their own people as well—be it by persecution or taxation too heavy for simple folk to endure.

"You are not saved by confessing to a curé," Pasteur Brousson told his listeners. "But by faith in the grace and cleansing blood of Christ. Transubstantiation, relics, worship of saints, the virgin Marie, and angels are all Satan's frauds for simple-minded idiots and undermine the saving power of Christ's blood, and will, in the end, bring God's wrath upon the Catholic Church. Come out of Babylon now, and return to the Eternal God!"

Idiots? The word sent an icy shiver through Jehan. He looked at Amelia for her reaction to such judgemental words and could see she was taking deep breaths, trying to remain expressionless. But he sensed her tolerance was wearing thin.

Brousson closed his eyes and leaned his head back, his face now dripping with sweat. "There is sin in the camp of Israel. I feel it here amongst us." The once gentle pasteur's eyes opened wide; piercing, possessed, surveying the people. "Those who have abjured their faith have betrayed our fellow believers. They are Judases with wicked, unfaithful souls, deserving of eternal damnation! Oh, ye miserable sinners who have abjured, return from your wandering, return to your Saviour."

Jehan wanted to melt into the stone wall of the cave. To disappear. His chest tightened. These were not the words he hoped to hear. He felt shame, not the joyous rapture that Cavalier spoke of. He knew it was meant to push him into submission, but it was only pushing him further away.

Several stoneware mugs were being passed among the people. A few people tossed back the contents, leaving trails of white liquid on their faces, then handed them back to be refilled from a cauldron set near the entrance.

"Those who have wandered like sheep away from God humble yourselves," Pasteur Brousson called out. "Examine your hearts. Repent! Reject worldliness and Catholic errors, and return to Christ and his truth."

When the mug, with its strange contents, came to Cavalier, he passed it on to Jehan.

"What . . . no. What is this?"

"'Tis only posset. I do not partake, but others say it helps them to relax into the Glory of God."

Posset. Jehan knew he wanted no part of drinking intoxicating beverages on this trip. It was a long way back in the dark, and why should they need to relax with drink to connect with God?

"Let us prepare for Communion, my Children of God." Brousson leaned over to fill the chalice from the bottle of wine. "Be it known . . . the right of participating in the Lord's Supper is only for true believers in good and regular standing. I invite those who are truly worthy to step forward to receive both bread and wine. Yet no backsliders, no nouveaux convertis, no unfaithful brethren should approach the table and partake of the emblems of Christ's body, unless you repent. Sinners repent to become worthy and join the Children of God!"

No nouveaux convertis? Jehan's shoulders sank in resignation. Clearly Brousson would never fully accept him into their group without fully repenting. But Catholicism had never been his choice so how could it be his sin?

Just then, a frail woman stepped through the crowd. "*Me repentis. Per la gràcia de Diu. Me repentis de mon pecat!*" Ragged clothes hung in folds over her thin body. She seemed to be in great distress and began weeping. Suddenly, she fainted, crumpling to the ground, hitting the side of her face hard against the wet stone floor of the cave.

Those around her stepped away, staring, but doing nothing. Brousson was immune to the disturbance and did not cease his imploring the sinful to step forward.

Jehan pushed through the crowd, his heart pounding, knowing he had to help the poor woman. He took off his hat, gently raised her head, and placed it under. "Madame, Madame, can you hear me?" She moaned and stirred, but was still weak.

Cavalier and Amelia came up beside him. She threw back the hood of her cloak and started unpacking herbs from a large pouch hanging from her belt. "This woman looks to have not eaten for many days."

Jehan watched Amelia work, seeing her hair fully exposed for the first time, glistening in the lantern light. She held a hand to the woman's head. "She is feverish. Did she drink of that posset?"

Cavalier looked puzzled. "I do not believe so. But her family has been near starvation the past few years, after they lost their chestnut grove to the extreme winters."

"Can you find cold water?" Amelia asked him.

Cavalier nodded. "There is a spring that pools deeper in the cave."

"That will do. Empty a mug of that poison, then fill it with water and bring it to me." She worked quickly, sorting the appropriate ingredients and crumbling them in her hand.

Jehan examined the woman's face and head for signs of swelling and found a knot forming near her temple. "Cavalier!" He stood and threw off his waistcoat, then pulled his chemise over his head and tossed it at him. "Soak this in the cold water. She is injured and we must get the swelling down."

The crowd was lost in some sort of delirium as Cavalier pushed his way to the rear of the cave. Moaning and weeping, they implored the grace and consolations of the Gospel.

Jehan grew anxious at the waiting, his chest now clenching like a vice. When Cavalier tried to return, two women caught up in their rapture blocked his way.

He called out to Jehan, "Can you reach through?"

Jehan took the mug and the chemise, icy wet and dripping. He quickly handed Amelia the mug, then rolled the chemise and rang it out. Kneeling next to her, he laid the bundled compress over the bump on the woman's head.

"Here, please mix this . . . vervain and arnica . . .into the water," Amelia instructed. Then placing her hand over the compress, she closed her eyes and whispered, "*In nomine Patris et Fili et Spiritus Sancti*. Amen."

Cavalier came down beside them, taking a long breath. "I thank the dear Lord that the two of you are here. Our people truly need your help, whether you join us or not."

A powerful hand abruptly gripped Jehan's arm—hard and brutal, yanking him onto his feet and bringing him eye to eye with one of the large sentries. The man ripped the dagger from Jehan's belt and began shouting, "*Traïdor*, Judas!"

Jehan had completely forgotten about concealing the dagger and his purse when he had removed his waistcoat. He raised his hands in surrender. "Wait. *Se vos plai, esperatz*. Hear me out. Cavalier . . . tell him I have something in my purse to show I am not a traitor."

Cavalier tried reasoning with the man while Jehan untied the purse on his belt. The man's eyes lit up. He seemed to be holding his breath in anticipation of a small fortune. But when Jehan pulled out his medallion, the man snorted and frowned, then tucked the dagger into his own belt. "*Bon. Mas dab jo*. Fine. But with me. *Lo pòdi aver quand me'n vas*."

Amelia reached up and laid her hand on Jehan's. "The man will return it to you when we leave."

He looked at her hand for a long wistful moment as she held it there, the skin youthful, her fingers long and graceful. Not like those of a woman who worked the land. He kneeled back down to check the injured woman's head. The swelling had already subsided and her eyes were more alert. Perhaps it was the cures, but perhaps Amelia's words and touch channeled God's healing. He turned to a young man who had been hovering nearby as they worked. "Do you know this woman? *Sabes aquesta femna?*"

The young man nodded.

"It appears she will heal," said Jehan. "But if she shows signs of confusion of the brain, be sure to give her a poultice or tea of calamint. From the mountains."

"Oc, *montièr* mint. *Polastre.*" The young man nodded again.

Jehan reached into his purse for a few deniers and placed them in his hand. "And she will need nourishment. Use this to buy her some food."

Amelia smiled with a look of approval. Jehan reached out and touched her shoulder, saying softly, "'Twas for you, Amelia. I carried the dagger for you. To keep you safe."

CHAPTER 20
INTENDANT BASVILLE'S SCAPEGOATS

13 May 1696
Intendant Basville's Office, Montpellier, France

The waiting was insufferable. The incessant ticking of the mantle clock—its hands nearly meeting for ten minutes before the tenth hour—caused Intendant Basville's head to pound with each step of his pacing. He had not slept all night, waiting at his office for word on the assembly raid.

"There should be a messenger by now proclaiming a successful outcome."

Basville's annoyance grew when his spy, Fallere, who sat on a stool near the door, removed his second-hand goat's hair perruque to scratch at shorn blond stubble, then stuffed it into the pocket of the old brown overcoat he wore.

Fallere cleared his throat. "Sieur, surely the soldiers have completed their task. Can I not have my payment and we can both get some sleep?"

The spy started to stand, but Basville walked over and pushed him back down onto the stool like the schoolboy he likened him to.

"No, you cannot. You will go nowhere until we get word. I am beginning to think you contrived this entire thing. I haven't heard from you in weeks and now you show up wanting payment before we have the heretics in hand. Tell me, how exactly did you acquire your information?"

"Truly, I did not contrive it," said Fallere. "I found a note dropped outside an inn east of Sainte-Enimie. I asked around and found a fool willing to decipher the location for a few deniers. He swore it was La Baume Dolente."

Intendent Basville thought he heard the clatter of fast moving hooves on the cobbled road. He went to the window and opened a shutter to a blast of sunlight. "Do you hear that, Fallere? Do you hear a horse approaching?"

"Yes, Sieur."

Unaccustomed to the intense light, Basville tried to blink away sun spots as he looked for an approaching messenger. But at the moment, his eyes served no better than his ears.

When a knock came at the door, he was certain. "This must be the news. Answer it Fallere." Basville's head throbbed harder with every rap as he sat to rest in his desk chair.

"Enter," Fallere said.

He opened the door to a young soldier standing in the hallway, tidying his hair and military justaucorps. He hastily straightened and saluted. "A message for Intendant Basville from lieutenant-general Broglie."

"Yes, yes. What is it?" barked Basville, waving the lad in. "What is your report?"

"The unit rode upcountry from Alais, then stationing horses at the base of a steep cliff due to unsuitable conditions, the unit approached upwards to the said Baume Dolmente . . ."

"Get on with it. What was the outcome?"

"Yes, Sieur. The unit approached on foot at dawn and sought out the said dissenters, investigating all accessible portions of the cave and the surrounding woodlands. Footprints were found, but there was no sign of the said dissenters, Sieur. That is all there is to report."

Basville slammed his fist on his desk. "Fallere! I was right not to pay you upfront. You bring me any more false leads and you'll be off to the galleys."

"False leads, Sieur? Since there were footprints, they must have been there earlier. The man I paid translated the message to 'at the time of light', and that is exactly the information I gave you. It was you and lieutenant-general Broglie who presumed that meant dawn. Perhaps it is code."

"Code. Code! You need to break that code then. You've wasted the few soldiers I'm given during this blasted war as if they are merely a pack of hunting dogs. I need these men focused on successful missions."

Basville wanted to deride him further, but held his tongue. He couldn't let the messenger return to Broglie with information to create false reports of his inability to manage. To the Intendant's relief, Fallere, the fool, plopped his wig awry on his head, slipped past the messenger, and exited out the door without pressing further for a reward.

"Give Broglie a message," Basville said to the young soldier. "I want no more reports like this. Ever. Period. He, too, is culpable. If he can't locate dissenters based on the leads, he must continue to seek and destroy their nest of treason. No more coming up empty-handed."

Basville refused to take the blame for the failures of others, but it was his reputation that was at stake. The veneer of order he depended on was wearing thin. Every last man, woman, and child would be arrested if that's what it took to clear the Languedoc of heresy.

CHAPTER 21
TIME TO HEAL

20 May 1696
Castelbouc Gorges du Tarn , Gévaudan, France

J ehan stepped off the cobbled path that wound its way through the Castelbouc village as it ascended the forested cliffs of the Gorges du Tarn. A beam of sunlight called him toward a patch of *muguet* —the tiny, delicate lilies-of-the-valley—dancing on low, thick masses of bright green leaves. His mother had told him it was tradition since the time of King Charles IX to take them as a gift of affection and to bestow good luck. So he knelt on one knee and plucked a handful, the warmth of the fleeting spring sunlight on his back.

As he walked on to Menina Elise's cottage, he pondered about the next assembly location. Would it be in a cave as was the first one on the Sunday past? Or would it be in the forests just outside of the local villages, like the two other smaller gatherings that were called in during the week?

When Jehan came around one of the stone houses, the cottage came into view. Menina was just stepping out the door, a basket over her arm.

"Good day, Jehan. I see you've come for Amelia by the looks of that bouquet," she said, her eyes lighting up and a merry smile taking years off her weathered face. She turned and called back through the open door. "Amelia. Jehan BonDurant is here for you." Menina stepped back out to the street, patting Jehan on the back. "I'm off to the baker's. 'Twas good to see you."

Jehan tipped his hat, then turned toward the open door to see Amelia walking through the common room toward him. Light from the rear garden window cast around her, transforming her into a pale silhouette. Romulus and Remus came running past her in their excitement to see Jehan. They showered him with a slathering of licks and nudges until he took turns rubbing their heads with his free hand.

"Jehan . . ." Her voice sounded feeble, fragile.

"How are you doing?" Concern gripped at his stomach. "You do not seem well."

"I need rest, is all."

She came closer to the door, and he could see she was pallid, with a darkness circling below her eyes. He stepped inside, then brushed a few strands of her hair from her face, tucking them behind her veil, and laid the back of his hand against her forehead. Its natural salubrious warmth reassured him a little.

"'Tis not an ague," she told him. "But after three assemblies in one week, I can do no more good without rest and solitude. My prayers will have more effect when I can speak to the Holy Spirit and the Sophia without distractions."

Jehan had not anticipated her need for rest. He had been so driven while serving the poor Cévenols at the assemblies, offering them his healing skills and coin for food, and he had assumed it nourished Amelia's soul in the same way.

She closed the door behind him, then whispered to the dogs. They went to lie by the hearth of the common room but kept four watchful eyes on Jehan's every move.

"I had hoped we would attend another assembly today," he said, "since the people always seem to need our help. But I shall gladly stay and help you recover in their stead."

He thought he glimpsed a sort of desire light in her eyes—the desire for him to stay—yet her words did not give away such emotions. "I am grateful for your offer, but time in solitude is what I need to heal my soul. Then I will be fully ready to help others again. 'Tis something you might consider for yourself."

His palm became sweaty as he still clutched the small bouquet. Why would she suggest such a thing? He had too much to accomplish to sit idly, contemplating his own well-being. "I fully understand that time alone, to rest and revive, is what you are in need of. Yet for me, the time I spend healing others keeps me feeling an aliveness."

"We are alike in that way, Jehan. We both want to help others. Yet there is a connection between this urgent need to heal others and the need to heal yourself." Her eyes were a little weary, but they penetrated his being. "You are searching for a way to heal your very soul. You and I both suffer from the tragedy of having lost our parents at a young age, and we cannot heal if we pretend we are not hurting . . . if we constantly feign strength and vigor. 'Tis noble to heal others, yet you avoid the need to look inside and heal your own soul."

Jehan ran the week's events through his mind, then through a series of justifications, searching for some way to prove he had no need to look inside, for some way to deny his need to heal. Yet the need was reflected in her sweet, sad eyes. It was there—the same pain he held from his own childhood. The pain he always found himself pushing down.

He took her hand in his as he could no longer deny she was the one meant to guide him; toward healing, toward what would mend his soul and open the way to the call of a spiritual path he was destined for.

"Dear Amelia. I am so sorry that you, too, had to suffer the pain of losing your parents. Menina shared your story, but I did not realize it still burdened you. This is how you know and understand me more than I have been willing to understand myself." He took her hand to his lips and pressed them in a kiss against her cool, tender skin.

With her free hand, she stroked his hair, and the sense of home came again—the same warm feeling he'd felt the first day they had met.

"Jehan . . ."

He lifted his head.

"Do you plan to hold on to that bouquet as long as you have held onto your anguish without tending to it?"

He could not help laughing at himself, and at the joy her perceptiveness brought him. He took a deep bow. "Pardon, these are for you, Mademoiselle." Then handed the bunch of tiny, white bell-shaped flowers to her. "They bring my affections along with good fortune as you revitalize. I am afraid I did cling to them for far too long. They are now bruised."

She smiled with a little color returning to her cheeks. "Have no regrets, Jehan. Muguet is resilient and it, too, will revitalize after some time in the pureness of still, clean water. Yet you will need to wash your hands of the toxins left behind."

"I am grateful for your guidance, Amelia. You are helping me to see what I need to discover my soul's true spiritual nature. If I can still myself long enough, I might finally find it. I promise you I shall go immediately to the well to rinse."

In one hand she held the bouquet, the other she held against her heart as she smiled. "In these moments of respite, we can move past trying to learn who we are and set an intention on who we want to be. This is our quest, and the journey never ends."

Jehan closed his eyes and reverently lowered his head to her for a moment. "I shall take my leave now so you can rest. May your rest restore your wonderful vivacity." His feet weighed to the floor as he turned with great reluctance to leave, but he moved on—to give them both time to heal their souls.

CHAPTER 22
RUMINATIONS

25 June 1696
Château de Cougoussac, France

The mistral winds had been fierce during the weeks since Jehan's return to Château de Cougoussac, causing delays in the spring plantings. His commitment to helping Benat and the tenant farmers had left him little time for himself. By the end of most days, he was exhausted, having worked until dark and then spent the evening keeping the books proper for the tax collector.

Often, he awoke to find he'd fallen asleep just as he started to write in the old journal. He would manage some notes on cures that Menina Elise and Amelia had shared, but never followed through on the hope of elucidating his thoughts on choosing a spiritual path. Amelia had opened his mind to ways of connecting to Spirit that he had never before imagined, and her guidance delighted him. But he needed time and healing—as she had pointed out—to let it settle in his mind.

He had taken a few minutes, two weeks past, to write to Amelia thanking her for her courage and wisdom, and telling her that he had only two certainties thus far; neither the Catholic faith nor the teachings of the Children of God felt like the path that he sought. So, now, all he could do was wait for her reply.

In recent days, the wait had turned his mood sullen since word came around of Intendant Basville's increased, but fortunately failed, attempts at assembly raids. The splendid code Cavalier had worked out for the time of the assembly at La Baume Dolente apparently had worked and had thrown the Intendant's soldiers off by hours. But it was a near miss and the potentially dreadful outcomes had begun creeping into Jehan's thoughts. So he prayed for his new friends, realizing they would likely continue to attend assemblies despite the increased danger.

The late June morning started calm, clear, crisp, making it perfect for a ride out to Genoüillac. He would finally have a chance to reflect on the strangeness, and sweetness, of his time with Amelia and Cavalier. Once Jehan got out on the road, the gentle swaying of Luisant's saddle lulled him into a daydream about returning—to be by Amelia's side again, aiding and healing the poor souls who clung so desperately to their religion. He could understand her need for peace and rest after she had taken on so much of their grief, praying for the people night and day.

The sweet smell of the bright pink lilies along the roadside, with their curling, freckled petals, penetrated his brooding thoughts, lightening them. A gentle reminder to treasure the good memories during his ruminations.

While herding his unruly thoughts about the assemblies, it suddenly came to him—he had been curious about the posset the assemblers drank, but had never taken notes when Cavalier and Amelia shared what they knew during the return to Le Villaret. So he pulled at Luisant's reins and stopped her under the shade of a beech tree. He took the journal and supplies from his saddlebag and performed the usual writing ritual—a few drops of water from his costrel and a bit of ground ink stick dropped onto the inkstone. Dabbing his quill, he wrote;

~ Posset ~
Special ingredient believed to be henbane. Source Cavalier.

Note: Ancients would burn and inhale henbane smoke with claims to transport to the other world. Brought the ability to communicate with féeries and other beings. Source Amelia.

That all sounded wondrous, entering the realm of féeries and such, but he hoped to experience the presence free of the aid of magic potions or subjugating religious leaders. Like Amelia, he just needed to be in nature, in silence. She was féerie enough for him, and their communication was light and effortless.

BonDurant Townhouse Genoüillac, France

The townhouse was quiet, except for a few giggles from the children's bedchambers. Jehan tiptoed down the marble floors of the hallway, thinking to catch a glimpse of his niece and nephews at play. He paused at the open door to André's chamber when he saw Lucrèce standing in front of the mirror above the mantle. Her dark hair was unbound, descending the length of her back.

She lifted the bottom corner of the mirror, pulling a tiny Bible from what appeared to be a recess in the wall behind. Jehan watched as she twisted the ends of her hair around the tiny thing into a high *chignon* and held it in place. She held up a hairpin as André came into view; his back to the door, his face reflected in the mirror, pale, frowning. He tucked the hairpin in place as she took another from the mantle.

"I will pray with you . . . if you will just stay here," said André, his bloodshot eyes pleading to Lucrèce's reflection. As he stared, his eyes moistened. But then, abruptly, they darted away from her reflection, seeming to catch sight of Jehan in the doorway.

"Jehan. We did not hear you come in." André looked as startled as a ghost caught in the moonlight.

"Pardon. I heard the children and thought to read to them. Are you about to set out?"

Concern etched André's brow as he paused before he spoke. "Lucrèce is going to visit Madame Lauren."

"My husband, you can be truthful with Jehan." Lucrèce smiled at André in her loving, reassuring way. "I have told you of his experiences on his trip and, on occasion, he joins us at these prayer meetings."

"Yes, André, please know I can now be trusted to use discretion. I apologize if I have not done so in the past, but things have changed." Jehan stepped into the room and pulled the door almost shut, not sure if the staff's loyalty had been affected by increased rewards. He continued in a hushed voice. "I have no desire or intention to reveal anything to the officials. I, too, must use caution since I am beginning to explore and embrace many ideas contrary to the Catholic faith."

"And so I am beginning to learn," André mumbled, looking from under his eyelids. He shook his head, moaning a bit. "If *only* you had followed through with a betrothal to Louise de Montcalm . . . then the authorities would surely look the other way. Jehan, you need to understand the breadth of the times ahead. Last month, the Intendant sent orders for his lieutenant-general Broglie to escalate his assembly raids. And he has sent letters weekly to the council demanding full compliance with his desire to clear the Languedoc of heresy." André's tone was reserved and distressed, his spark of confidence missing altogether.

"I have recently heard about these attempted raids," said Jehan. "Thank God they are not meeting with success."

"'Tis only a matter of time, though. For all these years, I've had to fend off attention toward Lucrèce, worrying she would be arrested and leave our children without a mother. And now I must . . ." André dropped his head and his voice weakened, trailing off into a murmur, "worry over you as well." He had mellowed over the last few months, but not in a healthsome way, seeming to be lost in dispirited resignation.

"I shall be careful André, so try not to trouble yourself so." Jehan placed a hand on André's shoulder—their roles now in a sort of countermarch. "I decided not to take part directly in the desert assemblies. But I do want to be of service to the people there. They are so downtrodden and in desperate need of healing and cures. Most are starving, having survived on acorns and grass the past few years when even the chestnut harvests failed." Jehan looked to the ceiling and heaved a breath. "And to think I once derided the opportunity to eat chestnuts." He directed his eyes back to André, hoping to ease his distress. "At the chateau, we are fortunate to have had a better year so far. And since I no longer see a need for frivolous clothing and luxuries, I now have the estate caught up on all taxes, and tithes, and old debts. That should keep us in good standing, and the authorities' eyes off of our family."

Lucrèce took a silk scarf from her wardrobe and draped it over her shoulders. "I must be off. 'Tis nearly time for prayer." She stepped into the hall and turned back around. "I think the two of you might like to spend some time sharing a glass of wine this evening. To calm your nerves a little."

Her intentions were good, but it was clear André had become dependent on drink. "Certainly, we shall spend some time together," said Jehan. "I can blend a tea with lemon balm and Saint Jean's wort, and save the wine for an occasion. Before you leave, Lucrèce, have any letters arrived for me?"

"Oh, I nearly forgot. In your bedchamber. In the top drawer of the commode. Unfortunately, no more correspondence from your sister. There is another letter, but it has no name written upon it."

André accompanied Lucrèce down the hall, saying his goodbyes while Jehan went to his bedchamber. His heart fluttered like the wings of an excited bird as he opened the commode drawer and removed the letter. He broke the seal, unfolded the parchment, and scanned it. *From Amelia. Praise God.* There was no mistake, even though she had used caution and left the letter unsigned.

Mon fidèl amic, I hope this letter finds you well. I understand your reluctance to join the Children, yet your desire to see them in good health. Perhaps, as I, you will choose your own path. You are invited to my library to study all the world's religions and philosophies, and follow the threads within them that lead to love and compassion. I am grateful for your humble and patient temperament. Upon solemn meditation, I find I am called to continue, by your side, in service to the Children. Many will attend the fête de Saint Jean. I would enjoy your escort to the Knights of Saint Jean de Jérusalem Commandery at Gap-Francès where the feast is celebrated. If you can arrange, please come to my grandmother's house before the eve of the fête and she will give you directions to my cottage. I do so look forward to your return. Since your departure, the joy felt in service to the people has diminished.

CHAPTER 23
DIVINE DIVERSIONS

22 June 1696
Amelia's Cottage, Castelbouc , Gorges du Tarn Gévaudan, France

Sunlight filtered through the forest canopy, brightening the bluebells scattered among stones and ferns as they danced in the breeze. There was a buoyancy in Jehan's step as Amelia's cottage came into view for the first time. Magical as any féerie house he could conceive; small and round, with a moss-covered conical roof, brambles and ferns nearly cloaking the ancient hewn stonework. The narrow door of dark knotted oak—bark still devotedly clinging—could have been mistaken for a tree trunk.

A short distance from the cottage, a crystalline brook flowed between rocks and over the path on its way down a gentle slope. The sound of splashing came from upstream, but the girth of an old twisted beech tree blocked his view. He stepped up to it, placed a hand on the gnarled trunk, and peered around it.

As if in a cloud of moonlit white silk, Amelia sat on the sunny edge of a pool, her light chestnut hair unfurled and free. She appeared like a beguiling, fantastical dream of Mélusine in a gossamer chemise with a long, feathery white tail extending from her right side.

He turned away and moved back around the tree. Heat flushed his face with embarrassment over the inappropriateness of seeing her bathing. *Mélusine? Could it be true? Not just my imaginings?* Too many hours of reading *Le Conte des Feés* to the children must be the cause of such notions. He let some time pass, hoping she would not be offended.

Thinking he should call out to her, Jehan peeked back around the tree, but she was gone. Disappeared. *How could that be?* He walked to the spot where she had been and looked further uphill, raising a hand to shade his eyes from the bright sunlight.

"So you've come."

Jehan startled and turned in the direction of her voice. Amelia emerged from her cottage, fully dressed in her faded blue linen gown with wet ringlets of hair appearing from under her star-covered veil. "I sensed it was you there . . . waiting behind the tree."

Romulus pushed past her and came running toward him, tail wagging. The dog splashed through the brook and sat by Jehan's side, nudging his hand. Amelia walked a few paces, coming to stand just across the brook from him.

"So that was *your* tail, eh?" Jehan playfully rubbed the dog's damp head. "Amelia . . . I thought . . . you looked so much like Mélusine sitting there. I do believe the children's féerie tale book is corrupting my reasoning."

"Is it now? Are you sure?" She smiled with spritely eyes, like he fancied a féerie might have. "We look for féeries to escape the chaos of the world. 'Tis easy to conjure them by will alone, by huddling in the shadows of a beautiful, magical realm. Our will has that power, so we must choose wisely how we use it. Remember, every word you utter, every thought you have, is an act of creation."

He had longed for her wisdom and playful challenges. "'Tis good to be here in the forest again. I have missed the peace."

"I am pleased you could come," said Amelia. "Have you had troubles?"

Troubles? André's last words before he left had weighed on him the entire journey. *'If only you had followed through with a betrothal to Louise de Montcalm . . .'* That certainly troubled him, but at least this time, he had not let André's disapproval rile him into anger.

"'Tis just that being here gives me space from the shame others can inflict, intentional or not." He rubbed a hand across his forehead. "I have allowed guilt to be my master for so long, but spending time in the forest, and with you, is teaching me I can change how I respond."

"For those who love nature and take communion in her embrace, she will penetrate any dark musings brewing in you. So . . . shall we share some time in meditation and let the forest take the sharp edges from your worries?"

Jehan smiled broadly to signal his delight and held out a hand, helping her across the brook. Once she was safely across, he removed the dagger from his belt and laid it between the twisted roots of the old beech tree; an act of reverence for God's natural cathédrale, in the same manner he would leave a sword at the portico of a church built by man. It now made sense why Pasteur Brousson did not want weapons at the assemblies.

They walked back uphill, along the brook, without saying a word. Jehan sensed they had reached a favorable spot, and at that very same moment, Amelia stopped.

"I feel this is a good place for us," she said.

How did she do that? Her thoughts were so often synchronized with his. They had both chosen the spot where the brook formed into a series of small pools and sparkling elfin cascades. "Indeed. 'Tis lovely here by the water."

He helped her settle down atop a large granite boulder, then lowered onto the ground next to her.

"Water is the most important element. From it, life emerges. Through it, we can pass from weakness to strength, from sickness to health, and from this world into the Heavens. Remove your boots and place your bare feet on the ground. This way you can connect to the direct knowing . . . to the remembering." She wrapped her veil close, then folded her hands in her lap and stared into the water. "But ask now the beasts, and they shall teach thee: and the birds of the air, and they shall tell thee. Speak to the earth, and it shall answer thee."

Jehan removed his hat, his long dark locks falling around his face, and placed both hands on the ground, running his fingers through the humus, and lichen, and twigs. He filled his lungs with the fresh air, earthy yet pungent with pine, then released it in a long slow exhale that loosened his taut shoulders. The warmth of the sun, restrained by filtering leaves, danced across his face.

Amelia began to chant, "aaaaaaa, eeeeeee." She stretched her hands out. "iiiiiii, òòòòòòò." And circled them to her heart. "ooooooo."

The sound quivered through Jehan's body and he closed his eyes.

A delicate fragrance of honey, vanilla, and new-mown hay began to seduce his worries away. *Sweet woodruff, surely.* Sounds magnified; gurgling brook, rock thrush melodies, deer scrambling over fallen branches, turtle doves chirring, dragonfly wings beating, a flower petal falling to the forest floor. The grasses sighed. The trees whispered and took remnants of busy thoughts. Voices came upon the wind like a dance of life and sang songs of joy to him. They called to him to listen and prepare, to be tested and strengthened. The sounds faded into a deep silence. He felt a nakedness, but no shame, and then, as if his heart had broken open, a current rushed in and flowed through his body. Alive, grace-filled, the Spirit was within, reminding him who he was. At one with all of nature, in a reciprocal kinship with the wild creatures, the soil, ferns, and flowers. The trees supporting and sheltering. Floating in the eternal light of the Divine, he held there, prolonging the experience, lingering, basking, reveling, until he heaved a long, deep sigh, letting the burden of his guilt—of his own accuser—finally depart.

He lifted his head and opened his eyes as he brushed back his hair. The vibrant forest surrounded him in a shimmering, pulsating vitality that he could actually see. Sparkling white and pink crystals within the rocks were suddenly visible and buzzing. Hope was palatable because Spirit was truly here, and now inside him as well. Energized with the strength to stand for right action and compassion, to be in loving service, he was revived.

Not wanting to break the wonderment, he gently touched Amelia's shoulder and whispered, "I felt my soul soaring like a bird just now."

She looked down at him with a radiant smile.

"Amelia, I truly felt the presence, and my heart is *utterly* full."

There was a great expansiveness in his chest, an awakeness he had never known. "I can understand now why people drink posset if it brings them to Spirit in this way."

"The presence is always here. When we choose to hear it and go into silence, it becomes known to us. The posset is a dangerous way to bring it on."

On that, they agreed, and he knew he would never partake in it.

There were other curiosities about the experience that he longed to know more about. "Your chant . . . it was the one you were singing on the first day we met, was it not?"

"Yes. The Spirit spoke to me just before you came into the forest that first day. It inspired me to sing *Lo Boier*, the ancient Cathar song. Just as I sang, 'The pilgrims that will pass by will take from the holy water,' I heard the commotion with the boar. You are the pilgrim and I see you are thirsting to drink from the holy water. I sense you are seeking radical enlightenment, just as I and so many others."

Jehan explored her eyes, as lovely as a blue-green brook where small brown pebbles had fallen. "Is this what the song means?"

"'Tis what it meant to me at that moment, but traditions says it holds hidden meaning about the path to the Divine through the feminine aspect of the Beloved Disciple, Saint Marie de Magdala. I believe you are open and ready to learn, and your soul is ready to remember, so I invite you to come into my library."

With this new connection to the Divine and ancient knowledge unfolding to Jehan, he felt a lightness and freedom like he had never experienced. "Yes, please, I am open to learning all the world's wonders."

Once Jehan entered, he was convinced the smallness of the cottage's exterior was a magical trick of the eye. Inside, there was an open room, possibly twenty pieds in diameter and nearly as vast as the prieuré's library, with concentric shelves filling every inch of the walls; save four window nooks and a small desk. There were tiny labels on the shelves, hammered tin, etched and inked with the Latin titles, '*philosophi, medici, theologi, historici ecclesiastici, sanctorum Patrum, textuum liturgicorum, bibliae sacrae, concilia advocatorum, lexicorum, historicorum, mathematicorum*'.

They spent the next few hours enraptured by highlights from the great works, Jehan reading and Amelia, his delightful muse, prompting him to consider the truth in the writings. They each curled into the warmth of opposite window nooks, discussing Pico and his concept of Grand Universal Wisdom, then sat together cross-legged on a thick wool rug searching for tomes on the Gnostics and ancient Egyptians, and ending up side-by-side on the bench at a table filled with writings on the Greeks philosophers.

Jehan turned a page. "Here is something interesting from Aristotle's treatise on *Politics*. We studied only *Physics* and *On the Soul* at the prieuré. 'Tis saying tyrants preserve themselves by sowing fear and mistrust among the citizens by means of spies, by distracting them with foreign wars, by eliminating men of spirit who might lead a revolution, by humbling the people, and making them incapable of decisive action. This is exactly what our own King is doing! Whether he has been advised, or it is his own choice, we cannot be sure."

"I feel fairly sure no one is holding him captive and threatening him, so those choices are his responsibility, but perhaps he lives in fear himself." Amelia reached over to the book and turned several pages. "Aristotle also says, 'He who has overcome his fears will truly be free.' This is most important to keep in mind. If you keep dominion over your thoughts, you can experience the true meaning of freedom."

"I never paid much attention to what scripture says of this notion. Admittedly, I was often distracted during sermons and readings. Have you a favorite passage?"

"I do." Amelia smiled, rose from the bench, and went to a lower shelf. "In the New Testament." She sat down again with a small Bible and leafed through. "This one, from the first Epistle of Jean is simple, and is my favorite. 'Perfect love casts out fear.'"

"Yes," said Jehan. "Simple and one to hold in the heart."

She handed him the Bible, and he turned to the only passage he could remember. "From Timothée's second letter to Paul. For God hath not given to us the Spirit of fear, but of power, and of love, and of a sound mind."

Amelia nodded with a reassuring smile. "Yes, of sound mind. God has given us the ability to choose our thoughts and push out fear. Through the power of those thoughts and through love."

"Yes, yes!" He leaned toward her and placed a hand on hers. It finally made sense what this passage meant. Why would Father Chabert have not explained this? "Amelia, thank you. I will carry these words in my heart." He took his hand away and placed it on his chest, then bowed his head to her.

She got up from the table, then reached for another small book, this one neatly tucked and protected by other larger tomes on a shelf above the little desk. "Here it is. What I have been meaning to show you." The hide cover was stiff and cracked. "From this old recipe book of cures, you will learn more than the Universities teach. But . . ." She looked from the corners of her eyes and smiled, "you will find even more lessons in the forest than in these books. Trees and stones will teach you what you cannot learn from the masters."

"I would imagine nature, being God's creation, is what inspired the masters in their writings."

"Precisely what I would imagine." She laid the little book on the desk and turned a few pages. "The recipes here seem to have been influenced by the Trotula. I have compared and found many are the same."

"The Trotula?"

"The writings of Trota, the female physician from Salerno who influenced Montpellier school of medicine on the healing of women. These have been most useful for Menina over the years."

"What does this say?" Jehan pointed at the parchment pages, running a finger over the drawings of herbs and flowers, suns and moons, then ran a finger over the heavy texture of the parchment and ink. The ink had faded in some places, and others were dark, newer. Scratches and symbols were interspersed.

"It is hard to decipher some of the writings. I see Latin, and the King's French, and is some of this langue d'oc?"

"It contains all of those, and other words that seem to be Hebrew. I have been working on translating them since I was eleven, so for nearly half my life now, and there is still more to learn. You see this," Amelia said, pointing to the page.

תלול ומרכך שלוש אונקיות שומר

"It says steep and macerate three ounces fennel," she explained.

"Perhaps I would like to learn Hebrew. Menina tells me that my dagger came from a Jew named Ben Durant from Aragon. What of your ancestors?"

"My ancestors' history has been well hidden. But, when I was small, Menina recited stories of the Cévenols, like us, whose roots are in the refugees who fled from Jerusalem to France. Marie de Magdala and the Christian Jews. And we are also descended from the Good Ones, *Bon Hommes*, who were Cathars and secretly worshiped Esclaremonde the Great for her good deeds. These stories inspired me to learn about ancient teachings."

"The boatman mentioned these to me. I suppose there is no pure French race then."

"Now there would be a féerie tale." Amelia giggled in that light, merry way, in such contrast to her solemn moments. "People have moved throughout the world for all of history. I know from the tomes here that this land has been home to many. The Gabali Celtae, the ones who honored the earth and practiced the solstice rituals, once populated this land . . ."

"Do you mean the ancient Gabali that Prieur Chabert calls long dead pagans?"

Amelia smiled. "Yes, but you will see for yourself tomorrow at the fête of Saint Jean that their rituals are still very much alive. The fête not only honors the birth of Saint Jean, but is also still very much a midsummer fête."

Jehan wondered if Gellion and Prieur Chabert had any notion that this went on.

"And there are other people who have called this land home," Amelia continued. "Romans, Francs, Wisigoths, Huns, Moors, and like your probable ancestor, Ben Durant, Jews fleeing persecution . . .

we surely are enriched by the blood of multitudes, each a strand woven into a strong cloth."

"Yet now we are being forced to uniformity by our own authorities," Jehan said. "They take our freedom to choose and force us to be what we are not."

"There are still choices, but they might not be easy. I find the only way to deal with an unfree world is to become free in my own heart and mind and actions, so that my very existence is an act of rebellion."

Twilight had come upon them much faster than Jehan had wanted, but he knew it was time to leave for the inn. He readied while Amelia put away the remaining tomes and pamphlets.

"For the fête," she said, "I shall pack all we need and meet you tomorrow morning at the inn. Surely, you will be pleased to meet Commandeur François Timoleon, of the Knights' of Saint Jean. He has much to teach on practical medicine from his years with the Hospitallers."

Jehan stepped out onto the threshold, reluctant to leave, but the arrival of the next day would be its reward. "I look forward to tomorrow." He paused and looked deep into her soulful, animated eyes. "Amelia, I am ever so grateful for the knowledge you have so kindly shared." He tipped his head in a reverent bow, holding his hat close to his heart, now swelling with affection for her. "Good night, dear Amelia."

He walked out onto the path, and as he was about to cross the brook, stopped and turned around for another look at this amazing young woman. She still stood in the doorway, her hand placed over her heart as if echoing his expression of the undeniable love growing between them.

He smiled, then leapt over the brook and walked to the old beech tree to retrieve his dagger. When he turned for one last delight in her angelic face, she had disappeared into the cottage.

CHAPTER 24
FÊTE DE LA SAINT JEAN

23 June 1696
Order of Saint Jean de Jérusalem, Knights Hospitallers
Commandery
Mont Lauzère Gap-Francès, France

The rapport Jehan felt with François Timoleon was nearly immediate. His demeanor was easy but assured, and his intent brown eyes reflected the mercy he spoke of. As the recently appointed Commandeur of the Order of Saint Jean de Jérusalem outpost on Mont Lauzère, he could easily abuse the power accorded him over vast land and lease holdings, but he expressed his intention to encourage peace and equity in the domain. He had sworn an oath to be serf and slave to the sick, so the two of them found much to discuss as they laid out linen bandaging and medicines—provisions for the usual carefree, drunken crowd soon to arrive for the fête.

Jehan continued in an exchange with the Commandeur on the best remedies for burns—likely to be needed that night—then paused to look out the window of the small building that served as hospital for the remote hamlets around Mont Lauzère.

Close by, Amelia assisted in the preparations for the vigil. A delight to watch her work, Jehan noted the cooperation and orchestrated movements among the women as they dressed the arched doorways of the commandery's grand maison and chapel. They strung garlands of green birch, long fennel, millepertuis, yellow stonecrop, and white lilies, aided by a few stout Knights on ladder duty whose black woolen surcoats, embellished with large, eight-pointed white crosses, were in stark contrast to the gaiety of the scene.

Jehan placed a hand on the windowsill and leaned out, curious to see what was happening in the field. His heart lifted when he saw the color that abounded; wildflower bouquets adorned long trestle tables, and beyond, merchants assembled tents and canopies in brilliant shades for the annual fair to be held in two days. Young men and maidens arrived in droves, each carrying a log or branch for the quickly growing pyre to be lit at the eleventh hour. The older children lit lanterns and candles, brightening every niche and table as daylight faded. And the littlest ones played tag and danced in circles in the tall grass.

Just as Amelia had promised, the old midsummer Gabali Celtae rituals, with all the symbols of rebirth and renewal, were still alive and well, just cleverly disguised—or not so at all—in the celebration of the Knights' beloved saint.

Commandeur Timoleon joined Jehan at the window with a subtle smile of contentment and said, "It pleases me greatly to see people from all faiths and walks of life together in hopeful celebration. They have come for the bonfire of good amity and to praise God for his benefits bestowed on them."

"How does the Bishop feel about those of other faiths in attendance?" Jehan asked.

Timoleon's brows lifted. "The Bishop has no say," he said in a resolute tone.

Perplexed, Jehan questioned how this could be. "Not that I judge, good Sieur. Yet I thought the Knights of Saint Jean served under the Holy Catholic Church of Rome."

"Not in my lifetime," said Timoleon. "We have always been self-governing and exempt from authority save that of the Pope himself. But many commanderies have separated from Rome, and we remember well the reason our own commandery became independent." He paused to make the sign of the cross. "Let us join the others outside. We can talk more while we survey all the goings-on."

They walked out into the courtyard and as they strolled the grounds, Timoleon continued his explanation. "In the year of our Lord, 1592, with the encouragement of the Bishop of that time, Catholics raided our fête, stealing everyone's proceeds, some fifty or sixty thousand livres, and wounding many guests." He took a deep breath, emitting a small sigh, and his shoulders dropped. "Even taking some prisoners. Since then, our order here on Mont Lauzère has been committed to keeping peace among all religions and creeds, regardless of what the Bishop thinks about it."

Jehan found his respect for Commandeur Timoleon growing quickly with his expression of a desire for harmony and stability. These must be the same qualities that Amelia appreciated, and why she was comfortable spending time here.

The Commandeur stood tall as he spoke again, "'Tis my duty and honor to serve all who reside within the commandery's realm . . . to protect them from injustice, no matter their beliefs. To us, a sick man or woman represents the person of Christ and should be treated as such. I suppose it's what makes them all feel safe coming to the fête. Though I am always surprised to see so many Reformed here since they proclaim to have abandoned idolatry." He tilted his head with a look of weary resolve. "Yet as long as they find their way to God, I am pleased."

Just after they passed the women at work, the Commandeur stopped and held his chin between his forefinger and thumb, scanning the crowd. "Do you think they have heard the latest news?"

"Pardon, which news?" Jehan asked.

"Yes, which news is that?"

Amelia. Her voice was unmistakable now—mellifluous and delicate as silver bells.

Jehan turned to see her standing behind him. Shifting a bit, he made room for her to join their conversation.

"Early this past week, Intendant Basville sent out new descriptions of the Reformed pasteurs," answered Timoleon.

"Indeed, I did hear that," said Jehan. "Word spread round

Genoüillac when a leaflet was posted in the marketplace. He has raised rewards again, I'm told. Amelia . . . has the news reached the villages in the Gorges du Tarn?"

"Not that I am aware," she answered. "He must be more determined than ever."

"Yes," said Timoleon, rubbing his forehead. "The Intendant is most definitely determined and willing to escalate tensions. Just a few days past, he ordered his lieutenant-general Broglie to capture Pasteur Henri Guerin and put him to the wheel." He heaved a sigh and made the sign of the cross again. "I do *not* condone their tactics. Although practicing the Reformed faith is contrary to current laws, no man deserves to die simply for preaching the word of Christ."

"I feel the same way," said Amelia. She hooked her arm around Jehan's and rested her hand on his forearm. "And you, Jehan, would you agree?"

"Most assuredly. 'Tis unfathomable to think how they could justify any sort of the cruelty."

"So . . . Mademoiselle," Timoleon said, "please pass word along to any of the Reformed you speak to tonight. And any Jews, Roma, Saracens . . . anyone, for that matter, even Catholics, that might assist the Reformed. They must all take heed."

Twilight approached, and Amelia's eyes flashed out across the festivities and games. What was she looking for? Jehan observed the last of the sweetmeats had been finished, yet there was plenty of wine still flowing, causing some to teeter among the tables and get restless. Her eyes seemed to land on a cluster of men who appeared to be having some serious discussion. And it was beginning to look ugly with heads shaking, hands flailing, grimaces.

Amelia tapped his shoulder. "We must find out what is happening there. It does not look good."

Nothing surprised Jehan any longer about Amelia, even such fearlessness in the face of a possible scuffle.

When they came closer to the group, he recognized several of the

Children of God. There was Cavalier and his young friend Pierre Laporte—the one who went by the name Rolland. Jehan recalled his broad pock-marked face hidden behind a moustache, large gray eyes, and flowing brown hair. Next to them was Abraham Mazel, whose black eyes and cropped black hair made him easy to spot. And, off to the side, was one other young man who seemed familiar, but Jehan could not place. The group was deep in an animated debate over persecutions and new taxes with an older fellow who looked to be taking a browbeating.

"Messieurs, I beseech you," Amelia interrupted. "Can we not be at peace for a few days? 'Let us love one another, for love is of God; and everyone who loves is born of God and knows God.'"

Cavalier bowed to Amelia. "Pardon, Mademoiselle. Yes, Messieurs, we should stop this bickering. It is getting us nowhere."

Rolland held a hand toward the older man. "Monsieur Rouvière, here, thinks he knows what's best for us, even though he still lives as a nouveau converti."

"As you can see, my friends are a little flustered over his suggestions," Cavalier said, then turned to Monsieur Rouvière. "But I, for one, appreciate the kindness of your offer to assist us and your desire to keep peace, even if my comrades do not."

"Thank you, Cavalier," said Monsieur Rouvière. "And thank you, Mademoiselle, for settling down these simmering tempers."

Tipping his hat to her, Rouvière—older, and likely wiser, than Cavalier's simple, adolescent shepherds and carders—bore the signs of a gentilhomme. Although he did not partake in the preponderant habit of perruque-wearing, he was attired in a well-tailored, high-quality, yet somber ensemble.

"We have not met," said Jehan, slightly bowing his head. "Jean Pierre BonDurant, of Cougoussac and Genoüillac, and this is Mademoiselle Amelia Auvrey. These fellows are good-hearted, yet I know they can be insistent with those of us who cannot yet find our way to renouncing our nouveau converti condition." He rolled his eyes to the others. "Are we not all entitled to freedom of conscience? Is that not what you want our King to realize?"

"Yes, you are right," said Cavalier. "You and Rouvière should be in fine company, so we'll leave you be. Come now, friends. 'Tis near time for the bonfire to be lit."

Cavalier herded his compatriots away—except for one. The young man Jehan could not place, who held back, off to the side, but within earshot.

Rouvière and Amelia began to talk while Jehan studied the man. Vaguely familiar and quite the contradiction, wearing the old brown overcoat of a farmer or shepherd, yet with stubbly blonde hair as if he usually wore a perruque, which might reveal him as a merchant or professional. So, why would he dress this way while the poor folk put on their finest for the occasion?

The man's eyes narrowed and his lips tightened when he seemed to notice Jehan returning his prying stare. Shifting sideways, the man leaned back against a table and shoved both hands deep into his pockets, but continued to glare askance at Jehan.

Rouvière quieted his tone as he spoke to Amelia.

"Pardon, Monsieur Rouvière," said Jehan, emulating the hushed caution. "I missed what you were just saying."

"I was explaining I had suggested to those young men that they consider fleeing to Geneva or Rotterdam. I've been discreetly organizing courier and guide services with family members who've taken refuge in these locations, so I offered to assist those who cannot afford the journey as an alternative to the rebellion they seemed to be instigating."

"Rebellion?" The blood began to pulse in Jehan's ears.

"With the higher taxes to pay for the King's aggressions, at war, and at home, and now the news of increased rewards and more pasteurs being put to death, the Children of God have been collecting arms. Preparing for the Apocalypse, they say. I cannot bear to see more death and destruction like we faced in the '80s. We need peace in the region."

"Then they *have* heard the news." Amelia's eyes were brimming with calculation. "I will do what I can to reason with them. They have put much trust in Jehan and me since they count on us to heal their sick and injured."

"What is the safest way you have to send messages?" asked Jehan.

"My uncle is a pasteur in Geneva. He has become a bit careless in his messages to our family, so I am looking for any good alternatives."

"A bookseller from the Hautes-Alpes, who frequents our markets, Jean Giraud, can help you," said Rouvière.

Jean Giraud. *Of course.* The bookseller from the Uzès market. *Galileo and féerie tales.*

Laughter rose and fell in waves from around the bonfire as it boldly leapt into the night. The last stragglers at the tables ran to watch the midsummer ritual. Amelia scooped up two bouquets, took Jehan's hand, and tugged until they were both flying like moths drawn to the flame. She handed one bouquet to him and waved the other through curling tendrils of smoke.

"What are these flowers?" he shouted over the revelry.

"Saint-Jean's bouquets . . . with seven herbs and flowers. Fennel, rosemary, foxglove, elder flower, millepertuis, male ferns, and wild roses." Her delicate laugh ebbed and flowed on waves of heat like an apparition. "Brandish yours in the smoke. To bless the maidens and help them become fertile."

Jehan and Amelia stepped into a large circle of thirty or more people, each waving a bouquet through the smoke; scenting the air with a sweet, spicy, sensual aroma. The maidens ducked in between, creating an inner circle around the fire, holding hands and singing—in langue d'oc, or some other ancient language, Jehan could not say. The young men followed and each came to stand behind a maiden. Then, seizing the maidens by the waist, the men lifted and swayed them nine times above the fire.

As Jehan and Amelia continued circling in the outer ring of people, he caught sight of the unknown young man again; firelight etched the man's features, causing the darkness beyond to deepen. Another time around, and he was still there, closer, and this time Jehan recognized the eyes. Amber, reptilian-looking. *Fallere!* Jehan could not believe he let this get by him; that he had not recognized him sooner. After they circled once again, Jehan stepped out of the circle, but Fallere was gone. The lizard had shed his green coat, but he was as sly and slippery as ever.

A few drops of rain fell across Jehan's face as Amelia followed him out of the circle. He glanced up to see a halo forming around the full moon. Gathering clouds grew in long, glowing fingers across the star-filled sky.

"Should we find cover and be off our feet awhile?" he asked, sensing tonight was not the time to worry about Fallere.

"The tradition is to stay awake for the rising sun, but we should rest." Amelia looked around at the complex of buildings. "The grand maison is always crowded and noisy. Too much snoring for my taste. But there are several outbuildings to shelter in."

She picked up a satchel she had left by the table where they supped, and Jehan grabbed one of the lanterns.

They walked uphill to a small water mill along the stream, very near the source—the birthplace—of the Tarn River. Believing it to be a good place to rest, Jehan went to the door. Reaching for the latch, it swung open with the slightest nudge. He lifted his lantern to rustling, movements, moans, and giggles. Buried deep in barley straw, under layers of blankets, were three or more couples merrily enacting the fertility rites.

Feeling his blood coursing, heating his face in response, he spun around and shut the door behind him.

"'Tis occupied. We will need to search further." He laughed and wiped beads of perspiration from his brow. "An appropriate place for creating new life, I suppose . . . here, so close to where the river is born."

The sprinkles of rain suddenly became a shower, so Jehan pulled off his justaucorps and held it over them. Puddles began to form in the dirt path—stages for spritely little drops dancing and glistening in the moonlight.

"There is a shepherd's *cazelle*, just there. Let's go!" Amelia ran up the path ahead, holding her veil in place, laughing and splashing.

JULES LARIMORE

He darted after her, his own laughter joyous and nearly uncontrol-lable, until they came to a little stone structure with a sturdy schist tile roof. She ducked inside and he followed, finding it comfortably warm and dry. Permeated by the sweet, grassy scent from a bale of newly cut barley hay, the cazelle was deep enough to shelter them from the rain, yet open on one side to nature and the night sky.

Jehan fixed the lantern on an iron hook on the underside of the roof, then broke apart the bale, creating a soft mound of straw against the back wall. Amelia pulled a rose madder-tinted woolen blanket from her satchel and spread it out. She let herself fall back, drifting lithely down into the resting spot with a sigh. Her blue veil slid off onto the blanket, and a torrent of chestnut hair flowed across it, the scent of it like dew-covered roses.

She patted the blanket next to her. "Join me. Surely your feet will be happy for the rest."

He sat down next to her and took a deep breath. True, the long day and all the traveling had left him fatigued, but elated all the same.

"There was a time when I thought a down-filled mattress was the best place in the world to rest, but I am so grateful for this sumptuous spot here next to you, sheltering from the rain."

Amelia tucked a hand under her head and looked up at him, her eyes luminous. "I thank you, Jehan, for getting me here safely. Romulus is a wonderful protector, but he does not make the best escort when there is a crowd. You have such a kind soul."

Her wide eyes held his for several long moments, and she smiled. A sweet smile that whispered the special secret alliance, the connec-tion that had grown between them. He lowered his head back on the blanket and turned to her, feeling a heat rush over him, wanting badly to kiss the sweet curve of her lips, but knowing he should not.

"My soul responds to yours, dear Amelia. You call it to your heart. I love when you share the world through your viewpoint . . . always so full of love and compassion and enchantment. You've brought magic to my life from the very beginning."

Lifting her free hand, he kissed it, putting his lips to her supple skin, white and beguiling as a moonbeam. "And I love these delicate hands that work so many miracles."

Her breath quickened in time with his. Without words, they held their connection. Radiant, entrancing energy flowing through hands and eyes for a long, long while. Jehan felt a bliss so powerful, so moving, he thought he could stay there for hours, days, forever, just gazing into the depths of her eyes. They lay there listening to the pattering raindrops, rhythmic like the blood coursing through his veins, until they dwindled and gave way to the mesmerizing calls of night birds and crickets.

Jehan watched Amelia's eyelids become heavy with each passing blink, and then she drifted to sleep. The lantern sputtered out, and he realized the moon had set, making the star-filled night seem vibrant— gold and hints of red against a dark indigo sky. He rolled onto his back to take in the twinkling, hypnotic majesty.

Trying his best to honor the vigil and stay awake, exhaustion began to get the better of him and eventually lulled him into a drowsy, dreamlike state. He was still aware of Amelia's breathing and tiny moans, and could hear rustling straw as she shifted. She let go of his hand, then her warm touch moved onto his chest and she leaned her head on his shoulder. He looked through lidded eyes to see if she was awake, but her eyes were closed.

"Amelia," he whispered.

"Yes . . . Jehan," she uttered wearily.

He brushed her hair back across her shoulder, then held a hand to her soft cheek. He knew he should resist touching her any further, but she leaned into his hand and he could not help but respond; wanting so much to hold her close, to sleep in her embrace. He wrapped her in his arms and slowly, gradually they twined into each other. So much stirred in him, but he could not dishonor her. *Resist. She does not know what she is doing.* He breathed deeply to calm his desires. Once they eased he lay there, tranquil, feeling blessed with newfound peace, grateful to be snug in her arms.

24 June 1696

Jehan woke to the song of a distant rock thrush. Dawn was breaking above knolls and tufts of pink heather, through smoldering smoke that hung in the air.

Leaning to kiss Amelia's forehead, he said softly, "*Ame. Mon Ame.*"

She sat up, blinking the sleep from her eyes. He pulled a few pieces of straw from her hair, and a half-hearted smile lifted her cheeks. But then she bit her lower lip and looked away as if she suddenly remembered their embraces.

She picked up her veil. "Time for Mass," she said, rising and draping it over her head.

"I do not hear bells tolling."

"They will . . . soon." She stepped outside the cazelle and crossed her arms tightly around her chest. "Since on this day of Saint Jean's birth, they are meant to chase away evil spirits."

Had he done the wrong thing? Touching and holding her as he did? A holy woman. Had he been possessed by evil? The thought filled him with regret that silted around his heart.

CHAPTER 25
SURPRISE ENCOUNTERS

14 July 1696
Genoüillac, France

Spectators filled the Place de Colombier for the weekly pétanque game, leaving little room for the few market vendors who had ventured up from Uzès. Jehan wandered the field's perimeter to search for the bookseller, marveling at how, even from a distance, the stench of midsummer bodies and garlic wafted in the air.

A hush fell, then a loud clack of the boules sounded, and a cheer went up from the crowd. Jehan stretched to his full height to see who had scored, but instead was distracted when his eyes fell on Curé Gellion on the far side of the field. For a moment, Jehan yearned for a cloak of invisibility or the stealth of a small cat eluding a hound, allowing him to slip around bystanders' legs and skirts and out the other side. Yet he knew it was time to deal with things differently and stand up to Gellion's intimidations.

The curé was likely just making his usual rounds, looking to stir up some heretical controversy or the other. But something more seemed afoot since, somehow, he had convinced Prieur Chabert to join him. Unless he was troubled over someone, or something, Chabert wouldn't be out on market day.

"BonDurant," Gellion shouted, as he shoved his way through the crowd, the sleeves of his black robes flapping around upraised arms like a bat swooping at a swarm of insects. Lid-less beady eyes, ringed by darkness, had discovered the desired prey.

Locked in the throng, Jehan could not move. With no way to avoid the curé now, he tipped his hat and feigned a cursory smile. Gellion came close enough to reach through the celebrating spectators. Red-faced and scowling, he grabbed the cuff of Jehan's blue justaucorps, the way he had when Jehan was a child.

"Why were you not out for the Pentecost or Corpus Christi processions last month?" he demanded.

Jehan jerked away. "Take your hands off of me. I have no need to run from you," he said, trying to convince himself as much as he was Gellion. He could now easily wrestle the frail curé off, if need be, but disgust still caught in his throat whenever memories of an unscrupulous frère's touches assailed him.

He quickly shook off the recollections, relieved to see Prieur Chabert catching up. Like a saint in his white scapular and tunic, ready to contend with Gellion's dark furor, the good prieur came to stand behind Gellion for lack of space in the sea of bodies.

"Good day, Prieur," Jehan said, leaning around Gellion to speak to Prieur Chabert. "I am surprised to see you out in this crowd."

"We have been concerned . . . since we have not seen much of you these past weeks," said Prieur Chabert.

Curé Gellion glared at Jehan. "Yes, where have you been?"

"All is well. I have been traveling, spending time at the Knights of Saint Jean commandery assisting their patients with treatments and celebrating the holy day of Saint Jean."

Jehan felt no need to share details. If he displayed worry over Gellion's query, it would only make him suspect something and it might push the rabid curé into one of his unsanctioned inquisitions.

"Curé, you need to get accustomed to the fact that Genoüillac is no longer my permanent place of residence. I cannot be in two places at once."

Gellion retracted slightly.

248

Standing him down seemed to be working. Pointing out how detrimental these processions had become might work even better.

"Besides, I am quite relieved I was *not* here for the Corpus Christi procession. I hear the Reformed were heckled for not removing their hats, and fights broke out."

Prieur Chabert made the sign of the cross and looked to the ground. "Yes, and sadly, there were severe injuries and a few deaths on both sides."

"God have mercy!" Jehan sensed the blood running to his face. He drew a deep breath to ease his ire and steady his rising temper. "Will these divisions . . . and this violence never cease? Can we not make every effort to live in peace?"

Adjusting himself so Gellion could not see, Prieur Chabert's eyes widened as if he understood far more than those words conveyed. He ever so slightly shook his head in warning.

Jehan was tired of holding back. Hadn't they wanted him to be a positive influence in the community? "This violence has gone on too long. 'Tis tearing our communities apart when we need to heal. The time has come to use empathy instead of armory."

"Deluded boy," Gellion squawked. "Do you assume your judgment to be wiser than that of the Holy Roman Church? And the King? Those insolent Huguenots are to blame. They refused to offer the respect due the Blessed Sacrament and started the violent actions by throwing rocks. Intendant Basville is ordering more villages to send up men for his bourgeois militia. That should put an end to it."

"Dreadful notion," muttered Jehan.

Gellion tilted his head and squinted. "What was that?"

"Devotion," Jehan said, exerting a confected smile. "André tells me you hung your red banners upon my townhouse for the Pentecost procession. Let that be my show of devotion."

"Sieur BonDurant does make a good point about living in peace, Curé," said Prieur Chabert. "Following the commandments and loving one another is the path God would have us choose, and Jehan holds a fine example of that for the people of Genoüillac. Let us move on now. You mentioned you wanted to check on Monsieur Laurens and his wife."

"Uhh . . . yes!" Gellion responded. "Easier to implicate. They have had some strange comings and goings." He eagerly departed, grumbling and jostling his way through the crowd.

Prieur Chabert proceeded to leave, but hesitated. His brows drew together as he regarded Jehan with a look of consternation.

"I am doing well, Prieur, I assure you," said Jehan, putting a hand on his shoulder. "I have found much solace in nature lately, a Divine connection. With traveling and managing my lands, I have little time to be in Genoüillac."

Prieur Chabert glanced around the Place de Colombier field, then he leaned in close. "I will be of aid to you if ever your situation calls for it," he said in a near whisper, then turned and hastened to follow Gellion on his next mission.

What was it that Prieur Chabert knew but could not say?

Despite the hope for a Grand Alliance peace treaty that would restore rights to the Reformed—or perhaps because of it—the air seemed charged with trepidation in every corner of the region of late. Escalating debates and arguments, divisions among neighbors and families, talk of rebellion, and now these deaths during Corpus Christi that Chabert mentioned.

Once both Chabert and Gellion were out of Jehan's sightline, his chest relaxed and he took off his hat. Clasping his forehead, he felt the blood coursing near his temples and causing a dull ache. He tossed back his hair, then donned his hat again and searched methodically across the field for the bookseller.

There he is. Monsieur Jean Giraud. Jehan recognized him from their interactions at the Uzès market the previous fall. He made his way through the crush of people. It required patience, but he found that easy to conjure after dealing with Gellion.

Arriving at the stall, Jehan nodded and tipped his hat. "Monsieur Giraud. I am Jehan BonDurant. When we met last, in Uzès, you offered other services and placed your card in the books I purchased."

"Certainly. I remember. You drove a hard bargain for a copy of *Les Contes des Fées* . . ." Giraud paused, shaking his head with a sardonic half-smile on his face, "Yes, yes, and a most prized volume on astronomy, as well. One that I had reserved for another customer."

"You have a good memory, Monsieur." Jehan looked around to be sure they could not be overheard. He would need to speak in some sort of cipher. "You come highly recommended by a Monsieur Rouvière from the Mont Lauzère area, so I'd like to conduct some business with you. The library at my château is in need of . . ." Jehan put a finger to his chin and looked at Giraud. ". . . updating," he said, pointing his finger to the sky. "Yes, updating. 'Tis the best place for . . . um . . . new learning. Will you come to Cougoussac . . . just outside of Chamborigaud?"

"That can be arranged. I can follow you there after market."

"Splendid, I shall . . ."

Jehan looked over Giraud's shoulder, noticing there were knights, mounted high on large white coursers, heading down the Régordane road toward the market. Their black cloaks and tunics with white cross insignias immediately gave them away as Knights of Saint Jean. As they drew nearer, he could see it was Commandeur Timoleon with one of his men. And between them—Amelia. Jehan's heart leapt. Wearing her cloak and hood despite the heat, she rode a smaller, speckled gray Auvergne mare, while Romulus stayed close by the horse's side, trotting in double-time to mimic the mare's stride.

Jehan realized he might miss them if he could not make it over to the road before they passed. The pétanque game had ended, and the crowds had thinned, so there was a chance.

"Pardon, Monsieur Giraud, I must go. But I shall meet you back here after the market and you can follow me to Cougoussac."

Jehan darted and dashed toward the road, catching Commandeur Timoleon's attention, who stopped and waved toward Jehan. When he arrived in front of the little retinue, Amelia held her hand down toward her golden-eyed wolf-dog, and gave a gentle command, "Romulus, stay."

Though the dog obeyed, his tail wagged vigorously, so Jehan gave him a quick rub between the ears. He had no idea what brought Amelia to town, but his heart rejoiced over the occasion.

"Good day, Sieur BonDurant," Timoleon said while helping Amelia dismount.

Jehan bowed his head. "Thank you for bringing Amelia safely into town."

He walked nearer, and could see she held a myrtle branch with fragrant snow-white blooms. "Amelia. Have you been well? I have written thrice in the last few weeks, but have not gotten your response. Have you received my letters?"

She looked down for a moment; her face hidden behind the hood. What distressed her so? Despite the awkwardness of their night in the cazelle at the Fête de la Saint Jean, they had departed on warm, friendly terms after celebrating mass and accompanying her back to Castelbouc.

She turned to him, cheeks flushed and dewy. "I did receive them, Jehan. I have been quite busy preparing for my annual pilgrimage to Sainte-Baume for the celebration of Marie de Magdala with little time to reply. That is where I am headed now."

He touched her elbow and coaxed her to a quiet spot a few steps away. They sheltered in the shadows along a vine-covered garden wall, the commotion around them paying them little attention. She bit her lower lip, as she always did when something troubled or embarrassed her, and timidly pulled her arm away. Perhaps she had wanted him to return sooner, but how was he to know with no reply to his letters?

"I am sorry I have not come again to see you," said Jehan. "You know how much I care for you, but André has been warning me about how dangerous travel is becoming. He gets word at council meetings from the inner workings of the Intendant's office."

The doleful expression on her face told him that was not what she wanted to hear. She turned her head away, so he felt he should explain further.

"I wanted very much to see you, but thought it best not to visit without your invitation. I would have come if you had written to let me know of the next, assem . . . uh . . . the next time you needed my assistance. Why are you planning this trip to Sainte-Baume when it could be perilous?"

She turned and looked up at him. Her eyes glistened and held an anguish like he had never seen. "I *must* go, Jehan. Of all the apostles,

Marie de Magdala was the one who persevered and was rewarded with the presence of the risen Christ. 'Whosoever perseveres to the end will be saved.' It is my time to reflect on her example, to persevere against temptations of the body and worldly goods."

She folded her delicate hands over her heart and stepped closer to him. Close enough, he could feel her breath, sweet on his lips, as she whispered, "Your touch still lingers on my skin."

A flush of heat radiated to his core; he ached to reach for her. He placed a hand over hers but quickly removed it, sensing there were now eyes, somewhere, watching them, though it wasn't apparent whose. Commandeur Timoleon and his knight had turned the other direction; the bookseller was engaged in another sale; the market-goers were in their usual frenzy to purchase and be off; and Curé Gellion and Prieur Chabert were nowhere in sight.

"Amelia," Jehan said, his tone quiet and full of caution. "I relish even the imagining of lying next to you . . . when every color is brighter, every sound more melodious, every scent sweeter."

She held out the myrtle branch. "It was considered sacred to Venus."

Surely, she could read the confusion clenching his brow. He took the branch from her, letting his fingers brush against the back of her hand.

"'Tis the only way I can show the pure love I feel for you," she explained. "There is no other way. 'Tis as if we lay by a river, but thirst, or are in the midst of a banquet, but hunger. And then you are gone. I love my God, and I know he is the one love who will never abandon me."

A sudden heaviness fell over Jehan. He should have listened to the regret he felt that morning after the fête; should have been honest about his feelings, talked to her, given her his apologies.

"Amelia, I would never abandon you, if it were your wish. Your eyes are now my holy sanctuary. I will honor your virtue and ask for nothing more." He breathed in her rose-scented skin, realizing she, too, had fears. Rightfully so, after losing her parents at such an early age. He parted his lips to speak but faltered, searching his mind for a way to stay gentle with her tender heart. "Even if your wish is for us to spend our time apart . . . you will still forever have my love . . . without condition." The strong connection he always felt with her suddenly seemed to wane; blocked somehow. "Is there no hope?"

"There is hope for a purposeful life for you. I see the good man you have become . . . when you pause and breathe, gathering strength to choose a better path. When you take a moment to let love guide you, there is where your hope lives. You have learned to find answers and direction in the sanctity of silence and stillness." She held a hand to her heart and bowed her head as a tear trickled down her cheek. She quickly turned and walked back to her horse.

Should he go after her? Everything in his body wanted him to run to her, to bow on one knee, swear his fidelity, and ask for her hand in marriage. He had found his muse, the one he wanted to spend his life with, yet she only wanted God. No, he could not let his own desires steal her happiness.

Amelia glanced back at him for a quick moment. "In the deepest part of our hearts, we both know the truth. We know this is our fate. I must go, but I shall let you know of my safe return."

Jehan slumped back against the garden wall, heavy, numb. As he watched Commandeur Timoleon help her mount, he prayed he would see her again.

CHAPTER 26
INDECISION

30 August 1696
BonDurant Townhouse, Genoüillac, France

L ate afternoon sunlight flooded the *solaire* of the Genoüillac
townhouse. The August heat, cunning and serpentine, had found
its way through cracks in the thick stone walls. It was no use shut-
tering the windows on such a day, so Jehan flung them open. The lace
curtains rippled a bit in the slight, sultry breeze that brushed across his
face. After setting his empty wine glass on the sideboard, he removed
his waistcoat and tossed it on a chair, then opened his chemise to
the air.

Pacing barefoot across the cool stone floors, he continued his
conversation with Lucrèce. "I am infinitely indebted to you for being
my faithful confidant. If I could win Amelia's love as easily as
knocking a sword from an opponent's hand, or creating a tincture to
heal the plague, I would ask her to be my wife."

Lucrèce and the folds of her gold linen gown were draped across
her settee, fluttering fan in one hand and handkerchief in the other.
She tilted her head and gave him a withered smile. He could not tell if
she tired of listening to his lamenting over the love he knew could
never be, or the heat, or both.

"Although I had originally sought a more successful financial match for you, I understand your heart is now entwined with Amelia's. 'Tis good for you to share your feelings or they will bottle up inside and break you."

"Of late, I have been greatly troubled over her safety. These past seven weeks, since she left for Sainte-Baume, have seemed near a lifetime to me. I have found little motivation to leave my room until today, but I had to speak to someone about it."

The hallway floorboards suddenly creaked outside the solaire, and the door swung wide. André walked in, neatly dressed for business but looking fatigued, his shoulders slumped, his face pale and creased with worry. He stood by the settee, resting a hand on Lucrèce's shoulder while he addressed Jehan. "Amelia? Do you mean Menina Elise's granddaughter? So, is she the *real* reason you abandoned the betrothal to Louise de Montcalm?"

"Abandoned," Jehan said flatly. With the simmering heat, he had little energy for debate. "Interesting choice of words. I reason that, since I never asked for her hand in the first place, there is nothing that I have abandoned."

"Well, there is logic to that reasoning," André said, oddly matching the calm Jehan held over the subject. "Or perhaps she simply would not have you . . ." His eyes evaluated Jehan with that familiar look of judgment formulating in his mind. ". . .you and your wild appearance. What has gotten in to you that you now dress like an unshaven peasant with no footwear to your name? I thought fine fashion was of utmost importance to you."

Jehan rubbed the growth on his face. Had it been three days, or maybe four, since he shaved? During his travels, he had gotten out of the daily habit. He found little interest in his appearance of late, his mind constantly occupied with concern over Amelia. Leaning his head near his shoulder, he sniffed, catching his own fetid odor. Was Lucrèce only tolerating his distasteful presence because she had no choice?

He lifted the wine carafe and filled his empty glass, then downed its contents before he replied, "'Tis true. We do speak of Menina's granddaughter. She is *not* the reason I have no interest in Louise de

Montcalm. However, I have been spending my time with her, working to heal the sick and injured around the Gévaudan. Mostly at the assemblies."

"Assemblies!" André waved a hand through the air, then clinched the nape of his neck, his calm erased by Jehan's truth. "You place yourself in grave danger by doing so and implicate the rest of us. Amelia is safer at Sainte-Baume than in the Castelbouc, so you must stop this foolish behavior."

"Safer? What makes you think you know about her safety?"

"I just came from the weekly council meeting. The Intendant has learned the Children of God are organizing for rebellion and he wants to be prepared this time. He sent a courier to let the council know he is currently focusing on the Gévaudan, so Castelbouc is at risk. And our area, south of Mont Lauzère, will be next."

A sinking sensation fell across Jehan. Someone at the fête must have gotten word to the Intendant. *A spy?* It might be any number of people from the large crowd that had gathered. *Surely not Cavalier.* But perhaps someone who was part of Cavalier's inner circle of friends. *Rolland or Abraham Mazel?* Those two were unlikely to have betrayed Cavalier, as they were local shepherds and carders who had been his childhood friends. *But Fallere.* He was new to the group. It had been just the previous fall when he pestered Jehan while in search of an assembly. The man always made him suspicious, and he *had* acted rather strange at the fête. Perhaps Jehan should have listened to his initial instincts instead of looking for fault in them.

"You realize what this means, Jehan?" asked André.

"It sounds as if we have dark days ahead unless we learn tolerance for each other."

"It means you could be called up for the militia. As noblesse, it is your duty, and I can only leave your name off the list for so long."

Militia. Jehan's gut tightened at the thought of taking up arms against anyone. Once he had set his course, training as an apothecary, it never occurred to him he would be called up. He had to stand firm. "I cannot serve in the militia," he said, shaking his head to emphasize his unwillingness. "I could never bring myself to cause harm to *anyone.*"

André threw up his hands. "This is the law, Jehan. Do you even begin to realize how difficult this is for me?" he complained, flailing his arms about as he spoke. It appeared Jehan had pushed him too far. "I have my duties on the Council, but I do everything I can to protect all of you . . . Lucrèce, you, Jeanette, the Laurens, cousin Moyse, and our other friends who still want to be involved with the Reformed faith. I would feel such shame and grief if anything happens to any of you. Yet, you, Jehan, most of all, put me in a precarious situation."

Lucrèce rose from the settee and went around the back to stand before André. She laced her fingers together as if praying for his forgiveness. "I am sorry, my love. . . so sorry for the burden it places on you." Her weary eyes gazed around the *solaire*. "The sun is setting now. 'Tis time to brighten the room." She kissed André on the cheek and went to light the candles atop the mantel.

"I wish not to imperil any of you," said Jehan, running a hand through his tangled hair. "I want to stand with courage for the truth, but with gentleness, not with violence and divisive anger. I cannot be party to this militia any more than I can be party to the rebellion the Children of God seem to be planning."

"You have no choice," said André. "As long as you remain in the country, they can force you. Otherwise, you could face fines, or land in prison or the galleys."

"Perhaps Jehan has not heard all the news," Lucrèce suggested. "There are many occurrences that point to a dire situation looming. André, tell him *all* of it."

Jehan felt his legs going wobbly like a newborn fawn, so he leaned on the sideboard, then sunk in the chair next to it as his head began to spin. He glanced at the carafe, but decided against more wine, needing to listen intently now—if that was at all possible in his condition. His recent reclusiveness had surely left him somewhat uninformed. "Please . . . tell me everything you know."

"I shall leave you two to talk," said Lucrèce as she lit the last candle and left the room.

Pulling a chair alongside Jehan, André began sharing. "There was a Pasteur Jean Roman captured after an assembly on Marie de Magdala's day."

"'Tis always sad to learn of a pasteur's capture," said Jehan, "but it happens with regularity. How is this any different?"

"It angered the Children of God and this time they took measures. The next day at a fair in le Dignan, the word spread rapidly. A group of about forty organized then marched to where the pasteur was being held. They surrounded the house and broke open the doors, without a bit of resistance from the twenty or so guards, and rescued the pasteur who has now fled the country. The Intendant was furious over another failure, so it is now his justification to intensify soldiers, and spies, *and* militia in the area." André paused and rubbed his neck again. "I could use a drink. Pour me some wine, please, Jehan."

Jehan complied. After all, how could he judge André's indulgences any longer when he had been drowning his own woes for the past few weeks? He clinked the carafe against an empty glass and knocked it over, but righted it. His vision blurred and his hand wavered while he poured, causing some to dribble down the side.

André picked up the glass and drew a long drink. "Do you realize we are both quite fortunate we were never called to serve in the war? I have some control over orders for the local militia, but I have no control over orders from the Royale Army. Hopefully, we have gotten round that now . . . I am sure you know France has been negotiating in peace talks with the Grand Alliance countries."

"Yes, *that* I know. So perhaps there will *finally* be an end to the war. There is talk around town that they might add treaty clauses to protect freedom of conscience for all. Possibly, even, a reinstatement of the Edict of Nantes. Will not William de Orange see to that?"

"Well, that is what everyone hopes for . . . but there's another incident that has weakened the chances. It began last month with the betrothal of Princess Marie Adelaide of Savoy to the King's grandson, Louis, Duc de Bourgogne. It was just the first step in a truce between the Duc de Savoy and King Louis that has now become official. With Savoy on the King's side, William is less likely to push for protections for Protestants, despite his commitment to the faith."

Jehan clutched his forehead with both hands and leaned his elbows on his knees. "Yet more dispiriting news," he muttered through unruly strands of hair about his face. He sat upright and looked at André. "I wish I could do something to bring peace to our land, and not be a part of what divides our people further. Uncle Barjon continues to write and encourages me to join his group in Switzerland, and I have been considering it. I long to live in a peaceful place, but it would also be for your sake. Surely . . ." Jehan swallowed hard, trying to clear the lump in his throat. "It would be easier to be rid of me."

"Well, if you had just said so sooner, you would have relieved me of much anxiety," said André, patting Jehan hard on the back. "That would be best all around."

Jehan cleared his throat and leered sidelong at André, vexed by his indecorous self-concern. "I am still only considering it. 'Tis a hard decision to make . . . to leave my homeland . . . and all my family and friends." Although, at times, he wondered if he would miss André at all. "There is much preparation that would need to occur first. And I am not sure I want to commit fully to the Reformed faith. I would rather retain my freedom of conscience so as to find my own path to God." He took a deep breath, knowing his immediate fate rested in André's hands, and asked with all the respect he could muster, "Would you be able to hold my name off the list for a while? I would be truly grateful for more time."

"I can try to arrange it, but cannot guarantee for how long," said André, squeezing the back of his neck. "A payoff may be required."

"Let us hope not," said Jehan. If he were to use his money for something, he would much rather give it to some poor soul who could not afford to flee the country.

André huffed. "I am telling you, at some point, your money may be the only thing to keep you out of the militia. Are you being careful with your correspondence to Pasteur Barjon? The post is no longer a trusted method for any mention of these things."

"I do realize this country has become too dangerous to freely write about anything to my uncle that might violate these incredulous laws against non-Catholics. So yes, I am being careful. I have been using a bookseller."

André pulled his chair closer to Jehan, and spoke in a hushed tone, "If you decide to go, I know of a scheme that has worked for others. 'Tis a false loan scheme. We write up and certify a document claiming

I loaned you money that you are paying back. Then I hold the money and distribute it to you, in small amounts as needed, through a courier, or perhaps this bookseller of yours."

"Hmm." Jehan folded his hands and gazed upward, hoping to collect his thoughts. He could not imagine carrying large amounts of money while attempting a dangerous—and illegal—flight from the country. So this plan might serve him well. "I shall take this scheme of yours into consideration," he said.

"You might also consider selling off some of your properties," said André. "I know the prieuré has never had good access to water, so the Bishop would likely authorize Prieur Chabert to make a purchase of your mills and water canals."

"You believe he would? That could be helpful. I want to be sure to leave funds to maintain the other properties. And for Françoise, if ever she changes her mind about returning home."

"Yes, but you will need to find a way to do the asking yourself," said André.

"I . . . I shall think on all of these strategies and formulate a design. Though, please, do what you can to hold my name off the militia list for now."

A contented smile seeped from André's lips. "I will, as long as we keep focused on taking these steps to prepare you for when the time is right." He seemed rather happy that his ideas might be set into motion soon—as if he wanted to be rid of Jehan all along.

Jehan's chest grew hollow and heavy. He sighed, looking at André. "Life no longer holds much meaning for me here . . . with no hope of entrance to medical school or Françoise's return from the convent, and now that Amelia . . ." Jehan stopped himself from saying more. Amelia always reminded him of the power of his words. He dared not speak a single word of giving up on her yet. Instead, he would listen to the inner voice, the knowing, that said she was alive—the one that connected them so strongly. He would hold firmly to the hope that, in time, she would change her mind. He would make preparations, but he must try to see her before making a decision of such gravity. Before deciding to stay—or to go.

31 August 1696
Château de Cougoussac, France

Wind wailed through the treetops, rattling the château's shutters. Jehan glanced up from his reading as leaves and small broken branches suddenly began pelting the library window glass. He looked toward the forecourt, where the sky overhead boiled with dark clouds, dust whirled across the gravel, and rows of lavender whipped to and fro.

He ran out of the library to the hall window that overlooked the kitchen garden and thrust it open. "Biatris. Come in now," he shouted. "There is a storm coming."

"A few minutes more, Sénher Jehan. I must get what we need for sopar."

He rushed down the three flights of stairs, careful not to slip on the worn stone, and burst into the kitchen just as Biatris entered from outside carrying a basket brimming with vegetables.

A gust sent the strewing herbs in a wave across the floor as she shut the door tight behind her. She rustled over them, scenting the air with meadowsweet and rosemary, and walked to the old oak table in the center of the room. "Too much goodness to let waste in the storm, Sénher. You see, we've *carchofa* now for the magic ink," she said with a proud smile, holding a sizable, vibrant green artichoke globe. "For the ink that cannot be seen. Like the bookseller, Giraud . . . like he instructed you."

"'Tis splendid, indeed. But you can be injured in a storm like this." Jehan valued her company during these lonely days. She, too, had become his confidant, patiently listening to stories of his times with Amelia. He could not even begin to think how he'd manage the château without her.

Biatris set the basket on the table and walked to a tall cabinet near the door, taking out a mailing sack of thick layered linen. "Since we talk of the bookseller . . . I *remembri* . . . a package came this day . . . from his *servici*." She laid it on the table, then unloaded her basket.

Jehan lifted a leg over the bench and straddled it, joining her at the table. He loosened the jute tie from the package and removed two books from inside the well-padded linen sack. "Aah, Molière," he said, running his hand across the fine, gold-tooled filigrees and title embossed on its leather binding.

"The Doctor in Spite of Himself. A fine selection," he said, chuckling over the humor of Monsieur Giraud's choice.

Feeling around the colorful, marbled end liner, his fingers came across something under the back cover. He picked up one of Biatris' cooking knives, then took the book to the hearth and removed the lid from a kettle of steaming water. Holding the book over it, he gently prodded with the knife's tip until the liner released and he was able to extract the hidden object. "Here it is . . . the letter I was expecting."

"From your Uncle Barjon?" asked Biatris. "The pasteur in Switzerland?"

Jehan scanned the letter, then looked up and nodded.

She raised her hands over her mouth, then steepled them under her chin. "You are making your preparations, then?" Her anxious eyes blinked, again and again. "To leave?"

Jehan had not anticipated such a reaction from Biatris.

"André warned me, just yesterday, that I might be called to join the militia, and I cannot bring myself to fight . . . for either side. So, it is looking like I have no other option agreeable to my nature."

Biatris shook her head and gazed down.

"I have no fixed designs yet," Jehan continued. "But I have asked my uncle to convey an estimate of costs for the journey and determine if his group would be willing to accept me. I know they want able-bodied men and women, but I must be sure there would be no animosities."

"Ani . . . mos . . . what is this, Sénher?"

"They may not be happy to receive me. There are more than fifty in their group who all share one small house, sleeping nearly twenty in a room." Jehan looked around the spacious kitchen. "Can you imagine, Biatris, if we slept twenty in this room?"

Moon-eyed, Biatris exclaimed, "Oh, *mon Diu! Non!*"

"And the Swiss are growing weary of supporting them. They may soon need to find another place." Jehan looked over the letter again. "Uncle Barjon has the costs listed here, yet it is still unclear if his followers have taken a vote to accept me."

"Sénher, *please*. Do not give up on your lady," Biatris pleaded. "Not yet."

"No, not yet," he assured her. "I still have hopes she will write. Although Aarau, the city where my uncle's group is, sounds like a beautiful land where I could live in peace and no longer be a burden to André. I believe the group would like to have me there, in part, because they know I have assets. But that is not enough reason to leave."

Jehan watched Biatris' eyes fill with tears, something he had never seen. She was always so undaunted and positive. Perhaps she would truly miss him, but she might also be afraid about her future, so he needed to assure her.

"Never worry, Biatris. If I do leave, there will be funds for you to remain on here at the château. And Benat, too. I want the estate maintained for my sister if she should decide to leave the convent and return home."

Jehan set aside the first book and stared at the title of the second. "*The Learned Ladies*. Just like Amelia." Surely this title was a sign it was time to write to her. She would appreciate the wit in using the book to conceal a letter. But would she know to look within the liner? If she did, and then found the blank parchment, she was intuitive enough that she would likely realize it contained invisible ink. But how would she know that holding it to a flame was the method for making it visible?

"Biatris, I shall retire to the library for a bit. I have some thinking . . . and some correspondence to attend to before supper."

She smiled and winked. "Oc, Sénher. So you will finally write your lady." She patted his cheek, then went to the cabinet and brought back two small dishes. After she spooned flour from a crock into one bowl, she put it into the empty basket along with the empty bowl, an artichoke, and the knife. Pushing the basket over to him, she said, "You will need these. I call for you when sopar is ready."

Nothing got past Biatris these days. Jehan was glad she accepted and supported his secrets. He took a deep breath. *Secrets.* During these times of oppression, secrets were the curse that bound his family of nouveaux convertis to her family of Calvinists—whether they practiced their faith hidden in homes, or barns, or chestnut *clèdes,* or caves. And it seemed the curse would not be over any time soon.

The sky had grown unruly and dark as dusk with the afternoon storm. Jehan lit a single candle that cast a warm glow around the library and settled in at his grandfather's desk. It looked more like a counter in the apothecary shop, with the writing accoutrements for surreptitious correspondence spread across its surface. He set to work concocting the special ink, dropping small pieces of artichoke heart he had cut into the dish and crushing them with a spoon, along with a little water from the washstand pitcher. It made him think of the simple times in the distillery room, times of experimentation, of learning old recipes and developing new. Times before he knew the joys and heartbreak that awaited him; times before the challenges he now faced.

While waiting for the words to compose in his mind, he slowly dabbed the quill several times in the liquid. He held his hand over the parchment for a moment, then the words started to form—carefully chosen words to avoid detection or implication, but words that expressed his love and concern.

Dearest,

My deepest wish is for you to be well and happy, and to have found the guidance you sought at Sainte-Baume. I have longed to hear of your safe return, but with no word, could only trust that your brave escorts and your intuition have landed you home unharmed and fulfilled.

You have remained constant in my thoughts and prayers, and now I must tell you that the activities we disdain, those that solicit violence, have been ordered to resume. An observer has been present among the Children, so I fear spending time with them would be unwise unless I am steadfast by your side.

Here I must make my full confession. What I feel for you is love, and I am utterly incapable of not feeling it for you. If I lose you, I lose my dearest friend. But my confidence in our love has held like a force that no one can move, and I feel destined to be by your side in peace and freedom someday. I do not know what God has in store for us, but we could weather the uncertainties together. I may soon be called to the militia, so if you should no longer wish for my friendship, I shall prepare to take leave.

Your Devoted Friend

Using the technique Monsieur Giraud taught, he folded the letter slightly smaller than the book and carefully inserted it in the liner that had been left unglued on one side. With the feather end of the quill, he mixed water into the bowl of flour, making a simple paste to seal the liner. Once the paste had dried, he reached for the inkpot with the visible, black ink and penned a message on the liner that he prayed to the good Lord she would understand.

To my dearest friend, the wisest woman I know, who has taught me to look deep inside. It is only with the heart that one can truly see. What is vital is invisible to the eye, but revealed by the flame of love.

CHAPTER 27
CONFESSIONS

22 March 1697
Dominican Prieuré Chapel, Genoüillac, France

The yule log had long since burned out and winter languished, bringing gray days, snow, and sleet with plenty of time for contemplation. Yet Jehan's thoughts were still as scattered as the dust that swirled around the prieuré chapel. Faceted early morning light punctuated the blackened wood of the confessional screen, but it failed to brighten Jehan's mood. He stared at the tiny particles sent aloft on the bright rays as Prieur Chabert entered the chapel.

Confession had been one practice of the Catholic faith Jehan was not eager to let go of, since it eased his guilty feelings. He had continued with the curé from Chamborigaud during his monthly visits to Château de Cougoussac's chapel. But it had been a long while since he'd confessed to Prieur Chabert.

Jehan had recalled Chabert's promise at the market the past summer—to aid him if needed. And, with still no word from Amelia, it seemed the time was right to confess his thoughts about leaving the country. Jehan fingered his rosary beads, worrying that Prieur Chabert's offer might not extend to concealing plans for such illegal activity. But, fortunately, he was a man dedicated to peace and perhaps would understand.

The confessional door softly moaned as the prieur closed it behind him and took his seat to initiate the ritual. Jehan began while Chabert intently listened to his confession—of his prideful nature of late, of not keeping his family's best interests in the forefront by dutifully joining the militia without delay. Some small bit of relief came to Jehan once he confessed the sin of pride. He could be accused of other, more serious sins; sacrilege for questioning transubstantiation, or divination for using the new healing skills Amelia taught. Yet he no longer believed these to be sinful. *Merely intelligent choices for those who value free will.* Still, it would be far too dangerous to confess such things, despite the closeness of his relationship with Prieur Chabert.

"You see, Prieur, I am profanely resistant to partaking in any form of violence, so I feel I might need to take flight to save my family from the Intendant's wrath."

Chabert showed compassion for Jehan's reasons. Then, in his own act of confession, he requested Jehan's confidence. "The circumstances of our world often overwhelm me with grief. I fear God's judgements for the continued intolerances and divisions will have many innocents caught in the midst, just as you were. Yet let us not put faith in the power of our problems. We instead shall have faith in the power of God to solve them. But he needs our hands and feet to do the work, so I am willing to do more for you than just look the other way. I shall discuss the purchase of your mills with the Bishop. Nonetheless, I do worry for your safety. I must ask that you continue your strategy of reengaging in worship at the prieuré on a somewhat regular basis. This will go far in keeping suspicions at bay until the time comes for you to leave. I shall contact you once arrangements are in place."

"God bless you, Prieur."

As Prieur Chabert left the confessional, Jehan's body crumpled; a falling sensation tugging him toward hopeless surrender. Must he really leave everything and everyone behind? Was it the only way? He pulled the silver Huguenot medallion from his purse and closed his hand around it while holding the rosary in the other, as if they could help him choose. But feeling tethered to both now only made his decisions more difficult. The Prieur's footsteps faded out to the cloister gardens, so Jehan rose, leaving the chapel to make the ride back to the château.

"Well, my fille. 'Tis done," he said to Luisant as he untied her from the portico column. He mounted and rode out the prieuré gates, knowing nothing could change what he had just done.

Recounting his words as he rode along, he weighed the soundness of his confession. He had been careful not to mention any of the false loans he and André had drawn up. Not about the one in November. Nor about the two others drafted and signed the past week after Pasteur Barjon had written again. Sharing such information would put André in an even more precarious situation. His cousin had already risked so much for his family, and now Jehan finally understood his moods and need to control.

Then fear hit Jehan as if he rode into a stone wall. *Has this been a mistake?* Would the prieur keep his confidence?

Through ordered logic, Jehan tried to quell the doubts, reminding himself how anxious the Bishop would be to gain better water rights for the prieuré. But his doubts sought to consume him. His mind rolled with horrendous outcomes, his stomach quivered. Amelia would have reminded him these doubts would create mountains, but faith would show the way. He faltered without her regular guidance. Maybe it was the many days of fasting for Lent. He felt open, and raw, and vulnerable. For all his designs, he still had little hope.

Château de Cougoussac, France

Though it was midmorning when Jehan arrived back at the château, heavy frost laid silence over the field along the Leuch River. Not a mouse or rabbit in sight. Yet, the river raged, swollen from the late winter rains, washing branches of fallen trees along with it. As he rode up the path to the château, he considered the flood his actions had now set in motion. Actions that might have a devastating effect on so many dear to him, possibly sweeping them into the prisons and galleys. The thought brought on a strange melancholy, leaving a hollow ache in his chest.

"Good day, Sieur," Benat called out as Jehan entered through the gate of the rear courtyard. "I have a delivery for you when you get your horse settled."

"I was not expecting a delivery. Perhaps it is some sort of supplies Biatris has ordered."

Benat ducked inside the stable then came out with a small barrel hoisted on his shoulder as Jehan dismounted Luisant.

"I'll take her from here now," Benat said. "Go see what delights wait inside your cask, then come tell me later while we continue some practice at cobbling. While we're at it, we can make a shoulder strap for your apothecary bag. I've finished pruning, so not much more to do till the ground thaws."

He transferred the barrel into Jehan's grasp.

"You are a good man, Benat. I am grateful for your discretion with my plans. And for the lessons."

When Benat learned Jehan had designs to leave the country, he had intensified his series of instructions, telling Jehan he must learn every skill possible to position himself in a *réfugié* community. The Refuge countries valued those adept in trades and crafts since they already had enough professionals of the healing arts, or law, or other pursuits of the highborn.

Jehan steadied the barrel on his shoulder while he maneuvered around Benat's dog—circling in search of a treat—then walked into the kitchen.

Biatris sat at the kitchen table, looking down, stitching and snipping on a pile of his clothing, with no reaction to the chill he brought in with him. "Almost done, Sénher," she said, not bothering to look up. "Many places to hide money now. See . . . in hem and in lining, here and here." She pointed out the various locations. "And a hidden pocket, just here."

Jehan set the barrel on the table with a thud, and she looked away from her work. He took the hand she had thrust into the hidden pocket and lifted it. Bowing, he kissed it and said, "I thank you, Mademoiselle. It has been an honor to have you in my household." He knew these moments might be some of the last to offer his gratitude, and in doing so, his shroud of sadness lifted a bit.

Her already rosy cheeks bloomed a deep crimson hue that spread over her entire face. "No one ever calls me Mademoiselle."

Jehan set her hand back on the table and patted it. "Now then, we have a delivery here. Have you placed an order recently?"

"No, Sénher."

"Well, then, let us see what mysterious contents lie within."

Jehan took a long iron cooking fork from a peg near the hearth and pried at the barrel lid. He moved the fork round to three spots, each time putting pressure on the handle. Finally, the lid released, clattering as it fell to the floor. He peered in and pulled out several handfuls of straw and a lidded rush basket. After opening the basket, he found more straw, then explored within until his fingers located a roundish object.

"Eggs," said Jehan, holding one up to show Biatris. "Who would send us a barrel of eggs? We have an endless supply from the coup."

Biatris reached toward a large stoneware bowl and slid it over. "I will help, Sénher."

He continued his search through the barrel while Biatris sifted through the basket, placing the eggs in the bowl as she found them. It was a bit of a hunt, but layered deeper in the barrel, buried well within the straw, Jehan found a few jars of honey.

"Castelbouc honey! Amelia! This is from Amelia." A lightness tingled through Jehan, and his vision blurred with the tears he fought back.

"Oh, Sénher. This is wonderful."

"Indeed," he exclaimed as he rustled around in the last of the straw. Surely there was some sort of letter.

"This last one . . ." said Biatris, examining the large brown egg, "*n'ei pas bona*. I fear it has gone bad. . . . no weight." She turned the egg over and over in her hand. "Oh, but look . . . a small hole." She shook it causing a rattle.

They looked at each other and smiled triumphantly.

"Surely it contains a note," said Jehan.

"Surely," Biatris cheered.

She cracked it on the rim of the bowl. Amidst fragments of eggshell, a bit of parchment, wound tightly into the tiniest little scroll, fell out onto the table. Her eyes widened at the sight.

Jehan picked up the petite letter, his heart racing as he unrolled it to its full size—a narrow strip about a hands-length long—then read it silently.

Forgive my delay in responding to your letter of August past. Within days of my return home, Menina was taken with apoplexy and palsy of the entire body until recent weeks when she regained use of all excepting her weak left limbs. Today is the first moment I found to open the book you sent and discover your message. Realizations have come twice over since we last met. In meditation in the cave of Sainte-Baume, Blessed Marie de Magdala asked me to understand the true meaning of friendship. As is her relationship with the Christ, it is a true love that goes beyond our human horizons. It is an eternal light as much as it is the flame that burns in us for each other. And Menina's illness has taught me to hold dear the time we have yet to develop that eternal connection, as angels of the Most High, before one or the other of us leave this physical realm. I would be most pleased to resume our work together as your chaste but loving companion. I shall be making visits to the ill and expectant mothers now that Menina cannot travel. Please come after Holy Sundays when there will be much to do and much to learn.

Blessings, your true friend. A

Jehan could not contain the smile that crept onto his face.

"Sénher? What is it? It makes you happy, I see."

At that moment, he was as joyous as a songbird ready to fly home after a long winter. "This changes everything, Biatris," he said, setting the letter on the table and reaching a hand toward her. "Please, be in no hurry to continue adjusting my clothing. I must go to Castelbouc, so I shall not leave the country at present. In my last letter to Amelia, I offered to help her tend to the sick, and she has accepted. 'Tis far too dangerous for her to travel alone now, so it seems my work here in France is not finished."

He would need to be patient, though, and savor his joy while he waited during the coming weeks until Holy Sundays had passed.

"But, Sénher, does this truly change things? Will trouble not follow you still . . . if you don't join the militia?"

In truth, it changed nothing for André and the family. Could he be indifferent to their situation for the sake of his desires alone? He felt the smile fade from his face.

"I shall provide André with a little money . . . in case he needs it to tie things over and keep my name off the list a little longer. It seems during these times, there are consequences for most any action I choose. So, for now, I choose to hold faith that I can be of charitable service here at home . . . without endangering anyone."

"You have a good heart, Sénher Jehan. I will hold hope for you as well."

"Thank you, Biatris. He rolled the little letter and placed it in his pocket. "I will write to Amelia so she fully understands my situation, then take leave for the chapel . . . and pray for us all."

His chest tightened as he tried to drive down his conflicting emotions. But he held on to the gratitude. Gratitude for a reason to stay.

CHAPTER 28
EDEN

30 April 1697
Castelbouc Gorges du Tarn, Gévaudan, France

Jehan stepped out the rear door of Menina's house onto the granite stoop. It was a simple entrance to the modest gardens. Yet, in his mind, the welcome was grand as any entrée to Versailles. A frog trumpeted with bellows and croaks, as birds of splendid colors fluttered about or sat on the *plessis* fences, performing their lavish melodies. The beds wore a wealth of spring flowers, and herbs, and cool weather vegetables like the threads of a courtier's emerald brocade gown weaving in and around each other.

It took a moment to spot Amelia on her knees amongst the profusion of plant life around her. She wore no veil, her light chestnut hair tied up at the nape of her neck with a few strands vining down beside her face.

Such a gentle gardener; she had transformed the plot so that native vines and greenery now cradled the ordered rows. Wild parts, tame parts, chaos, and rhythm all in one beautiful system.

As Jehan quietly walked down the path toward Amelia, Menina whispered from the doorway, "I'll leave you to talk."

It was good to see Menina doing better, though she now relied heavily on a wooden staff to get around, and her left side arm remained paralyzed. She shut the door behind him—heavy oak on rusted iron hinges making a long, low creak, then a dull thud. The sound silenced the birds and the frog, and caused Amelia to glance up. On seeing Jehan near the door, her smile outshone all the gleaming rays of afternoon sunlight that spilled through the sparse canopy of trees.

"Jehan!" She jumped up and brushed clumps of dark soil from the creases of her coarse hempen tunic. She rushed toward him, padding barefoot down the path, and took hold of both his hands. "I am so very pleased to see you."

He stood still, treasuring the warmth of her hands in his, the energy of life-giving loam still between her fingers. It was enough just to look into her eyes again. There, in those small compasses of color, Jehan had been guided to ancient and natural wonders. In their depths, he could see her purity and higher resolve, infinite and divinely influenced.

She gazed back up at him, her face smudged with soil, and he felt a euphoric connection to her secret desires.

"You say so little, Jehan, for one who has no shortage of emotion in his writing."

He could feel heat rush to his cheeks. "I am reading your eyes, Ame. Without speaking, they confess the secrets of your heart."

"And only *you* share the wisdom to read my heart. With this sort of wisdom . . . this knowing . . . a quietness often comes naturally. There is less need to say anything at all."

Jehan took her hands to his lips and kissed them. There was now such sameness of spirit with the two of them; now that they let love in, let it be no more than it was—simple, pure, uncomplicated— without expecting more. He held her hands to his heart, then released them with ease, allowing space in their togetherness. Jehan inhaled the sweet spring air that was somehow infused with the scent of new beginnings and Divine mystery.

Suddenly, the feisty frog began croaking again, distracting them, as if it needed some attention.

"You have created such a paradise here," said Jehan, gesturing. "I am amazed at how enormous things are, even with May still a few days on. The plants were not near this size last year."

"I have two secrets that have been used since ancient times. The first is . . . that I pay regard to the phases of the moon and also its position to the heavenly bodies. It takes a bit of learning, but I can teach you. Come to my cottage tomorrow and we shall study writings on the subject."

"I would very much enjoy that. Any knowledge to improve plantings is knowledge one should embrace."

"My second secret is very simple. I expand my love to the nature spirits of the plants. And to the bees and birds and worms since they, too, play a part in . . ."

The frog croaked again—louder, bolder.

They looked at each other and burst into laughter.

"And, yes, even to the frogs," Amelia continued, an amused singsong in her voice. "To all the living things that play a part in nurturing the land. While looking after Menina these past months since her apoplexy, I have spent far more time in her garden. It responds when I focus on the oneness of all creation . . . the life-giving force from the Creator that flows through us. 'Tis the same way for those who are ill or injured. They can be assisted by this same focus."

"Eden . . ." Jehan gazed out over the abundance. "This garden is a perfect little Eden. Especially with you here, mon Ame."

"Oh! That calls to mind something I picked up for you on my travels last summer." Amelia suddenly sounded as excited as a child. She tucked the hem of her skirts into her belt. "Wait here, I shall return in a wink."

Jehan watched her run into the house, then stared up at the azurine sky as he waited and listened—a drawer rumbled open, then it banged shut.

She appeared at the door, not quite in a wink, but nearly. "I was certain this would interest you." She nestled a loose strand of hair behind her ear while carrying a small book over, then sat down on a bench by the well.

"Something on new healing methods?" Jehan asked, coming to sit alongside her.

When she turned back the cover page of the slim publication, he saw it had stitched, heavyweight parchment for a binding instead of leather, and realized it was actually a lengthy pamphlet of some sort.

RECUEIL
D E
QUELQUES MEMOIRES
S E R V A N S
D'INSTRUCTION
Pour l'Etabliſſement
DE L'ISLE D'EDEN

A AMSTERDAM,
Chez HENRY DESBORDES, dans
le Kalver-Straat, prés le Dam.
M. DC. LXXXIX.

"I found it at a bookseller's stall. You see, it is titled *Instruction for the Establishment of the Isle of Eden*," Amelia said, "to provide a place of refuge. It includes an entire memoir of a visit to a remarkable island near Madagascar in the Indian Ocean. Every splendid detail of this wondrous place is described." She turned a page and pointed. "See here . . . the author states 'Its bounty and beauty could make it pass for an earthly paradise.' I have not read the entire pamphlet, just bits of it. There is no winter, and the flowers bloom all year long. There are forests and freshwater streams, and a cornucopia of natural fruits, beans, and roots. There are fish and birds, and fertile soil for planting grains and vines, or sugar and cotton. All of this, but no venomous creatures or plant life."

He slid a hand under hers, helping her support the pamphlet as she turned another page. "Astonishing." Now that she agreed to see him again, he had no intention to leave France unless he was required to serve in the militia, but he wanted to indulge whatever vision she had. "Tell me more."

She scanned over the page for a moment. "Here, the author calls for colonists who desire 'a society composed of honest men, established in a fertile and agreeable place with the blessings of health, liberty, tranquility of the conscience, justice, charity, and above all the hope of safety.'"

"It sounds ideal. Yet, I am not ready to leave . . . now that I have our friendship again. Although there might be brief times I cannot be here, these forests and this garden . . . they are *our* little Eden."

Amelia bit her lower lip. "You know, Jehan, *I* am not your promised land. You shall never find it in a person. And, with or without me, as long as you stay, you might never find the type of freedom you seek. Not with the looming threat of being called up for the militia."

Perhaps she was right. Had he stubbornly lost himself in some delusion? His mouth began to go dry and he could not bring himself to form words in response. *But no.* It was not denial. Foolhardiness maybe. He realized the risk but wanted desperately to keep the faith that peace would come soon.

She glanced down for a moment, looking through a few more pages of the pamphlet, then her eyes lit and she smiled. "I would be delighted to live on this Isle of Eden"

"You would think of leaving?"

"I could never think of leaving Menina. And I pray she has many more years to live. But if I were left alone in this world, it is the sort of place I would consider."

She ran her finger over the page she had turned to. "This says the project sponsors have worked out a generous plan to provide land and seed to those who have no money, in exchange for a tithe of the first harvest. And see what it says here . . . 'There will be a fund for daughters and ladies, who find themselves without relatives, to provide a house intended particularly for them, so that they can live there in an honest society by attending to works suitable to their quality. There will be a hospital established to support the poor, the sick, and the infirmed.' Perhaps that could be your contribution. To work at their hospital."

"But there is still hope for peace here. You have likely not heard, being so isolated here . . . there is a Protestant committee that has been meeting with William de Orange, King of the Dutch Republic . . . and England now as well. They have been asking that he only accept terms to a peace treaty with King Louis that include religious tolerance. We have no word yet on whether final terms have been decided, but the war seems to be drawing to a close, so we can keep it in our prayers."

"That would be a blessing . . . and a miracle to have religious tolerance again," Amelia said. "But if there is no such peace in this land, you might need to leave the country. Other European countries have strife and intolerances of their own. But, if you were to settle in a peaceful Eden such as this, you would be free from choosing a side."

It seemed hard for Jehan to grasp the Isle de Eden as a logical choice—traveling for endless months through many countries, over immense oceans on stormy seas—when, if he were truly ready to leave, in little more than a week he could escape to Switzerland and easily come home once peace resumed. Would she understand his hesitation? Suddenly they no longer seemed to be of like mind.

"I suppose . . ." His thoughts froze as he searched for their connection.

"Jehan," she broke in; her smile radiant, her eyes wide, excitement animating every part of her being. "It would make me happy to know you are safe and thriving. Doesn't it sound wonderful, living in peace on an island paradise?"

He had never seen her so aflutter, and he certainly did not want to try to settle her down on the notion. It was like asking a flame to not give light. She would have to come to it on her own.

"It does sound wonderful, mon Ame, but only if we were together."

She folded her hands over her heart, and her delighted face calmed to a serene glow. He could see the restraint she practiced for so many years came easily to her when she set her mind to it. "Let us pray for peace first though, and for Menina to live healthy and happy for many more years."

"Yes, and we shall save this splendid idea of escaping to Eden only for truly desperate times. For now, we have much to be grateful for here."

Her brows pulled together. "I must admit, my resolve to live in the present has waned since Menina's illness. You are right. We have much to be grateful for and much to plan for over the coming months."

Seeing the sadness come into her eyes was hard after she had just been so elated. He wanted to hold her in his arms, but instead, took her hand and held her with his eyes. The time had come to use the power of his words, just as she had taught him, and instill some hope, some encouragement in her. "Beauty surrounds us, Ame, and we can share our gifts with the people here. As long as we have a charitable purpose, we are blessed, and there is promise of a bright future. Where shall we start?"

Her cheeks lifted as a smile came to her lips. She sprung to her feet and began walking back and forth in front of the bench. "First, we shall make some rounds to see which families are in need . . . and which women are due to give birth soon. And, of course, spend time with Commandeur Timoleon at the Knights of Saint-Jean commandery hospital . . . for the fête, at least." She stopped and put a finger to her chin. "Hmm . . . and perhaps you would consider staying close by for Menina while I am on pilgrimage to Sainte-Baume in July."

Jehan admired her ambition and was thrilled she had come round. "Most assuredly. I shall reserve my usual room at the inn."

"If times are no longer desperate, is there need to continue our correspondence in a secret fashion?" she asked. "Do you think the delivery of eggs is a suitable method?"

"Eggs, yes. But, Amelia, now that I know they come from you, please do not endanger yourself by sending your honey. That helped me to know the basket was from you, yet it is easy to trace back to you. Next time I come, I shall bring a few of the château's messenger doves. We shall train them to do our bidding. Surely, that will be the safest way until this peace is official."

"Yes, that does sound much safer," she agreed. "The Children of God are using an olive vendor who travels the markets to spread word of the assemblies. He holds aside a variety called Sollier's Rougette from the rest of his products, so one must know to ask for them. So . . . shall we say . . . if you want to attend an assembly . . . you will purchase the olives, then send me a message by your dove about the meeting."

Sollier. The name seemed familiar. He stared off across the garden, trying to recall.

"Jehan. What do you think of that plan?"

He drew his eyes back to her and took her hand, hoping she had not felt unheard. "Yes, mon Ame, your plan is a wise one. On my way here, I twice saw soldiers patrolling the Route Royale. Though peace is near at hand, we can be none too careful when it comes to the assemblies."

CHAPTER 29
MAY DAY

1 May 1697
Amelia's Cottage, Castelbouc, Gorges du Tarn Gévaudan, France

A melia's cottage door stood ajar; the glimpse into her world of secret knowledge amidst bramble-covered stone walls beckoned Jehan in. He held a bouquet of muguet behind his back as he pushed the bark-covered door further into the room and entered.

A beam of light from the east window shone across Amelia as she turned around. Pristine now in comparison to her day in the garden, her face was luminous, the blue of her gown and star-covered veil vibrant as the spring sky.

Jehan presented the muguet with a bow. "I am pleased to offer my affections once again, mon Ame. Our tradition continues . . . our own Fête du Muguet on this first day of May. 'Tis quite remarkable that nearly a year has passed since our first meeting."

A little blush came to her cheeks. "Indeed. And a remarkable year it has been." She took the bouquet, added it to a vase of fragrant purple orchids already adorning the small table in the center of the room, then poured clean water into a washbasin. "Let us rinse our hands."

Jehan dipped his hands into the water alongside hers, lightly brushing them. Though he would always honor her wishes to remain chaste, he still relished the intimacy that they shared. It was his sacred challenge to love her, and be loved by her, but only in this way, allowing them both to heal and be healed. If he could, he would erase all distance between them.

Amelia turned to speak, her lips within inches of his, her breath caressing his face as she spoke. "Connecting with the phases of the moon taps into our deep desire to be in tune with nature. Are you ready to learn about planting to the phases of the moon?"

"Quite ready. As you know, my desire to connect with nature is very deep." The thrill of new knowledge shared by his beloved companion brought his mind to a hopeful place again, and he tossed aside any worries over threats that might force him to flee to some other Eden.

"I have pulled some references," said Amelia, "to help you understand the theories behind this." They settled in at the table, laden with stacks of tomes. "These by Newton and Galileo teach us about gravity, so someday you might want to read them. But all you need to learn for planting is actually quite simple, and goes back to ancient times."

Jehan leaned an elbow on the table and propped his chin in his palm, listening intently to her.

"Just as the moon's pull causes tides to rise and fall, it also affects moisture in the soil. 'Tis said that seeds will absorb more water during the full moon and the new moon, when more moisture is pulled to the soil surface. The seeds swell, resulting in greater germination and establishment of the plants. 'Tis best to plant certain types of plants during the waning of the moon and other types during the waxing."

"Fascinating," he said. "It makes good sense. How will I know which to plant during the waning and which during the waxing?"

"Annual flowers, and fruits and vegetables which bear crops above ground are best planted during the waxing of the moon . . . from the day the moon is new to the day it is full. As the moonlight increases night by night, plants are encouraged to grow leaves and stems."

Jehan wondered why everyone did not practice this easy method.

"So such plants as lettuces, basil, and cabbage. And apples and figs . . ."

"Precisely! And you will plant flowering bulbs, biennial and perennial flowers, and all vegetables that bear crops below ground, such as onions, carrots, and beets during the waning. From the day after the full moon to the day before it is new again. As the moonlight decreases night by night, plants are encouraged to grow roots, tubers, and bulbs."

"'Tis true. It really is quite simple."

"And if you want to bring more balance and precision, you can explore the newer theories presented in this manual by an Englishman on the best astrological times."

Jehan ran his fingers across the binding. "I have not learned the English language but I can make out the words astrologue, and herbs, and Nicholas Culpeper."

"Yet the plants are listed by their Latin names," said Amelia. "So you will still find it helpful. Perhaps you will want to study English or other languages you might find if you decide to go in search of Eden."

"Well, even if I do not go, knowledge of any sort might help me become as wise and courageous as you one day. So perhaps I will. Do you know why more people do not practice this planting by the moon? Did someone in the past declare these methods to be heretical or tied to witchcraft?"

"Menina tells me that is exactly what happened. During the period when huge numbers of women were sought as witches, and burned or drowned, certain male clerics and physicians looked for more reason to eliminate women from competing with their own healing practices. So they declared the women's practice of herbal medicine, including these planting methods, to be the sign of a witch."

"'Tis dreadful to think of it. I am glad you and Menina are here in the Gorges du Tarn where your secret garden is safely hidden behind stone walls and concealed by the mists, and where no one pays much attention to such things. I pray it stays that way."

PART THREE
The Reckoning

Nasturtium officinale: *cresson,* watercress

Latin, *nasus* meaning nose and *torquere*, to torment or smart the nose. The smarting sensation which its pungency causes to the nostrils has the effect of sharpening the senses, clearing the mind so that decisions can be made more easily. Applied with leaven it brings boils to a head. Good nourishment as salad, yet beware of lookalikes, *Berula erecta*, Lesser Water-parsnip and of *Oenanthe crocata*, Hemlock Water Dropwort which grows nearby; both are deadly poisonous.

CHAPTER 30
PROPHETS

14 August 1697
Mont Bougès Cévennes Mountains, Gévaudan, France

Spring had passed into late summer in what seemed a heartbeat. André had successfully used his connections to keep Jehan's name off the militia list, so he had busied himself with his healing practices and did not look back. Between assisting Amelia throughout the Gorges du Tarn and upper Cévennes, and attending Mass at the prieuré on Holy Days of Obligation to mollify Curé Gellion, his days had been full. He met Amelia at assemblies whenever time allowed, but already, the long days of August, as the hills turned golden, signaled autumn with the distant smell of burning stubble.

The next assembly was to take place at the wood of Altefage on Mont Bougès. As Jehan rode Luisant upwards on a crooked draille to meet Amelia and Cavalier, he recalled the directions. They had been neatly hidden in layers of waxed linen that sealed the Sollier Rougette olive crocks, just as Amelia had said they would be.

Sollier. Sollier. The familiarity of the name came to mind again, but he could not recall from where, so it must have been of little import.

Jehan's thoughts readily drifted elsewhere as he journeyed. He had been learning more about the Reformed faith at Lucrèce's prayer meetings and at the Children of God assemblies. But he saw marked differences between the two teachings and needed to carefully weigh which style of worship spoke to his own conscience. As much as he had tried to get past his early judgments and stay open to both, he still could not find complete solace in either. Yet meditation in nature always brought him close to the Holy Spirit.

Jehan reflected on the wealth of ancient knowledge that had been revealed to him here in the mountains, and felt grateful for discovering the reverent connections he had sought—and found. This was now his beloved place of refuge, a place to be himself, a place to spend time in service and by Amelia's side.

This land had offered a haven to many like himself, but he could not deny that the new roads built for the King's troops now threatened the sanctity of the Cévennes and the lower Gévaudan. He had already spotted a couple of soldiers on patrol, far below, on the portion of the Route Royale that ran along the Tarn River, but he was safe at these heights. If the persecutions worsened, and he was forced to flee, it was this magical land he would miss most, far more than his elegant homes and properties.

But for now, there was sickness to attend to and babies for Amelia to deliver—in homes of Reformed, and Catholic, and Jewish, and Saracen families, and at the Roma camps. It did not matter the faith or ancestry; they were all souls in need and Jehan and Amelia were glad to be in service to them. He felt certain he had been born with these values; with a God-given love for humankind.

After Amelia had returned from her annual pilgrimage to Sainte-Baume, Jehan had spent time with her at the Knights' commandery hospital where Commandeur Timoleon had become his exemplar model. While there, Jehan had learned many new methods for diagnosing and healing, his journal of recipes and treatments now filled with new notes; on spare pages, in margins, and on scraps of parchment tucked between pages already full. The Commandeur had taught him to read a pulse, to reckon the level of ague, and to diagnose by the twenty colors of urine as to which diseases they indicated. Jehan's favorite, and often the fastest method, was to read one's health from the colors of the skin and eyes. Although the frères Hospitallers often turned to bloodletting for cures, Amelia had started to convince them her herbal remedies were all that was necessary.

As sunset neared, Jehan arrived at a clearing in the forest where several Children of God followers had already gathered in preparation. He dismounted Luisant, secured her to a tree, then adjusted the shoulder strap that held his apothecary bag neatly at his side. With caution, he removed his dagger from his belt and hid it inside his saddlebag. He was never quite sure he could trust it in the hands of the designated sentinels, whose poverty might drive them to steal it.

He secured the flap on his saddlebag and turned to find a new, unsettling development with the sentinels—they were armed. Two young men, older boys really, stood by with carabiners, watching him closely. Where would these poor shepherd boys have gotten guns? Jehan held up his medallion, and they gave him cocky grins, chins high, as if overly proud of their new authority.

Jehan surveyed the clearing, sensing Amelia was already there, somewhere among the people.

A figure in hooded cloak and breeches slipped from around a cart, as silent as a *fée*, silhouetted by the last shimmers of sunlight slipping below painted clouds. A voice, muffled by the hood, spoke. "I felt you near."

His skin tingled in response, her voice like a soft breeze caressing his soul. "And I you, mon Ame." He stepped close to glimpse her face.

She pulled down her hood, revealing a grave expression.

"Amelia, what is it?" Jehan took her hand, reading her need to settle some deep emotion under the surface of her usual calm, dauntless nature.

"So far, everyone has arrived safe and uninjured, but there is much to concern me tonight. The people have become aroused and agitated by fear. Word has come from Pasteur Jurieu in the Dutch Republic that terms of a peace treaty have been established."

"But I don't understand. Is a treaty not a good thing? To end this cursed war of nine years over and bring freedom of conscience again?"

"Yes, however, there were no terms for religious tolerance of any sort, as we had hoped. Or restoration of rights for the Reformed, or *any* Protestants for that matter." She tightened her hand around his. "Come, come, you will want to read the pamphlets for yourself," she said, leading him to a barrel near the cart labeled 'Dry Herrings, Dutch Republic'.

Jehan peered inside. Instead of herrings, it was filled with pamphlets from Pasteur Jurieu. He picked one up and glanced through the eight pages of printed and stitched parchment.

"Jurieu is the same pasteur that so many of the noblesse have been upset with," Jehan said. "When I met a group in Alais last year, they gave me a one-page leaflet that expressed concern that he would bring even more trouble for Protestants on the whole. I understand Jurieu's vexation at the Catholic church, but what he says here seems a bit of an exaggeration."

He smoothed the pages and read a few lines.

BE ON GUARD WHEN DEALING WITH POPERY; It can be said that, in this Religion, lying is everywhere, for anything goes when Seducing. It is a dreadful tissue of fables, lies, false facts, suppositions, frauds, double-dealings, and fake news.

"Some Catholic church leaders could be accused of such things, thought not all," said Jehan, thinking about the compassionate Prieur Chabert.

She reached over and turned a page. "There are other statements here of even more concern. See, here . . ." She tapped at the page with vigor, her brow creased in a way Jehan had never seen. "This Pasteur Jurieu says the other Reformed pasteurs who espouse toleration of all religious creeds have joined in a conspiracy against truth."

"Yes, I remember now," said Jehan. "He believes his own personal take on the Reformed religion to be the only true faith."

"This is a bigoted outcry against all who do not blindly follow Jurieu's teachings," Amelia said as she looked to the sky, holding her palms toward the heavens. "Against the rest of humanity! He is not allowing freedom of conscience, any more than the King."

Amelia's face had reddened, and now Jehan felt his own blood rise in irritation.

"I never thought others would believe such outrageous conspiracy notions," he said. "How could anyone who has suffered persecution embrace *that* seduction?"

She inhaled deeply and moaned, "Fear." She folded her hands in front of her chest and took another breath. "People want to be part of something . . . part of a cause. So they flock like sheep to powerful men, honoring them with great authority. It helps them feel less fearful, but it can lead to dangerous places. Jurieu is manipulating their minds and sparking fires by brandishing his own lies."

A stout man wearing a coarse dirt-laden overcoat and breeches, who had been standing close by, stumbled over. White liquid sloshed over the rim of the mug he carried as he snatched a pamphlet from the barrel.

"Jurieu *es pas taradièr*," shouted the man, shaking the pamphlet in Amelia's face. "He is no taradiddler. He tells no lies. *La vertat es la nostra*. Ours is true faith!" A huge, drunken grin spread over his dark, leathery face.

From across the clearing, a young woman called out, "Pay him no mind." She lifted her skirts of fine black linen and hastened over. "My father has been fasting for days, and drinking too much posset, and he understands little of the world, even when sober."

"No harm done, Mademoiselle," said Amelia.

Jehan no longer liked to judge a person by their clothing. It was such a risky notion and one could be misguided. But by the young woman's attire, she did not appear to be a peasant. And her command of the King's French confirmed she had some sort of education. "You seem to know more of the world. Perhaps you can explain to your father that Jurieu is lacking tolerance. True enlightenment would mean tolerance for all, not just a single creed."

She sighed with a nervous smile while she held her teetering father by the elbow. "I have tried. He is as stubborn as his mules and frustrates me to no end. He believes these assemblies are all the enlightenment he needs."

"Oc, *filha*. And drink *es bon*," said the man.

Jehan glanced into the man's mug. "I have long wondered what is in these drinks. Cavalier tells me they use henbane."

"On occasion, they do," the young woman answered. "It is usually just curdled milk with barley wine and spices. But now there is some sort of magic bread they set out for the Eucharist. Lately, it seems anyone who takes Communion falls into an inspired trance, not just those who drink the posset. So, beware if you partake."

"We are only here to attend to illness or injury," said Jehan. "So we won't be taking Communion. Though, I am wondering . . . I have also seen a brown powder being added to wine and used on those who have agitations. We are not permitted to come close when they are prophesying. Have you knowledge of what that might be?"

The young woman supported her father as he leaned in, very close to Jehan's face, and whispered in a raspy voice, "*Es pas bon, te farà dormir.*"

"He says it will make you sleep," the young woman translated.

Jehan looked at Amelia. "*Papaver rhoeas*, field poppy opium, is my guess. Not as dangerous as the imported varieties, but it will bring sleep."

She nodded. "Just what I was thinking. Shepherds and carders offer it to epileptics and restless children in mixtures when they cannot afford apothecary cures."

"'Tis all madness to me, but I am glad you are here to help." The woman struggled to hold her father upright. She eased him to sit on the ground and knelt beside him as he began to doze off in a soused stupor. "We have a longstanding divide in our family. Some of us quietly follow the Reformed faith under the guidance of the traditional pasteurs, and with these conservative inclinations . . ." She paused and looked around, then lowered her voice. "We tend to see the Children of God as false prophets and fanatics. We still want our babes baptized by the Reformed pasteurs, but the Children of God brethren reject infant baptism. They feel revelation is more important to save the soul. A sister of mine, who is a follower, once screamed at me after she had given birth, 'Let no Blackcoats come here. No pasteurs. No baptism.' I try my best to make no judgment. I would prefer not to be here, but I must come to keep watch after my father."

"That is most kind of you," said Amelia, her eyes expressing sincere compassion. "You are a devoted daughter. Let us know if your father's condition worsens this evening."

"*Benlèu, los fidèls seguidors*! Welcome, faithful followers!" The joyous shout of a man came from the far end of the clearing, just as night came on and the amber glow of horn lanterns appeared.

Jehan and Amelia turned to see a wooden and iron ladder-like framework—apparently a makeshift pulpit—being hastily covered with black aprons by Cavalier's friend, Rolland Laporte. A tall, boney middle-aged man stepped upon it. The man was dark-visaged and of a wild and mystic appearance, with hair hanging over his shoulders and missing his upper teeth.

Amelia leaned over to the woman beside her. "*Parlaràs lo francès del rei?*"

Jehan could make out that she was asking if the woman spoke the King's French

"A little."

"Do you know this man? I have never seen him before."

"Pierre Seguier," the woman replied. "But we call him Esprit. He serves in place of the pasteurs who've fled the country. We pray he will bring the Holy Spirit to us."

This Esprit continued his announcement, in a mix of the King's French and langue d'oc, full of energy and enthusiasm. "There are other *fidèl's* wandering near at hand. Let us *benlèu los*. Show them the way by *cante* Psalms 68."

The voices were few at first,

"Let God arise
let his enemies be scattered . . ."

but like a contagion, they rapidly grew in number and intensity,

". . . let those who hate him flee before him.
As smoke is driven away,
so drive them away
as wax melteth before the fire,

let the wicked perish at the presence of God . . ."

"I have not heard this one sung before," Jehan said to Amelia, folding his arms across his chest. "I have always thought it vengeful . . . not expressing the forgiveness as Christ would call for."

Amelia grasped Jehan's forearm, clearly seeking his full attention. "Jehan, if they are singing this, they might be preparing to fight. I have had strong intuitions of late telling me so."

Cavalier emerged from behind a group of men and strode in Jehan and Amelia's direction, singing the Psalm triumphantly with the others. "Awesome is God in his sanctuary, the God of Israel. He gives power and strength to his people . . ." He stopped as he came near. "There you are, Amelia! I wondered where you'd gotten to. Good evening, Jehan."

Jehan tipped his hat. "Does everyone fare well so far tonight? Do you need our assistance?"

Cavalier breathed deeply. "That is something we need to discuss. You see . . . they've asked that you no longer attend to the people."

"I do not understand," said Jehan.

"They have decided your laws of physics and medicine are unchristian. They are worried you will interfere with the inspirés when they preach."

"We only want to help," said Amelia. "But we will honor your wishes."

Cavalier gave a slight bow of his head. "Since you have come far, you may stay. Perhaps tonight, our inspirés will persuade you to finally join the Children of God."

Jehan leaned over to Cavalier as they walked, keeping his voice low. "Have you been keeping an eye out for spies tonight? Any sign of Fallere?"

"No, I've not seen him." answered Cavalier. "But I don't believe he could be the one reporting us to the Intendant. He seems so devout."

Jehan knew Cavalier was wise for his age, but his good heart often left him vulnerable. "Well, you know, a good spy would have you believe . . ."

Two women turned to shush them.

They complied at first, quieting as Esprit began to speak, but this time, it was in his own tongue. Jehan looked at Cavalier and signaled his confusion, so Cavalier raised a hand to the women and shook his head, as he quietly translated for Jehan.

"Faithful followers. Children of God. By now you have read the news that the provisional Treaty of Rijswijk has been signed. But with no clause to return our right to worship, our hopes that William de Orange would be our saviour are crushed. Now that the soldiers will return from the front, they will be charged with waging more drag-onnades on us, and the horrors will escalate again. Pasteur Jurieu, in his pamphlets, tells us the End Times are near, and only God can deliver us from this oppression."

Esprit paused when murmurs swept through the hundreds of women and men that had now gathered, mostly young, with hardened hands and sunburnt faces.

When they stilled, he continued, and so, too, did Cavalier.

"Jurieu tells us that the Children of God should conquer the antichrist and bring the second coming of the Messiah. And, in his Mystical Manna writings, our sorrowfully missed Pasteur Brousson now agrees. My friends, the Kingdom of Heaven will be ours if we follow their guidance!"

Many in the crowd began nodding, confirming.

"Oc, oc!"

"Amen!"

But there were also those with stern, ambivalent eyes who looked askance at reactions from the others, or those who needed explanation before they agreed. Before long, nearly all heads nodded in agree-ment. Jehan wondered whether this was staunch belief or just the appeal of belonging to something bigger than themselves.

When the swell of people began shifting about, he noticed move-ment off to his side. He turned to see Cavalier's friend, Abraham Mazel, sneaking up on Cavalier.

Mazel leaned in from behind and poked Cavalier in the back ribs. Cavalier startled and turned, holding his fists high, his eyes wide and steely, reflecting his unflinching courage.

Mazel threw up his arms in surrender and squawked. "Amen, brother!"

"Careful there, Mazel," said Cavalier. "You know I am always on guard. I wouldn't want to hurt you."

They put their arms over each other's shoulders and broke out in laughter.

Mazel leaned his head against Cavalier's. "I acquired a bit of the Communion bread early. Want some?"

"No, Mazel," Cavalier said. His smile vanquished. "There will be enough inspirés before the night is out."

Esprit shot them a nod and a grimace, obviously annoyed by the disturbance, then resumed his persuasive speech.

Amelia leaned in and took over with the translation. "Our flock has been left without the pasteurs we favor, so now, the Holy Spirit must fill the angels amongst us. Let us listen for a message from tonight's inspirés . . . from the mouths of our youth . . . and our women. That is proof of the Holy Spirit, since they are uneducated and surely cannot possess the wisdom of our good Pasteur Brousson." She looked up at Jehan with an amused smirk just as Esprit stopped his discourse, then scanned the crowd in search of their next prophet. When he resumed, it was in angry bellows, but Amelia translated calmly, without the same outrage. "The King burdens us with more new taxes, driving us into poverty, then tells us we cannot practice our faith. Jurieu says we should take up the sword, and it is time we prepare. God is on our side."

Mazel began shaking, as if in response to Esprit's call. First his hands as if they'd gone numb, then his entire arms. "Owwwhhh," he moaned. "It burns inside me."

Jehan wasn't sure if he was fooling. Perhaps he really was in pain. He reached for Mazel, but Cavalier grabbed his arm.

"Leave him be," said Cavalier.

Mazel kept shaking his hands, then his feet. He arched his back and began moving and jerking as if in an odd sort of dance. "I feel it, friends . . . burning . . . I feel the . . . Spirit!" He wailed, then wriggled again. "The Spirit is in me!"

"Let us form a circle around him," said Amelia, "to catch him if he begins to fall."

Mazel shook his hands harder, and his head twitched about. "Yeow. Ooowwwh."

Jehan's chest tightened. "He is having some sort of seizure." He had no idea what ailment would cause a fit with this burning sensation.

A woman ran up with a mug of water and emptied a small pouch of brown powdered substance into it, then pushed it to Mazel's mouth. "Drink. Drink," she shouted.

Mazel shook about for another few minutes, then his head abruptly slumped, and he groaned as the movements settled. He folded slowly to the ground, like a young sapling wilting in the fire, with Jehan and his friends gently assisting.

Jehan did not care for the earlier directive to leave him be. It was something he simply could not do, and it would be on his conscience forever if he let Mazel die. So he quickly kneeled and checked Mazel's pulse.

Mazel sat silent as Jehan examined him, needing to pull open his closed lids to examine the irises.

"But Jehan," said Cavalier.

He held his hand up to Cavalier, hoping to silence him while he continued to work.

Mazel's eyes shot open, and he stared as if in a trance, mumbling, "I tell you, my children." Then he quieted again for several minutes, his eyes glazed over, while Jehan measured his pulse. In a sudden movement, Mazel stood, shouting, "I tell you, my children. My children, listen!"

Heads turned their way with hundreds of wide, expectant eyes on Mazel.

Esprit jumped off of the pulpit. "Rolland, come help me get Mazel up here."

The two moved through the whispering crowd and guided Mazel back to the pulpit as he muttered and moaned. They pushed him up onto the pulpit and supported him as he wobbled about.

Mazel looked over the crowd with half-veiled eyes, then inhaled and projected over the clearing. "My children!" His hands still twitched as he lifted his arms. "The fall of Babylon is near. The fulfillment of prophecies is here." He paused and looked around again. "I am prepared, with sword in hand, for a *camisade* to take back our land!"

The crowd shouted, cheered, and clapped.

"I can take this no more," Amelia cried out. She circled around the side of the crowd, and Jehan and Cavalier followed until she was near the pulpit. She tugged at Mazel's arm. "I feel the Spirit coming into me. I want to speak."

Jehan stepped near as Mazel stumbled off the pulpit ladder, and the woman who had Mazel drink from her mug rushed up to Amelia with a pitcher full of posset.

"They like it when the women speak," the woman said, animated with excitement, holding her mug to Amelia's face. "Drink now so the Holy Spirit will live through you."

Amelia pushed the woman's arm away and climbed onto the pulpit. Jehan could not guess what Amelia was about to say, but was impressed by her unusual boldness.

"People, good people." Amelia waited a moment until the crowd settled. "Hear me now. He who does not love, does not know God, for God is love! You have had hard times, I know. I, too, lost my father, a devout Calvinist, to the cruelties ordered by our King's Intendant."

The crowd grumbled, and she waited until they were quiet.

"But there has to be some way we can find to turn the other cheek. Love one another, even thine enemy. Repay to no one, evil for evil. It is written, vengeance belongs to God alone!"

The crowd suddenly stilled, with only whispers darting around the clearing. Some had understood and translated into the langue d'oc for others, then heads began nodding in agreement.

"We cannot control what happens to us in life," Amelia continued, "but we can always control how we respond to what happens to us. For those who do not wish for violence, you need not comply with this call to arms. You can rise above those who have killed and injured your families by choosing peace instead. Surely, there are leaders among you who want peace."

Then there was a deep grumbling, and a man shouted, "Oh, *fas cagar*! You piss off!" Gasps could be heard, and many brows raised until the man's unceasing rants set off a wave of jeers.

Amelia jumped down and pushed through the crowd, but her slight stature was getting swallowed below several tall men. Jehan caught up and reached in front of her, using his long arms to clear the way, then turned to see Cavalier moving around the outside of the crowd. They all reached the entrance of the clearing, where Luisant was tied, at nearly the same moment.

As she pulled up her hood and turned to Cavalier, Amelia's face flushed with frustration. "I understand the desire for revenge. I have struggled with it myself knowing the Intendant ordered my father's death before I was old enough to know him. Yet it is the people's fear and your magic drinks and bread that makes them desire to be martyrs with a violent end. There are likely prophets among these people, but it is also likely that it is not the Holy Spirit that comes to those who turn to these potions. You have told us there is sometimes henbane in the posset, but what exactly is this poison in the bread they are being fed?"

Cavalier looked around him, then answered, "They've not told me, but I believe it is *seigle ergoté*, the spiked rye. I remember talk of the rye fields being contaminated when I was a child. The poor were starving and ate it anyway, and ended up with Saint Antonie's fire. So, by accident, I think they've discovered, in small doses, that it brings these ecstatic moments."

Jehan worried over the deep anguish Amelia held in her eyes, knowing her heart must be torn open by this riotous disharmony so contrary to her true nature.

She slowly shook her head. "You know as well as I, Cavalier, we can only find enlightenment in the Most High, not in these outside influences."

"Yes, I agree," said Cavalier, looking shamefaced from under his lids.

"I feel there is nothing noble in your cause under this sort of leadership," she said. "But do as you may. 'Tis hard to reason with those who have fallen under the influence of fear. I am sad, though, for many of these people likely do not want to consume these things nor agree with the violence that is being encouraged. They only want to be part of something. To feel needed." Luisant whinnied and nudged at Jehan as if she understood the danger in staying, so he calmed her with a stroke on her nose.

"But Amelia, most of us here are in agreement. Only by showing power will we be treated fairly." Bitterness lingered in Cavalier's tone.

"You know, Cavalier, this stance is a dangerous one," said Jehan.

"I know, but we are preparing," he responded, his face now veiled with sweat. "For your safety, if you do not want to participate in our movement, you should no longer attend." He reached for each of their shoulders. "Amelia . . . Jehan . . .you are my friends and I will miss you at our gatherings. I beg you both to use caution as you leave. I've been watching and studying the dragoon patrols from the mountain tops. They have increased and will, more so, as the soldiers come home from the front lines. Remember, *les barralhos an ès è las parets aurelhos*. Hedges have eyes and walls ears."

"And so do spies," said Jehan. "Yet it is your trusted friends you ask to stay away."

Jehan untied Luisant and mounted her in haste. He left a stirrup open for Amelia's foot, and reached for her hand, hoisting her as she swung a leg over the horse's back and wrapped her arms around his chest.

He lifted one of her trembling hands and kissed it, then held it back against his chest. "We are blessed by the light of a full moon tonight. I shall take you home safely where you can sleep."

Jehan turned Luisant toward the path leading out of the clearing, and from the corner of his eye, in the feeble lantern light, he glimpsed a familiar face. He paused and turned for a better look. "Fallere," he said under his breath. How many times would his warnings to Cavalier go unheeded?

"What did you say?" Amelia asked.

"Nothing, mon Ame. I shall have you home soon." He cued Luisant to move on as the moon rose over the treetops, its silvery glow casting the way.

CHAPTER 31
HIDDEN FROM VIEW

16 August 1697
Gorges du Tarn, Gévaudan, France

In the few days since the assembly at the wood of Altefage, danger lingered in the mists. Divisions over religion had increased, and with rumors circulating of soldiers about, Jehan had decided to stay on at the Le Villaret Inn to be close to Amelia and Menina.

On the third day, in the early morning hours before daylight, a knock came at the door of Jehan's room, pulling him out of some frenzied dream; the details immediately forgotten. Could the innkeeper's wife be here to clean before cock-crow? He unbolted the door and opened it just a sliver to see two faces in the flickering glow of a single candle; young men, one lanky and golden-haired, the other stout with a moustache and a mass of tangled dark hair akin to Jehan's own upon rising every morning.

He blinked and squinted in the dim light. "Cavalier? Rolland?" he said, fighting the urge to throw them a minced oath for waking him. "What are you doing here at this hour?"

"We must speak in private," said Cavalier.

They huddled in the small room while Cavalier explained their urgency. Intendant Basville had posted a list of names; a condemning list reporting those who had purportedly attended the last assembly. Jehan's name was on it—along with Cavalier's, Rolland's, and others. Surely it was Fallere who had betrayed him. Betrayed them all. Yet it was his word against theirs, and it was their good fortune that the assembly had broken up before soldiers arrived. The Intendant had no real proof, but it had been a narrow call, so Jehan decided it best to head back to his Château de Cougoussac.

Cavalier offered an escort as far as the Pont de Quezac. "Safer in numbers," he said.

Jehan agreed, but had to get word to Amelia first. So, in the soft, gray pre-dawn light, as the cocks began to crow, he crossed the Tarn River to Castelbouc. It had been a dry summer, and the river was at its lowest, so there was no need to wait for the boatman.

Upon his arrival at Amelia's cottage, he found her already up, but in her morning gown. She helped him realize the folly in returning to the château. His homes would be the first place they would come searching to question him.

"Of course, mon Ame. I am not thinking clearly. I can only hope André and Benat will come up with something to explain my absence."

"If you wait to return, it will soon be forgotten," Amelia said, offering a gentle reassuring smile. "There are not enough soldiers to cover the entire Cévennes, so they will move on to catch easier prey in the act of their so-called heresy. I shall aid you in locating a place to hide . . . just until things settle."

"Ame, I cannot let you take that risk."

"Cannot? You know by now, my loving friend, my fierce protector, I do not follow anyone's commands."

He had no time to respond as she steered him outside.

"Wait by the old beech tree. I shall be ready in a wink."

In minutes, she had changed into her traveling clothes and packed a satchel. They quickly made their way along the path into Castlebouc to prepare for their departure. After rounding up the local baker's son to watch after Menina, and situating Romulus and Remus to keep guard, Amelia and Jehan were ready to set off.

Menina kissed Amelia's cheek. "Remember the place of our cere-
monies at Les Bondons? I trust you will be safe there."

"I love you, Menina." Amelia lifted her grandmother's frail left
hand and held it to her cheek. "We shall return in a few days."

"Oc, oc. Off with you now."

When they reached the river, they carefully hopped and lept over
large boulders, faintly glowing white in the dim light, and onto the
other side. As they walked up the path to Le Villaret Inn, they found
Cavalier and Rolland waiting outside, hands nervously positioned on
the pistols stuffed in their belts.

Amelia took a step back with a quick, deep inhale that made her
shock quite evident.

Jehan felt his brow crease as he stared at their guns, then shot a
fierce glare directly at Cavalier.

"We may need them for protection," Cavalier said, apparently
feeling the scrutiny and disapproval. "Don't worry, we are well
trained on how to use them."

"I have decided I should go into hiding," said Jehan.

"What about you two?" Amelia asked, not taking her eye off their
pistols. "What is your plan?"

"We're heading to a place Mazel and Esprit have set up on Mont
Lauzère . . . Bouzèdes hamlet," said Cavalier. "Join us. 'Tis the safest
spot until things simmer down."

Jehan looked to Amelia, knowing those two had markedly
disturbed her at the last assembly.

She glanced down, biting her lower lip, but then nodded, seeming
to acquiesce. "'Tis the direction we need to head. We can go with you
as far as it suits us."

Luisant. "I must get my horse," said Jehan.

Cavalier shook his head. "You'll have to leave her. The trails will
be too treacherous."

"Well, I must be sure she is tended to. Give me a few minutes."

Jehan stepped inside the inn and went straight to his locked room
to retrieve his belongings. He rummaged hastily through his saddlebag
for the necessary items, his heart convulsing as the seriousness of the
situation was finally sinking in.

The journal, writing tools, and Eden pamphlet—he stuffed into a hidden pocket on the inside right of his waistcoat. *The certificate of Catholic conversion*—into the outside right pocket of his justaucorps for easy access. *And the dagger*—that he had so foolishly left buried at the bottom since the night of the assembly, he tucked into the sheath on his belt. *But the Huguenot medallion*—his entrance pass to the assemblies, would have to stay. He certainly didn't want to be in possession of it if stopped by soldiers. So he dropped it into the saddlebag and covered it with his cravate. He filled his costrel from the pitcher on the washstand, then slung it over one shoulder, the apothecary bag over the other.

Daylight brightened the room through a small east-facing window, so he rushed downstairs and located the innkeeper near the kitchen. After explaining he needed to be gone a few days, they agreed on a payment to hold the room and stable his horse for several days in advance.

Jehan hastened out to meet his three companions just as dawn broke in shards through the silvery mists. Amelia and Rolland had stayed near the door, but Cavalier paced in the road, eyes intense, watching in all directions.

When they walked over to him, Cavalier stopped. "'Twill be fastest to head upriver on the road," he said, taking command of their little group, despite being the youngest among them. "Let's go."

"Wait," Rolland took hold of his arm. "On the road? Are you sure? That could be straight into the hands of Intendant Basville's Inspector General, Abbé du Chaila. He is stationed in Pont-du-Montvert."

"We'll use caution and only go as far as we can," Cavalier responded. "If we see soldiers, we'll head up the cliffs."

While Cavalier's confidence was undaunted, the discussion only brought pictures of a disastrous confrontation on the Route Royale to Jehan's mind. Yet he was certain Cavalier and Rolland knew the drailles, and caves, and woods better than anyone.

The road along the river was full of blind curves with steep gorge walls on either side, making it difficult to see very far ahead. They were a little past Espagnac when they nearly came head on with two soldiers as they appeared around one of the bends.

The men spotted Jehan and his party from a distance, shouting at them to stop. "Halt there! We must see your certificates of conversion."

Cavalier silently grabbed their arms and herded them back round the bend in the road, out of the soldiers' sight, then fled for the cliffs. He ducked behind tall broom shrubs and they all followed, quiet as stalking cats. They waited.

Within moments, the soldiers ran past and around the next bend, not realizing the group had left the road—the plan had worked.

Cavalier held a finger to his lips, then darted off. He knew the way and wasted no time ascending a draille on the steep northern slope of the gorge, serrated by centuries of winter torrents. Amelia followed right behind him, then Rolland. Jehan took the rear as the others scattered up the cliffside ahead of him at a fevered pace.

Before long, he lost sight of them as they moved into the treeline, covered in an eddy of fog. But he could still hear the sound of loose rock crunching underfoot, somewhere above. He took a right fork in their direction, onto an extremely narrow path—one better suited for a calm, persevering goat—and moved, light of foot, for several minutes until the clashing of water against stone, somewhere nearby, silenced their rapid ascent.

The high fog had easily concealed his location from anyone below, until—in a sudden moment—it was divided by a swirling wind, and strands of sunlight burst through. Jehan's chest tightened as his confidence faltered. His eyes darted around, looking for cover. To disguise his movements, he kept close to the surrounding trees. He would need to be vigilant and slow his pace to stay under the cloak of the forest's cover. Its deep greens and dark shadows playing against the gray stone cliffs gave some hope of staying undetected from below. He forged onward, taking heed of his positioning, until, several paces ahead, the narrowing draille came to an abrupt end at a sheer cliff, compelling him to pause.

Where are they? He had completely lost track of his companions.

A breeze whirred across his throbbing ears and caused his dark hair to flutter about his face, blocking his view and stinging at his eyes. He leaned against a tree to catch his breath. Trying to determine his best course from that point on, Jehan brushed his hair from his face and searched around the rocks above. Should he follow the others who had scattered up the cliffside ahead of him, or would he endanger them more by his presence?

A few drops of sweat trickled down his throbbing temples; one, then another. With no clear path forward, capture and condemnation seemed nearly certain now. Yet there was no longer any sign of their pursuers—no discernible sounds of horses or soldiers below.

A curtain of mist swirled in again and obscured his view, preventing him from determining the soldiers' whereabouts. *Perhaps . . . Perhaps they had eluded them all together. Perhaps the danger had passed.*

Then, as quick as it came, the undulating fog thinned once again, exposing a nearby waterfall cascading down the cliff wall. Jehan's fatigue gave way to a dangerous entrancement as he stared at the water. His eyes followed the water, down, down, down the steep cliffs, then spilling over the road and into the river. It drew his eyes to a cluster of stone buildings—a small village by the river's edge.

He could hear some sort of noise below. Sheep bells; faintly in the distance. Almost undetectable at first. Then he spotted the flock traveling downriver along the road. As they came nearer, the soft, tinkling cadence eased his tension a bit. But, little by little, the sound succumbed to a discordant, angry clanking and rumble. Something else was there below, but the blood pounding in Jehan's ears made it hard to know what, or who.

Suddenly, the presence of the King's dragoons became unmistakable when they came around a bend and into view uproad from the flock; a regiment of some fifty or sixty armed horsemen.

Jehan recoiled at the glimpse of their scarlet coats through the ebbing mists, flowing like flames from a dragon ready to devastate and devour. He froze for a moment; old trauma, trying to take control of his composure. Their foreboding noise echoed off the walls of the gorge as they charged past the shepherd and through the herd, forcing them off the road.

Regaining his senses, Jehan raced to the draille's end and climbed upward on the rock face and onto a small ledge outcropping. Backing against the cliff wall, his entire body shivered with dread, knowing his respite was over.

A gust of wind surged through the gorge as if to purify its stone walls of the approaching malevolence. It lifted a hawk towards its nest, only a few arm lengths from the ledge where Jehan stood clutching at the rocks for stability. He noticed the hawk's shadow dance on the sheer cliff face next to him and prayed its movements would not draw the dragoons' attention.

When he turned back to surveil their location, his right foot slipped off the narrow ledge. His fingers grasped wildly at the wet rocks until he had a firm grip. He hung precariously on the precipice, grateful for the strength with which he was blessed, praying it would be enough to endure. His arms began to tingle, causing debilitating despair to sweep through him, leaving him breathless and hindering him from continuing the ascent.

"Jehan." Amelia's calming voice whispered from above.

Thank God she is near, after all.

"Seek it in your mind's eye. Imagine your foot back upon the rock. Then envision yourself making your way up to me. Focus and 'twill come to pass. You have the power to close out the fear."

He looked up at her and his throat tightened. *Not so simple, this stopping fear.*

Suddenly, his body flinched, loosening small rocks under his once stable left foot, scattering them down into the gorge. He focused his eyes on the blank slate of the cliff face. As he took a deep breath, he tried to block out the image of his menacing pursuers.

With great care, he lifted his dangling right foot and tested a new spot on the ledge. It seemed sound enough to support him. Once he had his footing, he paused and turned again to monitor the dragoons.

A blazing streak from a lit torch sailed into the village chapel window below. Then came the sound of thrashing against wood. His eyes tracked it to a nearby house where two soldiers were kicking at the door until it splintered and crashed. Within seconds, they were brutally dragging the entire family out by hair and limbs. Jehan desperately wanted to come to their aid, but it would be a futile attempt at his distance.

His arms fatigued, the tingling turned to numbness. The ferocious pounding in his chest only added to his distress. Despite the soldiers' fixation with scouring the village, he imagined they could hear his heart thundering like a drumbeat, and the fear he had tried to dismiss only increased.

"Jehan," Amelia called again, breaking his rambling thoughts. "Have faith . . . they will not reach us here. The terrain is too steep for their horses." He glimpsed up to see her small, steady hand reaching toward him from the cliff's crest.

She had unraveled the truth that gave him the strength to forge ahead. *Renounce the fear. Envision a favorable outcome!*

She edged her outstretched arm further toward him, and her fingertips brushed against his hand. The energy of that touch and the radiance in her eyes enlivened him to move forward. *Just a bit more.* He hiked one leg up to a higher spot and planted his foot. *Must get her away from these barbarous madmen!*

Jehan grasped the rock above with one hand and took her hand with the other, then drew a calming breath to summon the courage from within and create the outcome he desired. *Freedom! How beautiful your promise.* With the potent aid of her sturdy hold, he thrust himself up and over the crest in one swift motion.

They rested in the hills just above the Gorges du Tarn. Jehan and Amelia sat on one side of the chestnut clède while Cavalier and Rolland sat opposite. Their strategizing had become a heated debate when Rolland had revealed that their destination, Bouzèdes, was the rebels' hamlet and that they were hoarding weapons there. Amelia would have no part of it.

Sunlight poured through the open window of the small stone building, indicating mid-morning approached. Jehan knew they were wasting time now. They had needed the rest, needed to pause for a few sips of water, but now they needed to make a move.

"This clède is the first place the soldiers will look when they realize we aren't back in Espagnac," said Cavalier, squeezing his hat between his hands. "Bouzèdes is the only safe place, I assure you."

"You cannot convince me to join you at this rebels' lair," insisted Amelia. "Not now that I know you are hoarding weapons. And I shall not tell you as such again, Cavalier. You are always pushing your ideas on me."

Jehan had had enough. "She has made herself clear, Cavalier. And I, too, cannot be a part of this. I am not willing to further endanger my family over your group's notion that violence will bring the second coming of Christ and enter you into the Kingdom of God."

"You see, Cavalier," Rolland jumped to his feet and barked. "*Never* trust a nouveau converti." He laid one hand on his pistol and shook a finger in Jehan's face. "If you dare breathe a word of this, we will remember you!"

Amelia cowered and looked teary-eyed at Jehan.

Cavalier leapt up. "These are my friends." He grabbed Rolland's shoulder with a warning in his eyes that was abundantly clear. "In spite of our differences. Do not get any ideas about hurting them in any way."

"I know a place we can go," Amelia said, her voice wavering with the agony of fear. "Up near the Cham des Bondons."

Jehan stood, then reached for Amelia's hand, helping her up.

Cavalier held out his arms in fidelity. "Forgive me, friends, for my unrelenting manner. Pasteur Claude Brousson returned just yesterday from the Dutch Republic to guide us once again. So, our enthusiasm for the cause has been renewed."

Rolland clinched his fists and his body stiffened. His gray eyes blackened with vengeance. "And he agrees with Jurieu that *now* is the time for us to be brave and bold. He says the crown of glory will be obtained for all those who will conquer, and that is what *I* plan to do!"

Cavalier turned his back to Rolland, blocking him from Amelia and Jehan. "If you decide to leave the country," Cavalier said, "get word to me and I shall make arrangements with Monsieur Rouvière for a guide. Besides storing weapons and food at Bouzèdes, it is an established point for making the flight to Switzerland."

"Thank you. I shall let you know," said Jehan, reaching out and shaking Cavalier's hand. "I wish you both well." Jehan turned and looked at Rolland. "Both of you. And I wish you the freedom of conscience you seek . . . that we all seek."

Amelia's eyes cast down. "Thank you both for getting us this far. The truth is, I am frightened by this talk of weapons. And I cannot be so far from Menina. She's all the family I have left."

Jehan mirrored Amelia's silence as they walked, sensing she needed time for quiet reflection. He knew her well now; knew what moved and enchanted her, knew what distressed and frightened her. It was evident to him this talk of rebellion had triggered her sorrow over losing her rebel father for the sake of religion. It had broken open her childhood injuries, bringing the fear of losing her family to the surface.

These long held wounds of abandonment, wounds they both carried, were strange; unlike the physical wounds they treated, these wounds were invisible yet refused to close completely, remaining tender when touched.

As Jehan followed her over undulating, windswept hills toward a rise in the distance, thoughts rolled through his mind; about these fears and how they might each release them. Amelia had guided him while he hung desperately from the cliffside, and it worked like a miracle. Was there something he could do to ease her mind? He had wondered once before why Prieur Chabert did not teach the power releasing fear could have. *Power withheld?* Perhaps Prieur Chabert had rendered subtle control over him by keeping him fearful. Jehan pushed his memory, trying to recall. Chabert had said 'let us not put faith in the power of our problems.' Surely, that was his way of saying there was power in releasing fear and worry. *But . . . the Children of God?* They actually nurtured fear, and it was spreading like a plague.

With the Gorges du Tarn falling behind them, Jehan let his

thoughts rest. He settled into the calm quiet of heathered moors studded with clusters of trees and yellow broom growing amidst limestone rocks. When they ascended a rise, they found a golden wheat field stretching out across the hilltop, and off in the distance stood three tall granite stones rising from the ground, about twelve pieds apart.

Jehan was curious, but said nothing until they came closer and he realized the stones were nearly twice his height. "These stones, they cannot be natural."

"No, but legends say they have been here many, many years. Menhirs. Standing stones from the ancient ones. Spirits of this land." She raised a hand over her eyes to block the sun and searched around. "I am hoping to find a certain cave. I have only been there once . . . as a child . . . with Menina and a group of women healers for a spring ritual. I remember the stones that we passed by . . . first these three, then there should be a group of six in the valley below, close to the entrance of the cave."

They wove down the far side of the grassy hill to a small wooded valley and located the six menhirs positioned at the juncture of two streams.

"It will be upstream a bit from here, but I am not sure which stream to follow," said Amelia as she pulled off her cloak and pushed it into her satchel. She looked around, studying the two paths alongside the streams, then set off on the one to the left.

Jehan tarried for a moment, noticing the red threads of the Roma tied to a branch across the stream, on the right path, but then hastened to catch up with Amelia.

As they continued upwards, the trees opened into tall grasses again and the Cham de Bondons plateau became visible. Near the plateau's edge were two *puech*, isolated hills, perched on top. They were light in color at the base, each topped with a ring of grass.

"Amelia, are these puech the reason this place is called Bondons?" Her cheeks lifted.

Finally. Jehan was relieved to see her lovely smile again.

She halted and set her satchel on the ground. "Yes, Jehan. Bondons, for bouncy breasts." Her voice held a bit of joy again, almost a giggle, and her eyes brightened. "You see, this is a sacred place. The ancient ones stood atop Mont Lauzère and saw these two puech as breasts." She swept an arm around the landscape. "And between them, the belly. They called this giant woman, *Mare Tèrra*, mother earth. The cave we are looking for should be somewhere below her belly. 'Tis said to be her womb. To honor her, the ancient ones erected the menhir stones as phalluses, near her womb and upon the plateau. And every year they came back to erect more. There are hundreds all across Les Bondons plateau."

Jehan reached for his costrel and offered her a drink. "Fascinating. And the ritual you spoke of?"

She passed the costrel back, and he let its quenching liquid fill his mouth while enjoying her tale.

"Until recent years, women would come here hoping to increase their fertility by sitting atop the stones. One of the local curés decided that mounting iron crosses on top would put an end to that, but he did not realize there were so many. I think he is the one who named this valley Malaval, the bad valley. And the cave, Malapertus, the bad passage."

Jehan could not help but smile, imagining the frustrated curé.

Amelia wore a frown of concern and her eyes began darting about. She paused, studying something off in the distance, then wrinkled her brow and continued looking around.

"I am sorry to distract you from your search, Amelia."

"It is not you. I . . . I think I am lost. The cave entrance *should* be near, but I do not see it."

"I saw the twisted red threads of the Roma near the menhirs. If they are still near, they might know the way."

They retraced their steps back to the juncture of the streams where the red threads were tied and took the right fork this time. Within a short time, they smelled wood smoke, and could see tucked off in the trees was a cluster of tents. Jehan thought it wise not to startle anyone by suddenly invading the camp.

He did his best golden eagle whistle, then called out, "Syeira. I am a friend. Are you there?"

"Who's there?" A gruff man's voice responded.

Jehan caught sight of several Roma peering around the trees, and sure enough, Syeira was among them. He saw her smile, then come out into the open.

"Jehan BonDurant," she declared. "My friend from Genoüillac. The one who gave us food and offered us work."

She took the hand of a young man who had come out to stand beside her and began walking toward Jehan and Amelia. The others also came forward and began chattering, many exclaiming their thanks to him.

"Jehan, I am happy to see you." Syeira's features had matured since they had met, some eighteen months earlier. "Please meet my husband, Manfri."

"I am delighted for you, Syeira," said Jehan. "It seems you have married well. And I am delighted to meet you, Manfri." He gave a quick bow of his head to Syeira's husband, who returned it with a smile and nod. Jehan then put an arm around Amelia's shoulder. "This is my dearest friend, Amelia Auvrey. We have come to ask for your help in locating a certain cave."

"Aaaahh . . . she is the first one," said Syeira. "From your palm reading."

"Yes, Syeira," Jehan said. "She is the truest friend and the purest love my heart will ever know. As clear and steady as the evening star."

Amelia looked up at him, her eyes brightening with a sweet smile of reassurance mirroring his affections.

They entered the camp with Syeira and Manfri long enough for Amelia to recount the story of their situation. After a short while, Syeira led them to the cave—not much further up the path—and left them to settle while she and Manfri set off to gather food.

Grotte de Malaval Cham des Bondons Gévaudan, France

Of all the caves Jehan and Amelia had seen over the summer, this was surely the most beautiful. Snow white crystals covered the ceiling, some spikey and long, some branching and lichen-like, all with droplets of water falling from them; others appeared like piles of snowballs stacked around the cave's floor. It was magical and pure. Nothing bad or *maléfique* about it

"'Tis a true blessing that Syeira was nearby with her family." Jehan tossed off his hat, removed the apothecary bag and costrel, then took off his justaucorps—now bearing soil and a few small tears—and laid it out for Amelia to sit on. The cool air of the cave penetrating his chemise was a relief after the morning of stress and exertion in the hot sun. "I understand now how the Roma must feel . . . needing to stay hidden, far from the view of zealous authorities."

"Yet you would never know it causes them any fear," said Amelia. "They seem so happy."

"Yes, they do seem a rather happy troop of souls. I believe Syeira is overjoyed to have found a husband to love."

Amelia sat cross-legged, then propped her elbows on her knees and buried her face in her hands. "I let myself slip into so much fear today." Her voice quivered between light sobs. "And it leaves me feeling separated from God."

"'Tis understandable, mon Ame." Her suffering, her anguish, was palpable and took hold of his heart, so he tenderly rubbed her shoulders. "'Tis our human nature. We were all in great fear today."

He hoped, with a little prompting, she might recall her own teachings and begin to feel stronger. "Tell me, how is it that you and Menina do not live in constant fear after knowing what happened to your parents? How have you overcome that so well?"

"I must be in constant practice." Amelia sat up, her eyes reddened from tears, and took in a few shaky breaths. "Fear is a choice . . . if we let our attitude, our minds, create pictures of future suffering . . . it diminishes our joy." She paused to wipe her cheeks with the back of her hand, then inhaled deeply. "It cuts off the flow of our vital life force and subjects us to a host of ills. You see how the Roma focus their attitudes on living cheerfully despite their situation. When we let our minds think of past dangers and calamities, it prevents us from being grateful for the moment."

Jehan could see a faint spark returning to her eyes as she shared. It helped to keep her talking, and teaching, so he continued with his questions. "I remember a phrase from Aristotle that made no sense when I first read it. 'We are what we repeatedly do.' Is that telling us that if we want to change our condition, we need to change our attitude and behavior?"

"Exactly," said Amelia. "We cannot live in perpetual bondage by our fears, but we can trust in Spirit and in the Sophia Wisdom to guide us." She took Jehan's hand in hers. "Let us close our eyes for a moment and focus all our thoughts on love and uniting our souls with the divine light of the Holy Spirit."

Several minutes went by while they sat in meditation. Jehan felt muscles throughout his body, taut as a hemp rope, begin to release. His mind calmed and he let go—even the worries over Amelia's tender state. Yet the connection to her was still there.

"I choose to release my fears," said Amelia.

"Amen," Jehan said and opened his eyes to see a slow, subtle curve return to Amelia's lips that assured him she, too, was feeling much better.

An hour or more had passed since Syeira and Manfri had gone to collect food.

Jehan knew Amelia must be as hungry as he. "Let's take our minds off our hunger and this accursed situation." He reached deep into the hidden pocket of his waistcoat for the L'Isle de Eden pamphlet. "I have been meaning to read more of this all summer. This Eden holds much promise and, at the moment, seems like a sound solution."

He took a few minutes to look over several pages, then read aloud about the exotic birds and giant turtles and coral and trees of ebony, cedar, and redwood. While he read, Syeira and Manfri returned, silhouetted by sunlight pouring in from the cave's entrance. They

walked with care among the rocks and other-worldly crystal forma-
tions on the cave floor.

Syeira set down a small soup pot and knelt to spread a colorful
cloth bundle that had been filled with blueberries, elderberries, chestnuts, dried cèpes, onions, chickweed, watercress, a piece of fried
bread, and several squares of linen. It was a feast from the bounty of
God's nature the likes of which Jehan had never seen.

"Thank you, Syeira," he said.

Amelia folded her hands at her heart. "You and Manfri are such a
blessing."

"You will need your nourishment to sharpen your senses," Syeira
said. "We all need to be wary in coming days. This food will clear the
mind so choices can be made."

Jehan recalled reading in his pharmacopeias that the watercress would
aid in this matter, and she had brought a large quantity of it. "Yes, with the
state of things, we will each need to make choices soon. Decide to join a
side, or hide like this for God knows how long . . . or flee the country."

"We heard you reading," she said. "Tell us more about Eden.
Manfri and I want to find someplace to begin our *familija*. To have
little ones."

In his arms, Manfri carried faggots of heather, branches of ever-
greens and white oak, and a large water jug. He crouched nearby,
setting down the supplies, and began preparing a fire. "*Va.* Yes . . .
place we no longer forced by King to hide. King's laws . . . bah . . .
hateful, and force us to always move."

"Our men," said Syeira. "They're ordered to life in prison if
caught."

"And wives to have heads shaved," Manfri added, putting an arm
around Syeira. "These laws worse than when Persian king banished
our people many, many years ago."

Jehan shook his head and huffed, appalled by the actions of the
man he must call his King. What Amelia had surmised months ago
was now so very evident. Louis—the so-called Great, the Sun King,
the Grand Monarch—himself lived in constant fear. Of nearly everyone, of nearly everything, of losing power. One fear playing into the

next. What else would explain his bigotry and drive him to order such horrid things?

Recalling some talk he had heard in town, Jehan realized just how much he had in common with the Roma. "I have heard the King's laws order Roma children to be taken and locked away in the Dominican schools, just as they do with Huguenot children . . . as they did with my sister and me."

"Yes, and that's why we must leave," said Syeira, laying out the berries on a square of linen. "But, for now, we are blessed. Many value our dancing and music and fortune telling, our *baxtali* . . . our happiness. They're not likely to report. Even the soldiers. But . . . we want to cast a plan."

Jehan and Amelia ate from the berries while Manfri lit the fire, then poured a little water on his hands, cleaning away the dirt. He offered them water for washing, then dried his hands on a square of linen and asked, "Your *cino ginadyi* . . . um . . . your pamph, does it talk of storms in Eden? Like Cévenol episodes?'

Jehan browsed over a few pages. "It says there are storms called hurricanes, but they do not uproot trees or destroy fruit as in the Antilles and Americas. The trees adapt by growing low and broad instead of tall."

Amelia yawned, laying her head against his shoulder. Syeira cleaned her hands, gave them each a portion of watercress and chick-weed, and began preparing a soup. Jehan continued to read aloud between bites, with Manfri sitting before him, attentive and wide-eyed.

Turning to the last page, Jehan found an elegantly handwritten note. "What is this?"

Amelia lifted her head.

"In the back, it says that a Monsieur 'le Marquis Henri Duquesne, the author of these Memoirs, was ceded the Isle of Eden for this project. It says he had everything nearly ready for embarkation when the donations were revoked and thus caused the project to fail . . . to the great prejudice of Monsieur Duquesne."

Jehan's shoulders sank. He should have known the dream of Eden was too good to be true. He looked back at the front cover, searching for a date.

"1689. I had not paid attention before to the date."

Amelia sat up. "Eight years ago . . . yet, surely there are other places."

"*Va*, there are," said Manfri. "At Marseille, I see many, many pamphs . . . tell of many, many places. Floride, Caroline, Irlande."

Amelia put a hand to her heart and looked at Jehan. "Surely there is an Eden somewhere. A place where there is only room for compassion and cooperation."

"I am not sure . . . what if . . . "

She tilted her head, smiling, with pure love in her eyes. "When we fully commit ourselves to our designs and believe, without fear, that we can do whatever we put our minds to, the grace of God shall be with us and, like magic, opportunities will unfold before us."

"It would be difficult to leave you, Amelia. Even for a short time." Jehan felt his heart tug, his breath catching in his chest.

She leaned her lips close to his ear. "My dearest friend," she whispered, softly and rather sadly, "My heart cannot contain everything I feel for you. I could not bear it if you were to abandon the peace and good fortune that awaits you, for my sake. You know I would never leave Menina alone. Yet, although I dislike to think of it, I realize she won't always be in my life. Like the Tarn River, God's plan has a natural course that changes over time. When she is gone, I shall have no family, only Romulus and Remus, but they, too, are getting older. If I am left alone . . . I shall join you in your Eden."

Jehan reached over and brushed Amelia's hair from her face. He wiped a smudge from her cheek and smiled. "One could start another Eden project. I have my money, and perhaps can find others who are interested." He felt a sudden weightlessness, his mind emptying of his concerns. "Yes! There *will* be another place for us to call home, and I *shall* find it. And Syeira and Manfri can join me if they choose."

Syeira and Manfri looked at each other with elated smiles. He lifted her, spinning her around.

"*Parikerav tut!*" cried Manfri.

"Yes, thank you, Jehan," said Syeira as she slid down out of

Manfri's arms. "We will go to Monsieur Narbonne's soon and wait there."

Amelia's eyes glistened with emotion. "I have been thinking . . . I should take Menina to the Knights of Saint Jean Commandery hospital, and we will live there until this unrest subsides. 'Twill be more secure than Castelbouc, and they may be able to provide her better care than I."

"That is very wise," Jehan said. "On my next visit, I shall be sure to bring a messenger dove to the commandery and begin training it for that location. I do not think the Intendant's soldiers, or even Fallere, will connect my name to Castelbouc, so I have faith we can return there safely tonight if we stay to the hills and mountains. We should wait until dark, after the last patrol, to cross the river. I shall hire a cart from the inn to transport you and Menina to the commandery. . . and see if the innkeeper has something I can use as a disguise so I can escort you on my way back to the château."

A faint look of amusement came to Amelia's face. "You could dress as a holy woman. And I . . . I could be some young shepherd fellow. You can wear my veil and one of Menina's old shifts."

Jehan's chest lightened, and he smiled. "I shall have to pin the veil across this stubbled face of mine, but I think it will work."

He could breathe again, knowing Amelia and Menina would be protected and cared for. It would make it far easier to reconcile the leaving.

CHAPTER 32
INTENDANT BASVILLE'S SAD MINISTRY

16 August 1697
Bastille's Office, Montpellier, France

"Once again, you failed me, Fallere." Basville caught himself clenching his fists, so he opened them and flexed his fingers to dispel the arthritic pain. "You must have fabricated some of the last names you gave me just to increase the reward. How are we to capture those barbets and force abjurations this way?"

"Nothing was fabricated. I cannot say for certain that all those in attendance at the assembly were Children of God rebels or even Huguenots. But they were all in the vicinity. My job is to provide you with information," asserted Fallere. "Not to capture anyone. That is lieutenant-general Broglie's domain and failure."

Basville caught his breath in disbelief. *How can this tawdry Fallere be so bold? And how dare he show up at my office, garbed in that livid green ensemble again!* "Broglie took this as far as he could. He sent soldiers to question these individuals and they could not come up with any proof of misdeeds. I cannot have Broglie's soldiers wasting their time. We need to increase the number of malcontents we execute or, at a minimum, force them to abjure. So we must catch them in action."

"Abjurations are not my responsibility, either. You have the Abbé du Chaila for that." Fallere lifted his chin defiantly. "And you will never encourage them by the methods he uses."

"So you suddenly have the courage to speak to me this way?" asked Basville, trying to keep his voice taut, composed, but the contempt boiling under the surface heated his face. "And you offer some newfound methods that you pulled from . . . where? From thin air?"

"I've been working amongst these people for two years now," Fallere responded. "So I can speak with some authority on what they will and won't respond to."

"I do not have to listen to this insolence." Basville huffed and stood, hoping it would intimidate Fallere into silence.

"You pay me for the truth, Intendant, so I shall speak the hard truth."

Basville raised a hand and wagged a finger at him, but could not think how to respond. A seed of self-doubt was taking root with each of Fallere's declarations.

"Intendant, what you need to understand is that, with their rights taken away and their pasteurs banished or killed off, these people have nothing else to live for other than their religion. Like a wolf pack, they will fight you till death. Don't you think it is time you changed your methods? You need to use a carrot rather than a stick to draw them in."

"I am merely doing as Louvois instructed." The thrum in Basville's temples turned painful as he caught himself defending his position with this little man. "Some years ago, he wrote that His Majesty wished the Intendants to push to the last extremity against those who want the stupid glory of being the last to give up their religion. And I've received no orders to the contrary since that time."

Fallere put his hands on his hips and squinted one eye. "But Louvois is *dead*."

"Well . . ." Basville began pacing, feeling trapped by his own oblivious loyalty. "I am certain Madame de Maintenon prefers us to continue, and she is my friend."

Fallere scoffed, "So you do this for your friend, who is likely the very one who manipulated the King into these extreme edicts and measures in the first place. She is a clever and skillful woman, I would say."

Basville stomped his foot. "Go, Fallere! Just leave!" He shoved Fallere toward the door while struggling for breath. "I no longer have need . . . of your services. Do not . . . show your face to me again . . . or you *will* go to prison."

"God-speed to you then, Sieur."

Fallere left shaking his head, triggering a primal urge in Basville to pick up the vase on his desk and throw it at the door: his hand instinctively wrapped around it, but then he held back. He clenched his jaw, wanting to retaliate for the man's defiance, but not wanting to appear the beast he was accused of being, so he endeavored to retain his dignity.

Drawing in a long breath, he wondered if what Fallere said held any merit. Had he, in truth, fallen prey to the wiles of Madame? Part of his plan was to rely heavily on her favor to secure his dream of a more important ministry at court in his old age. And both she and the King wanted the Huguenots put down at any cost. But had his own radical method of increasing executions been the very thing that hindered his success?

Even if it were true, he did not care for the likes of Fallere, pointing it out to him.

Basville's thoughts vacillated between his shallow breaths. *What a sad ministry and a sordid business for an old councilor—to be a burner of houses, torturer of women, executioner of the convicted.* He pressed his hands to his temples. *I feel as if I'm losing my mind.*

He stared at the stacks of orders and edicts on the credenza behind his desk and thought over each one he could recall, trying to reassure himself his actions were justified. After all, it was his duty to serve the King, and God, and follow the letter of the law. Although the law provided no details, no guidance on what punishments he should use —those were *his* choices, and he was proud of them. The King had left it to his better judgment and seemed pleased with his performance. Basville took another deep breath and counted the ways; he had perfected the dragonnade, dwindled the number of Protestants, and followed every wish of the King and Madame de Maintenon. How dare anyone fault him for the harsh treatments he ordered.

'Tis entirely the fault of those Reformed dissidents. Accursed Huguenots! Basville knew he would find a way to control them, one way or the other. But what he could not control, or justify was the heady rush from the hatred that lingered in his Jesuit-influenced heart —the hatred for all who practiced the Reformed religion. For as the Jesuit clergy had taught, the Reformed always infected the righteous with heresy. And that hatred is what would keep him motivated in his diligent service to the King.

CHAPTER 33
STORM OF THE CENTURY

17 August 1697
Château de Cougoussac, France

The château's library abruptly darkened, and Jehan raised his head from the documents spread before him on the desk. Through the open window, he saw turbulent gray clouds looming overhead, blotting out the sun. The wind rushed in; papers scattered into the air and drifted onto the floor. The sky crackled and flashed, forked lightning ripping it open. Moments later, booms of thunder echoed through the mountains, and birds darted out of the trees. Rain pattered on the window, and shouts rang from the fields as another flash of lightning cracked.

Jehan saw Benat running out of the wheat field toward the cart path, so he leaned out the window and called to him. "Do you need help securing the animals?"

"I very well may. Looks like we're in for an early Cévenol episode." Benat swept his head around to the pasture upvalley where the sheep and cattle were grazing. "I see a few of the tenants working them around toward the grange. I'll head on up with the dog."

Jehan shuttered the windows and sprinted downstairs to the first floor foyer where Biatris was busy lighting tallow candles. Light flashed through the windows like the eyes of a wild beast, and the house immediately shook. The charge in the air caused Jehan's skin to pebble, and he felt the hair raise on his arms.

"God's fury is upon us," Biatris said. She folded her hands and looked up, her lips moving in a quick prayer. "Could be many hours of darkness ahead, so I've saved beeswax candles for later."

"Very good. Now, I must go out and keep an eye on the mill and the water levels, but please, Biatris, for your safety, stay inside."

She bobbed a fast curtsy, so given to obedience. "Yes, Sénher. No need. I harvested vegetables this morning. Chickens in the roost, baking is done, and plenty of firewood in the kitchen . . . at least for a day or so." She paused and sighed. "I hope your Amelia will be safe."

"Thank you, Biatris. You are a blessing. I worry about Amelia, too. But she and her grandmother are in good hands at the Knights of Saint Jean commandery. They are strong, courageous women, and I trust they will make it through unharmed."

Jehan grabbed his hat from the console table near the door and darted out to the front terrace to see how Benat was getting along in the pasture. Working alongside two of the tenant farmers, he seemed to have things under control with the livestock.

The rain became heavier, streaming off Jehan's hat, and the wind stung his face with an icy chill. He headed out the main gate and toward the fields along the river, nearly slipping on the muddy road in his haste. Within minutes, his clothes were drenched and the air filled with the smell of raw earth. As he ran between the rows of wheat yet to be harvested, through puddles and muck, and on toward the mill, bells began to toll over the hill in Chamborigaud. They had already rung for midday mass not more than an hour before, so this had to be the warning for the Cévenole episode. When he listened carefully, he could hear bells in the distance, ringing up through several villages toward Genoüillac and Mont Lauzère. It would only mean one thing —the floodwaters were coming.

He came to stand at the river's high bank, to observe the situation, but it was still in its late summer state, merely a trickle. *Perhaps the mills will be spared.* The Cougoussac mill was somewhat protected from floodwaters, sitting on high ground and fed by a water channel cut from far upstream. But his two mills in Genoüillac sat directly along the river, so the storm could ruin his designs to sell them for travel funds.

The sky flashed, and the air filled with a pungent odor. His stomach began to feel heavy, signaling him to shift his thoughts before he fell into fear. He held no power over the wind and rising water, but he did have power over his thoughts and attitude.

In the moments he'd been standing there, the lightning became almost constant; crackling, clapping, flashing like an explosion of munitions silhouetting massive, black, billowing clouds. Spine-shivers suddenly ripped up Jehan's back when a bolt thrust down from the heavens, splitting an old oak nearly 40 pieds downriver, shattering it into huge pieces across the field. He knew he should get indoors. He might not be so lucky on the next strike.

The bells tolled madly now and the riverbed, nearly dry minutes earlier, bled a dark gray tongue of water that grew and grew. Within seconds, it was several feet deep and approaching the top of the bank.

The smell of thunder hung in the air as he raced back toward the house and entered the front gate. Benat was close behind with his dog —muddy to its neck—at his heels.

"Benat," Jehan called out. "Come through the front. No time to worry about the mud."

A tumult of rain pelted the windows of Jehan's second-floor chamber while they arranged the room as their sentinel post. Biatris lit the sconce candles with a rushlight and, in their trembling yellow glow, Benat rolled back the old Persian rug. Jehan opened the shutters to a front window and drew up three wooden chairs so they could monitor the château's lands.

The casements rattled and, outside, massive old trees whipped in the wind, branches cracking and falling to the ground. Fingers of water, seemingly from nowhere, streamed down hillsides, filling every crack and crevice until great waterfalls covered the surrounding hills and mountains.

Biatris pushed her chair away from the window and sat clutching her apron. Neither Jehan nor Benat could stay seated. They stood side by side at the window alcove watching as the river became dark as ink; a black brewing liquid with violent whitewater currents no living creature could survive, its vicious claws spilling over the banks and ripping across the floodplain fields in a wall as high as a horse.

Jehan's shoulders tightened and he began pacing the room, taking deep breaths, hoping to quell the fear. He moved back to the window and saw the rain continue in torrents, with a heavy fog forming along the hills. The river's roar began to compete with the angry thunder.

"*Mon Diu*! It gives me a fit of nerves." Biatris covered her ears and pleaded, "*Vos prègui, mes òmes*, come away from the window."

Jehan could see the waters getting nearer to the château. He knew telling the others would only increase their worry and wondered if his practice of focusing away from fear might help them all.

He closed the shutters and turned from the window with a nod. "The waters are holding well below the château walls. 'Tis a good time to envision that we will make it through this. The words we say and the thoughts we hold will be heard, so let us see, in our minds, the sun breaking through the clouds and all being safe and well."

"Like a prayer, then. You are right, Sénher. The storm is a sign of divine punishment. God is angry with those who persecute us. Nothing more to do. Only pray we'll be passed over." Biatris lowered her head and pressed her hands together.

"Seems as bad as an episode some years back. But we survived," said Benat in his stoic way. His eyes searched around the room as if looking for something to distract him from the storm. "Jehan, do you think Prieur Chabert will agree to your plan to sell your mills to the prieuré?"

Jehan pulled the other two chairs close to Biatris and sat. "I do. The Bishop agreed to a sale last summer, eager to improve the prieuré's access to the water canal. But I delayed, not being sure if I was ready. He so desperately wants ownership of the mills that I believe my delay . . . and my attendance at Holy Days of Obligation . . . is what has spared me from interrogation over my name on the Intendant's list. Well, that, and Benat's creative talk the day the soldiers came calling.

"I only told the truth, Sieur. That you were off to purchase honey and take remedies to the sick. I had no knowledge otherwise. They mumbled something about you not being the sort, then left."

"I thank you, nonetheless." Jehan nodded in appreciation. "And, for once, I am happy for André's persuasiveness. From what he told me, it seems to have served in convincing the authorities their spy had failed them."

Benat tapped a finger on his chin. "I would imagine . . . after this storm there will be farms and estates whose repair will be beyond the means of many. So, if you sell your mills soon, the Bishop likely won't be suspicious of your intentions. As long as Prieur Chabert keeps your confidence, the Bishop is likely to think you simply don't want to bother with repairs."

"Indeed," said Jehan. "God's timing is turning my loss into a true blessing, just as I am finally ready to go."

"Will travel not be dangerous, Sénher?" asked Biatris.

Jehan had to keep his vision clear and trust it would all go well. There could be no hesitation, no falling into a dark hole of fear. "Amelia and I had little problem evading the soldiers last week. We kept to the highlands of the causses and plateaus."

"Sieur Jehan." Benat leaned over and placed a hand on Jehan's shoulder. "Have you heard? There are terms for a peace treaty that might be signed and official any day now. And the returning troops have been ordered to the Cévennes. Are you sure it is the best time to leave?"

"I did know," said Jehan. "I saw it mentioned in a pamphlet from Jurieu."

The thought of the pamphlet filled his mind with images from all the tumultuous events of the past week. So much had happened, but it had finally brought him to fully commit to his designs. Now all there was to do was trust, listen to Divine guidance, and let the opportunities unfold.

Jehan clasped one hand on Benat's and took Biatris' hand in the other. "I have made my decision to go. Sending the soldiers into the upper Cévennes will bring more resentment from the rebels, and I will no longer be able to avoid the Catholic militia. It will look bad for everyone when I refuse to join."

Biatris grew sullen and pulled up her apron to dab away a few tears.

"The storm might be a blessing to me in yet another way." Jehan saw Biatris' brows lift in puzzlement. "While I hold no wish for devastation, it would aid my escape if the bridges are damaged. That would prevent the dragoons from making their way here and perhaps delay the inevitable confrontation with the rebels."

They all grew quiet and the sounds of the continuing storm came back into focus.

After nearly a quarter hour, Jehan could no longer bear hearing only the howling wind and rushing water, so he struck up the conversation again. "I sent word to my friend Cavalier just yesterday to arrange a guide. So it will not be long now."

Benat took a long breath. "I assure you, Sieur, I will look after the château . . . and I will try my utmost to protect Françoise, if she chooses to return. For now though, with this unrest growing, I believe she is safer at the Theyrargues Convent."

"Thank you Benat. I am afraid you are right. Funds will be left in André's care for maintenance, and my hope is that rent incomes will suffice as they have always done." Jehan felt his throat tighten and combed his hand through his hair—the nervous habit he thought long gone. "You will both be in my thoughts and I shall send letters through the bookseller. If any harm befalls me, Cavalier will be the most likely to learn of it and has promised to get word to you."

By half-past three in the afternoon, a blanket of darkness made for perpetual night. The incessant rushing and raging of water had lulled the others to sleep; surely a symptom of the distress they were under, Jehan surmised. Not able to sleep himself, he went to the library and built up a fire to stave off the draft. He collected the documents and ledgers in disorder about the room—everything necessary to make the sale of his mills, and land, and livestock—then placed them in a portfolio. He absorbed himself in preparing to leave; drafting a letter to Amelia to send out by messenger dove when the weather cleared, weighing which items would be most practical for his journey, and compiling a list in his journal.

~ Necessities ~
certificate of conversion
rosary
purse and coins
jewelry and gems found in grandfather's desk
apothecary bag ~ evaluate most crucial ingredients
satchel
change of clothing
cloak
tinderbox
sword
dagger
folding razor
soap
linen squares

~ For Nourishment ~
2 loaves bread
salted fish
dried figs
chestnuts
almonds
linen foodstuff bag

~ For Eden ~

grapevine rootstock
seeds of mulberry

The storm raged on through the night, but finally, he exhausted himself enough to move to the upholstered chair by the fire where he closed his eyes and drifted into a fitful sleep.

CHAPTER 34
IN THE AFTERMATH

21 August 1697
BonDurant Townhouse, Genoüillac, France

There was terror on their faces at the retelling. The entire family had gathered in the salon—André, Lucrèce, all three children— eager to learn what Jehan had experienced in the storm and what he had seen along the route from the Château de Cougoussac.

"How are the conditions now?" André asked. "Are the water levels still rising?"

"The rivers have receded, but they are not pacified. Several feet of swift moving water remain, capped in white tops. Mist hangs on the hills, with a drizzle of rain drifting about, and the air smells of things both living and dead." Jehan paused when he saw the two older children grimace at his description, but he needed André to understand the gravity of the situation.

"Did your livestock make it through?" André asked.

"I believe so. I saw a few dead sheep in the floodplain, but I think they came from upriver. There are massive piles of debris everywhere, rockslides and mud flows that brought down boulders and trees. And now the roads are blocked in places. No carriage or cannon wagon can pass through, perhaps only the smallest of carts. Along the river, entire sections of the road are washed away, leaving gaping holes that would swallow an ox, and entire trees are uprooted and flattened."

Lucrèce shifted, letting the baby slip off her lap and toddle over to join his brother and sister on the soft carpet. "Have you seen the mills yet?"

"Yes. They are badly damaged," Jehan groaned. The minute he had seen their condition, he knew he would never get the price he had hoped for. "Floorboards were lifted. Must have been from the force of the swollen river. And some of the wooden gears and bins are broken. The garden and hempfield along the river are destroyed . . . filled with sediment, and logs, and furniture, and barrels." He took a deep breath. "Do you know if everyone in town is safe?"

"We've not heard of any deaths here," said André. "But there were a few injuries. 'Tis the illnesses from molds that will come later that I worry about. From the window, we watched the river rise so high there were vortices enveloping entire trees that cracked and crashed into the bridges, blocking the flow. Water breached the walls along the banks and turned the roads through town into muddy rivers that thrashed against the buildings and slipped under doors, flooding the ground floor of nearly every building. Fortunately, ours sits just high enough that we were spared, but the water was within a few inches."

Jehan knew there could be no more delay. He had to sell his properties while it appeared he was motivated because of the damage—not because he planned to flee. "André. Will you speak to Prieur Chabert on my behalf as we planned? I would like him to meet us here tomorrow with his witnesses and the notary. I am ready to sell."

Lucrèce gasped, not being privy to the plan.

"Yes, without question. I think the time is right." André got up from his chair. "I have something for you. I shall be back in a moment."

"Sell what?" Lucrèce asked, her face gone pale.

"Do not be alarmed," said Jehan. "I will not sell the townhouse, or the château, or any of the lands or mill at Cougoussac. Only the two mills here in town, and the adjoining gardens and fields."

With a small book in hand, André came back into the room to join them.

Jehan turned to ask, "Did you find anyone to purchase the livestock?"

"Jean Roure dit Masson says he'll pay 500 livres for the Cougoussac herds," André answered. "Of course, you should hold back some of the livestock for the staff and tenant's personal use."

"I could not agree more," said Jehan.

André looked at the small book in his hand, then held it out to Jehan. "'Tis titled '*The Method of Treating Wounds made by the Blunderbuss and Other Firearms*'. I have never had an occasion for it, but you might need it one day."

Firearms. Jehan prayed he would never need the knowledge, yet at least he would be prepared. "Thank you, André, but my satchel will already be full. Nevertheless, I shall read it tonight and commit it to memory."

CHAPTER 35
ON THE THRESHOLD

22 August 1697
BonDurant Townhouse, Genoüillac, France

F rantic knocking at the front door of the townhouse caused every muscle in Jehan's body to clench, hardening around his bones. He looked up from his book and across the salon at Lucrèce and André, their faces contorted with alarm, reflecting his own concern. Had the sound come from the apothecary shop door, it might have been a soul in need of medicines. Though urgent, there would be no danger in that. And it was too early for Prieur Chabert and the notary.

Jehan rose from his chair, yet no one spoke. Dark thoughts choked his mind as he walked toward the window. They were all on edge after the storm, and the threat of increased persecutions hovered over the land like the Cévenole episode that still lingered. Neither were going away without leaving their mark. Yet, surely, it couldn't be mercenary dragoons, already back from the war and hungry for action, since they would have kicked the door in. The memory of how they treated their victims was still vivid. Jehan tried to abate his worries by telling himself it might simply be local soldiers checking on victims of the storm and looking for handouts of wine. Carefully, he peered down to the street from behind the salon window draperies.

"Lucrèce. Is that cousin Moyse? The man is covered in mud."

She jumped up and came to look. "I'm not sure. If he would just . . . remove his hat."

"Wait, he looked up," said Jehan. "'Tis him."

Jehan ran out of the salon and sailed down the stairs and across the foyer. He unbolted the door. "Quick, come in," he said, as he tugged at Moyse's torn and filthy sleeve. Jehan slammed the thick oak door and bolted every last lock. "Are you hurt? Did you get caught in the storm?"

"The dragoons . . ." Moyse panted, his face flushed and bearing dirty streaks of sweat. "They were at Mahlieres, near my farm. It's as if they rode in on the tails of that wicked storm, conspiring to be the death of us all. Instead of helping the villagers, they've been driving them to Mass at swordpoint and looting shops and farms. And not only the Reformed, but all the Catholics as well. Some of the soldiers are already back from war and, having had a taste for blood and destruction, don't care who they hurt." He put his head in his hands and slumped back against the wall.

"Here. Sit. Rest." Jehan guided him to the foyer bench and sat next to him. He began to examine Moyse, first for signs of blood, then for other injuries; prodding, palpitating.

"Yeow! Right there," Moyse said. "That spot on my wrist. Been throbbing since the roof of my house collapsed on me during the storm."

Jehan felt about a bit more, not finding signs of a break.

"Come next door to the shop. I'll make up a poultice."

Jehan took Moyse's elbow and assisted him to the inside door that led from foyer to shop. "You can tell me all that happened, then we'll get you something to drink and eat. And you can wash up."

Jehan looked around the shop at options for poultice ingredients. Without access to Amelia's special remedies, he would have to make do with the standard choices. He gathered a handful of fenugreek seeds, mixed in a tablespoon of mustard seed and a pinch of salt, and ground with mortar and pestle. The poultice was easy, and the bandaging went fast: creating the word amulet would take more time.

Moyse's brows pulled together. "I've lost everything." He took a long, shaky breath with a grim twist to his mouth. "When the storm came, I could not herd my sheep to safety before they were washed away down the ravine. My *cardage* building is gone, only a pile of stones and schist now. My house is flooded and nearly ruined."

Jehan found a page of fresh parchment and tore off a small square. He carefully wrote out tiny words and *charaktêres* to set the intention for healing—hoping to recall the correct ones—along with a few to relieve Moyse of his fear. He rolled the parchment and tucked it between the layers of linen and poultice he had wound around Moyse's wrist.

"Thanks be to God that my barn is on high ground," said Moyse. "Away from the ravine. I stayed there till it was over. But then I came out and saw the havoc down the hill in the village. Swords flying high, people running about, horses trampling everything. I could not bear to see if anyone got caught under hoof."

Jehan laid his hands over Moyse's wrist. "Let us say a healing prayer . . . *Quicumque vult salvus esse.*" Jehan closed his eyes and focused all his thoughts on gratitude and envisioning Moyse's wrist becoming healthy and strong. After a few moments of silence, he said, "*In Nomine Patris et Fili et Spiritus Sancti.* Amen."

"There." Jehan took his hands away. "It should feel better by morning. So, how did you make it here with the dragoons about?"

"Hid in a tunnel. Under the barn. I dug it years ago during the last persecutions. I waited until all the shouting and screaming stopped, then made my way to the other end. It comes out just inside the forest. I stayed on the drailles until I came into Genoüillac. 'Tis quiet out there, but someone has plastered a decree from the Intendant all about."

Another decree? "What now?" asked Jehan.

"It said the councils are hereby ordered to begin collection of new taxes for repair of the roads and bridges effective 13 September. And along the bottom, in bold letters, was 'One King, One Law, One Faith.'"

Jehan huffed, his jaw tightened. "Were it not that he wastes tax revenue on his precious Versailles, and on playing at war in hopes of taking over the world, there would be no need for another tax. I can find no respect for a leader that persecutes the citizens and drives the country into ruin." He sat down next to Moyse on the bench. "Come to Switzerland with me."

"You are fleeing, then?"

"Yes. I am not sure where I will settle in the end, or if I may even return, but I plan to start with getting to Uncle Barjon's colony. Would you like to join me? Surely, there is a better place that awaits us."

"I have little reason to stay." Moyse looked at his wounded wrist. "I am growing old, and I would like to live my last days in peace."

"I am awaiting word on the next guided departure date. In the meantime, you can stay at the château and help us with repairs after your wrist heals. Now, I need to get you upstairs and out of sight quickly. Prieur Chabert and his frères will be here soon. If they question your state and appearance, they will easily surmise you are Reformed. And Moyse . . . the children have already heard some frightening stories, so let us spare them yours."

Sunlight broke through the clouds at last, streaming through the salon windows. Jehan glimpsed bits of blue sky on the horizon and hoped it portended good things to come. He would breathe easier when this transaction was finally finished. He had sorted the documents of ownership and André assisted in drawing up the letters of sale that lay on the table before them. All they needed was to settle on the price and obtain the signatures from all the required parties in attendance.

"I am sorry it took so long, Jehan," said Prieur Chabert. "After having a few carpenters look at the repairs to determine the cost, I am afraid 450 livres is the highest I can authorize if I am to avoid the Bishop's scorn."

"That is all?" Jehan knew his family had paid far more for the mills and land some generations ago. "But revenues should pay for repairs in a fortnight, maybe two."

Chabert pressed his lips together and glanced at his folded hands. "I wish I could do more. I want to help, but with so many fields destroyed just as it is coming on harvest time, there will be little to mill this year."

The other men seemed to grow impatient. The two frères who came as witnesses began to whisper.

The notary gravitated toward the door. "Prieur Chabert, I have other sales to attend. We will need to finish soon."

André picked up the quill that lay between them on the table and handed it to Jehan. "As your *curateur alitis*, my recommendation is to accept this price. There likely won't be other offers."

Jehan looked around the room at their faces. The torment in Chabert's eyes made him realize he had to settle. Both he and Chabert would never be able to shed the anguish that would be created if there were any further tension between them. Jehan took the quill, dipped it in the inkpot, signed, and passed it to André. It went round to each of the men, and with that, Jehan's fate was signed and about to be sealed.

He walked to the window and stared out toward Mont Lauzère.

Chabert came up next to him and placed a hand on his shoulder while André showed the others out. "Please take great care, Jehan. Stay at the château until the time comes. You will be in my prayers as you take the path of your choosing."

Jehan turned to Chabert. He was a generous man, after all, sharing what power he had—not trying to take it away—despite Jehan's momentary fears.

"Thank you for being my loyal friend throughout the years." Jehan took the good Prieur's hands in his and looked him squarely in his eyes. There was no mistaking the earnestness of the man before him. "A person's religion, the cut of their clothes . . . none of it means a thing. Without the kind of compassion you have shown, there is no righteousness. Know you will be missed, Charles-Joseph Chabert."

CHAPTER 36
FIND ME IN THE STARS

22 September 1697
Hamlet of the Children of God, Bouzèdes, Mont Lauzère, France

Jehan silently ascended the *drailles* of Mont Lauzère, toward the hamlet of Bouzèdes, along with his traveling companions, Moyse, Syeira, and Manfri. The sun retired behind the mountains in a celebration of lavender and pink that would leave an impression of his beloved homeland emblazoned forever in his heart.

After the storm, it had taken a full month to organize the guides for the flight to Switzerland: tending to injuries and flood repairs or grieving lost loved ones had disrupted the lives of so many.

Throughout the journey ahead, Jehan's last moments with his family and friends would be keepsakes to occupy his mind. He smiled when he thought of his appearance at the prieuré's Sunday mass that morning—for good measure. It had given him a chance for a second goodbye with Prieur Chabert and an opportunity to bid good riddance to the old stone walls. The others had stayed back at the château, but by early afternoon, Jehan had joined them to satiate their appetites at Biatris' abundant dinner table where they were accompanied by Benat, André, Lucrèce, and the children. It had been a joyous last supper of stew with sweet onions, and truffles, and fresh herbs, a cassoulet, mellow cheeses and tapenade, pears, soft wheaten bread with honey, olives, and endive—then later—the bajanac chestnut soup to help settle their bellies. Biatris had told the travelers, 'I send you off healthy, and hope you never forget me.' And they had all agreed it would be impossible, not after such a tapestry of love. She had packed a foodstuff sac for each of them with bread, almonds, chestnuts, salted fish, and dried figs, then they had all said a tearful farewell—even stoic Benat who had reminded Jehan now was the time to keep his sword close at hand.

When Jehan's group reached Bouzèdes, Cavalier had already arrived. He held out his hands as Jehan approached, taking him by the shoulders, and they greeted with a hug and several pats on the back.

"'Tis all arranged, my friend," Cavalier said. "Your guides are here with their mules and everything you will need."

"I am in gratitude, Jean Cavalier. With your skills and stratagems, along with your compassion and willingness to compromise, you are a born leader, young friend. I believe you will serve the Cévenol people well, just as you have done for us."

"I pray for God's mercy that peace will prevail and there will be no need for my skills to be used for rebellion. But we shall see. I might be of a mind to join you in Geneva, myself, if things worsen. May your journey be a safe one." Cavalier clasped Jehan's shoulder for a moment. "I must go meet with the guides. They have arrived and are preparing the mules. You have some time yet, so you should rest a bit."

Jehan removed his hat and bowed his head to show his respect. Cavalier walked away and began a quiet discussion with the two guides as they secured their mule pack in an enclosure near an outbuilding. One of the guides rattled a lantern. There was a gentle crackle. Then a soft amber glow slowly grew, casting across their faces, illuminating their sober, watchful eyes.

Moyse pardoned himself and stepped away to say a prayer of thanks in solitude. Syeira and Manfri already rested on a boulder overlooking the silhouetted mountains and valleys of the Cévennes—land that fell, and rose, and fell again, tumbling into the blue waters of the Mediterranean, disappearing slowly into the nightfall. It was tranquil and magical to be on the mountain at night, with twinkling lights from Genoüillac and hundreds of other towns and villages fading into the distance. And it reflected Jehan's growing excitement for the adventure ahead. Surely, to embrace this exhilaration would be a good remedy for his trepidation over the unknown future unfolding before him.

While Jehan waited for Amelia and Commandeur Timoleon to arrive, he began unloading the contents of his saddlebag into a satchel. In the past, he would have worried over their delay; wondering where they could be, letting a little impatience and unease turn to painful anxiousness. But the Knights' commandery wasn't far, and Jehan clung to an indescribable assuredness that all would go as planned. He settled into the trust, holding steady in the faith.

With his task of unloading completed, he secured Luisant on the enclosure fence. Her coat shimmered nearly silver in the rising moonlight, and he reached out for its silken feel under his fingers. As he stroked her long neck, his thoughts evoked the cherished moments from the last few years, and he reflected on just how profoundly his life had changed in that time.

"We have had many adventures, my fille, and I shall miss you. But I leave you in good hands with Amelia." He pressed his head against the horse's neck, tussling with an emerging melancholy. "Take care of each other."

Jehan gave the horse a soft pat, then went to sit under the bows of an ancient oak on a broad, smooth boulder. He listened for the tree's voice as he studied its craggy branches against the moonlit sky, turning this way and that. It spoke of the beauty in resiliency—in knowing when it was time to change course, moving gradually in a new direction when there was a better way to go. He felt closer to the heavens at this spot on the mountain. And after the past year of his soul's remembering, he felt closer to the Divine.

Suddenly, his mind and body seemed suffused with Amelia's presence—he could feel her near. From over his shoulder, he heard the quick padding of paws on earth and heavy panting. He turned and caught sight of Romulus in the dim light, running toward him, tail high and wagging vigorously. When the handsome white wolf-dog reached him, he nuzzled against Jehan's arm, then rolled onto his back.

Squinting, Jehan tried to make out the shadowy figures in the distance. The large white cross on Commandeur Timoleon's tunic became visible, subtly swaying as he walked two horses toward the outbuilding and secured them near Luisant. Then, from the darkness behind him, Amelia appeared, stepping into the glow of the guides' lantern. She paused to speak to Cavalier and the guides, and after a few moments, one of the men lit another lantern for her.

Warmth radiated over Jehan as she walked toward him, soft light tumbling in golden ripples down waves of chestnut hair that laid loose over her blue linen gown, the tiny stars of her veil dancing on an azure sea of silk as she moved. How could he be leaving his beloved, beautiful friend? The world would be set right if only she could join him. He knew it was a sacrifice that they both must endure for the sake of Menina, yet still, his longing would never cease.

Amelia came to sit under the great oak, setting down the lantern and arranging her skirts to sit on the boulder beside him. She gazed at him with eyes as clear and steady as the stars in the heavens above. They sat that way in a long, profound silence, reveling in their peaceful connection.

Under the brightening stars, Jehan's thoughts eventually took voice. "There was a time, even after my release from the prieuré, when I locked myself in a prison of fear and anger. But you, mon Ame . . . you found a way deep into my heart. And I was freed through your wisdom . . . and your love. You have brought magic to my world from the very beginning. 'Tis like a magnificent flame entered my heart that outshines any darkness lurking there. And that very light will lead me on my journey, yet keep us always together. 'Twill shine across the milky way." He languidly swept his arm toward the sky. "There, in those millions of winking stars."

Amelia slipped her hand into his, with the gentle touch of a guardian angel. "Yes, my dear one. No matter where we are, when we look up at night, we will see the same stars and we can think of each other. In that way, our pure, loving friendship knows no distance."

Jehan placed his forehead to hers. "You have shown me how to be free, Ame . . ." he said softly, "in so many ways I never imagined possible. You understand my need for freedom . . . perhaps, better than I. You have blessed me by choosing a friendship far deeper than any we could find in marriage. And I will consider the space and time that separates us, as the place where our souls can dance freely on the winds of heaven, and create room so we may love even more."

She closed her eyes and drew a long breath, as if savoring the sweetness of the moment.

"I want you to have something from me, Jehan." From her pocket, she pulled a silver cross on a plaited leather cord and held it in her palm. "A word amulet, for your protection. 'Tis not only courage that makes us invulnerable, but the wings of faith as well. With it, abysses have been crossed, seas have been parted. So keep these words close to your heart, and you will have the faith to safely find your way to your Eden."

The simple cross illumed and glimmered white in the moonlight. Crudely etched around the perimeter were the words, *ha brachah dabarah.*

"I speak the blessing," he said.

"You've learned well, Jehan. 'Tis an ancient piece that Menina believes was used against the plague in the times of the Merovingians. On the back, you will see I have added these words . . . faith, courage, good health, success, joy, love. Whatever words you choose, the Spirit will listen, so choose them wisely."

Jehan held his hand to Amelia's soft cheek. "We both must realize, mon Ame, there is a chance we may never find each other again. But we can hold faith that one day we will thrive in an Eden . . . somewhere . . . someplace . . . where our souls can run free."

"For now, faith is all we have," she said softly and nestled her head against his shoulder.

He inhaled the sweet rose scent of her hair that brushed against his face. *For now.* That was all the assurance he needed to keep his hope alive.

There were no more words to say; only the cherishing of these last moments together. They grew quiet as they watched the hushed comings and goings nearby. One of the guides disappeared into a cottage and came back out, with three others following him. Cavalier signaled with a hoot like an owl and waved to come over.

Jehan looked at Amelia and smiled. "I suppose that would be my call," he said, standing.

He reached a hand down for her, and she sighed, picked up the lantern, and took his hand to rise.

They made their way over to the enclosure where the others stood. Romulus came to sit near Luisant and the horse bent her head down as if to greet the dog.

"They have taken a liking to each other this past year," said Jehan.

"Most certainly," Amelia responded.

"I would like you to take Luisant. You can look after each other."

"I will take good care of her, I promise you. I understand . . . the high mountain passes of the Alps would be far too dangerous for her." She lowered her eyelids, slowly bowing her head in a nod of gratitude until activity among the others broke the moment.

Cavalier was lighting another lantern, then went to gather up Moyse, Syeira, and Manfri and brought them over near the enclosure. He introduced the small group from the cottage, two men and one woman, who were hatmakers under the employ of a Seigneur Malbois, already in Switzerland with his wife. The guides were

Massip, a sturdy man of about thirty, and Stéphane, a slender, younger man with a head full of golden curls to rival Cavalier's.

"These are your false passports," said Massip as he and Stéphane handed out the documents. "Keep these on you at all times. Each of you will be provided with a mule for the journey. We move by night, then rest during the day. We have arrangements for lodging and meals along the way with those sympathetic to your plight. Our last bit of business before we go is to collect half the arranged fee. The other half will be collected upon arrival in Geneva. Please give your money to Stéphane."

The travelers turned over the required money, then mingled together, forming a large circle. Amelia set down the lantern, then took Jehan's hand.

"This is a prayer that will serve you well, my friends," said Amelia, closing her eyes and bowing her head.

Without a word, everyone took the hand of the one beside them until they were joined as one.

"Holy Spirit, Sophia Wisdom. Teach me to do thy will, for thou art my God. Thy good Spirit shall lead me forth into a rightful land." She opened her eyes and looked serenely around to the group of peaceful faces glowing in the amber light.

She took a deep breath and spoke again. "Whichever faith you choose to practice in daily life, know there is a *prisca theologia*: a single, true theology of wisdom that exists, which threads through all religions, and which was anciently given by God to man. Always look for that common wisdom, and live with understanding, tolerance, acceptance, and compassion, and there you will find the peace and love you search for."

Jehan could feel the air saturated with prayers and dreams for a better future. He turned to Amelia, then freely and fully, took her in his arms, and she responded in kind, wrapping her arms around his waist, laying her head against his shoulder. He held a hand to her cheek and pulled her close. They remained locked in their embrace with a feeling of oneness—with each other and with something far greater than themselves.

A faint whimper came from some of the mules as they began to get restless and shuffled about on the rocky ground.

"Time to go, my friends," said Massip.

Jehan kissed Amelia on her forehead for a long moment, then slowly, reluctantly released their embrace.

The guides began bringing the assigned mules to each of the travelers and helped them attach satchels and bags. As the other travelers got themselves settled, Jehan took his mule by the bit, tugged it over to a large rock, and after adjusting his sword, swung a leg over and hopped on.

While the guides assembled the mule pack and their riders in preparation for moving toward the draille, Jehan reached a hand out towards Amelia. As she held hers up, their fingertips touched for a mere moment until his mule jerked forward, following the pack as they set off.

Amelia softly laughed in her familiar way, sweet and silvery like magic bells. "You will not have much control over him. Not like Luisant," she said, her voice fading as the distance between them grew.

"Then I shall let go and have faith," he called back to her over his shoulder as he held tight on the reins and adjusted himself in the saddle.

When he turned around to see Amelia one last time, she was captured in a magnificent moonlight aura, mounted high on Luisant, her hand placed over her heart and tears sparkling on her cheeks.

"Let's get you home," said Massip to the group.

Your heart is my home, mon Ame. Until next we meet.

As their band of refugees set out over the narrow moon-lit draille with the milky way in a cosmic dance, leading the way, Jehan thought he heard her whisper back. *Find me in the stars.*

GLOSSARY

- *airetikos* (Greek): heretics
- *bain-marie* (French): water bath or heated double boiler used by apothecaries for distilling oils, named for ancient alchemist, Mary the Jewess
- *bajanac* (Occitan): soup of dried or roasted chestnuts, goat milk, and water
- *balandran* (Spanish): style of cloak with armholes and collar
- *barbets* (French): water dog used for retrieving game, often covered in mud; derogatory name for poor, illiterate mountain people
- *batelier* (Occitan): boatman
- *batèu tres deniers* (Occitan): boat ride is three deniers
- *bohémiens* (French): outdated 17th c. term for Roma, ethnic group originating in Northern India, thought to have reached France in the 15th c. via Bohemia; commonly lived a nomadic lifestyle and also referred to as Bohimans (Occitan), Romani, Roma, gitanes/gitans (French)
- *bona nuèch* (Occitan): good night
- *bons òmes* (Occitan): good men
- *bonser* (Occitan): good evening
- *camisade* (French /Occitan): surprise attack occurring at night, from Occitan word camisa, for white shirts worn by soldiers to recognize one another in the dark
- *carchofa* (Occitan): artichoke
- *cardage* (French): carding of wool
- *causse* (Occitan): limestone plateau
- *cazelle* (Occitan): shepherd's stone shelter with a door-less opening
- *Celtae* (Latin): Gauls of Gallia Celtica, according Julius Caesar, called themselves Celtae in their own language
- *Cévennes* (French): range of mountains in south-central France; name comes from the Gaulish "Cebenna", thought

to translate to "ridgeline", Latinized by Julius Caesar to Cevenna

- *charcuterie* (French): cold cooked meats
- *chatelaine* (French): decorative belt hook or clasp with a series of chains each with useful a household item suspended from it such as scissors, thimbles, watches, keys, and household seals
- *chemise/camisa* (French): men's shirt or women's shift
- *chignon* (French): hairstyle achieved by pinning into a knot
- *clos* (French): walled vineyard or garden of a monastery, prieuré, convent, or abbey creating the cloistered area
- *coif* (French): a close-fitting cap worn by both men and women
- *cordonnier* (French): shoemaker
- *costrel* (French): wine skin made of leather for traveling
- *cravate* (French neck band or scarf; cravat in English
- *curator alitis* (Latin): judicial measure wherein an adult between 18-25 years can freely manage and administer their property, but must be assisted by their chosen curator for all acts of immovable property (real estate) disposal
- *curé* (French): parish priest, rector, abbott
- *denier* (French): French currency; coin, similar to a penny; 12 denier = 1 sou, 20 sous = 1 livre (similar to a franc, dollar, pound)
- *dikhlo* (Romany): woman's scarf worn with hair tied in bun or two braids under it, used traditionally to signify she is married
- *dragonnade* (French): French government policy instituted by King Louis XIV in 1681 to intimidate Protestant families into converting to Catholicism; billeting of ill-disciplined dragoons in Protestant households with implied permission to abuse inhabitants and destroy or steal their possessions
- *dragoons* (French): mounted soldier or hired mercenary, often ill-behaved, named for the guns they carried,

carbines or muskets called a "dragon" because they were carved with a dragon's head

- *drailles* (Occitan): trail or pathway used by livestock farmers in the mountains of southern France for the yearly sheep migration known as the "transhumance"
- *épisode cévenol* (French): succession of torrential rains and floods when cold air from the Atlantic coast meets warm air from the Mediterranean
- *es pas bon, te farà dormir.* (Occitan): it is no good, will make you sleep
- *éstables* (Occitan): stables
- *féerie, fée* (French): fairy
- *fille* (French): girl; nickname for female horse
- *fontange* (French): hairstyle and headdress popular in the late 17th century, created by Duchesse de Fontanges, of hair curled high on the head over a wire foundation with starched linen frill and lace on linen cap; by the end of the century, women of most classes wore them
- *frère* (French): brother/monk, at a prieuré, monastery, or convent
- *gentilhomme* (French):gentleman
- *haute couture* (French):high fashion
- *Huguenot* (unknown):French Protestants, mostly Calvinists, who faced persecutions; primarily used in 16th-17th c. as derogatory name, but later became a badge of honor
- *In nomine Patris et Fili et Spititus Sancti* (Latin): In the name of the Father, the Son, and the Holy Spirit
- *Intendant* (French): appointed position, reporting to the Controller-General of France, who oversaw finance, commerce, and sovereign council (courts)
- *Juderia*(French): Jewish quarter
- *justaucorps* (French): long, knee-length coat worn mostly by men, but also women, in the late 17th c. -18th c., with buttons along the entire length of opening, and with stiff,

wide skirting that protruded in back and fitted sleeves with deep cuffs

- *lacets* (French): switchback on mountain road
- *langue d'oc* (French): Occitan/language of oc, known as lenga d'òc by its native speakers; a Romance language similar to Catalan; the original common language in southern France and of the troubadours
- *lapin* (French): rabbit
- *lappets* (French): decorative flap, fold, or hanging part of a headdress, of linen or lace; with long ties that were left undone in warmer weather
- *las claus d'aur e d'argent obren totes las portes* (Occitan): gold and silver keys open all doors
- *lăutari* (Romani): professional clan of Roma musicians; the term is derived from lăută, the Romanian word for lute
- *Lavandula angustifolia* (Latin):flowering plant in the family Lamiaceae, native to the Mediterranean
- *Levantine* (French): referring to residents along the eastern Mediterranean coast
- *livre* (French): (French): currency in late 17th c. worth one livre (franc, pound, dollar)
- *lotjament* (Occitan): lodging
- *ma poulette* (French): my little hen; term of endearment for girls
- *maléfique* (French): sinister, bad
- *me repentis* (Occitan): I repent
- mécontents (French): malcontents; term referring to Protestants in the Cévennes who were assembling despite royal decrees against it
- *Mélusine* (French): legendary féerie/fairy woman whose lower body turned into a fish tail when she bathed
- *Menina* (Occitan): grandmother
- *méreau* (Occitan): plural - méreaux; token of good faith; circular token which Calvinist Huguenots used to determine who was qualified to receive the sacrament to distinguish them from Catholic spies

- *mes bons òmes* (Occitan): my good men
- *métayer* (French): peasant farmer who managed a seigneurie parcel of land in a partnership with the Seigneur who paid for stocking the land; the farmer worked it and paid rent as a percentage of the yield in crops or money
- *mistral* (Occitan): meaning "masterly"; strong, cold, northwesterly wind, usually in winter or spring, averaging 40 mph and up to 115 mph; accompanied by clear, fresh weather
- *modes d'hiver* (French): fashions of winter
- *mon Ame* (French): Jehan's nickname for Amelia; also meaning "my heart/my soul"
- *mon Diu* (Occitan): my God
- *n'ei pas bona* (Occitan): it is not good
- *noblesse* (French): nobility
- *nouveau converti* (Latin): plural - nouveaux convertis; newly converted to the Holy Roman Catholic faith; often done only to avoid persecution while still practicing one's true faith in secret, such as the Reformed faith, Judiasm, Islam, etc.
- *oc* (Occitan): yes
- *pasteur* (French): Pastor
- *perdon* (Occitan): pardon
- *perruque* (French): wig or periwig; common in the 17th -18th c.
- *petanque* (French): game using heavy metal balls, (boules in French), meaning 'feet fixed' or 'feet planted' (on the ground) in which the objective is to throw or roll the balls as closely as possible to a small target ball
- *pieds* (French): measurement equivalent to one foot/twelve inches
- *posset* (French, English): drink made of milk curdled with wine or ale, often spiced and used as a remedy for colds or to relax for sleep
- *prieur* (French):Prior; priest in charge of a priory, convent, monastery

- *prieuré* (French): Priory; monastery or convent governed by a prior or prioress
- *Qual son aqueles dos?* (Occitan): Who are those two?
- *Quicumque vult salvus esse* (Latin): Whosoever wishes will be saved.
- *Reformed* (English): Réformé in French; originally, people or church of several Protestant groups to distinguish them from "unreformed" Roman Catholics; after great controversy over the Lord's Supper in the mid 16th c., the name became associated with only Calvinist churches
- *réfugié* (French): from Old French "refuge" meaning "hiding place"; in English, the word "refugee" was first applied to French Huguenots who migrated after the revocation (1685) of the Edict of Nantes
- *remember* (Occitan): remember
- *réseau* (French): net, network, web, or connection
- *sabots* (French): peasant shoe generally made from a single piece of hollowed-out wood
- *sage-femme* (Occitan, French): wise woman; a midwife healer
- *savoir faire* (French): ability to act or speak appropriately in social situations
- *Seigneur / Sénher* (French / Occitan): Lord of a manor, fief, or kingdom known as a Seigneurie
- *seigneurie* (French): Land, estate, and other property owned and governed by a Seigneur or Lord, which provided certain economic, social, judicial, and honorific privileges and obligations
- *solaire* (French): room in grand houses and châteaux intended as a quiet, private place for the family, especially for women; south-facing windows were required for good sunlight since the room was used for reading, embroidering, writing, and more
- *sopar* (Occitan): supper

- *sou* (French): French currency used in late 17th c. worth 12 deniers (penny) and 20 sols was worth one livre (franc, pound, dollar)
- *Tanta* (Occitan): Aunt
- *Transhumance* (Occitan): seasonal movement of livestock between fixed summer pastures in the lowlands and winter pastures in the mountains
- *va* (Romani): yes; ava is also used
- *valet de pied* (French): footman
- *vos prègui* (Occitan): please

In Relative Order Of Mention
HISTORICAL CHARACTERS AND MENTIONS

"Jehan" Jean Pierre BonDurant (Bondurant) 1677-1735 - minor noble born in Genoüillac, France. The spelling of the family's last name has taken many forms through the years. The BonDurant spelling is rare, but used here to remind the reader that the characters have been fictionalized. Although there is no record of his using Jehan, the Occitan (*langue d'oc*) spelling of his name, some of his ancestors did. It is used in the story as a nickname, and the pronunciation is very similar.

King Louis XIV 1643-1715 - King of France 1643-1715.

Curé Gellion - Parish *curé* (priest) of the Saint-Pierre Catholic church in Genöuillac.

Prieur Chabert - *prieur* (prior) of the Dominican Order of the *Frères Prêcheurs* (Friar Preachers) of Genoüillac.

Gabrielle de Barjon 1642-1695 - Jehan's mother and sister of Pasteur Guilliaume Barjon.

Jean Pierre BonDurant (Bondurand), (the elder), Seigneur de Cougoussac 1636-1694 - Jehan's father, a Protestant Huguenot noble who was staunchly resistant to forced conversion, and served time in the King's Tower in Uzès.

Pasteur Guilliaume Barjon - Jehan's maternal uncle and Calvinist *pasteur* (pasteur) who led a group of refugees in Switzerland and Germany.

Françoise BonDurant (Bondurand) 1681-1695 - Jehan's younger sister.

André BonDurant (Bondurant) 1664-1710 - first cousin to Jehan's father. Master apothecary, and Council member for the town of Genoüillac.

Lucrèce de Durand 1675-1710 - wife of André Bondurant. Lucrèce's children during the years of this story are Dominique - age 3, Pierre - age 18 months, little André - newborn.

Marthe Dollier (Brousson) unknown-1739 - second wife of Calvinist

Pasteur (Pastor) Claude Brousson. She used the alias name Madame Beauclose.

Pasteur Claude Brousson 1647-1698 - charismatic Calvinist Reformed *pasteur* (pastor) who risked preaching in the Cévennes mountains even after being exiled. He used the alias names Paul Beauclose or Olivier Beauclose.

Pierre BonDurant (Bondurant) 1607-1681 - Jehan's paternal grandfather and Doctor of Law.

Intendant Nicolas de Lamoignon de Basville 1648-1724 - French magistrate and administrator under Louis XIV who was steward of Languedoc for thirty-three years beginning in 1685.

"Colbert" Jean-Baptiste Colbert 1619-1683 - Minister of Finances under Louis XIV from 1661-1683.

"Louvois" François Michel Le Tellier, Marquis of Louvois 1641-1691 - French Secretary of State for War for a significant part of the reign of Louis XIV who claimed credit for inventing the *dragonnade*.

Madame de Maintenon 1635-1719 - King Louis XIV's wife; one of his closest advisers and influencers.

Jean Giraud - Huguenot bookseller from La Grave in the Hautes-Alpes.

William de Orange 1650-1702 - Prince of Orange, Stadtholder of the Dutch Republic, King of England, Scotland, and Ireland; a staunch protector and defender of Protestantsism.

Moyse BonDurant unknown-1699 - Jehan's distant cousin in his sixties, wool carder and farmer, widower with no children.

Marie de Magdala (Mary Magdalene) 1st century - follower of Jesus of Nazareth and apostle to the apostles; revered in southern France as one of the first Christians to preach there; annual pilgrimages to the Sainte-Baume cave, (where she lived her last years), have occurred since at least the 5th century.

Jean Cavalier de Ribaute 1680-1740 - from a modest farming family; worked as shepherd, then baker; compelled by persecutions to take up the cause of protecting freedom of worship for the Reformed Calvinist Protestant group in the Cévennes known as the Children of God; later becomes a primary leader of the Camisards.

Commandeur François Timoleon de Montaud Labat - Comman-

deur of the Order of Saint Jean de Jerusalem, Knights Hospitaller
Commandery at Gap-Francis, Mont Lauzere from 1695-1707.

"Rolland" Pierre Laporte 1680-1704 - a young wool carder from
Massoubeyran, nephew of Gideon Laporte; inspiré and upcoming
leader of the Children of God, gifted with preaching learned from his
other uncles who were Reformed pasteurs (pastors).

Gédéon Laporte unknown-1702 - Rolland's uncle from Branoux;
blacksmith and veteran soldier in the King's army; Reformed
Calvinist and upcoming leader with the Children of God.

Abraham Mazel 1677-1710 - wool carder from Falguières; inspiré
and upcoming leader of the Children of God.

Monsieur (Pierre) Rouvière - *nouveau converti* from a prominent
wealthy family of peasant elites who held dynastic influence in the
community of Fraissinet-de-Lozère. Opposed the Protestant rebels but
still secretly practiced the Reformed faith and had two sons who fled
for Amsterdam.

"Esprit" Pierre Séguier 1650-1702 - wool carder, inspiré, early
leader of the Children of God.

Massip, (Jean) - guide who assisted refugees to Geneva.

FICTIONAL CHARACTERS

Elisette - portrayed as the young niece of Marthe Dollier

Métayer Benat - land steward of Château de Cougoussac; Catholic

Biatris Gasquet - cook for Château de Cougoussac; Reformed

Luisant - Jehan's faithful horse

Jacques Arnaud - innkeeper of the Le Cristal Blanc Inn in Alais;
Reformed

Sieur Sollier, Seigneur de Naves - minor nobleman with a sericulture
and olive estate in the hamlet of Naves near Les Vans in the Ardeche;
Reformed

Sieur Monteaux, Comte de Laroque - wealthy count of Laroque,
west of Alais, with much influence in the region. Owner of successful
wool and silk spinning and weaving mills; Reformed

Sieur Raymond Brun, Seigneur de Entraigues - minor noble from

CHARACTERS

Entriagues, east of Avignon, with agricultural landholdings and mounting debt due to new taxation and failed crops; Reformed
Colette Brun de Entraigues - daughter of Sieur Raymond Brun, Seigneur de Entraigues; Reformed
Monsieur Fallere - young man who is the son of a successful truffle merchant from Montaren under the employ of Intendant Basville as a spy
Menina Elise - a *sage-femme*, (wise woman), healer and midwife for the Castelbouc area; "Menina" is Occitan for grandmother; Catholic but descended from Jean Rey who is based on an actual historical character - a courier who became a Cathar parfait
Amelia Auvrey "mon Ame" - Jehan's muse; Menina Elise's granddaughter; beekeeper and healer; free-spirited holy woman; her mother died in childbirth and, a few years later, her father was captured while participating in a Huguenot uprising, sentenced to the galleys, then died trying to escape.
Romulus - Amelia's brave, loving wolf-dog
Remus - Menina Elise's wolf-dog, brother to Romulus
Stéphane Laborde - guide working alongside Massip
Syeira - young Roma woman from a *lăutari* musician family; dancer and fortune teller
Manfri - young Roma man that Syeira marries; name meaning 'man of peace'

The Muse of Freedom was inspired by a French Protestant ("Huguenot") ancestor, Jean Pierre Bondurant, who lived in the Cévennes mountains of southern France, a crown of natural wonders, surprises, mystery, and contrasts. The region changes from place to place, making it a maze of winding rivers, deep gorges, caves, waterfalls, causses (plateaus) rich in limestone, heather-covered moors, and aromatic plants and herbs that provide nature's medicines. The slopes are covered with a variety of trees, depending on the locale. There are the sweet chestnut forests, *les châtaigneraies*, that were planted by early Benedictine monks and commonly known as the bread tree for providing sustenance. There are also white oak, beech, Scotch pine, and spruce for building, and the mulberry planted centuries ago for feeding silkworms. In the river gorges, life flourishes with beaver or birds of prey such as the peregrine falcon or the Bonelli eagle nesting in the cliffs. At nightfall, bats come out of crevices in the cliff walls. The ancient woods are a refuge to many wild creatures, from the stately, agile wolf down to a multitude of rare beetles.

The relationship with stone here is ancient and sacred, starting with the menhirs for worship and the dolmen and barrows for burials. From generation to generation, the ancient knowledge of stone working has been handed down and continues to be crucial to building homes, churches, and field walls.

The livelihood of the region's people has been diverse, since farming alone was often difficult in the rugged terrain where terraces are required. Sheep and goat herding has been common along with the keeping of *magnaneries*, buildings for the raising of silkworms, and chestnuts have been cultivated as a source of flour.

The mining tradition is old in the Cévennes, with iron and silver mining works being known since the Gallic period. During the Middle Ages, the bishops of Mende and lords of Sauve-Anduze acquired much wealth from silver galena veins around Mount Lozère, and the first coal mining occurred near Alès during the 13th century.

The Cévennes are located in the area originally known as Occitània. When it traditionally became a part of France, (in what was essentially a hostile takeover), it became known as Languedoc, and since 2016, as Occitànie. These terms for the region come from the name for the traditional language, Occitan or sometimes referred to as Provencal. The word Occitan comes from "òc" which means "yes". This was the original language of southern France and, being the language of the Troubadours, was the primary language in Europe during the Middle Ages. Of the many dialects and subdialects, the Languedocian form of Occitan is the original language of the Cévennes mountains region. So within the novel, it is referred to primarily as *langue d'oc*.

Being steadfast in their traditions, the people of the Cévennes have made for rebellious souls when others have tried to force change upon them. Even after the Ordinance of Villers-Cotterêts in 1539, when it was decreed that the langue d'oïl, (precursor to modern French), should be used for all French administration, the Cévenol people clung to their traditional Occitan language. Occitan's greatest decline was during the French Revolution, when diversity of language was considered a threat.

The ancestry of the Occitànie people, and the core of their religious beliefs, has been shrouded in secrecy for centuries, leaving much yet to be discovered. Thought to have melded into the culture over time are the Gabali Celtae (Gauls), Phoenicians, Romans, Essenes—the earliest Christians including Marie de Magdalen (Mary Magdalene), Lazarus, and Martha—Cathars, Francs, Moors, Sephardic and Ashkenazi Jews, Roma, Spanish, Italian, English, Scottish, and others.

Often referred to as "the Desert" by Reformist preachers, the Cévennes offered a remote place to live for those who chose to practice their own spirituality outside the strict confines of the Roman Catholic Church, begetting much diversity. The desert was a place of tribulations, temptations, and despair, but also a place to hear the word of the Lord. Over the centuries, periods of conflict and persecution were interspersed with times of limited tolerance, so living in this area kept most out of the watchful eye of the State which became the strong arm of the Roman Catholic Church.

There had been earlier conflicts in France between Catholics and Protestants during the late 16th and early 17th centuries that settled somewhat during a short period of limited tolerance when the Edict of Nantes was signed into law on 13 April, 1598 by King Henri IV, Louis XIV's grandfather. But by the late 17th century, France was once again a land deeply divided by King Louis XIV's lust for wealth, war, and tariffs and his insatiable passion for religious persecution, all driven by a goal of authoritarianism perfected.

Colbert, the Minister of Finances under Louis XIV from 1661-1683 was known for encouraging major public works projects, increasing France's colonial holdings, and working to create a nationalist balance of trade by instituting tariffs and regulations on goods and the trade guilds. This was the beginning of Louis XIV's focus on authoritarian control and what many French perceived as the loss of their independence. The new tariffs drove prices on imported goods so high that only the wealthy could afford them. And the retaliatory tariffs from other countries restricted the export of French goods, causing many trades to take huge losses.

After the death of his first wife, Louis XIV secretly married Madame de Maintenon, who became one of his closest advisers and influencers. She and the Roman Catholic leaders pushed for edicts to force Huguenot parents to educate their children in the Catholic faith. These efforts eventually resulted in edicts that allowed the Catholic clergy to forcibly take children from their homes to be held at the priories, convents, and monasteries by Franciscans and Dominicans.

King Louis's desire for absolute control led Louvois, the French Secretary of State for War, to institute forcible military enrollment of the nobility and gentry, (unless one had the money to provide payoffs in exchange), curbing the spirit of independence Louis and his advisors sought to extinguish. Louvois's *modus operandi* was discipline and complete subjection to royal authority. He claimed credit for inventing the *dragonnade* in 1681, which was the use of mounted soldiers, referred to as dragoons, to intimidate Huguenot families into converting to Catholicism. The ill-disciplined dragoons were billeted, (troop quartering), in Protestant households with implied permission to abuse and torture the inhabitants, and destroy or steal their possessions, earning themselves the title "booted missionaries".

Then in the year 1685, Louis XIV ended the Edict of Nantes due to the pressure and influence of the Roman Catholic clergy within Louis' circle and that of Madame de Maintenon. His Edict of Fontainebleau called for the Revocation of the prior Edict, and persecution of "heretics"—Protestants and anyone not of the Roman Catholic religion—escalated into renewed violence, causing many to seek *Réfuge*.

The King appointed Intendant Nicolas de Lamoignon de Basville, a friend of Madame de Maintenon, as the French magistrate and administrator for Languedoc beginning in 1685. He was extremely zealous and accused of significant cruelty in his pursuit and management of Protestants and others not of the Catholic faith.

In 1688, Louis XIV initiated the Nine Years' War (1688–1697), often called the War of the Grand Alliance or the War of the League of Augsburg. It was a conflict between France and a European coalition fighting the aggression of France which mainly included the Holy Roman Empire, the Dutch Republic, England, Spain, Savoy and Portugal. Fought in Europe and the surrounding seas, North America, and India, it is sometimes considered the first global war. The war, along with Louis's extravagances at his Versailles court, drained France's coffers to the point that new taxes had to be instituted to cover the cost of the war—just as famines were occurring from the two years of cold, wet weather in 1694-1695.

Just as the poor in many parts of France were starving, the ensuing destruction and atrocities from Intendant Basville's persecutions were creating divisions between neighbors and within families. The situation had citizens questioning whether they should stay in the country, or leave to seek refuge in a new land. As a result of the persecutions and the poverty, a mysterious spiritual resistance arose in the Cévennes mountains to fight the absolutism of the kingdom—both against the demand for religious unity and the new taxes that created an unfair burden on the poor and working classes.

This is the story of the Cévenol people during that time, some of whom chose to live in secrecy, some who chose to rebel, and some took the path of the *refugees*, fleeing the country by the hundreds of thousands, stifling the French economy in a way Louis XIV never could have imagined.

Author's Notes

The Muse of Freedom is based on many real historical individuals, events, and locations, using all the known facts I could locate. Although the settings often seem fantastical, they are actual locations with the exception of Amelia's cottage. Many still exist in much the same form as during the late 17th century, but the revolutions and wars that have plagued the area have destroyed some of the structures. Several characters are the creation of my imagination to bring a diverse, multi-layered experience to the story. But even the historical characters had to be used fictitiously, acknowledging that no one can ever entirely know the true story of bygone eras. That effort is rendered impossible by historical negation and revision to suit a particular agenda; by manipulated, exaggerated, or misinformed legacy stories; or by a simple lack of complete information. So, I took my characters on journeys that seem befitting based on my personal analysis and inspiration, hoping to give the reader an authentic experience of life during these tumultuous times.

I have taken the liberty to fill in gaps using extensive research on the history of the era, including religion, politics, inheritance and marriage laws, lifestyles, taxes, rents, the functioning of seigneuries, trades and crafts, agricultural practices, medical treatments and apothecaries, clothing, foods eaten and beverages consumed, status of women and marriage, education of children, weapons, biodiversity, geography, the ancients of the region, and more.

Details on plants, cures, and recipes in this novel are taken from various sources from the 1st-18th centuries and compiled to fit the story. (These can be found in the Bibliography).

Jehan BonDurant was inspired by an ancestor, Jean Pierre Bondurant dit Cougoussac, who was born in 1677 in Genoüillac, (Genolhac), France. His family members, dates of major life events, religious circumstances, status, homes and properties inherited, and the flight out of France are all found in historical records.

Previous researchers have noted there are records indicating Jean

Pierre was schooled at the Dominican Convent. From the interconnection of many strands of documentation, I have made a presumption—or rather a logical deduction—about his being *forced* to live at the Dominican Order of the *Frères Prêcheurs* Convent of Genoüillac (Genolhac) from age seven to age eighteen, (in the novel, I call the convent a *prieuré* or priory to prevent confusion, since many Americans think of a convent as a place exclusively for nuns).

It was a common occurrence, at the time this story takes place, for children of Huguenot parents to be taken from them and raised in priories and convents. A series of edicts under Louis XIV in 1661[1], 1681[2], and 1686[3], demanded a Catholic education for all children, and later, allowed the removal of children from Huguenot parents who refused to convert to Catholicism. Records from 1681 show Jean Pierre's father and grandfather made a *pension* (payment), to Francois Gay, *prieur* (prior) and trustee of the convent.[4] This payment occurred when Jean Pierre was almost four years of age, which was a common time for noble children to have begun school.

My belief is this payment merely reflected instruction by the Dominicans while he was allowed to live at home, but an incident occured later that hints at Jean Pierre's removal to the convent. Dragonnades were unleashed on the Reformed residents of Genoüillac (Genolhac) in January 1684, and within a few weeks, on 13 February 1684, the records show Jean Pierre was re-baptized Catholic. I believe this is the point at which he was taken and forced to live at the Dominican convent. Another clue about this comes from a statement by researcher Edouard Goulon Sigwalt, "*at the death of his mother he was 18 and lived in the midst of 'new converts' where they were put up with, apparently a site made of those of the R.P.R (Huguenots).*"[5]

Jean Pierre's parents remained Protestant and did not abjure until about a year later, after his eighth birthday.[6] Their abjuration came two months after the revocation of the Edict of Nantes, so they certainly would have done this to retain their rights. But it could have also been a failed attempt to have Jean Pierre released from the Dominican convent. I presume it would have failed since records show his father had a history of breaking the law, and it is unlikely that the Intendant would have approved Jean Pierre's release under those circumstances. His father was imprisoned in 1679 for a month in the King's Tower dungeon in Uzès, for reasons unknown,[7] but I embellished this by adding that he had been arrested for trying to stop the destruction of a Huguenot temple. This is the same period when Louis XIV first ordered them destroyed.

In my story, Jehan's (Jean Pierre's) parents had agreed to give up his sister, Françoise, to be raised in the Theyrargues Convent, a château owned by Marie-Felice de Budos, Marquise de Portes.[8] There is no evidence of this, and all we really know is the date of Françoise's birth. However, this convent is where many girls of Huguenot parents were taken. Marie-Felice de Budos was a powerful and notorious woman who had mercilessly tried to convert Reformed Calvinist Cévenols. She had dubbed the convent a "hospital" to justify her stated mission as providing alms, but her letters show that her real intention was to have a place to hold and educate *nouveaux convertis* children in the Catholic faith. It is possible that if Françoise had been taken to a convent such as this, then she might have decided to stay and take her vows. Further research into the convents in the region just might reveal this, but I will leave that to other genealogists.

I chose not to follow the common genealogy found in books and online for Jean Pierre Bondurant dit Cougoussac which states that he was left in the "guardianship" of his father's cousin, André Bondurant. I believe this might be a misunderstanding since I have found no records that specifically state this. I studied the only two records that make any mention remotely similar—the registration of the sale of mills and land in the local archives and in the records of the Dominican Convent.[9] They both use the term *"curateur alitias"* or *"curateur"*. It is important to note that *"curator alitias"* is not the same as a guardianship in France. The French word for guardianship is *"tutelle"*. This difference is explained on the French Ministère de la Justice, Minister of Justice, website. *"The person under curatorship, (curator alitias), can freely manage and administer their property. But it must be assisted by its curator for all acts of disposition,"* [10] (of immovable property - primarily land and structures). Traditionally, young people between 18-25 chose a family member to serve as their curator, but it was their choice. Another point—as mentioned earlier —Jean Pierre was not living with André in the months between his mother's death and his eighteenth birthday. He was already living in a facility with other *nouveaux convertis*. Perhaps there is some other document that refers to Jean Pierre as being under André's "*tutelle*" which has the dual meaning of guardian or tutor. We know André was, in fact, tutoring Jean Pierre in the apothecary trade, but there is nothing I found to indicate André was his guardian.

I also believe there has been some confusion on the profession of Pierre BonDurant (de Bondurant), the paternal grandfather of our protagonist, Jehan (Jean Pierre). Primary source archival documents, including tax records, state he was a "*docteur ès-droits*", a doctor of law, so he was a lawyer but not a physician.[11] [12] Some may have confused "ès" with "et" and the mistake has been repeated in various later sources. In the story, I represent him as a lawyer only. It was Pierre de Bondurant's father, Jehan (Jean Pierre's) great-grandfather, who was a physician, which is clearly indicated in archival documents.

I have used some creative license and placed the birth of "little André", the son of André Bondurant and Lucrèce de Durand in 1695 instead of 1696, where he fit into the story very nicely.

Another case of creative license is in my depiction of Marthe Dollier (Brousson), the second wife to Pasteur Claude Brousson. I mostly refer to her as Marthe Brousson so as not to confuse the reader. Women during this time in France did not take their husband's names, but continued to use their maiden name. From what is currently known, Marthe Dollier Brousson, (alias Madame Beauclose), was reported to be in Switzerland where she received a letter from her husband Pasteur Claude Brousson dated by him on 30 October 1695.[13] I chose to locate Marthe in Genoüillac, (Genolhac), in September of 1695 with her preparing to flee to Switzerland. The friendship between Marthe and André is of my own creation with no evidence to show whether they may have known each other. As for Claude Brousson, records definitively show that he crisscrossed France in 1695, so

I placed him in the Cévennes in 1695 and 1696. While the timing not be accurate, it allowed me to give readers the experience of his impact on Jehan (Jean Pierre) and his family and neighbors. Much of Pasteur Brousson's dialogue comes from letters he wrote during the 1690s, so they give us some clue that he was not quite the pacifist saint that he has been held up to be by some religious leaders. Scholars Charles Bost, Walter C. Utt, and Brian Strayer have given substantial evidence in their writings to show this. The historical characters of Marthe Dollier and Claude Brousson give the reader some indication of the clandestine way in which those following the "Reformed Religion" were forced to live. Their strained relationship, as I show it in scenes cut from the final manuscript, (for copies of these scenes, sign up at **juleslarimore.com**), is documented in their letters to each other.

Les Conte de Fées was actually published in 1697, a year after it appears in this story. Once again, this is a small shifting of the factual date that worked well for the story, allowing Jehan to purchase an edition at the Uzès market in the fall of 1696. Féerie (fairy) tales and legends had remained popular since ancient times, but their popularity in printed form surged in the late 1690s and played a large role in the society of the era.

On the subject of books, the bookseller, Jean Giraud, was a known dealer for banned Protestant books who is thought to have been part of a network that helped provide safe passage for refugees during the Huguenot diaspora.[14]

In my story, I recount and elaborate on a true incident that happened in Génolhac on a frigid January night in 1696. A prominent nobleman, Monsieur Narbonne, hosted Roma dancers to the dismay of Curé Gellion and Prieur Chabert who called in the regional magistrate to break it up. But Narbonne stood up to them, refusing to end the soireé or to send the dancers out into the cold.[15] During the Renaissance, the Roma were referred to as Bohemiennes/Bohemians, (because they immigrated into France via Bohemia), or Les Tsiganes. I have Jehan use the term Bohemians at first, out of naivete, but he is later corrected by Lucrèce, who says they prefer to be called Roma. The wealthy were truly passionate about, and appreciative of, the Roma's dance performances, so it was customary to host them in their chateaux. But in the second half of the 17th century, the Roma's fate changed radically. On 11 July 1682, an edict "against the Bohemians and those who give them refuge" called for men to be arrested and sent to the galleys for life, regardless of whether any crime had been committed. Women were to have their heads shaved and could be flayed and exiled if they continued to "lead a Bohemian life".[16] [17]

I placed cousin Moyes BonDurant (Bondurant) in several places in the story, even though the only documentation I found on him is of his time in Switzerland with Pasteur (Pastor) Barjon's group. The ministerial records of Pasteur Barjon showed that he and Jean Pierre shared a small house at the Huguenot community in Aarau and that Moyes died while traveling with the group between Helmershafen and Karlshafen on 6 July 1699.[18]

While researching the name Bondurant/d and its variations, the oldest use I have found to date is for a Jewish man listed in the records of Aragon in 1263 as Bon Durant.[19] So I incorporated the possibility of a Jewish ancestor into the story. The prefix Bon was "popular among Jews and rare or not attested among Christians in Medieval Navarre."[20] (Navarre was a kingdom under Aragon's rule until 1134, then under France's rule from 1285-1328.) Bon equates to "good" but could also be a version of "Ben", the traditional Hebrew naming for "son of", much like "Mc", "Mac", "O", etc. The timing of this Bon Durant from the 1263 records is very interesting since the next oldest listing I've found of a Bondurant is one born in 1280 in Malilhères, near Génolhac. Jaime I, King of Aragon was known for tolerance, until after the Disputation of Barcelona[21] in 1263 took place, (which I lack the space to explain here and may be the reason for the records of Jews from that year). Through a series of events, Jews in Aragon began to face escalating tensions with Catholics who wanted to restrict their freedoms. During this era, Montpellier in Languedoc would have been attractive to this Bon Durant since it was under the rule of Aragon and had a past history of tolerance and partage. A Jewish district had been established there in 1121[22] and Montpellier University had granted Jews the right to practice medicine—an interesting tie-in to the many physicians and apothecaries among the Bondurants. However, with the takeover of

Languedoc after the Albigensian crusade by the French King and Catholic leaders, the level of tolerance toward Jews in the surrounding areas gradually shifted. The inquisitions of this crusade caused Jews and Cathars who survived the atrocities to convert to Catholicism or flee to the places like the Cévennes where they could live in hiding.

Amelia, my fictional female protagonist, teaches Jehan a word amulet that she inscribes on parchment—"Ha Brachah Dabarah" meaning, in ancient Hebrew, "I speak the blessing" or "pronounce the blessing.[23] This sort of amulet was commonly included as a prayer for healing in recipe books used by sage-femme healers in Languedoc during the Medieval period.[24] The recipe books were versions of "herbals" and "pharmacopeias" and earned the name "grimoire" because some of the writing was indecipherable to most people. Later Amelia gives Jehan a silver cross with this phrase engraved onto it. I created the sketch of this cross to resemble two Merovingian crosses found in the Lausanne Museum in Switzerland.[25]

I have Amelia go on pilgrimage in honor of Sainte Marie de Magdala (Mary Magdalene). Legends dating back to the ninth century say that after the death of Jesus, Mary Magdalene and several disciples escaped persecution in Palestine by boarding a small boat with no sail and no rudder and setting off across the Mediterranean Sea. Miraculously, they made it to the southern coast of France and landed in Les-Saintes-Maries-de-Mer as the first Christians in France. Mary Magdalene preached alongside Lazarus in Marseille before settling in a cave on the side of a steep cliff in the Sainte-Baume mountains. It has been a pilgrimage site for royalty and common people alike since the eleventh century.[26]

Records show the Order of *Saint Jean de Jérusalem*, Knights Hospitallers, were present on and around Mont Lauzère (Lozère) since 1166 when lands were donated to the order by the baron of Tournel. They developed the Gap-Francès Commandery, which included a chapel, a manor house, a hospital, and several smaller buildings. They continued to purchase land and, over the years, became the primary landholder around the area. Along with their patron Saint, they also revered Sainte Marie de Magdala.[27] The Knights often escorted pilgrims to Le Puy, Saint-Gilles, and Sainte-Baume. Francois Timoleon served as Commandeur from 1695-1707.[28]

The clandestine assemblies of the Children of God occurred quite frequently with an abundance of inspirés and prophesying. I have added an element to my representation of them that only one scholar, (that I have come across), has touched upon—the use, intentionally or accidentally, of substances that may have caused hallucinations, and intensified by fasting and starvation. In an interview on *The Thinker's Garden*, Lionel Laborie, Assistant Professor of the Institute for History at Leiden University stated, ". . . *there is evidence that the French Prophets drank posset—a hot drink made of curdled milk, ale and spices—during their assemblies. Other eyewitness accounts suggest they consumed some sort of "magic" bread, liqueur, and powder before falling in ecstatic trances. Like many devout Christians of the period, they also fasted regularly, sometimes for weeks, which certainly contributed to their religious experiences.*"[29] [30]

In the story, I suggest that some of the Huguenot inspirés' convulsions and visions could have been set off by *seigle ergoté*, rye grain contaminated with *Claviceps purpurea,* a fungus that grows on grains, especially rye, during cool, wet periods such as the one from 1693-94. This fungus can cause "attacks of excitement and fear of enemies caused by visual illusions, hallucinations, and bad dreams."[31] "The common symptoms include fits, hallucinations, and trances."[32] "People under the influence of this compound tend to be highly suggestible. They may see formed images—for instance, of people, animals, or religious scenes—whether their eyes are open or closed."[33] And ". . . hallucinations, such as being 'out of body,' 'seeing a great light in the night,' 'visiting Heaven and Hell; sensations of burning heat and terrible cold; trembling and twitching."[34] "People who experienced pleasant hallucinations or euphoria, at least part of the time, might claim to be favored by God."[35] Those who had pleasant hallucinations . . . saw in the persons around them, gods, saints . . . the victims were overcome with joy, prayed to these figures, sank to their knees before them . . ."[36]

Pamphlets of the era were not like our modern day notion, only a few pages long. Instead, they were typically bound with a heavier parchment and, due to the small, narrow format, they could be eight to ten pages or, sometimes, as many as eighty pages. I use the term leaflet to refer to what is called a broadside in Great Britain; a one-sided, single sheet of paper, usually a governmental announcement or a strongly worded attack, posted in a town square or on the backside of a settle in a tavern or inn. The wording I used for the fictitious pamphlet from the "Languedoc Collective of Noblesse" is a compilation of bits from factual pamphlets and writings. I used it as a way to condense otherwise lengthy documentation into the narrative.[37] The pamphlet by Jurieu that is mentioned at the assembly on Mont Boguès was real, but I quoted only a snippet. The Isle de Eden pamphlet was, as mentioned, actually printed in 1689.[38] [39] This advertisement and other such propaganda for resettlement "projects" had a significant impact on Huguenots' decisions to leave France.

Records indicate that Jean Pierre repaid multiple loans back to André. However, I found it quite odd that the records never showed the original loans. It was standard practice for all loans, or sales agreements, or marriages, etc. to be notarized and recorded. When I read the memoirs of a Protestant noble woman from La Rochelle, it all became quite apparent. She had developed a plan to transfer her money and property in what were essentially false loans. Later upon her arrival in the Refuge country, the other people involved would send her the money she had "repaid" to them. I theorize this is what happened with the "loans" that Jean Pierre "repaid" to André.

The Cévenol episode on 17 August 1697[40] and the sale of Jean Pierre's mills, land, and livestock are all well documented, true occurrences.[41]

In case you are wondering, the quote in the prologue is a modernized version from a 1942 translation of Pico della Mirandola's *Oration on the Dignity of Man* from the original Italian. It is interesting to see how one might note a slight shift in the interpretation, but I believe both convey the larger meaning. ". . . *with freedom of choice and with honor, as though the maker and molder of thyself, thou mayest fashion thyself in whatever shape thou shalt prefer. Thou shalt have the power to degenerate into the lower forms of life, which are brutish. Thou shalt have the power, out of thy soul's judgment, to be reborn into the higher forms, which are divine.*"[42]

And, finally, for those of you who are looking for "nothing but the facts" on Jean Pierre Bondurant, I suggest reading the books by Mary Bondurant Warren; The Bondurants of Genolhac France, The Bondurants of America—Jean Pierre and Ann, and The Bondurants of America: Ann Tanner's Ancestors.

ENDNOTES

AUTHOR'S NOTES

1. Bastide, Samuel, *L'Exode des Huguenots* - *Pages d'Histoire Protestante*, Musée du Désert. Moulins: Imprimeries Reunies, 1959. p.8. "*The first Edicts persecuting the Huguenots appeared in 1661 at the time when the king (Louis XIV) took over the reins of power at the death of Mazarin. He signed 309 of these before the Revocation. Under the pretext of permitting their adherence to the official religion, he ordered the heinous kidnapping of Protestant children above the age of 7 years.*"

2. Carbonnier-Burkard Marianne et Cabanel Patrick, *Une histoire des protestants en France*, Desclée de Brouwer, Paris, 1998 - as stated on the Musée virtuel du protestantisme. "*In 1681, children could be taken away from their parents' custody... Boys could be placed in a Jesuit grammar school and girls in a convent. Their conversion was declared valid as soon as they reached the age of seven.*"

3. Churchich, Elizabeth Ann, *Children Of The Revocation: The Reeducation Of French Protestants After 1685*, p. 255 - a dissertation submitted to the Graduate School – New Brunswick, Rutgers University. "*After Louis XIV's edict of January 1686, this became a central tenet of the enforcement of the Revocation in Paris, with La Reynie regularly assigned to move children into, or out of, convents and Catholic homes depending on the status of their parents. In May, Louis reiterated his commitment to this effort in a letter to Monsieur de Menars, the Intendant of Paris. He wrote, "I was informed that many new Catholics neglect to send their children to their neighborhood Schools, and to the Instructions and Catechisms that take place in their parishes; ensuring that they could remain without being instructed in their Religion ... my intention is that you make known to my newly Catholic Subjects, that I wish that they regularly send their children to the Schools, and to the Instructions and Catechisms." He continued, adding the prescribed punishment for neglecting this responsibility: the children would be taken from their parents and placed in convents or colleges, with the pension to be paid by their parents.*"

4. Bligny-Bondurand, M., *Inventaire sommaire des Archives Départementales, antérieures à 1790*. Gard, Archives Civiles - Supplement a la Serie C. - Serie D., Archives Religieuses - Supplement aux séries G et H. p.146. "*1681 July 14 Remission made by Pierre de Bondurant, doctor of law, and Jean-Pierre de Bondurant, sieur de Cogosat, father and son emancipated, to Francois Gay, prior and trustee of the convent of Genolhac, of a pension of 12 1.10 sols, in payment of a sum 17 1.10 sols (July 14, 1681). 1681 July 30 Subsequently, service of remission to debtor of pension.*"

5. Goulon Sigwalt, Edouard, *Jean-Pierre Bondurant (1677-1735), Huguenot refugee in Virginia*, Cahiers du Center de généalogie protestante, Notebook n°26

– 2nd quarter 1989, Translated by Dolores Artau for Dr. John C. Bondurant for inclusion in the Bondurant Family Association Newsletter, Vol.8. p.8.

6. Goulon Sigwalt, Edouard, *Jean-Pierre Bondurant (1677-1735), Huguenot refugee in Virginia*, Cahiers du Center de généalogie protestante, Notebook n°26 – 2nd quarter 1989, Translated by Dolores Artau for Dr. John C. Bondurant for inclusion in the Bondurant Family Association Newsletter, Vol.8. p.8.

7. Research conducted by Serge Bondurant from primary source documents in local archives with notes on Geneanet. "On 07/29/1679 power of attorney for Gabrielle de Barjon, wife of Jean Pierre Bondurand, lord of Cougoussac, knowing that her husband is a prisoner in the Roy prisons in Uzès, since last June 15, appoints his attorney general Jean Jacques de Passebois, from the place of Trumuejol, to get her husband out of prison. Photos 3050-51 AD30-2E23-273."

8. Elziere, Jean-Bernard, *Autour d'une lettre datée de 1664 émanant de Marie-Felice de Budos (1628-1693)*. Le Line des chercheurs cévenols, n° 200/3, juillet-septembre 2020, pp. 76-90.

9. *Mémoires de l'Académie de Nimes*, VII Série, Tome XVIII, Année 1895, APPENDICE N• 29. - DOCUMENT INEDIT *"Vente perpétuelle du moulin de Laribal faite au couvent des f. f. precheurs de Genolhac par le sieur Jean Pierre Bondurand Cogossac assisté et authorisé du sieur André Bondurand Master apoticaire, son **curateur alitias,** pour le prix et somme de 450 livres."* / "Perpetual sale of the mill of Laribal made at the convent of f. f. preachers of Genolhac by sieur Jean Pierre Bondurand Cogossac assisted and authorized by sieur André Bondurand Master apoticaire, his **curator alitias**, for the price and sum of 450 pounds.

10. *Guardianship, curatorship, safeguard of justice: what are the differences?* French Minister of Justice website. Updated March 23, 2022. Directorate of Legal and Administrative Information (Prime Minister) https://www.justice.fr/fiche/ tutelle-curatelle-sauvegarde-justice-differences

11. Pellet, Jean, *Une maison de Génolhac Une maison de Génolhac pendant 650 ans pendant 650 ans*, Lien des Chercheurs Cévenols, Hors série n° 38. Quoted from primary source tax records for the houses in Genolhac; *"Pierre Bondurand, docteur ès-droits, et son frère Jean, reconnaissent en 1670 tout 42 BC franc de cense ainsique 46 Bd acquis par les Quarante des Caladon fin XVIème."* / "Pierre Bondurand, **doctor of rights/law**, and his brother Jean, recognize in 1670 all 42 BC tax free as well as 46 Bd acquired by the Quarante of Caladon at the end of the 16th century."

12. *Bondurant Family Association Newsletter*, Vol. 1 No. 1, August 1987.

13. Tylor, Charles, *The Huguenots in the Seventeenth Century: Including the History of the Edict of Nantes*. London: Simpkin, Marshall, Hamilton, Kent & Co., 1892, p.293.

14. Wirts, Kristine, *Keeping the Faith: The Story of a Seventeenth-Century Peddler and his Protestant Community*. The Journal of The Western Society for French History, Vol. 42, 2014.

15. Asséo, Henriette, *Travestissement et divertissement. Bohémiens et Égyptiens à l'époque moderne.* Les Dossiers du Grihl, Groupe de Recherches Interdisci-plinaires sur l'Historie du Litteraire, 2009.

16. de Vaux de Foletier, François. *Les Tsiganes, dans l'ancienne.* France, Paris: Connaissance du Monde, Société d'Édition Géographique et Touristique, 1961, p.

152-160

17. Asséo, Henriette, *Le traitement administratif des Bohémiens*, in Problèmes socio-culturels en France au XVIIe siècle, Paris, Klincksieck, 1974, pp. 9-87.

18. Bondurant Warren, Mary, *The Bondurants of Génolhac, France*. Athens, GA: Heritage Papers, 2000. p.60.

19. Motis-Dolader, Miguel-Angel, *Guía de las juderías de Aragón : un apasionante recorrido por el Aragón judío*. Zaragoza: Prames Publishing, 2011. (Referenced on *Medieval Surnames Search Engine*, sephardicgen.com)

20. Becker, Lidia, *Names of Jews in Medieval Navarre (13th–14th centuries)*. Toronto: York University, 2009. "These names were popular among Jews and rare or not attested among Christians. Nomen Bono 'good name' equates to Shem Tov; Bonhomo 'good man' to Benjamin. It is however, questionable, whether translations from Hebrew played a dominant role in all the cases. It can be assumed that the augurative names like Bonhomo, Bonavita, Nomen Bono were chosen because of their positive connotations."

21. https://en.wikipedia.org/wiki/Disputation_of_Barcelona

22. Vayssettes, Jean-Louis. *Jewish settlements in Montpellier in the Middle Ages*. Ministre de la Culture, 16 Sept. 2021.

23. Kenyon, F. G., *Greek Papyri in the British Museum*. London: William Clowes and Sons, 1893.

24. Niiranen, Sussanna Niiranen, *The Authority of Words: The healing power of vernacular, Latin and other languages in an Occitan remedy collection*. The Philosophical Psychology, Morality and Politics Research Unit and Medieval States of Welfare, Academy of Finland, 2011.

25. Deonna, W., *Abra, Abraca: La Cr0lx-Talisman De Lausanne*. Genava : revue d'histoire de l'art et d'archéologie, 1944.

26. Sainte-Baume.org

27. Lannin, Sir William Henry, *A Historic Review of the Order of the Knights of St. John of Jerusalem, of Rhodes, and Malta*. Boston: The Four Seas Company, Publishers. 1922.

28. André, Ferd, *Notice Historique Sur La Commanderie de Gap-Francés et Chronologie de ses Commandeurs*. Bulletin of the Societe D'Agriculture, Industrie, Sciences et Arts du Departement de la Lauzère. Vol. 15. 1864.

29. Laborie, Lionel, Interview at https://thethinkersgarden.com/camisards-rebel-prophets-of-languedoc/

30. Laborie, Lionel, *Enlightening enthusiasm: Prophecy and religious experience in early eighteenth-century England*. Manchester: Manchester University Press, 2015.

31. Kilbourne Matossian, Mary. *Poisons of the Past*. Yale University, 1989. p.11

32. Kilbourne Matossian. p.77

33. Kilbourne Matossian. p.116

34. Kilbourne Matossian. p.125

35. Kilbourne Matossian. p.145

36. Kilbourne Matossian. p.125

37. Stanwood, Owen, *The Global Refuge: Huguenots in an Age of Empire*. Oxford: Oxford University Press, 2020.

38. Duquesne, Henir, *Recueil de quelques mé moires servant d'instruction pour l'e tablissement de l'Ile d'Eden* (Amsterdam, 1689), avertissement.

39. Stanwood, Owen, **Between Eden and Empire: Huguenot Refugees and the Promise of New Worlds**

40. République Française pluiesextrêmes.meteo.fr

41. **Mémoires de l'Académie de Nimes**, VII Série, Tome XVIII, Année 1895, APPENDICE N• 29. - DOCUMENT INEDIT *"Vente perpétuelle du moulin de Laribal faite au couvent des f. f. precheurs de Genolhac par le sieur Jean Pierre Bondurand Cogossac assisté et authorisé du sieur André Bondurand Master apoticaire, son* **curateur alitias,** *pour le prix et somme de 450 livres."* / "Perpetual sale of the mill of Laribal made at the convent of f. f. preachers of Genolhac by sieur Jean Pierre Bondurand Cogossac assisted and authorized by sieur André Bondurand Master apoticaire, his curator alitias, for the price and sum of 450 pounds.

42. Livermore Forbes, Elizabeth, **Of the Dignity of Man: Oration of Giovanni Pico Della Mirandola, Count of Concordia**. Journal of the History of Ideas, Vol.3, No.3. Philadelphia: University of Pennsylvania Press, June, 1942, pp.347-354.

ACKNOWLEDGMENTS

Jackson Larimore Snyder, my uncle, instigated this story about twenty years ago when he shared his genealogical findings on Jean Pierre Bondurant. It was then that my character of Jehan began to take form, evolving over time. As it turns out, Jean Pierre is actually a well researched figure with an estimated quarter of a million progeny, many of whom have been fascinated with his story, and, like myself, have been the diamond hunters on the quest for gems finding a road strewn with rubies, emeralds, and sapphires.

I would like to thank Jon Cotham for sharing my passion for historical fiction in books and on screen, for being a sounding board for ideas and plot twists, and for indulging me with extra support when deadlines were near.

I am also in gratitude to Loic Breton for sharing stories and a tour of the Bondurant home, now belonging to his family in Génolhac, France. His tour up Mount Lozére was a must do, where he says Jean Pierre Bondurant "surely" spent time at the Camisard hamlet of Les Bouzèdes. In our short visit, Loic gave me a feel for the real character and spirit of the Cévenol people.

My research was mostly bolstered by the work of a distant cousin and dedicated historian and researcher, the late Mary Bondurant Warren. Her three books on the early Bondurants are filled with well researched facts on the family.

Many thanks also go out to all the other researchers who laid the groundwork for this story including many scholars, past and present, whose archived research papers and books are now available. Most notably are Marie-Lucy Dumas, Lionel Laborie, the various authors of the 19th century publications of *Memoirs of the Academy of Nîmes*, and curé-doyen Father César Nicolas who assembled and published primary source historical records in *The Génolhac Dominican Convent: 1298-1791*.

A special thanks to my editor, Laurie Chittenden and to my family, friends, and fellow authors who gave input throughout the journey: Janet Wertmann who lended tremendous support, creativity, and laughs through every chapter of the journey; to Donna Scott for her dedication to elevating my first chapter; Colleen Adair Fliedner, Mirella Sichirollo Patzer, Rosemary Morris, Wayne Dawson, Katherine Pym, and the members of the Ventura County Writers Salon who all gave feedback on early chapters; fellow members of the Historical Novel Society who constantly inspire and educate me, including Glen Craney whose writing led me to discover the group; France's Splendid Centuries writers collaborative—Ann McClellan, Keira Morgan, Rosza Gaston, and Laura Du Pre; my Bondurant Family Association support team—Eve B. Mayes, Bruce Ramsdell, Su McDonnell, David Bondurant, and Marcelle Bondurant Hoffman —who offered support of all sorts, including enduring, enthusiastic encouragement; my book cover designer, Gram Telen; map brush designer, K.M. Alexander; and the many advanced readers and reviewers.

SELECTED BIBLIOGRAPHY

Baring-Gould, S. *A Book of the Cevennes.* London: John Long, 1907.

Browning, W. S. *History of the Huguenots.* Philadelphia: Lea & Blanchard, 1845.

Cavallier, Jean. *Memoirs of the wars of the Cevennes, under Col. Cavallier.* London: J. Stephens, 1726.

Cuttriss, Frank. *Romany life, experienced and observed during many years of friendly intercourse with the Gypsies.* London: Mills & Boon Ltd., 1915.

Dumas, Marie-Lucy. *Génolhac sur la Regordane, XIIe siècle à 1815.* Ponteils et Brésis, France: Gens et Terroirs des Hautes Cévennes editions, 2011.

Durant, Will and Ariel. *The Age of Louis XIV.* New York: Simon and Schuster, 1963.

Ehrenreich, Barbara and English, Deirdre. *Witches, Midwives, and Nurses.* New York: The Feminist Press, The City University of New York, 1973.

Kenrick, Donald. *Historical Dictionary of the Gypsies (Romanies).* Second Edition. Lanham, Maryland: The Scarecrow Press, Inc., 2007.

Laborie, Lionel. *Enlightening Enthusiasm: Prophecy and Religious Experience in Early Eighteenth Century England.* Manchester University Press, 2015.

Laborie, Lionel. *The French Prophets: A Cultural History of Religious Enthusiasm in Post-Toleration England (1689-1730).* Ph.D. Thesis, University of East Anglia, School of History, 2010.

Ladurie, Emmanuel Le Roy. *The Peasants of Languedoc: Translated with an Introduction by John Day*. Urbana and Chicago: University of Illinois Press, 1978.

Lamoignon de Basville. *Mémoires secrets de Lamoignon de Basville, Intendant de Languedoc*. Montpellier: Aux Bureaux D'Abonnement des Chroniques de Languedoc, 1877.

Lewis, W.H. *The Splendid Century. Life in the France of Louis XIV*. New York: Doubleday Anchor Books, 1953.

Nicolas, Monseigneur l'abbe C. *Histoire de Génolhac, Mémoires de l'Académie de Nîmes, VII Serie, Tome XVIII,* Nimes: Clavel and Chastanier, 1896.

Paspati, A.G.; Hamlin, C. *Memoir on the language of the Gypsies, as now used in the Turkish Empire*. Journal of the American Oriental Society 7:143-270, 1863.

Pinkard, Susan. A Revolution in Taste: The Rise of French Cuisine. New Youk: Cambridge University Press, 2009.

Rider, Catherine. *Medical Magic and the Church in Thirteenth-Century England*. Social history of medicine : the journal of the Society for the Social History of Medicine vol. 24(1), pp.92-107, 2011.

Smiles, Dr. Samuel. *The Huguenots in France*. (1812-1904) London: Strahan & Company, 1873.

Stanwood, Owen. *The Global Refuge: Huguenots in an Age of Empire*. Oxford: Oxford University Press, 2020.

Tylor, Charles. *The Huguenots in the Seventeenth Century*. London: Simpkin, Marshall, Hamilton, Kent & Co., Ltd., 1892.

Warren, Mary Bondurant. *The Bondurants of Génolhac, France.* Tricentennial Edition, Athens, Georgia USA: Heritage Papers, 2000.

Pharmacopeias

Bostock, John, M.D, F.R.S. and Riley, H.T. Esq., B.A. *The Natural History of Pliny. Translated with Copious Notes and Illustrations,* London: Henry G. Bohn, 1856.

Gerard, John; Rolle, John; Islip, Adam; Norton, Joyce; Whitaker, Richard; Fisher, Sidney T.; Dodoens, Rembert; Johnson, Thomas. *The herball, or, Generall historie of plantes,* London: Adam Islip, Joice Norton and Richard Whitakers, 1636.

Salmon, William, Professor of Physick. *Pharmacopœia Londinensis. Or, the New London Dispensatory.* London: Th. Dawks, Th. Buffet, Jo. Wright, and Ri. Chiswell, 1682.

Thompson, C.J.S. *The Mystery and Art of the Apothecary.* London: John Lane The Bodley Head Limited, 1929.

CÉVENOLES SAGAS

The Muse of Freedom is the first in a planned series of three novels that follow the life of Jehan BonDurant and his Muse in their search for "Eden" and their efforts to stand up for tolerance and compassion. These stories will take the reader on a journey through the "Réfuge" countries and other intriguing locations.

To learn about sequels, receive special offers, access the Book Club Guide, and read fascinating blog posts articles. Visit my website and sign up at
https://juleslarimore.com/

If you enjoyed this book, I would be grateful for your honest reviews on Goodreads and Amazon. Even if you have no time to write a review, a star rating to tickle the algorithms would be wonderful!

Adventure on my friends,

Jules Larimore

Printed in Great Britain
by Amazon

39718490R00229